Delphi scanned the area

He paused suddenly, looked directly at Ryan far across the bay—and smiled.

The sight was unnerving, but Ryan fired two more rounds directly into the cyborg's face. The 7.62 mm slugs slammed to a dead stop inches from his grinning visage.

Delphi shouted a command over his shoulder, and the cannons began to spit flames.

Bursting into action, the companions rose to race away from the edge of the cliff, but the barrage of shells arrived first, and the ground erupted in powerful explosions. Salty dust filled the air as a section of the cliff broke away, with Ryan several yards from safety.

"Ryan, no!" Krysty screamed.

No response came from within the swirling dust cloud.

JAMES AXLER

DEATH LANDS.

Desert Kings

A GOLD EAGLE BOOK FROM
WORLDWIDE.

TORONTO • NEW YORK • LONDON
AMSTERDAM • PARIS • SYDNEY • HAMBURG
STOCKHOLM • ATHENS • TOKYO • MILAN
MADRID • WARSAW • BUDAPEST • AUCKLAND

First edition March 2008

ISBN-13: 978-0-373-62591-8
ISBN-10:   0-373-62591-X

DESERT KINGS

Through the travail of the ages,
Midst the pomp and toil of war,
Have I fought and strove and perished
Countless times upon this star.
                    —General George S. Patton
                       1885–1945

THE DEATHLANDS SAGA

This world is their legacy, a world born in the violent nuclear spasm of 2001 that was the bitter outcome of a struggle for global dominance.

There is no real escape from this shockscape where life always hangs in the balance, vulnerable to newly demonic nature, barbarism, lawlessness.

But they are the warrior survivalists, and they endure—in the way of the lion, the hawk and the tiger, true to nature's heart despite its ruination.

Ryan Cawdor: The privileged son of an East Coast baron. Acquainted with betrayal from a tender age, he is a master of the hard realities.

Krysty Wroth: Harmony ville's own Titian-haired beauty, a woman with the strength of tempered steel. Her premonitions and Gaia powers have been fostered by her Mother Sonja.

J. B. Dix, the Armorer: Weapons master and Ryan's close ally, he, too, honed his skills traversing the Deathlands with the legendary Trader.

Doctor Theophilus Tanner: Torn from his family and a gentler life in 1896, Doc has been thrown into a future he couldn't have imagined.

Dr. Mildred Wyeth: Her father was killed by the Ku Klux Klan, but her fate is not much lighter. Restored from predark cryogenic suspension, she brings twentieth-century healing skills to a nightmare.

Jak Lauren: A true child of the wastelands, reared on adversity, loss and danger, the albino teenager is a fierce fighter and loyal friend.

Dean Cawdor: Ryan's young son by Sharona accepts the only world he knows, and yet he is the seedling bearing the promise of tomorrow.

In a world where all was lost, they are humanity's last hope....

Chapter One

Ryan opened his eye and discovered that the jump was over. He was sprawled on the cold floor of a mat-trans chamber, the electronic mists slowly fading. His SIG-Sauer pistol was digging into his hip and his leather eye patch was askew. Son of a bitch, what a nightmare he'd endured this time, the Deathlands warrior thought sluggishly, reality slowly returning like waves rushing toward shore. The dream about the Mutie Wars had been startlingly vivid.

Suddenly a severe pain hit Ryan and he grabbed his head in both hands until the throbbing subsided.

The jump-mares he suffered seemed to be getting worse. Mildred had told him time and again that it was a natural side effect of using the mat-trans units, instantly traveling from one redoubt to another, hundreds, and sometimes thousands, of miles apart. But nobody knew for sure. All of the whitecoats who had built the mat-trans units were long dead, and nobody had ever found an operating manual. Mildred had had a CD with codes, but that was long gone.

Personally, Ryan didn't care much about the pain. Jumping hurt, and that was simply the price they paid for being able to move freely around Deathlands. As Trader often said, pain was life. Only the dead felt nothing.

Weakly, the man rose onto his arms and rolled over to rest against the armaglass wall. The material was deliciously cool through his jacket, and he gratefully pulled in lungfuls of air until his mind began to clear. He checked his weapons: a Steyr SSG-70 bolt-action longblaster, a 9 mm SIG-Sauer hand-blaster and a curved panga.

Adjusting his eye patch, Ryan looked around the chamber at the five people sprawled on the floor. They were panting hard and drenched in sweat. The shock of instantaneous travel through the predark machinery was always painful to the companions, but obviously this jump had been particularly bad for everybody.

A low moan sounded from a redheaded woman. Krysty Wroth lifted her face and wiped away a string of drool with the back of her hand.

"Hi, lover," Krysty whispered hoarsely. The woman wore a shaggy black fur coat and green military fatigues. A gunbelt encircled her trim waist, supporting a holstered S&W .38 revolver, along with a couple of ammo pouches. A canvas backpack lay on the floor near her blue cowboy boots, the silver tips glistening in the harsh fluorescent light.

"Hey, yourself," Ryan replied, smiling back. "Triple bitch of a jump, eh?"

"Been through worse," Krysty said softly, then broke into a ragged cough. Once, they had jumped into a flooded redoubt full of rotting corpses. The stench was so overpowering that Krysty was still amazed that anyone had the presence of mind to hit the Last Destination button so they could jump out of there.

At the grim memory, she experimentally sniffed. The air of the redoubt smelled flat and artificial, with-

out any trace of other living creatures. Good. Several
times they had jumped somewhere only to find the walls
had been breached and there were coldhearts or muties
inside the redoubt. But this one smelled clean and
empty.

"Here, drink this," a stocky black woman said, proffering a battered canteen.

"Any chance it's water?" Krysty asked hopefully,
taking the container.

"Nope, a new batch of jump juice," Mildred Wyeth
replied, brushing a pair of beaded plaits from her face.
The woman was dressed in a flannel work shirt and
heavy denim pants tucked into U.S. Army boots. A
Czech-made ZKR target pistol jutted from her gunbelt,
and there was a worn canvas bag hanging at her side
bearing the faded letters M*A*S*H.

Back in the twentieth century, Dr. Mildred Wyeth
had been a physician who specialized in cryogenics
research. On a crisp December day she had entered
the hospital for what was deemed routine surgery.
But there had been complications and she'd ended up
in a cryogenic freezing unit, and slept through the
nuclear holocaust. A hundred years later she was
awakened by Ryan and the others to find a strange
new world of radioactive ruins, acid rain storms, mu-
tants and cannibals.

One of the physician's projects was to try to perfect
some sort of tonic that would ease the agony some of
the companions endured following a jump. Sometimes
the companions arrived at a redoubt racked with pain,
vomiting their last meal, totally helpless for several
minutes. In the Deathlands, that was a good way to get
chilled. So far, none of her concoctions had helped

much, but she always had hope for the next batch. These days, hope was all anybody had.

"Jump juice," Krysty said without enthusiasm. Then she sighed and took a sip. She paused to swallow, then drank some more. "Gaia, this tastes like coffee!"

"It is, mostly," Mildred replied, sitting upright. "U.S. Army-issue coffee mixed with sugar, honey, srag root and a few other things. I figured maybe a stimulant was needed more than a relaxant."

"P-pass that over h-here," J. B. Dix muttered, reaching out a hand. "Cold coffee sounds mighty good to m-me." The wiry man was dressed in neutral-colored clothing, Army boots and a brown leather jacket that had seen better days. A 9 mm Uzi machine pistol hung off his left shoulder, a S&W M-4000 shotgun was across his back and his backpack bulged with odds and ends. Their old mentor, Trader, had nicknamed him "The Armorer" long ago, and the title fit perfectly. There wasn't a weapon in existence that John Barrymore Dix couldn't fire in his sleep or repair in the dark.

Krysty handed him the container and he took a swallow. He paused as if half expecting his stomach to rebel at the brew, but slowly he began to smile.

"Dark night, this is your best mix yet, Millie!" J.B. exclaimed in delight. "I think we have a winner here!"

"Pity I can't make more." Mildred sighed.

Pulling out a pair of wire-rimmed glasses from his shirt pocket, J.B. placed them on his face. "Why not?" he asked curiously. Already he was feeling better, the vertigo of the jump fading.

"About half of this is three-hundred-year-old Napoleon brandy," she stated. "I doubt we'll ever find another bottle of it again."

"Shine is shine."

"Oh, no, it isn't. Trust me on this one, John."

He grinned. "Always have before, Millie." Reaching out to pat her hand in consolation, J.B. shared a private moment with the physician before passing the canteen to the next companion.

Brushing the snow-colored hair from his face, Jak Lauren took a long drink, some of the juice running down his chin. Lowering the canteen, the youth shook all over like a dog coming out of the rain. "Best batch yet!"

A true albino, Jak had been born in the swamps of Louisiana. The young hunter was dressed in loose camou clothing. Odd bits of razors, glass and feathers had been sewn into his jacket, making it camou for the new world. When hiding among the ruins of predark cities, Jak could all but disappear among the wreckage. And it would be painful if anyone grabbed him by his jacket. A massive .357 Magnum Colt Python hand-blaster rested on his right hip and countless leaf-bladed throwing knives were secreted upon his person. A knife was sheathed on his belt, and the handle of a small knife peeked from the top of his left boot.

"Hey, over here," Ryan said, reaching out.

Turning, the teen relayed the partially filled container. Ryan took a couple of swigs, then handed the canteen to a tall silver-haired man slumped against the wall. Wordlessly accepting it, Doc Tanner drained the container before giving it back to Mildred.

"Th-thank you, my dear Ryan," Doc whispered. "That was needed m-much more than I could p-possibly express."

Tall and slim, Dr. Theophilus Algernon Tanner was

dressed as if from another age in a frilly white shirt and a long frock coat. An ebony walking stick lay across his lap, the silver lion's head peeking out between his strong fingers. A mammoth LeMat percussion pistol was holstered at his side, along with several pouches containing black powder and wadding for the Civil War blaster.

"Well, jumps always hit you and Jak hardest," Mildred said, screwing the cap back on the canteen. "Probably from all the…" She paused awkwardly.

"Indeed, madam," Doc whispered hoarsely.

Although only in his late thirties, Doc appeared to be in his sixties from an unexpected side effect of being trawled through time. The whitecoats of the twentieth century had performed experiments on Doc for years, trying to solve the mystery of why he was the only time traveler to survive the experience. Exasperated by Doc's many escape attempts, the whitecoats had hurled him forward in time. Realizing a mistake had been made by doing that, agents of Operation Chronos still hunted for the man. One notable agent was Delphi. Part man, part machine, and all devil, Delphi had laid a devious trap for Ryan, knowing full well that Doc would be traveling with the man. The trick had nearly worked, but Doc escaped at the last moment, leaving Delphi buried alive in a collapsed tunnel. The rest of the companions believed that Delphi had bought the farm, but until Doc saw the cyborg's lifeless body, he would never stop waiting for the demented monster to return.

"All right, let's see where we are," Ryan said, levering himself off the floor. The companions assumed their usual positions and drew their weapons as the one-eyed man walked to the chamber's door and pressed the lever. The door opened onto an antechamber.

Each mat-trans unit had its own unique color, possibly to identify the location to travelers. But that was just a guess. Nobody knew for sure why the armaglass was a different color, or where all of the military personnel disappeared to after the nuke war. Or where they took the megatons of supplies previously stored inside the underground bunkers. The redoubts contained a thousand mysteries, the color codes being only one of them.

However, one constant in every redoubt was that the antechamber was usually small and always empty, except perhaps for a small table or chair, and was devoid of dust, a sterile void. But this room was large and stuffed to the ceiling with wooden boxes. There had to have been a hundred of them filling the room, each one absolutely identical to the other, aside from a black serial number stenciled on the side.

"What is all of this stuff?" J.B. demanded curtly.

"Dunno. Those aren't predark mil numbers on the sides," Ryan said slowly.

"It almost looks like somebody did a run," Krysty stated. Her long red hair moved as if stirred by secret winds that only she could feel. "They jumped into the redoubt, tossed out the boxes from the mat-trans unit, then jumped out again."

"A raiding party?" Doc muttered. "That could very well be, madam. As I recall, we did something similar ourselves once."

"Yeah, chill Silas," Jak growled, clicking back the hammer on his Colt Python. Dr. Silas Jamaisuous had been one of the predark inventors of the mat-trans unit and crazier than a shithouse mutie. "Think might be someone's private cache?"

"Perhaps," Mildred said slowly. "But look there!"

Squinting slightly, Ryan followed the woman's finger and saw a crushed flower protruding from the stacks of boxes. A Deathlands daisy. The leaves were still green and the blossom was only starting to wilt.

"That's fresh," Krysty declared, raising her S&W .38 revolver. "Can't be more than a day old, mebbe two at the most."

"Which means that somebody has very recently been inside the redoubt," Ryan growled, holstering the SIG-Sauer and sliding his Steyr SSG-70 longblaster off his shoulder. He worked the bolt. "All right, triple-red, people. Doc and Jak, Krysty and Mildred, stay inside the mat-trans unit so that nobody else can jump in here with us. J.B., check for traps. I'll stand guard."

With practiced ease, everybody did as they were told without comment.

Warily going to the nearest stack of crates, J.B. tilted back his battered fedora and carefully examined the boxes without touching anything. There were no trip wires that he could see, pressure switches or anything else dangerous in sight. But that didn't mean the stack was safe.

"Well?" Ryan demanded, the deadly Steyr balanced in both hands.

"Tell you in a sec," the Armorer replied, pulling out a small compass and waving it over the piles of containers. If there was any kind of a proximity sensor hidden among the boxes then the compass needle would flicker slightly from the magnetic field. However, the needle remained unresponsive and steady.

"Okay, we're in the clear," J.B. announced, tucking the compass away.

Casting an uneasy glance toward the exit door of the antechamber, Ryan went to the nearest pile of boxes. Choosing one, he briefly inspected it before drawing his panga and using the blade as a lever to force open the lid. The nails squealed in protest, and out puffed excelsior stuffing. Placing aside the lid, Ryan removed a fistful of the soft material and froze motionless.

Lying nestled in the stuffing was a severed human hand.

Chapter Two

Suspecting a trap, Ryan nudged the grisly object with his panga and it shifted, exposing two more hands underneath. All of them were identical, down to the pattern of the hair on the back of the hand and a scar near the thumb.

"What?" Jak muttered, craning his neck for a better look.

"Don't touch them!" Mildred warned, scowling at the hands in frank disgust. "Don't get anywhere near those things!"

"Saw hands before." Jak snorted in wry amusement, then frowned as he noticed the silvery wiring dangling from the wrists.

"Robotic hands," Ryan growled, stabbing one with the panga. A drop of clear oily fluid leaked out and was quickly absorbed by the excelsior. "Only seen those once before."

"Most assuredly, sir, and I was there!" Doc whispered hoarsely, his face contorting into a feral snarl. Angrily, the man slapped the box and it fell to the floor, a dozen of the hands tumbling into view. Each was absolutely identical to the other.

Slowly approaching, the rest of the companions gathered around the stacks of boxes, staring in astonishment.

Prying off the lid of another box, Ryan saw that it was full of white foam peanuts. The foam would dissolve in gasoline, turning it into a crude form of napalm that would stick to almost anything. That doubled the chilling power of a firebomb. Vaguely, Ryan remembered Mildred saying how the foam would last forever and never rot away, and before the Nuke War it had been as common as dirt. But these days it was more rare than an honest baron. Everything made of the stuff had been consumed during the endless fighting after skydark. Molotov cocktails were very deadly weapons, and easier to make than a blaster.

Tipping the container, Ryan spilled the peanuts to reveal a set of four internal organs. They were made of a shiny brown plastic edged with an assortment of clear tubes and more silvery wires.

"Those are livers," Mildred stated. "My God, if this means what I think it does…"

Nervously, the woman adjusted the med kit hanging over her shoulder. Or rather, what she called her medical bag. She had found the empty canvas bag a while back and slowly filled it with what meager medical supplies she could gather: a plastic bottle of boiled cloth, leather strips to use as a tourniquet, a razor-sharp thin-bladed knife found in an art gallery, a few herbs and moss she knew helped ease itching and minor infections, some plastic-wrapped tampons reserved strictly for deep bullet wounds, a plastic bottle of alcohol, some plastic fishing line for sutures, a curved upholstery needle and one small tin of aspirin. Not much, but it was a start.

Hurriedly opening another box, Krysty dumped a couple of plastic human hearts on the floor. At the impact, they started to beat, but soon stopped. The companions began to rip through the crates and boxes, finding more hands, limbs, lungs, kidneys, something that looked like gills of all things, and several flexible armor plates that none of them could recognize as part of a human body. Then a face clattered to the littered floor, landing upside down.

Using his ebony stick, Doc flipped it over and inhaled sharply. Although stiff and lifeless, the face was painfully familiar to the man, the smooth features so lifelike that he half expected the disembodied face to blink open its eyes and start to talk. Jak kicked foam peanuts over the face until the grotesque visage was once more out of sight.

For a couple of minutes nobody spoke and there was only the muted hum of the sterilized air flowing from the disguised wall vents.

"So, he's back," Doc said woodenly, the words sounding strangely flat and emotionless. "The foul cyborg has returned!"

For a moment the universe reeled and Doc was back in the underground tunnel fighting the hated manchine, the only illumination coming from the muzzle-flame of his booming LeMat and a sizzling laser beam fired by Delphi. Then the explosive charges detonated and the ceiling started to fall, as the river began to rise over their heads....

With an effort of will, Doc returned to the reality of the present. If Delphi had been here, then he might walk through the access door of the antechamber at any second! Drawing the LeMat, he pulled back the heavy hammer of the single-action blaster.

"John Barrymore, do we have any grens?" Doc barked, turning to face the door across the chamber.

"Got better than that," the Armorer replied, pulling a squat mil sphere into view from his munitions bag. "I've got an implo gren! Been saving it for an emergency."

"Well, this is it, sir!" An implo gren was a predark marvel that didn't explode outward, but instead created a gravitational field that pulled everything nearby inward to compact into a small, hard sphere. A single implo gren could reduce a U.S. Army tank down to the size of clenched fist. Nothing could survive that. Not even a cyborg.

"All right, if he is here, then let's finish this now!" Ryan declared roughly, sliding the Steyr off his shoulder. "We're gonna recce the entire redoubt, from the fusion reactors in the basement to the garage on top. And if we find Delphi, then we pin him down with blasterfire long enough to get clear and let J.B. use the implo gren."

"Sounds like a plan to me," Mildred agreed, pulling out the Czech ZKR. Back in her own time, killing a person was the worst crime imaginable and carried the most stringent punishments possible. At first Mildred had found it difficult to reconcile taking a life with her oath as a doctor. But "kill or be killed" was the mantra of a new America.

"How much space needed for gren?" Jak asked.

"We need at least thirty yards," Krysty replied, her animated hair flexing and turning in response to her heightened emotional state.

"I… My friends, while I truly appreciate these sentiments, honor forces me to remind you that we do not have to stay," Doc noted hesitantly in his stentorian voice. "We can simply leave and jump to another redoubt. With luck, Delphi will never find us again."

"Or nightcreep next week!" Jak shot back scornfully, drawing his Colt Python. "Not run. Ace now!"

"I agree," Krysty stated forcibly. "We should stay."

"But still, madam—"

"Dark night, if we rabbit now, we could find ourselves ambushed after every damn jump," J.B. added, using his free hand to adjust his fedora. "We arrive weak and sick, then in rushes Delphi." He vehemently shook his head. "I don't want to get chilled on my knees puking. That's a bastard-poor way to buy the farm."

"There is no good way to die, John," Mildred countered, patting his arm. She had seen death a thousand times before and Thomas Hobbes had been right—it was always ugly and brutish. "But I'd rather face it on my feet with a gun in my hand. Next time, we may not have an implo gren."

"Fucking A," Jak added emphatically.

"Has anybody considered the possibility that Delphi isn't even here?" Mildred added. "Or that he hasn't attacked yet because of the spare parts?"

"Too valuable to risk, eh?" Ryan said thoughtfully, rubbing his unshaved chin. It was an interesting idea, and opened a host of possibilities. Unfortunately there were far too many possibilities and not enough hard answers.

"Krysty, can you sense anything?" he asked hopefully.

"No...not really," the woman said hesitantly, trying to concentrate harder. Sometimes she could feel the presence of danger long before it arrived—hidden coldhearts, sleeping muties, even acid rain. Her talent had saved their lives more than once. It was also not very reliable, waxing and waning.

Closing her eyes, the woman tried to focus on the cyborg, but stopped after a few minutes. It was useless. The redoubt was full of automatic devices that kept the place spotlessly clean and scrubbed the air. How could she pinpoint just one more machine? Ruefully, Krysty glanced at the piles of boxes. Besides, exactly how much of Delphi was still norm anymore, and how much had been replaced with plastic and steel?

"Well?" Ryan prompted.

"Sorry, lover," Krysty answered regretfully. "But I'm still too weak from the jump."

Ryan grunted at that. Fair enough. It had been a long shot at best. "Okay, we do this the hard way," he stated. "Doc, you can stay here to guard the boxes if you want, but we're going hunting."

"Then consider me Ajax of Troy!" Doc rumbled, standing a little taller. "I shall not fall on my sword!"

Jak raised a snowy eyebrow.

"I shall not fail."

"Ah."

Then Doc's voice took on a more gentle aspect. "And thank you, my friends," he said, looking around at them. "I... Thank you."

Slapping the man on the back in reply, Ryan started for the control room with the others close behind, but Mildred stopped them.

"Wait a second," she said, a sly grin forming. "Leaving is actually not a bad idea."

"Really, madam!" Doc said askance.

Mildred snorted. "Not us, ya old coot. The boxes."

Ryan paused. He had considered smashing all of the parts, but that would take hours, and it was still possible that the cyborg might be able to use some of the bits. But he couldn't do drek if they were gone.

"Good thinking, Millie!" J.B. said, grinning wide. "Come on, let's scatter his shit across the world! Remember what Trader said—denying an enemy necessary supplies is halfway to winning any fight."

"The other half is blowing out his brains," Ryan added. "All right, I'll stay here and watch the exit through the control room. The rest of you get moving!"

As the others headed for the boxes, Ryan leveled his longblaster at the door leading into the redoubt. At the first sign of movement he would open fire. But even if Delphi was standing on the other side, he felt sure the cyborg wouldn't attack them straight on. The nuking coward liked to strike from behind, to lay traps or to hire mercies to do his fighting. Doc had almost aced the bastard all by himself, and this time the nuke-sucker would face all of the companions. The old man wasn't a blood relative, but some families were forged from friends in the heat of battle.

Blood brothers, Mildred called them. Ryan liked the term. It said a lot in a few words. Blood brothers. None of the companions were related, but there was no doubt they were a family. And kin helped kin.

Forming a ragged line, the other companions started passing the boxes along and stacking them in the mat-trans unit. When it was full, Krysty tapped random buttons on the control panel, left the gateway and closed the door, triggering a jump. A few ticks later, a white mist rose from the floor and ceiling, and the complex machinery performed its function. A series of ethereal lights danced within the swirling cloud, then the sparkles diminished and the mist slowly dissipated to show the unit was empty again.

"Dark night, look how many boxes are left!" J.B.

stated, studying the remaining pile. "Must be enough parts here to build a dozen copies of the bastard. Just how bad did you shoot up his ass, Doc?"

"As much as possible," the old man replied with a note of pride in his voice. "However, I have noted that there were no spare brains among this grotesque array of medical effluvia. These must be simply spare parts for the next time he is damaged."

"Which means he's not making an army of himself," Krysty said, hoisting another box. The lower they got in the pile, the heavier each box became and the parts got larger.

"Quite so, dear lady."

"Good," Jak snarled, taking the container. "One enough."

Accepting the box, Mildred added, "More than enough."

"Agreed, madam."

"If these important, then where guards?" Jak asked suspiciously, continuing the process. A lid shifted, revealing a pair of lungs. Fighting down a shiver, the teenager tossed the container into the gateway. For some reason, the body parts reminded him of the cannies they'd come across back in Louisiana.

"We're hardly out in the open," Krysty replied. "This is the center of a nukeproof redoubt. No place safer in the world."

In reply, the teen only grunted and kept up the pace. The mat-trans unit was filled a second time, and then a third, before the antechamber was empty.

"Done and done." J.B. sighed in relief, removing his fedora and smoothing down his hair. "Good luck to him finding those again!"

"Mildred, any idea what those thick plates were?" Krysty asked, dusting off her hands. "I've never seen anything like those before."

"No idea whatsoever," Mildred replied. "Maybe body armor, or something to do with his weapons systems, possibly even the force field generator or a communications device…it could be anything really."

"Including his hologram generator," Doc snarled in a manner that startled his companions. The dastardly cyborg had once almost lured him into a deathtrap by creating a three-dimensional image of his dear wife, Emily. How the soulless manchine ever got a recording of her was something that still rankled his troubled thoughts.

Ryan kept a careful watch on the door that separated the antechamber from the control room while the others caught their breath. They needed to be razor sharp before daring to leave the antechamber.

When they were ready, Ryan holstered the SIG-Sauer and opened the door. There came a series of muffled bangs as the mechanical locks disengaged, then the portal silently swung aside on well-oiled hinges.

With the Steyr leading the way, Ryan stepped into the control room of the redoubt. A row of comps lined one wall, the monitors endlessly scrolling with binary codes. Twinkling lights danced across the console, a few of the switches moving to new positions all by themselves. But there was nobody in sight.

Taking a position near the door to the corridor, Ryan stood guard and J.B. punched in the code, then eased into the hallway as the door snicked open, Uzi at the ready. He disappeared from sight for a moment, then stuck his head back into the control room.

"All clear," J.B. reported. "Nothing in sight, but the usual doors."

Gathering in the corridor, the companions waited, listening for sounds of movement. When satisfied, they advanced on triple-red, opening each door and checking every room. Normally, these were offices for the base personnel. But in this redoubt each room was piled haphazardly with mil supplies: one room full of combat boots, another stacked high with dark green fatigues, the next with bedrolls and after that backpacks.

"What did you say about an army?" Krysty asked sarcastically, pushing open a door with the barrel of her wheel gun. Inside were lumpy canvas bags containing compact tents. "There's enough stuff here to equip an entire ville of sec men!"

"Just no weps yet," Ryan corrected, checking inside a closet. He wanted to stop and loot the place, as he needed a new pair of boots bad. But first and foremost, they had to know if there was anybody else in the redoubt.

When the companions finished the level, they ignored the elevator and used the concrete stairs to proceed straight down to the bottom level. There was little to search there as the entire level was filled with a silently working fusion reactor located behind thick lead walls. Some of the controls on the master control panel were blinking in the red, but they had found other redoubts doing the exact same thing, and the machines were still working smoothly years later. Whatever the flashing lights meant, it had nothing to do with malfunctioning equipment.

Now with their backs clear, Ryan led the way up into the redoubt, going from floor to floor, checking every room for any sign of the dreaded cyborg. But aside from the cornucopia of clothing and bedrolls on the fifth level, the rest of the redoubt was empty of anything useful. There wasn't a scrap of paper in the wastebaskets or even a roll of toilet paper in the crappers. It seemed as if the redoubt had been effectively emptied long before Delphi started hauling in fresh equipment. Of course that left the big question of where was he getting the supplies?

In the kitchen, the companions found all of the refrigerators softly humming, clean and ready to be used, but totally devoid of anything edible. The rows of ovens worked normally, and the faucets delivered clean water. But that was all. There wasn't even salt and pepper in the table shakers or napkins in the steel holders.

"Okay, time for the armory," Ryan decided, shifting the pack on his back. His stomach was grumbling slightly, and the thought of the self-heats they had found the previous week made his mouth water, even though the food was usually tasteless. But this was not the time or the place for chow. Soon enough they would know if the base was empty, and then they could break out some food.

The others judiciously agreed and proceeded with extreme care, with J.B. checking for traps all along the way. They stopped a couple of times to listen to strange noises, creaking and a soft pattering from overhead, but there was nothing in sight and they proceeded, if a bit more slowly.

Reaching the next level, Ryan found the lock on the stairwell door was partially melted, a small, clean hole penetrating completely through the thick metal. Obviously the cyborg had been there. Must have used that damn laser Doc had told them about, the one-eyed man thought. Tentatively, he touched the metal with a fingertip and found it smooth and cool. But that meant nothing. The steel would have been room temperature after only a few hours.

Crouching to peer through the hole, Ryan saw only the usual corridor on the other side, a long, straight hall that led past the elevator bank and ended at a massive armored door. The armory. When the base was fully staffed, the corridor would be a death trap, with no place to hide or take cover from snipers. Now it was just a passageway, although once before they had gotten trapped inside a cage that dropped down from the ceiling.

Gently, Ryan pushed at the door with the barrel of his longblaster. As it swung open there came a soft exhalation of warm air, closely followed by a strange hum and a series of soft pattering again. But this time he heard it clearly. It almost sounded like rain. Had a pipe busted? Or mebbe a sink was overflowing on the top level.

Taking the lead, Ryan proceeded down the corridor, with the rest of the companions fanned out behind him so as to not offer a group target. They reached the door without incident.

Going to the keypad on the wall, Krysty tapped in the 3-2-5 access code. Nothing happened.

She repeated the code, and this time the lock disengaged. The door slid aside, revealing a bare floor covered with scratch marks. The companions discovered that the room was completely empty. Sadly, this was the condition that they found most redoubts: stripped to the walls, every blaster, lightbulb and fork gone, removed by the predark soldiers after skydark and taken—well, somewhere else. They had no idea where.

"Okay, let's do a standard hunt," Ryan said, removing his finger from the trigger of the SIG-Sauer. "Check under the racks for anything dropped, and be sure to look in the garbage cans."

Peering around a corner, J.B. called out, "I don't think that's necessary this time!"

Joining the man, the rest of the companions paused in puzzlement. The area past the corner was as vacant as the front of the armory—except for a long row of wooden coffins on the cold floor.

"Is this the abode of vampires?" Doc muttered uneasily.

"Far from East Coast," Jak said, referring to the ville the companions had visited once. The locals called themselves the People, and lived off human blood. They weren't exactly the vampires of legend that Mildred had shown them in the vids, but close enough.

"Ten…fifteen…twenty…thirty of them," Krysty said, her hand tightening on her S&W revolver. Her thumb brushed against the smooth steel where a hammer would have been located for most other blasters. But the Model 640 had an internal hammer, making it perfect for firing from inside a coat pocket.

"Odd place for a mortuary," Mildred stated.

"Mebbe they aren't for deaders," Ryan answered.

"What else would you put in a coffin?"

"Let's find out," J.B. suggested. Going to the first coffin, the Armorer knelt to check for traps, then pulled out a knife and wiggled the steel blade into the thin crack between the side and the lid. Pressing downward, he got some play, and moved to the other side to try again. This time the nails squealed in protest, then the lid came loose and crashed to the floor, the noise preternaturally loud in the cavernous room.

"Are…are those what I think they are?" Mildred whispered, looking inside.

"Son of a bitch," Ryan muttered, holstering his blaster. Filling the coffin were AK-47 assault rifles, Kalashnikov rapid-fires. The blue-steel barrels gleamed with oil, and the wooden stock shone with polish. He lifted one of the predark blasters, testing the weight in a knowledgeable hand.

"Seem brand-new," Jak said suspiciously, taking another weapon. He worked the bolt and raised the AK-47 so that the overhead fluorescent lights could shine down the barrel.

"Clean!" the teenager announced, releasing the bolt so that it snapped back into position. "All need ammo, and good to go."

Already at the next coffin, Jak got the lid off and chuckled at the sight of all the curved magazines for the weapons. Inspecting one, he naturally found it empty. The brass in an autoloader was pushed upward by a spring. Leave the weapon loaded for too long and the spring got weak and the blaster jammed in the middle of a fight. It was the price a person paid for having a rapid-fire that required constantly loading and unloading the ammo clips.

The third coffin was full of loose 7.62 mm brass for the rapid-fires. The next couple contained more clips, then more Kalashnikovs, more ammo and, finally, grens. Hundreds upon hundreds of them. Just simple HE charges, no thermite or Willie Peter. White phosphorous, as Mildred called it. But still, it was more grens than the companions had ever seen before except for the Alaskan redoubt.

The last coffin contained assorted survival supplies, folding knives, canteens, Aqua-Pure tabs and the like. A baron's ransom in irreplaceable tech.

Judiciously, J.B. and Ryan chose a couple of the grens and disassembled them on the spot. But there were no traps, no gimmicks. The explosive mil charges were fully functional, the small wads of C-4 moist and soft. Then the two men went back and used their knives to remove the lead for some of the cartridges and poured out the powder. They half expected it to be sand or sawdust. But the silvery dust looked normal, and when Ryan touched it with the flame of a butane lighter the propellant flared brightly and yielded no smoke.

"Smokeless gunpowder." J.B. chuckled in delight. Most of the blasters they found stored in the redoubts were loaded with cordite. Greasy stuff that gave off almost no smoke but smelled like a mutie's fart. This stuff gave off no smoke at all, none, and there was no smell. The Armorer knew how to make black powder and how to convert that into gunpowder. Fulminating guncotton, nitro, plas, those were no prob. Easy pie. But this stuff was a kind of predark chem far beyond his capabilities.

Sitting cross-legged on the cold floor, Jak began to insert live brass into an empty clip. When it was full, he placed it aside and started on another. Doc joined him at the task and they began stacking the loaded magazines.

The rest of the companions stood guard, keeping a close watch on the open door.

"Must be about a hundred of the rapid-fires," Krysty said slowly, biting a lip. "And mebbe a million rounds."

"Closer to two million as I figure it," Mildred said, scrunching her face. "Spare body parts downstairs and enough blasters here for an army. What is the son of a bitch planning?"

"Could be trade goods," J.B. theorized, running a hand along the satiny finish of a Kalashnikov. He took a clip from the pile and gently inserted it into the receiver, then worked the bolt to chamber a round. "A man could buy a whole ville with just a couple of these."

"Or take over a dozen," Ryan added grimly.

"Baron Delphi?"

"Why not? Last time he gave M-16 assault rifles to the people he hired to kill us and capture Doc. Mebbe now he plans to carve out an empire…" Ryan didn't finish the thought, but he could see that everybody else was also reaching the same conclusion. After creating his kingdom, the cyborg would come after Doc and the rest of them again. Only this time, instead of facing four coldhearts, the companions could be facing a bastard army. A real army, hundreds of sec men armed with rapid-fires. They had tangled with something similar in Shiloh, but back then the companions did a nightcreep and used the element of surprise. That would not be the case this time.

"What puzzles me is the use of these coffins," Doc said, placing aside another full clip. "It is most unlikely that these funeral containers were all that he could obtain to transport the blasters. It seems more likely that—"

"Fireblast, he must have been smuggling them out of someplace," Ryan said, completing the old man's thought, rubbing his chin. The last time, the cyborg seemed to have unlimited supplies. But now he was smuggling weapons? The only logical reason why he'd be doing that: the bastard cyborg had more enemies than just the companions.

"All right, everybody grab a spare blaster and some grens," Ryan announced, taking a loaded AK-47 and sliding the strap over a shoulder. "I want to check out the last few levels of this redoubt, then go outside and find out where we are."

"And then what?" Mildred asked, filling her pockets with spare ammo clips. "Should we send all of this stuff on another one-way trip to nowhere like the last batch?"

But before the Deathlands warrior could respond, the soft pattering sound came again, closer this time and from directly above them. As the companions looked curiously upward, the ceiling shimmered like a heat mirage in the desert and a dark figure came into view. Eight metal legs extended from a globular body with red crystal eyes on the front and a stubby little weapon of some kind mounted on the side.

"Droid!" Ryan cursed, diving to the side as he cut loose with a long burst from the Kalashnikov.

The stuttering stream of AP rounds hammered the machine, doing scant damage. Then the scuttling droid fired back, a sizzling energy beam from the tiny weapon hitting Ryan directly in the chest.

Chapter Three

A soft, dry wind blew over the weedy landscape, carrying the faint smell of salt. High in the sky above Nevada, dark purple clouds rumbled ominously and sheet lightning flashed brightly, momentarily parting the roiling cover to expose a fiery orange sky.

Lumbering out of the bushes, the monster slid down the steep clay bank and landed with a splash in the shallow river. Standing ten feet tall, the colossal griz bear studied the rushing water. The river was quite shallow in that area of the forest, no more than a few feet deep. Huge boulders jutted from the churning surface, the spray creating a shimmering rainbow above the flow. Wiggling through the rocky shallows were big silvery trout, golden salmon and huge schools of bright-orange sunfish resembling underwater fire. In the deeper parts black-hued catfish wiggled along the bottom eating everything they encountered without prejudice. They smelled odd, and the bear consumed them only when there was nothing else available.

In the warm summer months, the griz would travel downstream to the cliffs where there were freshwater crabs, huge blue things that tasted wonderful, the snapping pinchers easily avoided. Other forest predators savored the delicious rock-dwellers, but none of them dared to challenge the powerful griz. Wolves, cougars, even the giant bull moose avoided the monstrous killer. The griz was the largest creature in the entire mountain forest, and the unchallenged master of the entire valley.

There came a flash of gold in the rushing water and the bear lashed out a massive paw. The surface of the river smacked loudly, and a wiggling salmon bounced into the misty air. Quickly bending forward, the griz snapped powerful jaws shut on the flapping fish, the skull bones audibly cracking.

Contentedly sitting in the cold water, the bear used both paws to rip the huge salmon apart, happily gnawing on the tasty internal organs. Pale blood splattered the thick fur of the beast as it contentedly consumed all of the dying fish, then afterward it daintily washed the warm gore off its paws and lazily rose to head back for the bank.

However, as it neared the grass, the animal paused at the sound of rustling leaves and instantly growled menacingly, its haunches rising slightly in preparation for a jump. Then its nose caught a strange smell in the air. Galvanized in raw terror, all thoughts of fighting vanished. The griz turned tail to charge for the deeper water in the middle of the river.

But it barely traveled a yard when a humanoid figure jumped out of the treetop and landed squarely on the back of the forest killer. The griz bear snarled in fury as the hooting stickie slapped it with both hands, the deadly suckers adhering to the fur and flesh. With a jerk, the hands were raised, crimson gobbets of flesh ripping free from the startled bear. Violently shuddering, the wounded animal roared in agony and rolled over. But the stickie stayed in place and again plunged the sucker-covered hands deeper into the ghastly openings, pulling out more flesh with one hand and pieces of beating organs with the other.

Agony exploded inside the griz as blood sprayed into the air from the ruptured arteries. As the mutie consumed the still-living flesh, the griz mindlessly turned to run away, careening off a partially submerged tree and then slamming directly into a boulder. Broken fangs and blood erupted from the brutal impact, and the bear jerked back for a split instant, only to charge forward again, trying to reach the deep waters downstream. But its great strength was fading fast and every step was blinding agony, the sounds of eating from the thing riding on top stealing what little reason the animal possessed. It weakly tried to rub the stickie off by hitting a boulder, then the desperate animal rolled over again, keeping its attacker under the water for as long as possible before surfacing. But it was to no avail. Blood dripped off the big bear, the river running red.

Slowing noticeably, the bear could feel no pain anymore and somehow knew the end was near. Summoning its last bits of strength, the griz rose on its hind legs to bellow a challenge at the world, then it collapsed into the running water with a tremendous splash and lay still, its great lungs laboring to draw ragged breaths. Sight faded to darkness and a terrible cold filled the beast as its thoughts became confused and muddled.

Steadfastly continuing to eat, the happy stickie barely noticed when the whimpering bear finally stopped moving and collapsed dead in the cold water. When it reached the still-warm fish in the belly, the mutie hooted in delight at the unexpected prize.

As it extracted the partially chewed food, the stickie paused at the sound of a low rumble. Usually loud noises

were good. Explosions and fire always meant norms
were nearby, and they sometimes had prizes worth stealing. But this was different somehow, and it rapidly grew
louder. Timidly, the worried stickie looked at the stormy
sky, the roiling clouds of black and fiery orange crackling with sheet lightning. There was a kind of rain that
fell sometimes, every drop burning worse than the
orange-beast that consumed wood. Once it had seen another stickie caught in a downpour of the fire-rain before it could reach a cave. The flesh of the mutie
dissolved, exposing the white sticks underneath, then
those fell apart, and still the fire-rain continued, destroying animals and plants, until there were only rocks
and bad ground. When the rain stopped, the mutie had
fled far away, but still it feared the return of the bad water.

Sluggishly, the mutie recalled that the fire-rain had
a very specific smell, similar to old bird eggs, and
there was no trace of the fire-rain smell. This had to be
something else. Some new animal perhaps? Drooling
slightly, the stickie hooted in delight. The females were
always delighted to get new meat, and would reward
him by spreading their legs.

In a splintery crash, the armored war wag plowed
through the row of trees, the heavy treads flattening the
laurel bushes into pulp. Hooting a challenge, the stickie
rose to wave both sucker-covered hands at the strange
angular beast, then charged in attack. Jumping high, it
sailed toward the rolling thing, but suddenly there came
a series of loud bangs, the noises so close together they
almost seemed to be one long explosion.

Tremendous pain ripped through the stickie as the
heavy-duty combat rounds tore it apart. The mutie fell
into the dirty river alongside the cooling corpse of the

giant bear, slayer and victim joined together forever in death.

Rolling uncaring over the bodies, the lead APC crushed them in the mud and rocks as three more war wags appeared from the forest. Each of the armored machines was draped with sandbags for additional protection, the windows only tiny slits to prevent an enemy from shooting inside the vehicles. Instead of wheels, they rolled on armored treads, and the vented barrels of rapid-fires jutted from each side like the quills of a porcupine. On the top of the lead wag was a scarred dome, the stubby barrel of a 20 mm Vulcan minigun sweeping the opposite shoreline for any possible dangers. The next wag had a missile pod on top, the firing hatch closed at the moment, and the last two vehicles were armed with the fluted barrels of high-pressure flame-throwers. Blue-tinted smoke blew from the exhaust pipes rising from the roof of the war machines. The metal plating under the patched sandbags was badly scarred in several locations, but there were no breaches in sight.

As indomitable as mountains, the armored wags jounced across the Nelson River, the water sluiced off several layers of old blood, tufts of human hair and several mutie suckers coming loose from behind the ramming prow to wash away.

Sparkling with droplets, the war wags lumbered up the opposite bank, the prows rising high to crash down onto the grassland. The big diesel engines revved in power and the machines increased in speed.

"Smack on target." Zane Bellany chuckled, sliding shut the steel hatch on the left blasterport and holstering his rapid-fire. It took two tries because of the cramped quarters, but the man finally got the Webley .44 wheel gun back into leather.

As bald as a rock, Bellany sported an enormous head that seemed to merge with his incredibly hairy chest. His clothes were clean, but heavily patched, and crude tattoos were visible on every inch of his exposed skin. A machete hung at his side, tucked in a rattlesnake-skin sheath.

"Waste of ammo." The driver snorted, feeding the power plant more juice. The gauges on the illuminated dashboard flickered in response. As the wag surged forward, a piece of the aced stickie came loose and fell off the array of welded iron bars covering the windshield.

Unconcerned, Bellany shrugged as he reached for the half-eaten sandwich lying on the dashboard. "Don't worry about it," he said, taking a mouthful and chewing. "We got plenty."

Concentrating on steering the huge transport, the driver merely grunted in reply. He was a newbie to the convoy and still had trouble getting his head around the idea of having enough ammo. All of his life the man had watched grim people fight to the death with fists, knives and clubs over the ownership of a single live brass. Yet the four wags of the convoy had cases of the stuff.

Upon joining the convoy, the driver had been given, *given,* a leather gunbelt containing a pristine S&W .357 revolver, the double row of loops across the back holding a total of thirty live brass. Thirty! It was a fortune in brass, but that was nothing compared to the stack of boxes stored in the armory. Grens, rockets, all kinds of predark mil shit. Just fragging incredible. How the chief kept finding the tons of stuff he had no idea.

Along with the blasters, Chief Rogan often unearthed predark meds, crystals that you could dissolve in water and drink to cure the Black Cough, the Blind Shakes, all sorts of triple-bad ills. The meds were worth a thousand times more than any blaster, yet the chief regularly gave them away. At first that seemed like an incredible waste. But whenever they returned to those villes, the convoys were greeted warmly and nobody tried to jack them in the night, sell them rad water, or any of the other feeb tricks some locals used to rip off outlanders.

Finished with the sandwich, Bellany brushed the crumbs off his shirt and reached over a shoulder to grab a roll of paper. Carefully untying the piece of cloth holding it closed, Bellany studied the hand-drawn map, then checked the compass on the dashboard before raising his head to note the landscape outside. After the river was supposed to be a series of foothills, and than a deep valley…right. They were nearly at their goal. Rolling up the map again, he tucked it back into the honeycomb and grabbed a mike from a clip attached to the ceiling.

"Okay, everybody get razor," Bellany said, the words echoing throughout the long wag. "And somebody wake up the chief. We're almost there."

"And sooner than expected," a familiar voice said from behind.

Turning, Bellany smiled in greeting at the man standing in the doorway. "We didn't run into any trouble like last time, sir," he said, hanging up the mike.

"Then what were you shooting at?" Chief "John Rogan" asked, frowning slightly. The man was wearing a mil jumpsuit bleached a dull gray to match his pale combat boots. Two different blasters rode in a wide gunbelt and a short crystal wand was tucked into a shoulder holster. The others had no idea what the thing was, but naturally assumed it was a weapon of some kind.

"Just a stickie," Bellany said. "Nothing important."

Damn it, he missed stickies? Curse the bad luck for them to be found when he was out of the control room! "Stickies, eh? Well, as you say, nothing important," Rogan lied, limping across the cabin.

As the convoy leader took a seat, Bellany forced himself not to comment on the man's condition. Pale and thin, Rogan always looked rather sickly, a condition that had tricked a lot of coldhearts into trying to ace the norm for his blasters. But the chief was still here while the others were now residents in the worm hotel. In spite of appearances, Rogan was lightning-fast with a blaster and rarely missed. Privately, Bellany thought it was more than possible that the chief had just a touch of mutie in his blood, but wisely never mentioned the idea out loud. Chief Rogan hated all muties with a violence that bordered on madness.

Limping to the gunner chair, the man who called himself John Rogan awkwardly eased into the seat. Studying the grille covering the front windshield, he buckled on the seat belt usually ignored by all of the other members of his crew. There were some scattered bloodstains on the metal, but no appreciable damage. Good. It had taken him quite a while to steal these four trucks from the Alaska redoubt controlled by Department Coldfire, and getting replacements was totally out of the question. If another operative of Coldfire ever found him, or worse, somebody from TITAN, then the cyborg would be ruthlessly executed on sight.

But the fools cannot kill what they cannot find, Delphi noted sagely.

However, he was still annoyed about missing the stickies, though. The cyborg would have appreciated one last attempt at raising their intelligence. But so far, the only muties that Delphi had directly encountered were flapjacks, runts and those annoying little water rat things. Whatever the hell those were! That doomie called Haviva had warned him about teeth in the dirty water, and she had been right. Teeth in the water. The phrase had stayed in his mind. And the fat little muties had been nothing but teeth in the dirty marshland water. The horrible things aced four of his men before they could escape. *Teeth in the water.* Delphi was extremely glad the deadly rodents were far behind them now. On the other hand, he wanted to find just one more group of stickies. He still had some faint hopes for his broken children, but it was starting to fade away. They might simply be too stupid to ever train.

"How's the fuel?" The cyborg sighed in resignation, checking the array of flickering gauges.

"Halfway down," the driver replied, steering around the ruins of a predark house. The roof and walls had crumbled to the ground long ago, leaving only the brick chimney. But as the war wags rumbled past, the chimney visibly trembled and broke apart, finishing the destruction.

"That's acceptable," Delphi commented, watching the house recede into the distance behind the convoy.

For some bizarre reason the random destruction felt ominous, almost as if it was a premonition of doom. The cyborg tried to shake off the dire thoughts. He was a realist. He did not believe in omens and portents. That was merely voodoo nonsense for the illiterate masses. Yet the disturbing feeling would not leave the man-machine hybrid, and he stared at the cloud of dust rising from the wreckage until the natural contour of the land removed it from his sight. For a moment Delphi wondered if this might be the death waiting for him in the ruins that Haviva had foretold. But she had warned him of teeth in the water. There was no water here. Only crumbling brick buildings, blast crater and weeds.

"Sir, is there something wrong? Hey, Chief!"

With a start, Delphi realized that Bellany had been talking to him for a while. "No, just lost in thought over that redhead in the last ville," the cyborg lied quickly, then made himself chuckle. "By thunder, she was fantastic! Damn near aced me in bed, and that was before she pulled a knife and tried to gut me like a fish!"

"Just a greedy slut." Bellany snorted in disdain. "And you paid her two live rounds! Must have wanted it all, and she ended up with nothing."

"Sad, but true," Delphi said in agreement. Actually he had been forced to slay the whore when he lost control for a second during their sex play and accidentally revealed his true self, the beams of light from his cybernetic eyes shining directly into her horrified face. She'd shrieked in terror and he'd quickly pulled a knife to slash her throat, then cut his own arm to try to cover up the murder. Thankfully, the local sec men believed the innocence of the cyborg, especially when he insisted on having another slut finish what the first one had only started. A normal man denied release would seek completion, so he'd had to do the same. Anything else would have been deemed suspicious.

Annoying, but necessary. In the end it had cost Delphi another live round, but the cyborg had sex with another slut, finally crying out in pretend joy when inside he was seething with impatience to leave. Happily, if this mission was successful, he would never have to do such foul, degrading things again. He finally would have no need for the troopers of this convoy, or these ramshackle old war machines. He would be whole, complete, indomitable!

Struggling to control his breathing, Delphi rubbed his bad leg, remembering the disastrous fight in the underground tunnel.

Soon enough, Tanner, he silently raged. Oh, so very soon, revenge will be mine. Only this time, I'm not going after you. That would be too swift, too easy. This time I'm going to destroy your only reason for staying alive....

"Hey, look!" the driver called, applying the brakes and slowing to a complete stop. "Is that the place, Chief?"

"Looks like it," Bellany muttered, checking the map. "What do you think, sir?"

Rejoining the conversation, Delphi looked out the window. The wag was parked on top of a hillock, and down below were the sprawling remains of some pre-dark city. Most of the structures had been leveled and remained only as square outlines in the thick carpeting of weeds and scraggly bushes. A hundred cars were parked neatly in grassy fields that had once been a busy city street. Delphi realized that the bronze statue of the town's founder was nowhere in sight, the mall was now a scum-covered pond. The nuke damage to the town seemed minimal. Sierra Nevada College was a liberal arts college and not on anybody's ICBM hit list. However, its graphic arts department had a nexus generation IBM Blue/Gene supercomputer used to train students for creating state-of-the-art computer games and special effects in movies. And he wanted it.

"Hmm, I'm not sure," Delphi muttered, augmenting his vision for telescopic sight. The hundreds of assorted ruins zoomed into view and he studied them carefully.

Several of the college buildings still remained, the thick marble walls covered with moss and dense growths of wild ivy. Nevada had not been hit too hard during the war, but it had been torn to pieces by earthquakes, a volcano and the mindless rioting that soon followed skydark. Add to that the general destruction of the acid rain storms, and suddenly Delphi wasn't at all sure that he could find the graphic arts lab anymore. It seemed that implacable time was the ultimate destroyer.

As he searched for additional landmarks, the other wags arrived to park in a ragged line alongside the lead wag. The troopers inside the vehicles were talking animatedly, more than a few of them checking over their blasters, obviously preparing for a recce.

Accessing his mental files, the cyborg compared his memory of the university town to the present-day jumble of weeds and broken sidewalks. Overlapping the two images, Delphi saw that too much had shifted over time, and was forced to sneak a peek at his palm. The nanotech monitor embedded into his flesh crackled into view for a moment, then faded away again. The replacement hand was not yet fully interfaced with his internal circuitry, but the brief scan had been enough.

"Yes, this is it," Delphi stated, sitting upright. "Daniel, take us down the hill. But move slow! I cannot vouch for the stability of the subterranean aqueducts."

The driver blinked in confusion.

"Ah, sir…" Bellany started.

"The sewers are damaged and the streets may collapse," Delphi explained impatiently. "At the first sign of titling, head into the weeds." Then he diplomatically added, "You're my best driver, Dan. Try not to let me…down."

The man at the wheel smiled at the feeble joke. "No prob, Chief," he boasted, shifting into gear once more.

As the armored wag began to roll, Delphi activated the electric circuits to the 20 mm Vulcan minigun on the roof. He had a very limited supply of rounds for the Vulcan, mainly because at maximum discharge it could empty the entire vehicle of shells in under five minutes. Sluggishly a vid monitor on the dashboard flickered and scrolled into life, displaying a static-filled view of the land directly ahead of them. Touching the joystick, Delphi saw a graduated crosshairs appear on the screen. Even in his time period, this was an awesome weapon of destruction.

"Zane, contact the other wags," Delphi commanded, swiveling the Vulcan back and forth to check the servomotors. "I want Margaret and Vance to stay on top of the hill and keep a watch on us from a safe distance. Evan is to stay close."

"Already told 'em," Bellany replied, putting the hand mike back in its clip.

For the briefest second, the cyborg smiled for real. "You know me very well, Zane."

"That's my job, Chief." The bald man smiled, swaying to the motion of the wag. "To make sure your ass only has that one hole in it."

In spite of himself, Delphi snorted in amusement at the rank vulgarity, then jerked around and squeezed the trigger on the joystick. On top of the wag, the Vulcan roared for a brief second and a gelatinous thing exploded amid the branches of a large redwood a hundred feet away.

"Damn, you're fast," Bellany whispered, raising an eyebrow as the clear remains of the aced mutie dripped onto the dirt like clear syrup. "I never even saw the bastard mutie!"

"Which is why he's in charge," Daniel said, angling the wheel to roll around a large chuck of predark concrete studded with iron rods. "And why I drive, and Etta is the healer, and you… Ah, exactly what is it you do here again?"

Giving a half smile, Zane smacked the driver across the back of the head.

"Oh yeah, now I remember." He grinned, feeding the diesels more juice. The big engines responded with a surge of power.

As the wag crested over the hillock, a wide expanse of greenery spread out before it. The field of low grass became dotted with low bushes that merged together into a dense undergrowth. Obviously there had been a forest fire here in recent years, or perhaps acid rain, and the soil was only now reclaiming the lost territory.

The war wag went over the bushes without any hindrance, the plants scraping along the belly of the machine. Reaching level ground, now young saplings grew in abundance: pine, birch and willow. With no regard for the plants, Daniel drove the war wag right over the saplings, snapping off the trunks at bumper level.

The rad counter on the dashboard began to wildly click and Daniel abruptly veered away from the lake. It had to be a blast crater that had filled with water over time. Nasty. His granny had believed that when rain filled a rad pit, anybody swimming in it became a mutie. The chief said no, but it still sounded reasonable to him. Most folks were feebs, and how else could anybody explain why there were so many damn muties?

A perforated metal pole stuck out of the ground, and Daniel headed in that direction. Soon enough, bits of predark trash were visible among the weeds and plants. Two wags smashed together, a plastic toilet seat, a length of chain dangling off a cracked block of concrete.

Pieces of dark asphalt appeared here and there among the plants, and Daniel used them as a guide through the suburbs and into the ancient city. He had done this sort of recce many times before and knew what to look for.

Soon, the fledgling trees gave way to vertical walls of thick moss, and vines extended in every direction. Bright red umbrella bushes stood like fiery giants amid the greenery, clusters of tiny birds fluttering about inside the tangled maze of twisted branches. Delphi knew the strange bushes were not a mutation, but simply vegetation indigenous to Puerto Rico. How it got to North America was anybody's guess. Most likely, there had been a few samples in the college greenhouse, and after the nuclear war, they began to spread. Delphi had seen lions in Texas and elephants in Maine. When humanity tried to kill itself, the zoos of the world were left alone, neglected. Some of the starving animals weren't eaten and managed to escape and breed in the wild.

Which unfortunately did not explain the howlers, Delphi thought. Those mutations were not listed on any of his files or records.

Howlers were not genetic experiments designed to survive a nuclear war, or biological weapons, organic killing machines created by the military to combat the growing mutant population. No, they were something else. Something different and unknown. Privately, the cyborg feared they were true mutations, Mother Nature's savage response to the atomic rape of the planet. Someday, they would have to be eliminated, or else humanity would find itself embroiled in another war for survival.

More and larger buildings could be seen among the thick carpeting of moss, along with the occasional upright door or intact window. A gleaming white satellite dish thrust up from an ivy-covered building, the fire escape festooned with gently waving flowers.

The progress of the war wag slowed from the amount of debris on the old streets. More than once, the armored prow slammed into a bush only to discover a fallen-down bridge behind the growth or corroded remains of some large vehicle. Delphi recognized a few of them as Abrams battle tanks. Clearly, somebody had known what was going on inside the quiet college, but had arrived far too late to do anything about it. Just like sex and comedy, the cyborg mused, even in combat, timing was everything.

As the war wag reached an open area, Delphi called for a halt. Only a few yards away was a weed-encrusted fountain, the legs of a bronze statue rising from the amassed plants to end in ragged stumps above the thighs.

"This will do," Delphi directed, unbuckling his seat belt and standing. "We make camp here. There's good visibility in all directions. Nothing can get close without us seeing."

"You expecting trouble, Chief?" Bellany asked, rising to take a Kalashnikov assault blaster from the gun rack. Expertly, the troopers checked the load in the clip, then worked the arming bolt to chamber the first 7.62 mm round.

"No," the cyborg stated, taking down an AK-47 for himself. "Just preparing for it." He was wearing better weapons than this, but it would be good for morale for the others to see him armed like them. People were such fools.

"What exactly are we after here, anyway?" Bellany asked, slinging the longblaster over a broad shoulder and stuffing his pockets with spare clips.

"Shine, sluts and slaves?" Daniel asked hopefully, turning off the engines. The diesels sputtered a little then went still. On the dashboard, a second set of gauges and meters came to slow life, using the power from the nuke batteries inside the floor. Fuel for the motors was difficult to acquire outside of a redoubt, but the nuke batteries supplied electricity for decades before burning out.

"Hardly," Delphi corrected with a disapproving grimace. "There is a lot of old tech here that we can incorporate…ah, that we can use in the wags. Maybe even get the radios to work for farther than a couple of hundred feet."

Resting both arms on top of the steering wheel, Daniel gave a long, low whistle.

"Working radios," Bellany muttered. "That'd give us a chilling edge in any fight with anther wag. We gotta try for those!"

Which was why I offered the suggestion, fool. "Exactly, old friend," Delphi said, beaming a cold smile. "My thoughts exactly."

Just then the second wag rolled into view and came to a halt only a few yards away. As the engines died, the side hatch cycled open, lowering to the ground to form a short flight of stairs. Two armed troopers were standing inside the wag, the door of the security cage closed behind them just in case of any trouble. Bypassing the stairs, the two men jumped to the ground and stood in a crouched position to give the other troopers inside the wag needed clearance to fire. All of the men were carrying Browning Automatic Rifles, heavy bolt-action weapons from the Second World War. Only one person was carrying a Kalashnikov, a short redheaded woman who was the sec boss for the second wag.

Looking over the ivy-covered ruins, Cotton Davenport grunted in satisfaction, then unlocked the door to the cage and walked outside to join the troopers. Next came two more troopers, carrying Browning longblasters, but these had bayonets attached to the end of the barrels. The blades shone mirror-bright in the weak sunlight radiating downward from the stormy sky. Both of the guards wore bandoliers slung across their chests, the loops full of shiny brass cartridges.

"Okay, spread out and do a perimeter sweep!" Cotton commanded, her fiery curls shaking in the cool breeze. "I wanna fifty yard recce in every direction! You find anything, chill it."

Nodding, the four troopers headed off in different directions, their weapons held at the ready.

"Come on, Zane," Delphi said, starting along the central corridor of the wag. "I don't want to waste any of the daylight we have remaining."

"No prob. Got your six, Chief," the big man said, striding close behind.

Just past the food locker, Delphi noted the left and right gunners were alert in their metal cocoons, hands resting lightly on the handles of the Remington .50-caliber machine guns. Excellent. There should not be any need for the heavy weapons on this sojourn, he thought, but it never hurt. Briefly, Delphi wondered if he should have brought along the Kalashnikovs.

Turning into the mudroom where the troopers stored their acid rain garments, Delphi took down a hurricane lantern and slung it over a shoulder before unbolting the door to the security cage and stepping through to work the handle that activated the armored hatch. With the soft sigh of hydraulics, the section of the hull disengaged and swung down to the vine-covered ground.

Exiting the wag, Delphi pretended to stretch sore muscles because it was expected, then strode into the ruins. Bellany stayed at his side, as Cotton and four more troopers joined the procession. Two of them wore bulky backpacks and one man openly carried a crowbar. Everybody carried lanterns and grens.

As the group moved deeper into the ruins, the buzzing and chirping of the insect life went silent, and there was only the sound of the leaves crunching under their combat boots. Surreptitiously, Delphi checked the area with an infrared scanner inside his left hand, but saw no indication of anything large. But he stayed alert for anything cold-blooded that wouldn't have appeared on the scanner.

Vines were thick underfoot, making walking tricky business, and little white mushrooms were everywhere. The air smelled of damp earth, decaying matter and flowers. There was a small banana tree in the smashed display window of a clothing store and clusters of an unknown fruit festooned a public library. One of the troopers nudged another to point out a large spiderweb filling an alleyway between two buildings, and a large snake on a second-floor balcony stared unnervingly at the norms as they moved past.

The jungle of Nevada, the cyborg darkly mused. With the weather patterns of the world this badly scrambled, it was a miracle that anybody had survived sky-dark.

Behind them, the engines of the war wags gave off soft pings as they began to cool. Troopers watched the group from behind the gridwork covering the wind-shields, and high on the hill there came the flash of reflected light from a pair of binocs.

Going to the cracked marble basin of the old fountain, Delphi located the broken statue and pulled away vines until he found the rest of the figure. It was lying amid the leafy ivy and kudzu, the bronze turned a dark green from a century of corrosion.

"Is that their baron or some kinda god?" a trooper asked curiously. The statue was of a man carrying a longblaster and powder horn, so it had to be a sec man of some kind. He'd seen hunters wearing the same kind of fringed clothing back east. The fringe waved in the breeze and helped keep off the flies and skeeters.

"The great-grandfather of their baron, is more like it," Delphi replied, running calculations inside his head. If the Boston Minuteman had been facing the southeast, then the main road should be to their right. Hopefully, the physics lab was still standing, or else this whole trip would be a waste. Delphi only had limited resources since being thrown out of Department Coldfire, and every failure threatened his very existence.

Just for an instant, the cyborg relived the awful moment when a friend told him that the executive council had ordered his termination for the failure to retrieve the test subject, aka Doctor Theophilus Tanner. The occasional lack of success on a mission was to be expected in the chaos of the Deathlands, but Delphi had broken too many rules, slaughtered too many gene-pure people, in his mad quest for Tanner. All would have been forgiven if he had accomplished the task, but this level of failure meant his doom. Knowing he had only minutes in which to act, Delphi had reluctantly killed his friend and used his Ident card to raid the main warehouse for spare body parts and supplies, then established a supply cache at an abandoned redoubt. Now he walked the planet amid the dirty savages, posing as a trader, exchanging trinkets for food and buying the loyalty of men with guns and bullets, searching, hunting, committed to another desperate quest, this time to gain his own salvation.

"Well, nuke me running," a trooper muttered, rubbing the back of his neck. "Never would have supposed they had flintlocks back then. Thought that was something new."

"Yeah?" Cotton asked, suddenly interested. "And who the frag has new flintlocks?"

The trooper started to reply when something moved in the trees, jumping from branch to branch with blurring speed, and coming their way.

"Volley fire!" Bellany shouted, and the troopers raised their BAR blasters to unleash a crackling discharge. The hail of bullets tore through the treetops, sending a score of leaves fluttering to the ground. Then a bloody screamwing plummeted into sight to bounce off the marquee of a vine-covered movie theater. The lifeless body flopped to a fire bush and the leaves closed around the small, leathery body, wrapping it tight to extract every ounce of nourishment.

"Watch for the mate," Bellany commanded, using a thumb to switch his AK-47 from single shot to full-auto.

The words were barely spoken when a larger screamwing lanced out of the tree to swoop down and skim along the ground, its deadly beak and claws ready to kill. Without hesitation, the troopers opened fire, peppering the plant life with hot lead. But the winged mutie was too fast and the thing was almost upon them, shrieking in rage and fury, when Delphi fired once. In an explosion of gory, the head was blown off the screamwing and the body slammed into Cotton, knocking over the startled sec woman.

"Th-thanks, Chief," the woman panted, getting back to her feet. "Nuking hell, that thing was fast! How could you ever—"

"Yes, yes, you're welcome," the cyborg interrupted, already contemplating other matters. "Come on, I think the building is this way!"

As he rushed off by himself, the others scrambled to catch up with Delphi as he darted from a stand of banyan trees to a sagging church. An old skeleton was lashed to the cross on top, only the ropes and jungle vines holding the dried bones in place. A plastic rosary still hung from the broken neck of the Catholic priest, a fiberglass arrow shaft going through his ribs exactly where his heart would have been located; another jutted from the left eye socket.

Ruefully, Delphi knew that after skydark, most of the

survivors went temporarily mad. Terrified and starving, they turned against any symbol of authority, police officers, physicians, judges and even the clergy, killing the very people who could have helped them stay alive. Damned themselves to a century of barbarism by their own foolishness and fear. Not many people could read these days, and the word "whitecoat" was the most vile curse word. Advanced technology was suspect and considered magic by most norms. Traveling across the scorched continent, Delphi had no trouble finding sec men to join his convoy—blasters with unlimited ammo was a lure that none could resist—but very few wanted anything to do with the engines, power plant or electronic machinery.

"This place makes my skin crawl," a trooper whispered. "It's evil. I can feel it."

"Frag that noise," Bellany snapped irritably. "Watch for more screamwings and stay with the chief!"

Frantically, Delphi looked around, then charged in a fresh direction. Yes, this was it. He was close, almost there! The main street of the ruins was made of red bricks, partially crumbled back into the moist earth, witch weed and dill growing thick between the irregular rows.

A large metallic shape filled an intersection and Delphi thought it was another army tank at first. But as he got closer he realized it was the bent wreckage of an ICBM missile. Probably one of the many that had been shot down during the brief war. The ceramic nose cone was still attached, and the cyborg nervously checked for any signs of life from the thermonuclear death machine, or worse, a radiation leak. But the missile registered as magnetically inert, and there was only the low-level background radiation that blanketed the world these days. The weapon that had killed the world was dead, Delphi noted sardonically. A sword beaten, not into a plowshare, but into landfill. The irony was almost poetic. In primordial harmony, sheet lightning thundered in the stormy sky.

Moving around the missile, Delphi paused, then moved forward with renewed vigor. There it was! At last!

The graphic arts building of the college was still standing, the marble walls intact, even if the facade was slightly tilting to the left, so that the front door was now a trapezoid. The window glass for all five stories was long gone, but stout bars still covered the lopsided openings.

"What a rad pit." Bellany scowled, resting the stock of the Kalashnikov on a hip. "You sure there's anything useful here, Chief?"

"Absolutely," Delphi muttered, moving to the encrusted remains of the revolving door. The shatterproof glass was also missing from the frame, and he easily stepped through the portal and into the dim interior.

The terrazzo floor was thick with dirt, only a few very small plants having found the necessary purchase to grow on the resilient material. The furnishings in the lobby were draped with vines, the ceiling thick with cobwebs, and there was a definite reek of mildew in the air. Automatically, Delphi activated his nasal filters just in case there was any black mold in the structure.

"Use your handkerchiefs!" the cyborg snapped, pulling the knotted cloth over his nose and mouth.

Understanding the danger, the troopers rushed to obey, several of them sprinkling the cloths with a few drops of shine as additional protection.

Proceeding deeper into the building, Delphi felt his artificial eyes come alive and start to glow to counter the darkness. Instantly he countermanded the process and pulled around the lantern hanging at his side. Raising the flue, he flicked a butane lighter alive and applied the flame to the rag wick. When it caught, he lowered the flue and turned the wick all the way up for maximum illumination. The wick burned with an eerie blue light from the alcohol in the glass reservoir, which only served to give the darkness an additional unearthly feel.

As the others did the same, the lobby came to life and Delphi could now see the trappings of civilization. Dead security cameras mounted on the walls, an ATM in the corner, pay phones, an alcove filled with candy and soda machines. The ghostly echoes of a bygone era.

Going to the reception desk, Delphi held the lantern high. Most of the lettering had fallen off over the intervening century, leaving behind only a cryptic scramble of partial words and names. Useless.

Looking around the lobby, Delphi saw two sets of double doors at opposite ends. One set was broken and hanging from the rusted hinges, the other still in place, the glass in the observation port cracked but intact.

Ipso facto, Delphi mentally chuckled, heading for them. However, the doors proved to be firmly locked. The IBM supercomputer had cost the college several million dollars. He had expected some decent security. Just not this good. Could…could this have been one of the hardpoints where the redoubts had been designed? Suddenly the cyborg felt a tingling rush of excitement. This could be the answer to his prayers! Not just a college, but a top-secret military laboratory!

"Blow it," Delphi eagerly commanded, moving back a ways.

Now the troopers with the backpacks moved up, pulling out blocks of C-4 plastique. Taking over the work, Bellany cut the big blocks into small squares and attached them to the outside of the doors where the hinges should be located on the other side. Shoving in small detonators, the trooper trailed the wiring behind him as he got clear, then attached them to a small handheld generator.

"Hot plas!" he shouted in warning, then twisted the handle on top.

The little generator gave a low whine and the C-4 violently exploded, smashing the doors apart and sending a hurricane of exhaust across the lobby, creating a storm of dust. The entire predark building seemed to vibrate from the concussion.

"Davis! Hannon! Stay by the front of this drek hole and watch for stickies," Cotton commanded, wiping her stinging eyes with the back of a hand. "That fucking boom might bring every mutie in the area down our nuking throats!"

Coughing loudly, the two troopers shuffled away.

Hurrying closer, Delphi was stunned to see that the doors had not been removed, but instead were merely separated by a few feet, the adamantine portals still attached to the locking bar on the inside. However, the massive hinges were twisted and stretched like warm taffy, leaving a gap between the doors of about a foot.

"Shitfire, they sure built things strong before the big chill," Bellany muttered, impressed in spite of himself. "That plas charge should have knocked down the whole damn wall!"

"Ah, but this is no ordinary building," Delphi said, holding the lantern next to the gap. Past them was only darkness. "I think this might have been a mil base."

"A fort?" Still blinking, Cotton furrowed her brow. "Thought you said it was a school," she said.

"A little of both, and so much more," the cyborg said excitedly. "Now stay close and follow my lead!"

Turning sideways, Delphi managed to squeeze through the slim opening and held the lantern high. There was another long corridor ahead of him, but this one was spotlessly clean, without any dust, vines or mold. There was a breeze coming from behind Delphi carrying the rank smells of the jungle, mixed with the tang of ages-old dust. But the air past the doors was flat and sterile, tasting rather similar to that of a redoubt. Sterile and clean. Simply amazing, he marveled. The installation seemed to be intact. The seals had to have held for a full century! And if that was true…

Unable to restrain himself further, Delphi ran forward past numerous doors marked only with project codenames—Broken Thunder, Delta Dawn, Maelstrom and the like—until reaching a plain door marked simply as Coldfire.

Eureka! Breathlessly the cyborg tapped an entry code onto the keypad and there was no response, which was not very surprising. Even the vaunted nuke batteries had limits.

Glancing behind to make sure the others coming through the doors were not close yet, the cyborg pushed up a sleeve and opened a small service panel in his arm. Pulling out a power cord, he attached it to the port of the keypad and tried again. This time a green light came on, there was a click and the door swung open wide. But before Delphi could move, there came the sound of running boots. Quickly he reclaimed the power cord just as Bellany, Davenport and the others arrived.

"Don't like you going off by yourself, Chief," the bald trooper growled, peering suspiciously into the open doorway. "What if you found a stickie, or a greenie, hiding in here?"

"I was in no danger," Delphi replied tolerantly, pulling down his sleeve. "Now I want the rest of you to stay here in the hallway. I must do the next part alone."

"Sir, I just said—" Bellany started, but was cut off by a curt hand gesture from the cyborg.

"Oh, I'll be fine," Delphi reiterated, unable to look away from the darkness. Everything he wanted, everything he needed, could be only feet away in the Stygian gloom. "Besides—"

"No."

The word startled the cyborg and he slowly turned. "What was that you just said?" he demanded.

"I said no," Bellany repeated gruffly. "Where you go, so do we, Chief. End of discussion."

Impatiently, Delphi started to rally cogent arguments, but then saw the grim determination in the trooper's face and accepted the situation. The only way to stop the man from following would be to kill him. Delphi had no real problem with that, but there were too many others that would also have to be killed, and in the ensuing fight, some of their bullets might damage the delicate equipment inside the predark lab, ruining the whole reason for coming here in the first place.

"All right, we stay together," Delphi said, artfully masking his annoyance. "However—"

"I'm on point," Bellany said, stepping in front of the

cyborg and walking boldly into the blackness. Holding their blasters at the ready, the other troopers stayed close to Delphi.

The floor was bare concrete, thick power cables crisscrossing the expanse in a manner shockingly similar to the jungle outside. A huge supercomputer stood mute along a cinder-block wall, the huge tanks of liquid nitrogen used to cool the machine standing in a neat row inside a chained corral.

Mountains of machinery rose and fell around the group, the shadows cast by their alcohol lanterns making the equipment seem oddly animated.

"So what are we looking for?" Cotton asked, tightening her grip on the Kalashnikov.

Pausing in thought, Delphi debated how much to tell them when one of the troopers snorted in disgust.

"Blind Norad, it really stinks in here," he said behind the mask covering his mouth. "Kinda reminds me of a latrine."

Pursing his lips, Delphi started to mock the fellow. After all how could there be the smell of feces inside a lab that had been sealed for a hundred years? Then he smelled it, too. Fresh dung. But how was that possible unless…

"Muties!" Delphi shouted, smashing the hurricane lantern on the floor.

The glass reservoir crashed and the supply of shine ignited, creating a rush of light that caught something large and dark just outside the nimbus of illumination.

"Go back-to-back!" Bellany shouted, raising the AK-47. "Form a circle!"

"No, don't shoot!' Delphi cried, but then the shadows moved again and a trooper shrieked as his arm was torn off at the shoulder, taking his blaster with it.

As the others rushed to his aid, Cotton spun and triggered her rapid-fire. The muzzle-flash strobed in the darkness almost revealing something darting between the huge predark machines. The 7.62 mm rounds ricocheted off the hulking equipment, throwing off sprays.

"Damn it, that was an order!" Delphi raged, shaking his Kalashnikov at the norm. "I said no—"

But the sec woman fired again, a longer burst, just as Bellany fired his weapon in the opposite direction.

"Shitfire, there's two of 'em!" a trooper snarled, pulling a gren.

Aghast, Delphi pointed the rapid-fire at the man and was about to shoot when there was movement above the group and a large black creature landed in the middle of them, right on top of the smashed lantern. The blue flames rose around the mutie, apparently doing no harm to it whatsoever, but revealing every feature. It was a huge catlike creature, almost the size of a pony. The smooth fur was dead-black, the mouth a crimson slash, the long fangs dripping blood from the recent kill, and the eyes were solid yellow. Then a writhing nest of tentacles rose from the back.

"Nuke me, it's a hellhound!" a trooper screamed, backing away in terror. Then he convulsed and toppled over, revealing a second mutie retreating into the gloom with most of his spine dangling from its horrid jaws.

Dropping his AK-47, Bellany spun in a crouch, drew the Webley and fired. The booming muzzle-flame actually touched the hellhound, scoring a long bloody furrow along its side. Snarling insanely, the big cat charged through the crowd of troopers, bowling them over as it escaped into darkness.

As the gutted body hit the ground, the troopers began

firing their weapons in every direction, the discharges illuminating the predark lab. Delicate machinery exploded into pieces as the two hellhounds circled the group, going in different directions, constantly moving.

"Sons of bitches are trying to confuse us!" Cotton bellowed, squeezing off a short burst from the Kalashnikov. "How fragging smart are these muties?"

The light from the smashed lantern was beginning to flicker and die, and as the illumination diminished, the hellhounds came ever closer. Oddly, the monstrous cats seemed unconcerned about the other lanterns.

"It's not the light!" Cotton realized, shouting over her chattering longblaster. "They don't like fire!"

"Chief, is there anything in here we can burn?" Bellany demanded, working the bolt to free a bent shell caught in the ejector port. He got it loose and the bent casing flew away.

"I have no idea!" Delphi replied, feeling both of his hearts pound in his chest.

Suddenly one of the creatures leaped on top of a comp, only to jump off again immediately. The jar sent the big machine tilting and men scrambled away as it crashed on the floor with a deafening noise, smashing one of the lanterns. As the light vanished, a scream from the other side of the group told of another chilling.

"The eyes!" Delphi shouted. "Aim for the eyes or the ears! Those are the only weak points!"

Kicking spent brass out of their way, the troopers shuffled closer together for protection.

"You heard the man!" Cotton shouted at the top of her lungs. "Eyes and ears, boys! Send it to hell!"

Dropping back, Delphi sprayed an entire clip of

rounds at the hellhounds, then dropped the exhausted weapon and pulled a pistol from his gunbelt. At the grasp of his hand, the weapon audibly charged and an indicator light on top registered in the red. The battery inside the H&K needler was fully charged.

"Everybody out!" Delphi commanded, leveling the Kalashnikov and his pistol. "I can handle this alone!"

"No nuking way. We stand together!" Bellany snarled, snapping off shots with the Webley. Then the hammer clicked on a spent shell. Ducking, the bald trooper cracked the weapon to drop the empties and hastily thumb in fresh rounds. One live cartridge fell and rolled away under a wooden desk—and a hellhound jumped over the desk to land on top of Bellany.

Shrieking obscenities, the man went down, firing the handcannon point-blank into the chest of the thing. A single swipe of the powerful claws removed his throat, while the tentacles lanced outward, spearing two other troopers, scoring minor wounds. Their rapid-fires dropped with a clatter, firing off a few rounds before stopping.

Recoiling, Delphi paused for only a second, then aimed both of his weapons and fired them simultaneously. The chattering of the assault rifle completely masked the soft hiss of the H&K coil gun. The 7.62 mm bullets bounced off the body of the beast, but the 2.5 mm depleted uranium slivers punched clean through the sleek, muscular body.

Pumping out piss-yellow blood, the hellhound snarled over a shoulder, and all of its tentacles stabbed for the cyborg. He ducked, and they missed by less than an inch. Staying in a crouch, he fired again and again, scoring hits both times.

Now the others trained their blasters on the wounded beast, hammering it with lead and steel.

Gushing sticky golden fluids, the creature sprang for the cyborg and missed, but knocked the Kalashnikov out of his hands, the rapid-fire taking the needler along with it. But as the animal landed on the desk, Davenport shoved her Ruger .357 into one of its ears and fired. The backblast threw the woman down, but the head of the beast cracked open, yellow blood erupting from the mouth and exploding the eyes. Weaving drunkenly on its legs for a long moment, the beast went still and gently laid down as if it was merely going to sleep. As the head listed sideways, the life fluids ceased to flow from the ghastly wounds and the big hellhound went still.

Taking heart from the chill, the few remaining troopers cheered wildly, now able to concentrate on the last man-killer. Trying for the nimble creature, they succeeded only in finishing the destruction of the predark lab.

Recovering his needler, Delphi cursed when he saw another trooper fall and made a command decision. The resources of the lab were already lost. Time to save what he could.

"Use the grens!" the cyborg bellowed, pulling the crystal wand from his shoulder holster.

Taking defensive positions behind the toppled comps, the troopers readied the explosive charges, ripping off the safety tape holding the arming level in place.

As if understanding the danger, the hellhound turned and looped for the door. Already facing that direction, Delphi waited until it was directly in sight, then squeezed the wand.

A scintillating laser beam stabbed out from the tip, hitting the big cat in the neck. Yellow blood formed a geyser from the punctured artery and as it turned, Delphi increased the power to maximum and burned a long burst straight down its throat. The beast went stock-still as the mauling power ray burned down its gullet. Now the grens arrived, raining down around the beast and thunderously detonating, ripping the body apart into bloody gobbets.

As the smoky blasts dissipated, Cotton walked over to inspect the corpse.

"Yeah, that's aced proper," she said with grim satisfaction. Then the woman hawked and spit on the tattered remains. "All right, gather the blasters and boots! Leave the bodies. They'd only be dug up during the night by animals."

Moving slow, as if they were drunk, the exhausted men moved among their fallen comrades, taking what was necessary and ignoring the rest. Death was part of their job. Later they would mourn for lost friends, but right now there was still work to be done as quietly and efficiently as possible.

Realizing this was his best chance, Delphi holstered the laser, then took it out again, just in case there was another of the creatures hiding somewhere. Bioweapons! Somebody was going to pay for that dearly. There was no doubt in his mind that this had been a trap set just for him. How else could animals have gotten inside a room supposedly sealed for a hundred years? Clearly, they had been placed there recently, the doors resealed. And the people in charge of all biological weapons worked for TITAN. This was bad, Delphi acknowledged.

Going to the smashed comp, Delphi looked over the wreckage and sighed. He had hoped that something might have survived the battle, but the IBM Blue/Gene supercomputer was utterly destroyed. The huge comp was the finest and fastest of its kind in the predark world, and used some of the prototype for the circuits inside his body. The cyborg had fervently hoped to find something he could use here, but that was impossible now. The circuit cubes were broken, the digital wafers shattered, and the plasma chips warped from a series of massive short circuits. Gone, all gone.

With diminishing hope, Delphi went from one server to the next, finding only trash. The last two servers had bullet holes in them, yet were still serviceable and capable of working. Good news indeed. Except that they contained none of the experimental microprocessors that he required.

Then inspiration hit and Delphi walked to the control board for the supercomputer and raised the service panel to palm over the complex wiring. Incredibly, he received an answering tingle and dug among the morass of shielded circuits to retrieve a lumpy section of a slim piece of ribbon cable. It was a Thinking Wire, and almost as advanced as the version that he carried. Even more important, the microchips embedded in the cable seemed completely undamaged!

Keeping out of sight behind the raised lid of the console, Delphi opened a port in his chest and fed in the wire. It took a few moments for his systems to initiate the new hardware, and there was a moment of disorientation. Then whole sections of deactivated programs and hardware became active in his mind. His autorepair systems were back online! Scrolling through the command menu, he held out a palm and there appeared a barely visible sheen in the air. Frowning slightly, Delphi rerouted some power and the translucent distortion expanded to a full yard, then it turned transparent.

I have a force field again! Now he was safe from bullets, lasers, anything. Everything! Even a focused EMP beam designed to burn out his internal circuitry and render him powerless, paralyzed, a prisoner inside his own augmented body. Helpless prey for the agents of TITAN. If they were actively hunting for him, then it was time to turn and take a stand. No, he'd attack them! The balance of power had been redressed. Now the war began in earnest.

"Sir?"

Quickly dissolving the immaterial force field, Delphi looked up and saw Davenport standing nearby. How much had she just seen? Did she know the truth? "Yes, what is it, Cotton?" the cyborg asked in forced casualness.

That made the sec woman pause. This was the first time he had ever called her by her first name. Guess I've just stepped into an aced man's boots and am the new sec boss for the convoy.

"We're ready to leave, Chief," she replied, resting the still-warm barrel of her Kalashnikov on a shoulder. Bellany's gunbelt and Webley .44 hung over the other arm. "Unless there's something else you want to look for around here."

"No, I've found what was needed," Delphi stated, lowering the service panel and locking it closed once more. "Let's go."

"Where, sir?"

There was only one answer to that. "East," Delphi said, flexing his hands, feeling the power course within them. "Let's go home."

Chapter Four

Astonished by the sheer speed of the spidery droid, Ryan hit the floor braced for the searing onslaught of pain from the laser beam. Incredibly there did not seem to be any damage from the bright ray. But he felt fine, and even his shirt was undamaged. What the frag? Had the thing missed?

As the droid fired again, Ryan rolled out of the way and the rest of the companions triggered their Kalashnikovs in unison, peppering the machine with a hail of 7.62 mm rounds, the ricochets zinging everywhere. Then Ryan came up holding the 9 mm SIG-Sauer and put two Parabellum man-stoppers directly into the machine's eyes. The red crystal shattered and the droid began randomly lancing out with the strange white beam, hitting the walls, floor, coffins and Doc, to no effect whatsoever.

Snarling a curse, Jak cast away the useless AK-47, smoothly drew his Colt Python and stroked the trigger, sending a booming .357 round directly into head of the droid. With a loud ringing noise, the shiny metal deeply dented, the machine limply fell from the ceiling to crash on the floor, wildly shaking, the metallic legs flailing insanely.

Moving fast, Doc stepped in close, leveled the LeMat and sent a massive .44 miniball directly into the dent.

The metal split apart with a huge eruption of sparks and smoke began to rise from the droid as the legs slowly lowered to the floor and went still. Nobody moved for a few moments until they were sure the droid was aced and not merely faking.

As the companions gathered around the creaking machine, Mildred went to Ryan and checked the man over, looking into his eyes for any signs of dilation, taking his pulse, pressing an ear to his chest to listen to his heart, and even yanking up his shirt to see the skin underneath.

"I'm fine," the one-eyed man said patiently.

"Yes, you are," Mildred finally said, tugging down his shirt. "And I'm damn glad for that, but puzzled as all hell. Why are you fine?"

"I guess it missed me."

"No way, lover," Krysty said, turning. "I saw that white beam hit you dead-center." Her hair started flexing as the woman frowned. "At least, I think it hit you…"

"Hit," Jak stated in a no-nonsense tone. "Hit Doc, too."

"Indeed it did, my young friend," Doc rumbled, going to the weapon lying impotently on the floor. The man kicked aside a leg partially covering the device. "Which begs the question of why we are unharmed. Did the laser malfunction, or did it do something else to us that has yet to achieve full effect?"

"Like what?" Mildred demanded, resting a hand on the strap of her med kit.

The man shrugged. "Possibly we now have cancer or will go insane in a few days. You tell me, madam."

The physician started to rebuff the suggestion, then

had to reconsider. Whoever had set the droid as a guardian over the blasters would have been incompetent beyond belief to not make sure it was properly armed. So what did the white light do?

Kneeling on the floor, she ran fingertips over the beam unit, then J.B. joined her and they started to disassemble the outer casings.

"Think more?" Jak asked, studying the ceiling, his blaster held tight in a two-handed grip.

"No, if there were any more of the machines they would have joined the fight," Ryan said, holstering the SIG-Sauer. "I've seen droids with laser camou before, but never as good as this one. Until it moved, I had no idea the bastard thing was hanging above us."

"Aside from the odd tapping noise," Krysty added, removing the mostly spent clip from her rapid-fire and inserting a new one. "That must have been caused by the metal legs moving on the ceiling."

"How do?" Jak asked, easing his stance slightly. If the others said the area was clear, that was good enough for him.

"Magnets most likely," Ryan said with a shrug.

"And that's also what this is," Mildred said, studying the interior of the weapon. "Nothing but a massive capacitor and a magnetic array." She touched a golden coil. "See, that's the focusing mechanism. I've seen something similar inside a CAT scanner."

"Not las, but mag gun?" Jak asked quizzically.

"Yep."

"So what was the light?"

"That was from a halogen bulb." J.B. grunted, tilting back his fedora. "Nothing more than a souped-up flashlight, probably just there to help aim the magnetic."

"Aim the magnet, sir?" Doc repeated slowly, chewing over the information. "Are you saying this is some sort of scrambling device? Mayhap a kind of antirobot gun?"

"Could be, yeah. What else would a focused beam of magnetics harm? A comp, mebbe, or a—"

"Cyborg," Ryan interrupted in a hard voice. "This wasn't set here by Delphi to guard the blasters. Somebody else put it here to wait for him."

"A cyborg chiller," Jak whispered, impressed and uneasy at the same time. Then he eagerly added, "Still work? We use now."

"No, it's busted to drek." Mildred sighed, standing and dusting off her hands. "The circuit boards are fried, the ribbon cables melted, the focusing ring warped…" She dismissed the device with a hand wave. "The only way we could use this to hurt Delphi now is if we dropped it on his head from a great height."

"This means that most likely Delphi has not been here in a long while," Krysty added, ruminating out loud. "Weeks, mebbe, or even months."

"It also means that somebody else wants Delphi aced," J.B. stated. "Which is fine by me. The enemy of my enemy, and all that, eh, Doc?"

"True words, John Barrymore," the silver-haired man intoned. "Although, I have usually found that the 'enemy of my enemy' axiom loses all coherent meaning after the aforementioned protagonist is finally eating dirt. Then all bets are off."

"Fair enough," Ryan said savagely, working the bolt on a Kalashnikov. Then his stomach softly grumbled. "Come on, let's finish the recce of this redoubt. The sooner we know it's safe, the sooner we can have some chow." In an effort to save their stomachs, the companions had deliberately not eaten before doing the jump. It seemed to work, but now they were paying the price.

"I hear that," J.B. added eagerly, heading for the exit. "I'm not quite hungry enough for Millie's boot soup, but will be soon."

"Well, it kept us alive, that's for sure," Mildred shot back proudly. "Although it must have been a month before I finally got the taste out of my mouth. It made hospital food seem absolutely delicious in comparison."

"Indeed, madam, the flavor combination was rather reminiscent of the haute cuisine of Hades," Doc observed, glancing sideways and trying to hide a smile. "Although to be honest, it was truly the finest boot soup that I have ever had!"

"Aw, shut up, ya old coot," Mildred shot back, pleased and annoyed at the same time.

Reaching the exit, the companions paused to check over their weapons before proceeding down the long hallway. Jak was the last to leave and closed the armory door behind them. Even though the machine was smashed to drek, he didn't trust droids and felt better with a good foot of steel between them.

"Wait a minute, I may have something," Krysty said, rummaging in her bearskin coat pockets to finally pull out a handful of jerky. She offered it around and everybody took some. "Been saving it for a while," she said. "But it should still be good."

It took some determined chewing before the dried meat yielded any flavor, but as the reconstituted juices trickled down their throats, the hunger pains in their bellies eased.

Slightly refreshed, the group reached the elevators at

the end of the corridor, but instead took the stairs. They had been hesitant about using the elevator before as the noise would announce their presence to the whole redoubt. Well, the blaster fight had already accomplished that. But the cage was a deathtrap if they got ambushed. The stairs at least gave them some room to move.

Climbing and chewing, they proceeded to the next level and found the barracks empty and unused, but spotlessly clean. Ready to house hundreds of soldiers at a moment's notice. Ominous.

Continuing up the stairs, Ryan took the point and eased open the door to the garage level. The parking area was full of civilian vehicles from the predark soldiers rushing to the base to escape skydark: pickup trucks, a couple of Harley bikes, battered station wagons, an SUV and the like, but there were no mil wags in sight. Curious.

Staying low, the companions spread out through the ranks of the vehicles, checking out the workbenches along the walls, fuel depot, grease pit and wire cubicle where all the heavy equipment was stored.

"Okay, we're clear," Ryan announced, standing upright again. "Let's go outside so J.B. can find out where we are."

"And then we eat," Mildred declared, patting the MRE envelope in her coat pocket. Sealed in a Mylar envelope, the Meals Ready to Eat was military ration that was as fresh and tasty today as when made a century earlier. It was almost as if the government knew the nuke war was coming, Mildred thought, and had made preparations for some people to survive. The observation was not new, just disturbing. Politicians, smart enough to plan for war, but too damn dumb to hold on to peace. Thank goodness they were all gone.

Taking the zigzag tunnel to the exit of the redoubt, the companions abruptly halted at the sight of a vehicle parked just in front of the huge black doors. It was a huge smooth sphere, vaguely egg-shaped, mounted on a set of armored tank treads.

"Delphi!" Doc bellowed, brushing back his frock coat to whip out the LeMat and start fanning the hammer. The Civil War handcannon boomed and miniballs slammed into the wag.

"Hold fire!" Ryan yelled.

"See him inside?" Jak asked.

"No, I did not," Doc rumbled angrily, waving the LeMat to dispel the volumes of smoke pouring from the hot barrel. "But the windshield can be made opaque."

"So, mebbe he's not inside," Krysty said.

"Mebbe he's playing opossum," Mildred shot back tersely.

"Got the implo ready?" Ryan asked, working the bolt on the rapid-fire.

"All set to go," J.B. replied grimly, the sphere tight in a hand.

"Odd that he hasn't returned fire yet," Krysty said hesitantly.

"Got a test for that," J.B. said, and stepped around the corner to whip something forward, then duck back behind the wall once more.

After a few seconds there came a resounding explosion, followed by a thick ringing silence.

Tensely alert, the companions waited. A minute passed, then another, and some bitter smoke drifted along the tunnel following the gentle breeze coming from the air vents.

"That not implo." Jak scowled. "Reg gren?"

"Sure," J.B. replied, lifting the precious implo gren into view from a pocket. "I'm not going to waste this until I knew the son of a bitch is in there for sure. Lots of reg grens, but only got the one implo, remember."

Listening hard, Ryan couldn't hear any movement from around the corner, and bent low to take a quick look. The wag was exactly the same as before. Suspecting a trap, he rolled another gren under the wag and waited to see what would happen. After another minute, he stood in plain view. Still no response.

"Okay, it's clear," Ryan stated, walking around the corner. "There's no way Delphi would sit still for this long unless he's unconscious."

"Or aced," Doc rumbled dangerously, the LeMat held in a white-knuckled hold. "I do not honestly know which I would enjoy more, seeing him deceased or doing the job myself!"

"Bloodthirsty old coot," Mildred shot back.

"And you have never been his captive, madam," the time traveler growled. "While, sadly, I have."

Gathering around the huge wag, the companions now could see it was in poor shape. The treads had several shoes broken off or missing entirely. There was some sort of box on top reduced to little more than twisted wreckage, and the opaque windshield was badly cracked. The normally smooth white hull was badly pitted in spots, tiny rivulets of silvery steel congealed along the sides.

"That was his LAV," Doc stated in his stentorian bass.

Tilting back his fedora, J.B. gave a whistle. "Well, somebody kicked his ass, that's for trip damn sure," he said happily. "Mebbe he is dead. That'd sure solve a lot of problems."

"He was probably trying to get the LAV into the garage for repairs," Krysty guessed, running a hand along the armored hull. "Anybody know a way inside this thing, so that we can check?"

Almost too soft to hear, there came a low click and then a section of the hull jutted slightly. Quickly the companions stepped backward, bringing up their weapons, as the hatch cycled downward forming a short set of stairs.

Wordlessly, Ryan pointed to the left and right, J.B. and Krysty heading around the machine to attack from the other side.

Then his heart skipped a beat as a long, black, metal leg extended from the interior, closely followed by two more and the globular body of another droid. It took only a nanosecond for him to see this machine did not have a cyborg chiller mounted to its belly, but something else, a sleek, ferruled tube with pulsating fiber-optic cables and a narrow red lens that glowed like the eye of a demon from Hell.

"Las!" Ryan bellowed, throwing himself to the side and raising the Kalashnikov as a shield.

The same as before, he was still airborne when the beam stabbed outward. But this time it was a brilliant red beam the color of burning blood. Ryan felt the rapid-fire get hot in his hands, and when he hit the floor, he threw it away only a moment before the ammo detonated.

The blast rocked him, but he went with the force of the concussion, rolling away until hitting the wall. There was a pain in his side and another along his neck, but Ryan ignored those and pulled the SIG-Sauer as he stood, tracking and firing.

The beamed stabbed the wall next to him and he could feel the terrible heat radiating outward, it was so close. Ducking, he fired the SIG-Sauer twice, then spun and fired twice more.

Gotta keep moving, Ryan realized. Can't let it get a bead, or I'm the last train west! Move, Cawdor, move!

Firing and weaving, he got behind the egg-shaped wag and the droid went out of sight. Then it rose above the vehicle, the dead eyes searching for him. He locked gazes with the machine, and the smooth hull of the wag turned yellow, orange, pink...and the laser cut through the vehicle less than an inch away.

Raising his blaster, Ryan cursed. With the machine on the other side, he couldn't shoot through the LAV to hit it! Using the wag as a shield had saved his life, but now he couldn't fight back!

Suddenly there was a thundering detonation from the opposite side of the tunnel, and the droid dropped from sight as a hot wind breathed around the armored treads underneath, the metal pinging and cracking from shrapnel.

That had been a gren! Knowing this tunnel was the best place to bomb the droid, he yanked out his gren, pulled the ring, flipped off the spoon and lofted the bomb over the wag. Then he ducked.

If possible, the second blast sounded even louder than the first, and something heavy slammed into the LAV, making it shake.

Glancing upward, Ryan saw a cloud of smoke billowing in the tunnel, then Doc appeared from around the first turn in the passage and waved him on. That was all he needed. Breaking into a sprint, Ryan charged around the wag and across the empty space. Friendly hands grabbed his clothing and yanked him behind the metal wall just as the laser cut through the smoke, missing him by less than a hair.

"Everything!" Ryan commanded, holstering the SIG-Sauer and pulling the second gren from his pocket. He armed the charge and threw it hard at the opposite wall. The mil sphere hit and bounced out of sight into the next section.

The rest of the companions did the same, and the tunnel shook from the continuous bombardment of high-explosive plas. The lights went out with a crash of glass, the explosions casting distorted shadows as they went off.

Then the droid lumbered around the corner only a yard away from the companions. One eye was gone and a leg was bent, but it still moved with grim resolve.

"Dark night, the nuke sucker is armored!" J.B. shouted, throwing the unprimed gren in his hand with all of his strength. The metal sphere hit the remaining eye of the droid and bounced off harmlessly.

Then Jak and Doc fired together, the .357 Colt Python and the .44 LeMat sounding like chained thunder. Even as the droid came closer, the eye shattered, and it froze, motionless.

Moving around the corner, Mildred took a full second to aim, then gently squeezed the trigger on her AK-47. The fiber-optic cables of the deadly laser were ripped from their couplings and the housing bent slightly.

But as they watched, something rose from the top of the droid, a flexing cable with a tiny light at the end. It pointed at them, and the body rotated, the legs extending and contracting as the war machine glided forward.

Gaia, the thing had a spare eye? Krysty cursed bitterly as she moved away, dropping a clip and reloading fast. One droid to capture, a second to ace. Somebody wants Delphi eating dirt even more than we do, she thought. Now that it was out of the LAV, the robotic machine had them in a chilling zone, with nowhere to hide. Some dim recess of her mind rationalized that this was probably why it had laid in waiting inside the broken wag just like a real spider, waiting for the flies to get close before it pounced.

Retreating fast, Jak and Doc fired again, throwing more smoke than lead, with the others firing away with the Kalashnikovs. The combination was nearly deafening, and it became impossible to shout any suggestions as the desperate group ran along the zigzag tunnel, getting only a split second of respite before the droid appeared once more seeking fresh targets, the lethal energy beam constantly flashing out to punch small molten holes in the metal walls and floor.

Tossing grens, the companions scrambled around the last corner, then broke for the lines of parked wags. As the charges detonated, the laser cut through the swirling dark smoke, shattering the rear window of an SUV and exploding the front tire on a compact foreign car.

Ryan and the others barely got behind cover before the droid stepped out of the tunnel looming high, almost brushing the ceiling. Obviously it was trying to stay away from the grens, and with just cause. Two of its legs dangled uselessly from its armored body, a third was badly bent and there was a crackling electric display crawling around the ruin of the second eye.

At the sight, Ryan impulsively touched the patch

covering his own damaged orb and bizarrely felt a instant of sympathy. Then cold reason took over and he swung up the Steyr to fire at the busted section. That would be the best chance to reach the minicomp inside the machine. Holding his breath, Ryan put two rounds directly into the charred opening, then the laser impacted on the other side of the convertible he was behind. The beam sliced through the fabric as if it was mist and moved along the side in a sweeping maneuver. Ryan ducked and felt the heat of another near miss. Then he stood and fired again into the eyehole.

This time he was rewarded by a fresh geyser of sparks. The machine titled slightly, but then righted itself and advanced once more. Moving among the civilian wags, the droid stabbed out the laser again and again, breaking windows and mirrors as he tried to track the scurrying norms.

Ducking behind a sedan, Krysty got a clear view of the machine and rose to shoot at the laser. Already weakened, the casing was slammed away, exposing the delicate crystals and wiring. As the droid turned toward her, the woman stood her ground and fired again. In an explosion of crystal, the laser winked out, chips and wires sprinkling to the floor.

J.B. and Jak whooped in triumph. Then the dead laser dropped off the droid, a hatch flipped open on the left side and another weapon cycled into view—larger, covered with smooth metal, with a small hole at the end of the barrel instead of a crystal.

"Needler!" Mildred cried in warning, firing her Kalashnikov. The physician hit the weapon twice, the 7.62 mm rounds ricocheting off the dense housing as if the rounds were thrown gravel. Then there was a low hiss from the droid and the Cadillac the physician was hiding behind violently shook from the barrage of 1 mm fléchettes.

Ordering the companions to get down, Ryan threw a gren high to detonate in the air above the machine. It shook from the blow and hosed a stream of fléchettes in his direction, almost tearing the front off the battered old pickup.

By the Three Kennedys, this weapon is even worse than the laser! Doc realized, triggering the LeMat and AK-47. Internally, the man struggled to recall if he had faced such a device before. Most of how he escaped from the Chronos whitecoats was lost in foggy memories. There was something, a symbol, some sort of a circle within a circle…

Reloading the rapid-fire, Doc shook off the useless recollection. But even as he shot again, the old man made a mental note to tell the others about the symbol. It could be very useful later on. A circle in a square? A triangle…? It was gone, like so much of his past.

Mildred threw another gren and the droid picked it off in midflight, the plas creating a fireball directly above a limousine bearing mil license plates. The blast crumpled the vehicle, and incredibly, the theft alarm began to bleat.

Unable to shout directions again, Ryan made a decision and threw his last gren at the limo. It hit the floor and rolled underneath before exploding, the blast flipping the wag over to crash on a small compact car. But thankfully, the alarm ceased to sound.

Popping up into view, Jak snapped off two rounds from his Colt Python, then ducked down, a blurry stream of fléchettes going through the air exactly where his head had been a split second ago.

"This is my last gren!" J.B. shouted from somewhere among the parked wags, letting everybody know it was anything but a gren. Then a pipe bomb appeared, flying through the air, a dangling fuse sizzling and spitting.

But as if recognizing a superior threat, the droid moved sideways and walked over several wags to take refuge behind the fuel pumps. The pipe bomb fell on the roof of a Volkswagen Beetle and started to roll of when it cut loose. The wag was blown sideways off the floor and tumbled over a dozen other wags, breaking windows and headlights until it came to rest against the workbench, rattling the assortment of tools for a hundred feet.

Fuming with impatience, Ryan scowled at the droid and wiped his hands dry on his pants. With the droid poised above the fuel pumps, Ryan knew there was nothing they could do. Only grens seemed to damage the blasted armor of the thing, and if they used one now, it could ignite the stored supplies of condensed fuel, filling this entire level of the redoubt with a tidal wave of flame that could chill all of them for sure.

His mind whirled with a dozen battle plans and settled on the best. "Take it out!" Ryan shouted, and threw an unprimed gren.

A valley of grens sailed toward the droid. They landed, the tape still holding the arming lever firmly in place. But the machine responded anyway and hurried away from the potential firestorm.

"Run for it!" Ryan roared, and started for the door to the stairs.

Crawling over the lines of wags, the droid tried to cut the companions off, launching short bursts from the needler. But this time, they threw live grens and gained precious yardage with every blinding detonation.

Ramming open the door with a shoulder, Ryan rushed in and held it aside for the others. As they charged through, he slammed the door shut and dropped to the floor. Almost instantly, it shook violently all over, the hard metal denting from the incoming fléchettes. There was a brief pause, followed by another burst. Then silence. Something fumbled with the door latch. Another burst of fléchettes, and more silence.

As the seconds ticked away, Ryan crawled to the others and explained his idea.

Suddenly they heard the sound of the elevator starting to descend.

Moving fast, the companions rushed back into the garage level. Grabbing a fire ax off the wall behind the workbench, Ryan slammed it into the double doors of the elevator and twisted with all of his might. There was a metallic creak, a sharp crack and the portals slid aside, exposing the dark shaft.

Glancing down, Ryan could see the elevator cage slowly descending the shaft. Perfect.

Turning, he saw Doc arrive, dragging a thick hose connected to the fuel pumps, with Krysty at the controls.

Grabbing the nozzle, Ryan pulled the handle to maximum flow as the redhead threw the main switch. For a stomach-twisting minute, only air hissed from the hose, then the pumps sluggishly engaged, the hose went stiff and fuel gushed from the end to cascade down the dark shaft.

Out of breath, J.B., Mildred and Jak arrived with their arms full of the unprimed grens. Setting them down, they started to yank off the safety tape and pull pins as fast as they could.

Suddenly there was a pounding sound from the elevator cage in the shaft as the Niagara of flammable fuel arrived.

"Now," Ryan growled through gritted teeth, and the others started to lob the grens and two more pipe bombs.

When the last charge went over the edge, Ryan shut off the nozzle and backed away fast, the others helping him move it to a safe distance. Even as Krysty shut off the pumps, there were more bangs from the shaft, followed by a hail of fléchettes. Then the grens cut loose in a nuke storm of explosions, the detonations changing into a sustained roar as the hundreds of gallons of fuel ignited. The entire base seemed to shake from the confined blast, then a volcano of flame vomited through the open doors, reaching out for yards and licking at several of the parked cars.

Protecting the vulnerable fuel pumps with their bodies, the companions turned their backs to the blast and took the pounding. The heat cooked the air from their lungs and the muffled thunder inside the shaft seemed to go on forever. Then it eased somewhat and died away completely.

Gasping for breath, the companions staggered away from the pumps and returned to the elevator. Thick clouds of smoke blocked their view down the shaft. They listened closely for several minutes, but there was only the sound of the heated metal creaking as it expanded slightly. Then one of the braided cables that supported the cage snapped with a sharp twang.

"Th-think that did it?" Mildred wheezed, weaving slightly. She touched the metal doors of the elevator and instantly withdrew her hand. Damn, that was hot!

"Dunno. Only one way to tell for sure," Ryan replied gruffly, hefting a Kalashnikov. "J.B. and Krysty, stay here with Mildred. If anything goes wrong, pour more fuel down the shaft until it nuking floods! Jack and Doc, with me. And keep those big-ass blasters ready." The .357 Magnum and the .44 miniballs had a lot more penetration power than the 9 mm Parabellum rounds of the SIG-Sauer or the 7.62 mm rounds of the Kalashnikovs, and they might need every bit of it if the droid had escaped and now was loose in the redoubt.

Nodding agreement, everybody moved fast.

Going to the workbench, Ryan grabbed the ax and hurried down the stairs with the other two men. At each level, they paused to check the elevator doors, but saw nothing amiss. Finally they smelled smoke, and wisps of fumes faintly colored the air, the wall vents already struggling to clear atmosphere.

Reaching the bottom level, they ran past the nuclear reactor and paused at the sight of roiling clouds of smoke coming from the bulging elevator doors. Diligently, the wall vents were audibly trying to clear away the pollution, but more fumes were issuing from the elevator than the vents could dissipate.

Proceeding carefully, Ryan crept along the wall, with Doc and Jak close behind, their big-bore blasters at the ready. Gesturing, Ryan directed the men to take positions behind the massive steel pipes feeding water to the cooling units of the nuclear reactor. They nodded and assumed firing stances. Alone, Ryan moved closer to the elevator and strained to hear any movement behind the battered doors. But there was only the steady crackle of the dying flames.

Unexpectedly, a strange rushing noise came from

the ceiling and a deluge of white foam gushed out from hidden fire sprinklers. With a curse, Doc holstered his wet LeMat, the black powder rendered useless from the moisture, and swung up his AK-47, easing back the arming bolt as quietly as possible.

Covered with the sticky goo, Ryan eased closer to the double doors, waited a minute, then slipped the ax blade into the charred rubber seal. Bracing his boots against the slippery floor, he twisted the wooden handle and the doors squealed in torment as they were forced aside, then jammed solid in the wall. A wall of smoke rolled out to fill the corridor with Stygian darkness.

Quickly stepping back, Ryan blinked the smoke from his eye trying to see inside the cage, then something metallic moved and the head of the droid filled the opening.

The needler hissed, chewing a hole through the wall, missing Ryan by a good foot, then it started angling in his direction. Summoning every ounce of his remaining strength, the Deathlands warrior swung the fire ax with both arms and buried it to the shaft into the damaged eye of the machine.

Jerking wildly, the droid yanked the ax from his grip as it began shaking and shuddering, fat blue sparks crawling all over the damaged hull. The needler fired randomly at the floor and ceiling, then ran empty.

Ryan pulled his SIG-Sauer and put an entire clip into the other eyehole, hammering the metal aside. A moment later Doc and Jak were at his side, handcannons booming thunder, the heavy-caliber rounds hammering deeper, and farther, into the armored machine. For some reason that seemed to reduce the shuddering, and Ryan sensed danger, so he grabbed the ax to pull it free with a grinding noise, then slammed it in again.

The ceiling foam slowed to a trickle as the resilient machine turned toward Ryan. Doc drew his LeMat, shoved the barrel into a tiny rent and hoped the weapon would fire. The foot-long lance of flame from the pitted muzzle seemed to fill the interior, and the droid went motionless, then dropped limply to the floor of the elevator.

Not trusting the predark machine, Ryan retrieved the ax and hacked at the body of the droid until the protective armor sheathing came off, revealing the interior workings. Now the three men fired their weapons into the complex assemblage of advanced technology until the delicate circuitry was reduced to a pile of loose debris.

"Ashes to ashes, dust to dust," Doc mumbled.

"Frag that mutie shit," Jak countered, reaching into the machine to grab a handful of loose wiring and throwing it down the dripping white corridor. "Now, aced for sure."

"A most wise precaution, my young friend," Doc replied, wiping the foam off his face. "This is a particularly redoubtable opponent, and its demise is not yet assured."

"Now it nuking is," Ryan said, stuffing his last gren into the head of the droid and pulling the pin.

Running for cover, the three men just made it behind the water pipes as the gren detonated, blowing a blast of wiring and chips across the corridor for a dozen yards. The litter hit the floor and skidded along, leaving a score of tiny contrails in bubbly chems.

"Okay, back to the armory for more grens and

ammo," Ryan stated, touching his throat. The flame-retardant foam was stinging his many cuts, although none of them seemed life-threatening. Just annoying. "After that we hit the showers and leave."

"Are we to make a jump, sir?" Doc asked, arching an eyebrow.

"Hell no," Jak answered curtly.

"Damn straight," Ryan said, striding off in a determined gait. "We're going outside after that Delphi and end him." Just then, his stomach growled in hunger again, but Ryan ignored it completely. Food would come later. There was more chilling to be done this day.

Chapter Five

After rearming themselves, the companions went to the garage level of the redoubt and checked inside the egg-shaped LAV for anything useful. Delphi had a lot of advanced weaponry they might be able to use against him. Unfortunately the wag had seemed to have been stripped to the walls, possibly to make room for the droid to get inside to wait for the cyborg to return. Everything was gone, even the chair from the control board and the engine. The LAV was an empty shell.

"Pity." J.B. sighed, setting down a pillowcase full of grens he had brought along. "However, I can still leave him a little something to remember us by."

"Need any help?" Jak asked eagerly.

"Sure. You start stringing the trip wire."

Leaving the two men to their work, the rest of the companions gathered by the towering black doors.

"Did anybody else notice that the droid acted as if it could understand what we were saying?" Krysty asked.

"Maybe it could," Mildred suggested. "Intelligent machines were being experimented with in my time. I guess whoever Delphi worked for…"

"Coldfire," Doc said, expelling the word as if it were a piece of rotten food. "Department Coldfire. I seem to recall that it is a division of Overproject Whisper, the lunatics who built the redoubts!"

"Whitecoats," Ryan growled, putting a wealth of bitter feelings into the single word.

"Quite right, sir," Doc said. "Thank God that TITAN is around to keep…" The man paused, a strange expression on his face, then he turned toward the wag. "John Barrymore, how is the work progressing?"

Puzzled, the three companions glanced at one another.

"It'll go faster if you stop jeckling me!" J.B. answered from inside the vehicle.

"That's heckling!"

"Whatever!"

"Ah, are you okay, Doc?" Ryan asked, taking the man by the shoulder.

The old man turned to face him with a smile. "Certainly, my friend, never better. Why do you ask?"

"What was that you said about…Titan?" Mildred asked carefully.

"The Titans?" Doc repeated, stroking his jaw. "Why, those were the ancient giants that the Greek gods stole Mount Olympus from to control the Earth. Fascinating story, but why ever did you ask about them now?"

Nobody spoke for a moment. Clearly, something was going on with the man, but they had no idea what.

"Oh, no reason," Mildred said hastily. "I was just thinking how the droid was like something from Greek mythology. A guardian of the rainbow bridge."

"Tsk, tsk. That's Norse mythology, madam."

"Really? My mistake."

Just then, J.B. walked backward from the wag, holding up both hands. "Easy now," he warned. "Steady! This is tricky part!"

"Tell something not know!" Jak retorted, also moving backward down the short flight of stairs. In his hand, the teen was holding a spool of wire. The other end was inside the vehicle, and he was keeping the length very taut. As he reached the floor, Jak stepped aside and J.B. carefully closed the hatch on the wire, snipping it off the end. Then both men scrambled to get clear. After a few minutes when nothing happened, they relaxed.

"Done and done!" J.B. announced, straightening his hat. "When Delphi tries that door, we'll hear it on other side of world!"

"Not be enough left to load empty brass!" Jak grinned mercilessly.

"Then, pray, let us proceed," Doc rumbled, drawing the LeMat to check the fresh load in the blaster. "The sooner started, the sooner finished. *Ergo sum est*, eh, my dear Ryan?"

"Bet your ass," Ryan agreed, sharing a private look with Krysty and Mildred. They were unable to talk freely at the moment with Doc standing among them, but the man's bizarre behavior would be discussed later.

Positioning themselves in front of the blast doors in a combat formation, the companions stayed razor while Krysty punched in the exit code on a small keypad recessed into the wall, then pressed the lever. There came the expected rumble of heavy machinery under the floor, then the sound of working hydraulics, and the nukeproof doors loudly unlocked and opened with a low rumble. A wave of cold washed over the companions as they gradually saw a solid wall of rushing water completely blocking the exit.

"Dark night, we're under a waterfall!" J.B. exclaimed, resting the barrel of his AK-47 on a shoulder.

A fine mist was coming into the tunnel, making everything damp.

"Good way hide redoubt," Jak commented.

Going to the edge of the slippery floor, Ryan experimentally held out a hand and let the falling cascade impact his fingers. The water hit hard, but not with pummeling force, so this was clearly not a big waterfall.

"We're going to need some rope," Mildred said, holstering her blaster. "No way we're going to try to breach that without support."

A coil of rope had been spotted in the tool room of the garage and quickly retrieved. Lashing one end around Ryan, the rest of the companions took hold of the other end and tried to brace themselves.

"We could loop this once around the wag," Doc suggested, glancing at the vehicle.

Shifting his grip on the rope, Jak snorted in contempt.

"Too risky," J.B. answered. "Jak and I have that baby rigged to blow if Delphi farts too hard. Stay as far away from that wag as possible."

"Accepted."

"Good safety tip, thank you, Egon," Mildred said in a singsong voice that meant she was quoting somebody.

Wrapping the end of the rope around his own middle, Doc gave the woman a quizzical glance, but she could only shrug in reply. The film *Ghostbusters* was one of her favorite movies, but its humor was a little too bizarre to try to explain to a schoolteacher from the 1880s.

Seeing that the others had dug in as best they could,

Ryan shuffled forward again, moving closer to the edge, feeling the companions tighten the rope lashed around his waist. The cool spray felt refreshing on his face and, squinting his good eye, Ryan could almost see through the shimmering wall. Can't be that deep then, he realized. Shallow and slow. This was just camou, and not a barrier to keep out folks.

His sleeves were already soaked, droplets of condensed mist trickling down his face into his shirt. He had taken off his jacket, but the man still felt like he was carrying fifty pounds of clothing.

"Ready?" the one-eyed man called over a shoulder, fingering the edge of the doorway.

"Abso-fragging-lutely!" J.B. shouted back over the muted roar of the fall.

Taking a deep breath, Ryan placed an arm over his head and stuck his face into the rushing water. The falls pounded on his arms, but not hard enough to knock him over. Extending a foot, he felt nothing beyond the tunnel, then stabbed downward with the AK-47. There was no resistance until the longblaster was completely submerged. There was a ledge about four feet away. Good enough.

Pulling back, Ryan gulped some air, brushed the sodden hair from his face, hunched his shoulders, and walked out of the tunnel. There was a moment of disorientation as he fell, then plunged into water. It rose to his chest before his boots hit rock. With the water pouring all around him, Ryan held his breath and waited a moment to make sure it was stable. Then he tugged once on the rope, saying that he was still alive, and got an answering tug before moving forward once more. Carefully placing one boot ahead of the other, he moved from a ledge of smooth rock to an uneven surface that felt like pebbles and stones. He was drenched to the skin by now, and felt that his lungs were about to give out, when he suddenly stepped out of the waterfalls and into open air.

Drawing air through his nose, Ryan touched the SIG-Sauer at his side, scanning the area for any danger. He was standing waist-deep in a wide pool, or rather, a small lake, with steeply sloped sides of what looked like red clay. Were they back in Virginia?

That was when he noticed the moss covering the boulders jutting from the lake and the tall banyan trees lining the shore. Oranges grew in abundance, along with other fruits that Ryan could not identify. There were numerous birds sitting in the trees, none of them looking like muties, and then a monkey dashed along the treetops screeching and yelling as other monkeys gave pursuit. A motion in the water caught his attention, and Ryan saw a black snake with diamond markings of yellow and blue glide along the bottom of the lake. There was a large lump in its midsection proclaiming a recent kill, but he kept track of its progress until the snake was out of sight.

Glancing at the sky, Ryan saw the usual maelstrom of purple and orange clouds filling the heavens, the occasional bolt of lightning zipping from one to cloud to strike another.

Tugging on the rope for more play, Ryan started to wade toward shore. A school of tiny fish resembling an underwater rainbow darted past the man. That made Ryan ease his stance slightly. If there were any large predators in the pool, the fish would be long gone. But he still kept a careful watch for the return of the diamondback snake. Most animals killed for food, but there were some that aced others just because they could. Man was not alone in chilling for sport.

Reaching the shore, Ryan maneuvered clumsily through the ankle-deep mud and crawled onto dry ground. The grass was freckled with tiny flowers and he recognized them as the same type found inside the mat-trans chamber. The cyborg had been here.

Slowly straightening, Ryan let the water drip off his clothes as he studied the thick jungle. Straight ahead was a sort of path, the thick bushes mashed to the ground.

Past the bushes was a broken stand of bamboo, the splintered shafts scattered around and the stumps already a yard high. That looked like the passage of a heavy wag to him. Maybe even a war wag. With the egg-shaped wag inoperable, the cyborg would have needed new transportation. And there could have been anything parked in the garage, even an APC or a tank.

Kneeling, Ryan examined the crushed leaves, but there was no sign of tire tracks or tread marks. And bamboo was the fastest-growing plant in the world, according to Mildred. Under the right conditions it could rise several inches a day. Which meant there was no way to even guess how long it had been since the wag, or wags, forced its way through the dense foliage. But certainly no more than a week. That matched the condition of the flowers in the mat-trans. Delphi had been here only a few days ago.

A weak tug came on the rope, and Ryan jerked back twice in reply, saying it was safe for the others to exit. As the rope went slack, he holstered the blaster and started undoing the knot when the jungle around him went eerily silent.

Mouthing a curse, Ryan clawed for the SIG-Sauer as a large figure moved in the shadows under a banyan tree. Instinctively, the man fired twice and a bellowing roar sounded as something with four arms rushed into the light. Fireblast, it was a hunter!

Moving fast to the side, Ryan pumped five more rounds into the hideous creature before it was upon him. Wrapping all four arms around his chest, the gorilla-like animal squeezed with monstrous strength, and Ryan felt his ribs creak with awful pressure. Nuking hell, the mutie had seven rounds in it and was still trying to ace him! But the slugs were probably why Ryan was still alive. The 9 mm rounds weakened the creature enough to give Ryan a fighting chance.

Wiggling the SIG-Sauer against the dark fur, Ryan fired off three more rounds, keeping his head low so the mutie couldn't reach his vulnerable throat. The creature grunted loudly from the impact of each hot slug into its leg and upper thigh, then the grip loosened slightly. Wiggling an arm free, Ryan shoved the blaster under the snarling jaw and triggered the last two rounds. The muzzle-flame engulfed the beast's face, and its head rocked back from the triphammer blows of the steel-jacketed bone-shredders.

As the arms dropped away, Ryan kicked the mutie, but the blow seemed to have no effect as the dying animal staggered away, blood gushing from the ghastly wounds. Then it turned and insanely roared to charge again with a grim intensity. Normal or mutated, Ryan knew that look. It was going to take him with it onto the last train west.

With no time to reload, Ryan dropped the blaster and drew his panga to meet the charge with a slash of razor-sharp steel. The mutie stumbled to the side, trying to get around the man, and Ryan lashed out with the flat of the blast slashing the exposed throat from ear to ear.

Gurgling horribly, the hunter grabbed at the ruin of its neck, crimson life pumping onto the ground. Yanking the AK-47 off his shoulder, Ryan stitched the mutie from groin to crown and it stumbled away to collapse into the bushes. There was a mighty exhalation, and it went still.

Sheathing his knife, Ryan grabbed the SIG-Sauer from the grass and shoved the empty blaster back into its holster, never looking away from the steaming jungle. He'd encountered that type of mutie previously, and the hunters always traveled in packs. He had to get back into the redoubt fast. His ribs ached, but there was no wheezing when he breathed, which meant there were no broken bones. He was thankful for that.

Stepping awkwardly down the slope, Ryan saw something move in the trees and fired a short burst in its direction. If he hit anything, there came no answering cry of pain.

Wading back into the lake, he nearly slipped on a slimy rock, but caught himself from going into the water when six more hunters dropped from the trees and charged. Incredibly, they paused at the edge of the water.

Seizing the moment, Ryan fanned the rapid-fire, stitching the group of muties. That seemed to shatter their hesitation, and they jumped in and waded forward, with all four arms raised. Firing again, Ryan tried to jump aside, when he felt a hard tug around his waist. What in the… Damn! The nuking rope was still tied around his middle and was tangled on a rock!

Trapped, Ryan did the only thing he could and

jumped backward, slipping and sliding down the mossy bank to splash into the water. He had to cut the rope loose or he would never leave the water alive. Firing the Kalashnikov with one hand, the man clawed for the panga but felt only empty leather. Then he spotted it on the mossy grass, lying amid the delicate flowers.

Spreading out, the muties moved into the shallow lake and began to circle the man, grunting and slapping at the water to draw his attention. But he refused to follow their lead and turned around randomly, firing single rounds to conserve ammo. Smart, Ryan thought. I forgot just how nuking smart these things are. The second they see me try to reload, it will be all over. Suddenly he heard a fusillade of blasterfire, and two of the creatures toppled over, gushing blood from multiple wounds.

Krysty and J.B. stepped into view on either side of Ryan, their Kalashnikovs firing steadily, the spent brass arching away to splash into the dirty water. Two more creatures were chewed apart by the rapid-fires, and the remaining muties turned to flee back into the jungle.

"Watch the trees!" Ryan growled, dropping the clip and reloading.

Giving each of the fallen hunters a round in the head, Ryan saw one of them rise with a strangled cry, showing it had been faking, before it flopped back into the water and went still. Under the water, murky clouds of red were spreading from the still bodies, and the tiny fish were darting in and out of the unexpected feast.

Shaking the moisture off his glasses, J.B. started to say something when Krysty fired a long burst past the man. Retreating back into the shadows, a bleeding hunter disappeared into the lush plants.

"Cover me!" Ryan snarled, advancing toward shore.

Nodding, Krysty and J.B. raised their Kalashnikovs, ready to chill anything that moved.

Pausing at the shallows, Ryan scanned the area, then darted forward to grab the panga and rush back into the lake. Bellowing in pain and fury, several hairy muties jumped into view and rushed to the edge of the pool, waving their arms, snarling and spitting. But not one of the creatures entered the water.

"Why won't they follow into the water?" J.B. demanded suspiciously. He wanted to look down, but didn't dare take his gaze away from the hulking brutes. "Are there snakes or something?"

"I don't think they're allowed in," Ryan answered cryptically, sawing himself free and firmly sheathing the knife.

"They're guard dogs!" Krysty said in understanding.

"And we know that Delphi likes to use trained muties, so…" Ryan stopped short as a creature swung out of the trees on the end of a vine. It let go and sailed above the companions to land hard on the opposite shore. Trembling once, it sighed and went still.

Firing a single round into the moss on the shore, Ryan saw the mutie roll over lightning-fast and reach for that spot, only to grab empty air.

"Nice try, feeb." J.B. sneered contemptuously.

Turning its massive head, the mutie glared directly at the norm, then walked slowly back into the waving bushes and disappeared. The other muties did the same, and the jungle slowly came to life once more, the birds twittering and the insects chirping.

Staying on the alert, the three companions retreated to the waterfalls, and climbed back into the tunnel. None of them relaxed until the blast doors were closed.

To the concerned expressions of the others, Ryan explained what had happened outside.

"Hunters!" Jak cried. "Shit, what do?"

"Well, we're not going through that jungle on foot, that's for triple-damn sure." Krysty sighed, shaking her head. "Those things would ace the lot of us in minutes, no matter how much ammo we were carrying."

"You can load that into your blaster," J.B. agreed wholeheartedly.

"Pity we can't ride out of here," Mildred said wistfully, looking sideways at the white wag.

"Why can't we?" Ryan said, starting to smile.

The physician frowned. "I thought you said that thing had been completely gutted?"

"It is," J.B. answered. "But there are lots of civvie wags in the garage. "I'm sure we can do something with them."

"They're useless," Krysty said. "Those muties would rip off the doors easily."

"Not if they are surrounded by a protective grille," Doc stated thoughtfully. "Remember those bikes that Silas used in Tennessee? They had a cage around them for protection. Mayhap we can do something similar."

"Only one bike in garage," Jak replied, then added, "but lots of trucks. Those work good. Need cage."

"We can make them," Ryan stated, starting along the tunnel. "The redoubt had plenty of power, so the electric arc welders will be working. All we need is some steel bars."

"Where get?"

"The armory!" Krysty replied. "That has all the hardened steel we can possibly use."

"Blasters?" Jak asked. "We gut longblasters?"

"Why not?" Mildred said. "We have more than we can use, and the barrels are perfect for what we need. Strong and light."

"But ruin blasters…" the teen whispered, as if even contemplating such a thing was an unforgivable sin. Weapons were something you fought and chilled for, risked your life to get hold of, and held on to no matter what. To destroy dozens and dozens of working blasters seemed wrong.

"Come on," Jak said, brushing back his snowy hair. "If needs done, best do quick."

"Good man," Ryan said over his grumbling stomach. "But first we eat."

"Afterward, Jak and I have to defuse this," J.B. said wearily, scowling at the egg-shaped war wag. "There's no way for us to get another wag through this tunnel with this thing blocking the way. And one hard shove will set off a blast louder than skydark."

"Fair enough."

Turning away from the blast doors, the companions walked slowly into the redoubt already mapping out their work for the next few days.

Outside the redoubt, the hunters gathered in growing numbers along the edge of the forbidden pool, thumping their chests and howling in savage fury over their dead brothers floating facedown in the dirty water. They all knew the laws given to them by the god Delphi. Blood spilled must be paid in blood taken. The urge to kill burned in their minds, but they would have to wait for a little while longer.

Soon enough the two-legs would come out again, and then the feasting would truly begin.

Chapter Six

Softly, the digital clock chimed the hour.

Damn. Rising to his feet, Dr. Edgar Franklin smoothed down his hair and straightened his collar. TITAN expected him to perform certain duties, and this was the day he'd chosen to inspect the Rhode Island redoubt. Appearances always mattered to him. His usual attire was hospital scrubs and sneakers. Loose and comfortable, they let a man breath and think. But for this day's chore he'd decided to wear combat fatigues, a wide gunbelt holstering a military-issue pistol and knee-high jackboots. Couldn't be more uncomfortable if I was wearing a straitjacket, he thought.

Leaving the galley of the redoubt, the man took the elevator down to the middle level and walked into the waiting mat-trans chamber. Consulting his personal digital assistant for the correct code, Franklin tapped in the sequence of numbers and letters.

Instantly, the electronic mists rose from the ceiling and floor, masking his sight. There was a brief moment of disorientation, then the mists receded, revealing a different redoubt. But stepping from the unit, Franklin stopped in puzzlement. Where the hell was this? He wasn't in Rhode Island. According to the colors on the wall, this redoubt was located in Antarctica! How was that possible?

Leaving the unit, the man cross the antechamber and went into the control room. Pressing a palm to a blank section of the board, he accessed the secondary systems and ran a quick diagnostic of the unit to see what was wrong. Had there been a major malfunction? Had Whisper lost another redoubt? Several had been volatized in the nuclear war, an expected and accepted loss. Then a few were damaged by natural disasters, earthquakes, volcanoes and the like. Incredibly, one had been flooded, of all things, and another was nuked out of existence only a few years ago. Yet there was no scientific explanation of how a nuclear warhead from the war could have waited that long to finally detonate.

Some fool in TITAN security had suggested that a handful of survivors from the outside had used a tactical nuke to destroy the base, which was patently ridiculous. As if their uneducated brains could possibly learn how to operate a portable nuclear weapon, much less gain entry into a redoubt! The savages roaming the so-called Deathlands barely knew how to make fire. Their pitiful, ragtag civilization was reduced to the level of wooden clubs. Which were hardly capable of causing damage to a hundred-billion-dollar fortress. Still, it was a puzzling problem.

A light flashed on the console, announcing the diagnostic was completed. Leaning toward the monitor, Franklin chewed the inside of a cheek as all of the programs reported that the matter-transfer unit was functioning normally, every primary computer system in the green and every defensive subsystem fully operating within normal parameters. Strange. Very strange.

Consulting the PDA strapped to his wrist, Franklin returned to the mat-trans unit and slowly tapped in the

Rhode Island destination code once more, double-checking that he made no mistakes. Once more the mists rose, fell, and he checked the walls. God Almighty! Now he was in a redoubt at the Panama Canal.

"Son of a bitch," Franklin muttered uneasily, then tapped in the code for the main TITAN base.

The mists came and went, and this time the man found himself exactly where he was supposed to be. It seemed that only the redoubt in Rhode Island was somehow blocked. All right, logically, there were only three distinct possibilities. The first, and most likely, was that the redoubt had suffered a technical problem of some kind, dysfunction or malfunction. Or two, the redoubt had been destroyed. Not at all likely, but theoretically possible. Unfortunately the third option was the most likely, and the most unsettling. There was something blocking the mat-trans chamber at the redoubt.

Checking the files in the PDA, Franklin finally found the command sequence that he needed to impart whatever blocked his jump, and spent a good minute carefully tapping in the alphanumeric code. Stepping into the antechamber, he patiently waited, his pistol up and ready.

A few minutes later the white mist filled the chamber and then faded away to reveal a stack of wooden cases.

Curiously, Franklin holstered his weapon and entered the gateway to examine the odd boxes. Prying one open with his bare fingers, the man scowled at the spongy excelsior stuffing and impatiently brushed it aside to reveal a human arm with silvery wires dangling from the shoulder joint. Instantly he recognized it as an artificial limb used for battlefield repairs and to create cyborgs. But that was impossible. Every cyborg had been decommissioned by Coldfire. Except for one. The great traitor. The sworn enemy of TITAN.

"God help us, he's back," Franklin whispered, his face tightening into a rictus of blind hatred. "Delphi is back!" And then he realized he had a new duty to perform.

WHILE THE OTHERS WERE preparing dinner, Ryan got Mildred and Krysty alone for a few minutes in one of the officer's quarters by pretending his ribs were especially bad. That really didn't require a lot of faking on his part. When his shirt came off, dark purple and black bruises were encircling his entire torso, and on his back were the clear imprints of four inhuman hands.

Staying near the door to keep a watch out for Doc, Krysty frowned at the sight of the discoloration, but said nothing. Nothing she said would help the man heal any faster.

"And this happened after you shot the hunter?" Mildred said in amazement, running fingertips along his sides. "I've seen worse, but not on anybody who survived."

Ryan grunted at her touch. "Just glad I got in as much brass as I did. The son of a bitch was strong."

"More than you, that's for sure," the physician commented, shaking her head in disbelief. "Much stronger than any normal gorilla, and those are way stronger than humans already."

"Yeah, I know."

"Guess you do at that." Getting the med kit, Mildred rummaged inside. "I can give you some aspirin to help you sleep tonight," she said, retrieving the bottle.

Taking a small bandage from her bag, Mildred wrapped the man tight to help his ribs heal faster, fetched a glass of water from the bathroom and gave him the pills. Ryan dry-swallowed the aspirin, then drank the water.

"Okay, now that's done, let's get to the real reason we're here," he said in a controlled tone. Looking at the women, he met their gazes. "What the nuking hell was the problem with Doc? He starts talking about something called Titan then goes blank, like the man never heard of the people he was just talking about."

"He mentioned Coldfire, too," Krysty added. "But he's talked about them before. Only this Titan was new."

"Well, it could be some sort of a mental block," Mildred said, leaning back in her chair. "Maybe something happened to him that was so horrible he's blocked it from his memory." But even as she spoke the words, the physician began to frown. "No, that makes no sense. I know he was brutally tortured by Cort Strasser before you busted him loose, and he remembers every damn minute."

Although the two of them clashed sometimes, Mildred had the highest respect for the old scholar. He had survived experiences that would have destroyed lesser men, and she thought Doc was tougher than a boiled horseshoe when the chips were down.

"But if that's true, this is something else," Krysty said, her hair tightening protectively around her face. "Not a block, but more like…" She made a vague gesture. "Oh, I don't know, like a bungee cord. He's free to move about, say and think what he wants, but if Doc goes too far and mentions Titan, then it snaps him back hard."

"Depending upon how wide the perimeters of the block are, this might explain a lot about his odd lapses of memory."

"True."

"Could this be that stuff you told us about?" Ryan asked hesitantly. "Hypnotism?"

After a moment Mildred shook her head. "No, that's only a tool for psychoanalysis. The doctor induces a state of monomaniac to the patient, but it's easily broken. Hypnotism has been used a lot in movies to turn people into robots, but that doesn't work in the real world. Heck, hypnotists can barely make folks stop smoking, much less turn them into slaves!"

"Good to know. So, is there anything we can do?" the Deathlands warrior asked, feeling helpless. A knife wound he could stitch closed, set a busted bone, dig out a bullet, but with this sort of invisible wound, something inside the mind, that was beyond the man, and he had no problem saying so. This was Mildred's specialty so she was in charge.

"Unfortunately, no," Mildred replied, crossing her arms. "Damn it to hell, I wish there was something to be done! Oh, I've read several books, attended lectures, taken some mandatory classes, but still…" She shrugged. "Even if I had the proper psychotropic drugs, I'm only an amateur. If I tried digging around in Doc's head, I might make him worse, a lot worse."

"Great." Doc had always been a tremendous asset to the group, but if his mind was finally going, well, Ryan would do what he hoped the others would if he was going insane. Put two rounds behind his ear and remember him in a toast every now and then.

"Then we do nothing for the moment," Krysty said.

"Nothing, except offer him our friendship and support." Mildred sighed. "And listen closely if he ever mentions Titan again. With enough pieces of the puzzle we might have a chance of finding a solution. But until then…"

"It's like planning a nightcreep," Ryan muttered thoughtfully, trying to get a handle on the problem. "Until we know more about the enemy, what kind of sec men they have, are there dogs, boobies, and the like, any recce is just going to get us aced."

"And that's a pretty fair analogy," Mildred said with a wan smile.

From down the hall, they heard Jak call them for dinner.

Ryan and Krysty helped Mildred gather her med supplies, and the three of them walked from the room lost in their somber thoughts.

Heading to the kitchen, the three companions were greeted by a delicious smell. Inside the fragrant kitchen, J.B. was standing at one of the many stoves stirring something in a softly bubbling pot.

Taking warm plates from the steamy interior of a dishwasher, Ryan and the women joined the others at a long dining table, and dug into the simple meal, gray mil cheese on crackers, beef stew, canned bread with what passed for butter, freeze-dried coffee with sugar and powdered cream and pressed cherry-nut cake for dessert. The military rations were not particularly savory as durability and longevity, not taste, had been the prime considerations in designing the predark MRE food packs. But the food was hot, was somewhat tasty and everybody cleaned their plates.

Afterward, the dirty dishes were unceremoniously

dumped into an empty dishwasher, and the tired people trundled off to the barracks to choose rooms for the night, with Doc and Jak getting comfortable in an office to stand the first shift of guard duty. Normally, that wasn't necessary locked deep inside a redoubt, but this night it seemed a logical precaution.

With their Kalashnikovs nearby, the two men settled down at a wooden desk with large mugs of black coffee and a pack of playing cards. Personally, Doc would have preferred a game of chess, however, the uneducated, barely literate albino teen kept winning, and so the old man had abandoned the noble pastime of kings and emperors for the more dubious pleasures of gin rummy.

Meanwhile, the rest of the companions decided to raid the stockpiles of clothing. Ryan took several pairs of thick socks and a pair of boots, Krysty replaced her worn fatigues, J.B. found a shirt in his size and Mildred acquired a new fatigue jacket, along with several sets of bootlaces. Made of resilient nylon, the laces made surprisingly good trade items and could be exchanged for a plethora of goods and services at most villes. They all chose a few pairs of underwear, and Mildred found a box of combat bras and tried to find garments in the correct size for her and Krysty.

Moving to the laundry complex, the companions grabbed four of the bath towels on a shelf above a sink, quickly stripped, eyes averted, and donned a towel. They found that most of the bottles of bleach and detergent had only dried residue at the bottom. But some of them contained a scant few ounces of liquid that proved to be more than enough for the small loads. While all the clothes were tumbling in the dryers, the two couples hit the showers, finding stalls at opposite ends of the huge lavatory for a few minutes of privacy. It took a while for the dusty bathroom pipes to deliver anything but rusty sludge, but eventually, that cycled through and they luxuriated in a cascade of unlimited clean water. There was no soap or shampoo in sight, but the MRE packs had yielded tiny bottles of all-purpose cleanser, along with toothbrushes, tiny tubes of mint toothpaste and plastic combs. The men shaved using their knives while the women watched in amused fascination.

Clean and refreshed, the four weary people, wrapped in towels, reclaimed their clothing and trundled off to the barracks. Choosing separate rooms, they barricaded the doors, checked their blasters and settled in for the night. In a couple of hours, Doc and Jak would wake up J.B. and Mildred, with Ryan and Krysty taking the final shift until dawn.

Removing his towel, Ryan eased himself onto the soft bed, and was soon sound asleep. Studying the dark bruises on her muscular partner, Krysty decided he needed sleep tonight more than anything else and settled in beside him under the thick army blankets.

Across the hall, J.B. checked the heavy dresser jammed against the door for a second time, then finally nodded in acceptance.

"Come to bed, John," Mildred said from across the room, her voice low and sweet.

Hearing something in her tone, J.B. slowly turned. The lady physician was already in bed covered only by a cotton sheet. Seductively, she raised a shapely knee. With the light streaming from behind, he could see the delicious outline of her full figure through the thin material.

Immediately, J.B. started to respond to her sultry beauty. He had been with several women in his life, but she was the most beautiful, not only because of the face and figure, but for the person inside. Mildred had fought by his side through fire and blood, earning more than his friendship. She was inside him, bonded to his very soul. Lacking the right words, the man had never told her, but she was his world.

"Tired?" Mildred asked huskily, allowing the sheet to slip down a little, revealing her generous cleavage.

"Never that tired," the man responded eagerly, sliding the munitions bag off his shoulder.

Depositing it on the floor, the Armorer placed the Uzi on top of a metal desk, then laid the S&W M-4000 scattergun alongside. He let his towel tumble to the floor, then removed his wire-rimmed glasses and put them on the desk near the blasters. But starting forward, he saw her smile turn into a scowl.

"Ahem," Mildred said, looking upward.

Puzzled for a moment, J.B. then removed his beloved fedora and reverently set it aside.

"Honest to God, John, sometimes the way you treat the ratty old thing…" she muttered, shaking her head in mock anger.

Grinning apologetically, the man stepped closer and took her face in his hands. Gently, he kissed her on the lips, the light touch relaying more than mere words ever could. The electric moment built in intensity as their hearts quickened, and the caress enfolded to a passionate embrace, their arms wrapped tight around each other.

Her beaded locks clicking softly, Mildred opened her mouth to John and they kissed deeper, more ardently.

Their hands began to explore each other, each intimate caress fueling their mounting desire, his pale skin a perfect contrast to her dark beauty.

Breaking apart for air, Mildred coyly raised the sheet and John climbed onto the bed. Taking her in his arms, J.B. hugged the woman tight. Responding to the strength of the man, Mildred felt her nipples tighten.

Bending to kiss a warm breast, J.B. ran a hand along her stomach, then slid a finger inside the delicate folds of her femininity and expertly began a small circular motion. Gasping in delight, Mildred opened her thighs, and the man intensified his teasing caresses, invoking waves of pleasure until the woman thought she could stand no more and finally shuddered all over in velvet ecstasy.

Smiling at her pleasure, J.B. looked deep into her lovely eyes, asking a silent question. Whispering his name, Mildred nodded in response and reached out to stroke his shaft, caressing the stiffening flesh. As his breath started to quicken, she released him and spread her legs completely. Changing position, J.B. lightly moved across the yielding satin until fully anointed with her moisture, the scent of their passion filling the bedchamber.

Taking Mildred by the hips, J.B. eased forward, swelling as the electric flesh tightened around him. Murmuring wordless sounds, Mildred arched her back as he partially withdrew, then he plunged in deep, the woman crying out in pleasure at the penetration.

Clawing her hands down his back, Mildred thrilled to the play of the hard muscles.

As the man rose and fell, she yielded to the wonderful motion for several seconds, then began to move in reply, meeting his thrusts with her own, doubling their pleasure. Secret words were spoken as they rocked in unison, limbs entangled, their skin glistening with sweat. Then their movements became faster, intensified. Words were abandoned to primordial breathing. Their gazes locked, the man and woman joined, moving as one, striving, yielding, giving and receiving at the same time. Suddenly, Mildred gushed with new moisture, her nipples hardening, and they slammed together in a physical crescendo of sensual ecstasy, unable to breathe or to move or think, lost forever in the precious instant of perfection....

Slowly, reality returned and they collapsed against each other, panting, trembling from the glorious after-effect.

Still completely engulfed inside the woman, J.B. reached out to stroke her face, and Mildred took his hand to kiss the palm and press it to her cheek. No words for spoken, and none were needed. All that could be said had already been expressed, and for a few precious moments, there was nobody else in the world, no troubles, no danger, only the smiling lovers and the ethereal music of their soft breathing.

Chapter Seven

Swimming… Ryan was splashing and swimming in the cool green water of the nameless lake, odd columns of red rock rising upward like the weathered pylons from some ancient temple. The water soaked his clothing and filled his boots, weighing him down like sticky lead, draining his strength, but there was no way to get them while swimming, and he was tiring fast.

A raging fury filled the man and his exhaustion faded away to be replaced with a hard determination. Not gonna get aced out here in the middle of nowhere! Now move, you nuke-sucking bastard! Get some dirt under your feet and quickly find the convoy before it's too late! He raged to himself. Some small part of his mind said that it may already be too late. The Trader could be lying on the side of the road chilled by the stickies, or worse, the convoy had taken off and now was miles away. But he ignored that. Ryan had fought bigger men than himself, stronger, meaner, yet always won because he did not quit.

Unfortunately, there were only sheer rock walls in every direction he turned, unclimbable cliffs with no place to get out of the water larger than a spent brass. Then he caught a glimmer of white and instinctively started paddling in that direction. Could it be a sandy beach? A predark wreck? But as Ryan got closer, he saw there was an adobe ville sitting on a pebbled shore. Oddly, there was no wall surrounding the cluster of buildings, which naturally made him think it was a pre-dark town that had somehow survived skydark. Yet there weren't any telephone poles sticking out of the ground or cars parked along the curbs that he could see from this angle. Strange.

His rage was starting to ebb away, his strength fading when Ryan felt the toe of his boot scrape ground under the green water. Barking a short laugh of relief, the man dragged himself out of the lake and flopped bonelessly on the bed of pebbles. The smooth rocks were hot from the sunlight and the soothing warmth seeped into his aching body like a healing balm.

Catching his breath, Ryan rose from the stony beach and checked his weapons before stiffly walking toward the adobe ville, diligently searching for any signs of muties or coldhearts. He had been caught once with his pants down. Never again.

In spite of the heavy cloud cover, the day was hot, but there was a cool breeze coming off the desert carrying a faint taste of snow from the nearby mountains, and Ryan gratefully drank in the delicious sensation. The place seemed deserted, and there was nothing dangerous in sight. Yet he was oddly apprehensive. Then it hit him. The buildings were adobe, dried mud bricks, with wooden poles sticking out of the sides to support the red clay tile roofs. But most of them reached four, five, even six stories tall. Which was flat-out impossible for adobe. The mud bricks couldn't take that much weight unless there was another structure underneath supporting them.

This was a fake, Ryan realized. Someplace made to

look primitive to hide the real buildings. Could it be an underground cache like the Trader used, or something else?

Warily, the twenty-year-old man drew his Colt .45 autoblaster and worked the slide to chamber a round. The sound of metal on metal was reassuring, the tiny noise seeming to echo along the sterile white streets. That was when he noticed one building that seemed different from the rest. It was a little blurry, as if seen by tired eyes, or through a faint mist. Triple weird.

Advancing closer, Ryan studied the structure. It was a three-story adobe building, red-tile roof, wooden shutters over the windows and a weathered door with some kind of a glowing symbol set into the lentil. A sort of circle with an oval going across sideways with a large star set off center to the left.

There was a moment of disorientation and Ryan found himself standing in the middle of a weedy road, the sound of engines growing steadily louder. Then a war wag came over a low hillock, closely followed by several more. He could not believe it. That was the convoy! But…but hadn't he just been in a lake?

With a squeal of pneumatic brakes, War Wag One came to a rocking halt and the side door was thrown open wide.

"Well, nuke me!" The Trader laughed in delight, stepping into view. "Look who we have here!"

"Never thought I'd see your sorry ass again, Cawdor!" J.B. chuckled, lowering the barrel of his Remington Bolt-action. "Nice to have you back…." The wiry man stopped talking and squinted through his wire-rimmed glasses.

"Behind you!" the Trader bellowed, swinging up a blaster and firing.

Ducking, Ryan swiveled to see a white mist rise from a depression among the weeds, then a nest of ropy tentacles lashed madly about as a creature pushed through the weeds, the plants turning brown and withering at the passage of the hellish thing.

Snarling in rage, Ryan grabbed for the Colt at his hip, but found only bare flesh and rumpled blankets. Then there came the sound of a toilet flushing, followed by running water. With a supreme effort of will, the man opened his eye to see the bedroom of a redoubt. A dream. It was just that damn dream again, he thought.

"Morning, lover!" Krysty called, sticking her head out of the bathroom. There was a toothbrush in her hand and her smile was foamy. She was dressed only in pants and boots, her new bra hanging off a doorknob. "Nice to see you moving! I was thinking about setting the mattress on fire, but wasn't sure even that was going to work."

"Probably not," Ryan growled, taking his eye patch from a bedside table and slipping it back into place. "But I know of another way that would have gotten me awake trip-fast," he said with a gentle smile.

"Yeah, I thought of that, too." She chuckled, walking over, her full breasts swaying from the rolling motion of her full hips. Bending over, Krysty planted a long, minty kiss on his lips, then pulled back. "However, I'm starved and want some breakfast. Lots to do today."

"Yeah, fair enough," Ryan admitted, feeling a rumble in his gut from the mere thought of food. Suddenly his desire for the woman was gone, replaced by a different kind of hunger. Throwing off the blankets, Ryan set bare feet on the floor and reached for his pants.

There was a time and place for everything. He and Krysty would get some private time later on, but right now, there was work to be done.

After a hurried breakfast of beef stew, canned bread and black coffee, the companions went directly to work on the wags. They broke only for lunch, and by late afternoon, the job was completed.

Stepping back from the predark machine, Ryan wiped his sweaty forehead and studied the last weld on the final cage. It looked good, but he had to make sure. Grabbing the hot metal with a gloved hand, the one-eyed man shook it hard, but the gridwork stayed firm and unyielding. Done and done. They were ready to go.

After ascertaining that the cyborg's LAV was safe to move, the companions dragged it into the garage and shoved it out of the way in a disused corner. Then J.B. and Jak rigged the egg-smooth vehicle once more, this time adding a coffin full of live brass to the mix. When the wag detonated, the entire garage level would be filled with a maelstrom of shrapnel. To be honest, J.B. didn't know if that could chill Delphi, but it sure was going to be spectacular! Half of the Armorer wanted to see the staggering blast, but the rest of him wanted to be as far away from the maelstrom as possible.

When that was accomplished, the companions really got to work. The best of the civilian wags were carefully chosen and completely disassembled. Then everything not actually needed to make the machines move was meticulously removed. Each vehicle was reduced to bare framework, then rebuilt, the engines raised higher than the lake outside and the exhaust pipes altered to go straight up. Next, the companions added a reinforced fuel tank, an entire row of nuke batteries and a single seat for the driver. Then the crude speedster was surrounded by a strong cage made of blaster barrels removed from the stores of Kalashnikovs. The hollow bars were set with care at what the companions sincerely hoped was a couple of inches farther away from the driver than the reach of a hunter.

There were still a few extra Kalashnikovs remaining, so the companions each took two, and everything else in the armory had been either set with a trap or destroyed by the arc welder.

"Wish we had the time to add some spikes to the cage," J.B. said wistfully, running a handkerchief along the sweatband inside his hat. "Or make them stronger. If a weld pops, a bar could come loose, and then we'd be easy pickings."

"Not so easy," Jak replied, checking the load in his Colt Python, then closing the cylinder with a click. Holstering the blaster, he jerked a wrist and a knife appeared in his palm. The freshly sharpened blade gleamed like sin in the moonlight.

Tucking a toolbox between the row of nuke batteries, the man shrugged. "Yeah, I know," J.B. hedged uncomfortably, strapping down the sturdy case. "But still…"

"Don't worry, John, the doors will do," Mildred stated, tying a cloth around her hair. Knotting it tight under her chin, she made sure every beaded lock was safely tucked away. If a hunter got a fistful of hair, at the very least it would be incredibly painful as the creature ripped it out by the roots, and at the worst, deadly as it hauled the driver into range of their claws and fangs.

"Sure as hell hope so," J.B. said softly. Normally he

would have argued to wait for another day or two, so that he could add some refinements, but unfortunately, time was against them. The longer the companions waited, the farther Delphi got from the redoubt. Or worse, the sooner he'd jump to the redoubt, see that his spare parts were gone and attack from within, driving them out to the muties' waiting arms.

On impulse, the Armorer touched the implo gren in his munitions bag. One shot. That was all they'd have. One fragging chance to ace the cyborg. Grimly, the man donned his fedora. So he'd bloody make it count if he had to shove the damn thing straight down his throat first.

Seeing his dark expression, Mildred wanted to offer him some comfort, but continued lashing down her med kit to the metal floor right next to the Kalashnikov. Back in medical school, a wise dorm mate had once compared the male of the species to brewing beer: sometimes they just needed to be left alone. True words.

Over at the fuel pumps, Doc was holding a gurgling hose over a partially filled bucket. Slowly, the trickle of fuel slowed to a dribble, then stopped completely. All out. Hanging up the nozzle, he lifted the bucket by the handle and carried it to the last speedster. Using a cardboard funnel, the man carefully poured in the few pints of clear fluid.

Sitting behind the wheel, Krysty turned on the paper for a few moments to check the fuel gauge.

"How much juice did we achieve, dear lady?" Doc asked, setting the bucket aside and vigorously wiping his hands dry on a clean rag. Shooting a blaster with juice on your skin was a fast way to lose fingers.

"That put me at a little more than half a tank," Krysty said, frowning. "You sure there's no more?"

"Mayhap in another redoubt…" Doc answered guilelessly.

She grunted in reply. "Fair enough." After battling the droid, there had not been much fuel left in the main tank of the redoubt, so the companions split what little there was equally among them. Hopefully, it would be enough to get them through the jungle and far enough away from the hunters. On open ground, the creatures were relatively easy to ace. But in their natural environment, they were death machines. There was no doubt in her mind that the gorilla-like muties would have aced Ryan if they had been allowed to enter the pool. That had been a foolish mistake by Delphi. Many fights were lost because somebody acted stupe, more than anything else.

Climbing into the lead speedster, Ryan closed the hinged hatch and dogged it shut with a sliding bolt. The crude door was painted a bright yellow, oddly marking its exact position in the resilient cage. Wrapping a cloth around his own hair, Ryan strapped himself in place. Turning on the engine, he checked over the few gauges still attached to the skeletal remains of the dashboard. Oil pressure, temp, power, everything looked good. Then the man revved the engine hard a few times trying to make it stall, but the machine refused to flood or choke.

The others started their own engines, filling the garage with noise and exhaust fumes, the wall vents struggling to clean the atmosphere until there was a brisk breeze blowing through the level. Each seemed satisfied with his or her speedster, except for J.B., who still wished for something other than the Volvo SUV. It was a good wag, but relatively new and he had hoped for something older.

The Trader always said that old metal ran better, and it was true. The flashy models produced just before the Big Flash all had electric carburetors, fuel injectors, built-in comps, and the like. So even if they somehow survived the Nuke War without getting fried by the EMP blast of an atomic blast, the fancy engines were a real nuke-in-the-ass to maintain, to his mind. Cruise control, automatic seat adjusters, kill switches, theft alarms, low-jacks, and all of that technodrek had to be ripped out before you could even start to rewire the engine to make them run smooth. And there had always been a few speedsters that simply could never be made to work, until a gunner for the Trader had come up with a snazzy little bypass gimmick made from assorted bits of junk. With one of those, the Trader could get any wag to run.

Removing his glasses to polish them on a sleeve, J.B. grinned at the recollection. Dark night, I haven't thought about Hoban in years.

"Everybody hot?" Ryan called, glancing around.

Hands gave curt waves as the companions did a last check on their speedsters, making sure that all of the food and general supplies were lashed down tight, the rapid-fires loaded, spare ammo tucked away safely, along with the grens. Each person had an AK-47 set in a pressure-clip on the floor, far from the questing hands of the muties, yet readily available to them if the need should arise. But more importantly, every speedster had a rubber mat glued to the floor under the driver.

"Ready and willing!" Krysty answered, working the clutch and gearshift on what had once been a Nissan. "Just say the word!"

"Then let's roll!" Ryan shouted, shifting into gear and starting forward.

Forming a ragged line, the six speedsters rolled into the exit tunnel, maneuvering easily past the series of antirad zigzags.

"Half a league, half a league onward!" Doc sang out over the noisy engine of the Saturn SUV. It wasn't a very powerful wag, but for some reason he felt drawn to the machine. He had no logical idea why.

"Aw, stuff it, ya old coot!" Mildred shot back. "You know I hate that damn poem!"

"Hate Tennyson, madam? Impossible!"

"Mebbe just hate you!" Jak added, trying not to smirk.

Looking over a shoulder, Doc flashed his oddly perfect teeth. "Now that I believe!"

The massive blast doors at the end of the tunnel loomed. Braking to a halt, everybody got their rapid-fires ready, as Krysty hopped out to tap in the exit code on the wall keypad and press the lever. She immediately raced back to her speedster, and was safely inside the locked cage before the doors parted to expose the wall of water.

Anxiously, Ryan touched the fresh bandages under his shirt as he waited to see if any of the muties would come out of the rushing barrier. But nothing happened. The one-eyed man stomped on the gas pedal.

Shooting forward, he literally flew through the pounding water and was airborne for several seconds before dropping into the lake with a resounding splash. Veering away from a boulder, he jogged to the left just as Krysty burst into view, closely followed by J.B., Mildred, Doc and Jak.

The lake was chest-high on them, completely covering the tires. Choppy waves smacked the engines, making them sputter and cough, but then they surged with life.

Steering wildly, the companions did their best to avoid the assorted obstacles submerged in the shallow lake, and Mildred clipped a boulder hard enough to rattle her teeth. But the physician held on to the steering wheel with both hands and got the little speedster back under control before it smashed headlong into another large rock.

Watching out of the corner of his eye, J.B. whistled in relief. That had been close. Too damn close.

Shaking the spray from his face, Ryan searched for hunters waiting for them in the trees or bushes, but then the shore was upon them. Bracing for the impact, the man jounced up the mossy slope and went flying again for a moment before landing on top of the bamboo stand, sending out broken pieces in every direction.

Angling past a tree, he plowed into a bush, and a rear wheel slipped in the greenery turning him abruptly back toward the lake. Savagely twisting the steering wheel, Ryan fought to stay out of the water and managed to angle back into the bushes to careen off a banana tree in an explosion of bark. Fruit fell from above like green and yellow rain as Ryan rejoined the others rocketing through the dense jungle. J.B. gave the man a game thumbs-up, and Krysty nodded, then they were among the banyan trees. Hanging vines were everywhere, and the companions concentrated on their driving. Even shouted conversations were pointless over the six engines and the steady rustling of the plant life smashed aside by the steel cages.

Colorful birds exploded from the trees at their approach, and the little monkeys ran away, screaming and waving their arms in an almost human manner. Running over a hissing snake, Ryan dodged a large flower that turned to follow the speedsters, then something heavy landed on top of the cage, and a hairy arm clawed for his face. Hunters!

Leaning away from the limb, Ryan flipped a switch on the dashboard and the entire cage crackled with fat blue sparks. On the dashboard, a meter showed the first line of nuke batteries in the rear of the speedster draining slightly, but nothing serious.

With fat blue sparks crawling over it, the mutie blindly tried for the man, missed and accidentally touched the door. Now the second set of batteries surged, completing the circuit, and the mutie shrieked as it burst into flames from the massive electric shock.

Shifting gears, Ryan smelled ozone and cooked flesh, as the aced mutie tumbled away. Unfortunately the gas gauge was dropping at an alarming rate. Every time he fried a mutie, the power drain made the engine slow. But there was nothing that could be done about that now. He would just have to stay low, stay fast and trust that the welds were strong enough to hold.

A snarling mutie leaped from a bush, all four arms spread. Dodging the creature, Ryan saw the other companions in their speedsters darting about. Jak had an aced mutie on the front, partially blocking his view. The albino teen was fishtailing the speedster in an effort to get the smoking corpse off, but was having no luck.

A large mutie was clinging to the side of Doc's cage, holding on with both feet while four hands grabbed for the old man's long, flowing hair. Ryan could see the scholar stabbing the button on the dashboard, but nothing was happening. Fireblast, he thought, something had to be wrong with the bastard wiring!

Quickly angling in that direction, Ryan bounced over some exposed roots, nearly losing his seat, then saw Krysty slam her speedster into Doc's wag, crushing the mutie between their two cages. There was an electrical shower as their cages touched, sizzling sparks zapping the creature. A gory ruin, the charred hunter hung on with a single arm, then fell away to disappear in the clouds of bluish smoke pouring from the exhaust pipes. Only the arm remained to sway to the motions of the racing speedster.

A stuttering burst rang out, and Ryan turned to see Mildred trigger her rapid-fire at a hunter perched on top of her cage. Bleeding from a score of wounds, the mutie thrust downward with a stick, knocking the Kalashnikov from her grip. The AK-47 hit the floor and tumbled to the rear of the speedster, lying on top of the nuke batteries.

Stomping on the accelerator, Ryan went cold at the sight. If the metal blaster made contact with the terminals, Mildred would be fried alive!

Shouting a war whoop, Jak turned his speedster, streaked along an earthen mound and fired a single shot from his Colt Python. The Magnum round hit a tree branch ahead of the crouching physician, the wood exploding into splinters. Dropping free, the branch hit the bleeding mutie across the face, fangs and blood gushing from the brutal impact. As the mutie fell off, J.B. ran over it with his speedster, grinning like a madman.

Then Mildred slammed on the brakes and the Kalashnikov flew to the front of the cage and dropped onto the dashboard. Snatching the weapon with one hand, she rammed it back into the clip on the floor, then shifted gears to accelerate to full speed.

There were spaces among the trees now, and occasionally Ryan could see open sky. They had to be reaching the end of the jungle. He had no fragging idea what lay beyond, but without the cover provided by the trees, the danger from the muties would be eliminated.

Suddenly a rock bounced off the cage near Ryan, stony splinters peppering his face. Cursing vehemently, the man veered away from the attack, then realized his mistake and spun back again just it time to avoid a barrage of rocks thrown by other muties.

From somewhere there came the sound of shattering glass as a headlight was destroyed. Doc cried out in pain. A fist-size stone shot through the opening of a cage to hit the back of Krysty's chair, nearly throwing her into the dashboard. Suddenly they were out of the jungle, barreling along an uneven grassland that stretched to the horizon.

Loud cries from the furious Hunters could be heard coming from the jungle, but they were growing fainter with every heartbeat. The muties were not allowed in the lake, so maybe they were also not allowed out of the jungle? That made sense. What good were guard dogs if they could run away?

A low earthen mound sent Ryan airborne over a ravine, and he landed with a jarring crash on the other side, nearly losing control of the vehicle. The terrain was getting rougher, wild and jagged. With no other choice, the one-eyed man slowed his speedster. Unexpectedly, a blaster fired. Ryan turned to see Jak shaking his head vehemently and heading to the west. He was puzzled for a moment, then understood the teen was still following the trail of Delphi from the redoubt.

Downshifting the gears, Ryan and the others followed the albino youth through the churned countryside and onto a smooth grassland. Young trees dotted the landscape, but they were few and far between, and easily avoided. Slowing for a minute, Jak studied the ground, then took off again, the others staying in his wake.

Squinting at the grass, Ryan caught a glimpse of the signs of an old campsite, then it was left behind. Fireblast, had there been four cook fires? That could mean fifteen or so people traveling with the cyborg. Ryan wanted to go back to look for more details about the weapons and wags of the cyborg's convoy, but they were still too close to the mutie to risk stopping.

Checking the fuel gauge, the man grunted at the needle trembling near the quarter-tank mark. Half of their juice was already gone.

High above the racing speedsters, thunder rumbled in the turbulent sky, and there came the faint smell of sulfur. Ryan fought the urge to increase his speed and stayed close to Jak. If they lost the trail now, they would never find it again after an acid rain. On the other hand, if they were caught out in the open, after the storm there wouldn't be enough of the companions left to stuff into an empty cartridge.

Casting fast glances to the other companions, Ryan saw that they comprehended the situation and wanted to stay on the trail. There really was nothing else to do but keep moving and hope they outpaced the coming rain.

Concentrating on their driving, the companions sped along the untamed grasslands, listening to the distant thunder and waiting for the first sprinkling of fiery death from above.

Chapter Eight

"Yah! Move, you nuking bags of bones! Yah!" James Keifer shouted, cracking his whip in the air just above the running team of horses. Already straining against the leather harness, the animals surged forward, redoubling their efforts, and the buckboard increased in speed across the rough terrain.

The valley rose sharply on each side of the small convoy, jagged boulders dotting the landscape from where they had tumbled down the sloping hills. Sagebrush and scraggly juniper bushes grew in wild abundance, tall cacti growing higher than any norm, their thorny arms outstretched as if praying to a blazing sun god.

A dozen of the armed slavers rode their horses in tight formation around the rattling buckboard, the big men hunched low, their hands gripping blasters. One man had an arrow through his shoulder, the wound bleeding from the front and back, his shirt soaked black and crawling with flies. But the grim man was still in the saddle, his blaster raised, the hammer cocked and ready. The cargo had been aced, and now they were fighting for their lives. What a nukestorm of a job this had turned into!

"Any sign of 'em yet?" Stanley Frederickson demanded from the rear of the buckboard, pulling back the drawstring on a huge crossbow. The spread of the weapon was more than a yard wide, and few people could even load the massive bow, much less control the staggering recoil. The string locked into place, Frederickson pulled an arrow from the quiver on his back and knocked it in place.

"Nothing yet!" shouted one of the other slavers in the shaking buckboard. Facing backward, he stood with one sweaty hand holding a longblaster, the other wrapped tight around the iron bars of the cage.

Stout poles supported a canvas awning that kept the blazing sun off the heads of the remaining slavers. Blood stained the floorboards from a chance hit that chilled Vera Nazarene, the body of the aced woman tossed out to give the others more room to fight. The grim slavers had said nothing as they'd heaved their friend to the sand, consigning her to the scavengers.

"Think we lost 'em?" G. W. Barton asked hopefully, a bloody rag tied around his throat from a near miss by the attacking cannies. At every word, the trickle of red seeping from under the crude bandage flowed faster.

"No fragging way!" Keifer replied loudly, over the pounding hooves of the team of horses. He licked dry lips and started to add more, then changed his mind. "Yah! Yah!" he bellowed, cracking the whip again. "Come on, ya big bastards, move!"

Whinnying in response, the animals increased their efforts and the buckboard surged forward, which increased the wild shaking. Grabbing the low wooden sides of the buckboard, the slavers held on tight and prepared for another assault by the cannies. Longblasters were loaded, knives loosened in sheaths and the fuses checked on a precious few hand-bombs. The homemade explosives were clay jugs packed with black powder and loose pebbles. When the charge blew, the blast sent out a halo of rocks that chilled anything for ten yards, norm or mutie. The bombs were what the slavers used to blow up ville gates. The men they chilled on sight, but the females and babes would be sold or traded.

Lashed securely in the four corners of the buckboard, covered with heavy tarpaulins, were four large barrels filled to the brim with black powder and soft lead to be made into musket balls. A staggering bounty of ammo had been hauled from the Redbone Mountains and paid for with slaves—pilgrims, farmers, fools and feebs, anybody the slavers could capture alive in their nets. Then they rode the Great Salt, trading slaves to Dogrun for lead, exchanging the soft metal to Royalton for black powder, then trading the powder with Cascade for flints, the shiny, brittle little stones that made the powder explode. The barons of the villes of Royalton and Cascade pretended they had no idea that Dogrun used slave labor in their mines, and everybody got working blasters.

The hordes of muties roaming Deathlands never stood a chance against the booming muskets of the three villes, and there soon was a safe zone that reached all the way from Green Hell to the Flat Lake.

Unfortunately, it seemed that news of their wealth had spread.

At first, the slavers had thought this was a simple jack, some outlander mercies doing a nightcreep to get the cargo of ammo. But when the slavers tossed out Vera, the outlanders stopped to collect the body and one of them took a couple of bites out of the still-warm corpse.

"Fragging cannies," Wilma Fisher growled, tucking

her blunt flint into a pocket. Even after being sharpened again, the rock would be too small for a longblaster musket, but would work just fine in a handcannon.

Taking a fresh flint from the row of small pockets sown across the front of her rawhide shirt, the busty slaver tucked it into place and tried not to think about what would happen to her if taken alive by the cannies. Raped, of course, which might not be too bad, but then she'd be tied to a rock and slowly cut apart. The cannies believed that the death songs of people sweetened the meat. Maybe that was just a story, but Fisher would eat her own blaster before that happened.

Inserting a fresh flint, Fisher twisted the screw to lock the rock into place. A charge of powder and lead was already in the barrel, but the woman checked the cover of the flash pan to make sure the priming charge was still in place. With the fragging buckboard bounding and jerking all over the place it was surprising that any of the slavers still had teeth in their heads, much less powder in their weapons! she thought. But a sniff of the pan filled her nose with the reek of rotten eggs. That told her the powder was still place, primed and ready.

"Frag 'em all!" Fisher roared, her long hair lashing freely in the wind. "It's chilling time, boys!"

Nobody replied, saving their breath. Every slaver wanted to bed the woman, and nobody ever wanted to face her in battle. Fisher liked chilling more than getting rode, and she loved getting rode more than breathing.

Everything had gone fine on the way to the Redbone Mountains, lots of empty miles and a few stickies. Nothing serious. Several times along the way, Vera Nazarene had sworn that she saw a flash of reflected light from the sand dunes, or a rock formation, almost as if somebody was watching them through a longeyes. But that nonsense had been ignored. As if anybody had a working scope anymore! But it seemed the woman had been right. The cannies hit the convoy near the Dune Sea, and she had been the first to get chilled, a hole blown clean through her belly from a sniper.

Just then, a great cloud of dust rose from behind a hill to their east.

"Here they come again!" Barton yelled, pulling out two muzzle-loading pistols and cocking back the hammers.

If the Red Shakes hadn't taken so many of the slavers last winter, the convoy would have twice the number of blasters than it did now. More than enough to deal with any attempted jack! But now…

A moment later half a dozen predark bikes burst into view from out of an arroyo, sunlight glinting off the windshields. Carrying throwing axes, the cannies looked lumpy from the pieces of hardwood strapped to their bodies as protection from the soft lead bullets. Here and there was a flower of splinters sticking out showing where a lead ball had hit but failed to achieve penetration.

Following behind the group of two-wheelers was a massive war wag. The huge Mack truck was pulling a long, eighteen-wheeler, flatbed trailer with wooden walls added. The planks were studded with nails, and louvered shutters hung protectively over the big tires. Even the cab was coated with wood and nails, making it resemble a thornbush, and a colossal eye was painted across the planks covering the grille, the inhuman orb staring directly forward in singular purpose.

Wooden armor studded with nails, Barton raged, squinting at the bizarre sight. Who ever heard of such a thing?

The slaver found the painted eyeball oddly disturbing as he tried to aim at the war wag, which was probably what it was intended for—to scare people into running away so that they could be more easily run down. That realization brought a cold wave of adrenaline to his stomach. Nuke-sucking cannies were trying to play him!

Trying to ignore the big eye, Keiffer took aim and unleashed the crossbow, the arrow lancing harmlessly between the dusty covered riders and burrowing itself deep into the planks covering the front of the war wag, just missing the eye.

Fiendishly, the cannie driver of the Mack grinned in response, displaying sharpened teeth, and increased the speed of the big rig.

Cursing bitterly, Keifer started to reload the crossbow.

"Dumb-ass gleeb! Now watch how it's done by a real gunner!" Fisher snarled, raising her longblaster and firing. A foot-long lance of flame boomed from the end of the muzzle, along with a huge cloud of dark smoke. A split second later, the windshield of a bike exploded into sparkling pieces, the rider jerking backward as red blood exploded from his exposed throat. As the body fell, the bike veered away to disappear into a gully. A few moments later there was a fiery explosion and a huge gout of smoke rolled upward into the sky.

"That was for Vera!" the woman shouted smugly, pulling out a ramrod to start reloading her own weapon.

Just then, the buckboard hit a rock, sending her over

the side. The slavers watched in horror as the woman hit the ground, her blaster flying away. She was still rolling in the sand when the cannie bikers roared past, the leader swinging a hand ax. Still stunned from the fall, Wilma feebly tried to dodge, but the blade hit, cleaving her head wide open and splashing her brains onto a nearby rock.

Startled for only a moment, now all of the guards in the buckboard began hammering at the cannies with muskets and crossbows. Grinning widely, the bikers spread out and opened fire with their handcannons, the staggered volley of smoke temporarily masking the outlanders. But then they reappeared from the roiling fumes, throwing hand axes. The blades spun across the intervening space and slammed into the horses.

Screaming in pain, the animals reared, throwing several of the slavers to the hard sand, bones audibly breaking as the bodies crazily tumbled along like windblown leaves.

As the other riders struggled to control their mounts, Keifer knelt to fumble with a butane lighter, then stood and heaved a hand bomb. Instantly, the eighteen-wheeler slammed on the brakes, tires squeaking and screeching, while the sleek two-wheelers quickly separated. The clay jug hit empty sand and violently exploded. Two of the cannies wobbled on their bikes from the concussion, but none of them fell.

As the bikers sped away, more cannies stood up in the rear of the Mack war wag, and started firing predark handcannons at the slavers. Raising his arm to throw another bomb, Keifer as blown backward with most of his face gone, the hail of blood, brains and teeth splattering across Frederickson. The driver cast a single brief look backward, then crouched and started insanely whipping the horses.

"Yah! Yah!" the fat slaver bellowed, spittle flying from his mouth. "Faster, ya motherless gleebs, or it's the stew pot for all of you!" The whip cracked constantly, the pounding of the hooves sounding like distant cannon fire, it was so loud.

Fumbling to reload his musket, Barton could not believe what had just happened. The cannies had predark blasters? Then why were they throwing axes before? Mebbe to conserve ammo? He'd never seen live brass in his life, only black-powder blasters. So why were they using the brass now, unless… Nuking hell, this wasn't a jack!

"Ambush!" Barton shouted, firing his longblaster. "We're heading into a fragging ambush!"

His eyes going wide with understanding, Frederickson started pulling the reins to the left, toward the open desert. But the terrified horses didn't want to obey and kept going forward. Frantically, he whipped the animals, but that only made them slow down in confusion, and the bikers grew closer.…

SPUTTERING AND COUGHING, the engine of the modified Saturn died away completely. Pumping the pedal, Ryan tried to coax the speedster a little farther until coasting to a full halt near the foot of a large hillock. With squealing brakes, the rest of the companions stopped nearby, Jak's engine sputtering and dying before he came to a complete rest.

"Guess that's it." Krysty sighed, yanking off the handkerchief and running a hand through her hair. "We made it farther that I thought."

"At least we left the acid rain behind us," Ryan grumbled, cracking his knuckles. He knew the storm might still be coming this way, but even on foot they should be long gone before it arrived.

"Any sign of the hunters?" Mildred asked in concern, yanking out the spent rounds from her blaster and shoving in live brass.

"Don't see how," Ryan said, turning off the power to the cage, then throwing the bolt before unlocking the door.

Pushing it open with a boot, the big man got out and stretched with obvious relief, then reached into the backpack on the floor to unearth a soup-can-size object. With a snap of his wrist, the predark Navy telescope extended for a full three feet, and Ryan placed his good eye to the end and looked around, carefully studying the distant horizon. The telescope was an amazing little thing they had found in the ruins of the Virginia Beach Naval Station. The unbreakable plastic lens was kind of heavy, but the scope compacted smaller than binocs and was perfect for the one-eyed man.

Turning slowly, Ryan could only see barren desert. There were some reddish mountains to the north, along with several sand dunes, but nothing else. "Clear," he announced with some satisfaction, compacting the telescope. "Didn't think the muties could follow us this far, but it never hurts to make sure."

"Caution is the virtue of the wise," Doc proclaimed, awkwardly exiting the cage.

"So where are?" Jak asked, shaking his head and running stiff fingers through his hair. Then he paused. What was that smell...rotten eggs? He sniffed again, but this time there was only the dry desert breeze, as dead and sterile as the depths of a forgotten tomb.

"Looks like Australia," Mildred said, taking out a canteen to dampen a cloth and wipe down her face. But she knew they could be anywhere. These days, there were swamps in New York, and deserts in Kentucky. How anybody had survived skydark seemed a miracle.

"Tell you in a sec," J.B. said, removing the cloth from his hair. Crumpling it into a ball, the man stuffed the rag into his munitions bag, then reached under his shirt to pull out a minisextant. Facing the partly cloudy sky, he found the sun, got the half mirror into focus, then did some fast mental calculations. Tucking the little device away, he pulled a predark map from a pocket and spread it wide.

"Best as I can tell…we're in Colorado, near the Utah border, just above the Great Salt," J.B. announced, folding the plastic-coated sheet again and tucking it carefully away in his munitions bag. "If we had any juice left we could drive to Two-Son ville." The companions had been there a while back, and helped the local baron deal with a nasty infestation of stickies. It was one of the few villes in the world where they would receive a friendly welcome.

"Utah," Ryan whispered, a chill running down his back in spite of the dry heat. Briefly, he touched the leather patch covering his missing eye, remembering the nightmare once more. Then he shook it off. Mildred had said that a dream was just your brain cleaning out the drek of the day, and carried no special meaning.

"Something wrong?" Jak asked, a knife slipping into his waiting palm. Squinting hard, the teenager glanced over the sandy vista, but there was nothing dangerous in sight. Not even a screamwing moved through the lonely sky.

"No, nothing's wrong," Ryan answered, brushing back his long hair.

"The Zone," Doc repeated, his face darkening in somber thought. Clutching the silver lion's head on his sword stick, he twisted the handle and pulled out a few inches of the Spanish blade hidden inside, then slammed it closed again with a solid click. This was near where he'd last tangled with Delphi, and he wondered if the locale had some special significance to the blackguard.

The faint crackle of blasterfire reached them, closely followed by the muted roar of predark engines.

Instantly the companions drew their blasters and waited. Nothing happened. Then the sounds of blasters came again, accompanied by the rotten-egg smell of spent black powder.

"J.B., with me!" Ryan snapped, drawing the SIG-Sauer and starting up the sandy slope. "Everybody else stay with the supplies!"

Working the arming bolts on their Kalashnikovs, the companions moved protectively around the speedsters as J.B. sprinted forward to try to catch the other man. He joined Ryan at the crest of the dune. The other man was lying on his belly, head tilted as he listened intently to the soft sounds of battle. Lying down, J.B. crawled closer and concentrated. He distinctly heard predark revolvers and muskets firing, along with some sort of homemade explosive. Mebbe a pipe bomb or Molotov. Then he caught the death scream of a horse.

"Could be mercies jacking a convoy," J.B. guessed.

Saying nothing, Ryan took out the longeyes and crawled over the top of the dune until the other side was visible. Through the longeyes he saw a horse-drawn buckboard being chased by a pack of norms on motor-cycles with an odd-looking war wag bringing up the rear. The machine seemed to have wooden planks along the exterior instead of metal armor. Then the man noted the arrows sticking out of the wood, along with the splinter clusters of bullet hits. Off by itself, a second war wag was burning out of control, the occasional crackle of live brass coming from the fire as ammo cooked off from the heat. His guess would be a hit from one of the homemade bombs, but it was only a guess.

"Wood armor," J.B. muttered softly in disbelief. "Smart. It'd be easier to make than sheet metal and weigh a lot less."

"Certainly better than sand bags," Ryan said grudg-ingly. "One cut and the sand runs out, leaving you with an empty bag for protection."

"True. The stuff wouldn't stop a gren, but then, what would?" J.B. said, answering his own question. "Nice touch that big eye. Bet a live brass that throws off the aim of most coldhearts."

Grunting in agreement, Ryan changed the focus on the longeyes and looked along the rocky valley, finding corpses scattered around, and a smashed two-wheeler burning. A couple of horses were galloping into the distance toward a dry riverbed.

That was when he spotted the cage full of chilled people in the buckboard. Slavers! Were the folks attack-ing them sec men from some ville? He studied them closely and frowned at the sight of their pointed teeth, many of them wearing necklaces of dried human fin-gers and ears.

"Cannies," the Deathlands warrior growled in disgust.

"Which are the cannies?' J.B. asked, squinting at the fight. "No, wait, I see the cage. Dark night, cannies jacking slavers. Kind of makes you wish for the acid rain to come, doesn't it?"

Ryan nodded in reply just as a huge explosion cut off the team of horses pulling the buckboard, and the two merged, the fighting going hand-to-hand. Knives and hatchets were flashing in the bright sun, blood spraying, the cursing of the living mingling with the screams of the dying combining into the low growl of combat.

"Hell of a fight," J.B. said with a humorless smile. "This could be just what we need."

"Yeah, I thought of that." Ryan grunted, lowering the longeyes. "Notice those other bikes hidden in the crater?" There was a circle of tumbleweeds placed around the depression to help mask the presence of the machines.

"I'm not blind yet," the Armorer replied, squinting through his glasses. "Those must be the reserve troops in case the fight goes bad for the cannies. Too bad there's only four of them, and six of us, or else we could…" Sucking air through his teeth, he exhaled slowly. "You know, I just got a crazy idea."

"Way ahead of you, amigo," Ryan said, compacting the longeyes and tucking it away to bring up the Steyr SSG-70. "Better move fast, this could be over soon."

"I'm already gone," J.B. answered confidently, crawling backward until he was past the curve of the dune and out of sight.

Setting the barrel of the longblaster on the grainy sand, Ryan worked the arming bolt and fiddled with the focus on the telescopic sight. A few moments later he spotted a furtive motion near a group of boulders, and saw three of the companions running low across the valley floor toward the blast crater. A glance down the other side of the dune showed Mildred standing guard over the piles of supplies with the scattergun.

"Here we go," Ryan whispered out of the corner of his mouth, placing a finger on the trigger of the long-blaster and choosing his first target.

Chapter Nine

"Burn, ya bastards!" Dragon Webber screamed, wheeling around the buckboard and throwing a Molotov at the horses in the front.

The sloshing glass bottle hit the wooden harness and burst apart to cover the animals in flames. Screaming in terror, the horses began bucking and kicking, fighting to get away.

Lashing his whip at the cannie on the bike, Frederickson fell forward off the buckboard and was trampled to death. Then the leather reins snapped and the flaming horses bolted away in blind panic, trying to get away from the orange thing that was eating them alive.

Out of control, the buckboard wheeled wildly and plowed into a stand of cacti coming to an abrupt halt. The slavers in the rear were thrown around haplessly, Barton going over the side to land in the spiky plants.

Bleeding from a score of minor wounds, the slaver rose and fired both of his handcannons at the nearest cannie. The double load of lead slammed hard into the woman's wooden armor, cracking off a piece. Grinning in triumph, Iron Mary Cantone shot back, and the slaver dropped the blasters to clutch his missing groin, hot blood gushing between his fingers as he rolled about screaming.

Braking to a halt near the buckboard, Dragon swung

his ax, ending Barton's pitiful wails, then climbed off his bike just as another slaver launched a crossbow. The quarrel went straight through his shirt, missing the cannie by an inch and stabbing deep into the patched leather seat.

Whipping the ax forward, Dragon got the slaver directly in the face, the man falling backward, the fresh quarrel and unloaded crossbow flying from his limp hands.

Shouting a war chant, Hammer climbed into view from the other side of the buckboard, his ax dripping crimson and a scalp in his hands. Caught in the act of loading his musket, a slaver let go of the ramrod inside the barrel, swung up the weapon and pulled the trigger. The hammer dropped, sparks flew, the pan flashed bright, then the blaster seemed to bulge slightly just before it exploded. Dropping the shattered stock, the slaver reeled around clawing at the ruin of his face, one eye dangling down a cheek by a long string of whitish ganglia. Laughing, Hammer tossed away the scalp, pulled a knife and buried it in the chest of the mutilated slaver.

Dropping the spent shells from his revolver, Dragon thumbed in fresh brass when he heard a galloping horse. Spinning, he closed the partially loaded cylinder and fired twice from the hip. The slaver on the horse slid off the saddle to land on the sand with a crunch, her neck twisted at an impossible angle.

Hauling a weeping slaver up by his hair, Hammer slowly slit the struggling man's throat, then shoved him out of the buckboard.

"Come on, before the rest of these assholes come back!" Iron Mary snarled, kicking a corpse in the face just to make sure.

Wasting a second looking for more horseback riders, Dragon then joined the others in the buckboard. Ignoring the barrels of trade goods, they started stripping the bodies of blasters, when one of the supposed corpses rolled over to raise a crossbow. There was a sharp twang as the slaver fired.

Jerking to the left, Dragon felt the breeze of the arrow pass his cheek. Shitfire, that'd been close!

Knocking aside the crossbow, Iron Mary jumped on the dying slaver, slashing wildly with a curved knife. He tried to hold her off with bare hands to no avail. Blood flew everywhere, her laughter masking his shrieks of pain until the slaver went still. Panting from the exertion of the chilling, Iron Mary smiled as she raised the blade to lick the blood off the steel.

"Mighty sweet." The buxom cannie chuckled, sheathing the knife.

"We can do that later!" Dragon ordered, rattling the small door of cage. The bars were set too closely together to pull out any of the meat without hacking them apart first. "Now, hurry and find the damn key for that cage! The other slavers will come back soon, and I will not leave all of this behind!"

"Mebbe it was in the pocket of somebody who fell out of the buckboard," Hammer squeaked in a childish voice. The muscular cannie stood over six feet tall, but his head was grotesquely small for the gargantuan body, almost as if it had been an afterthought. A necklace of tongues hung around his throat, his exposed back covered with different tattoos of eyes to protect him from muties.

"So hop out and get it for us, will ya?" Iron Mary smirked, going through the pockets of a bald slaver. Then her head exploded.

Turning fast, Dragon fired his revolver at the group of slavers galloping toward them on horseback. The slavers shot back with colossal blasters, the lead balls actually humming as they went by the cannies.

Flipping an ax forward, Hammer got a rider in the leg. The slaver went tumbling off the mount to land with a sickening crunch. Another slaver threw a net at the cannies in the buckboard, but it tangled on the cage. Shooting repeatedly until his wheel gun clicked empty, Dragon dropped behind the wooden side of the buckboard and pulled a blaster from the holster of a corpse. Checking the load, he crouched and fired, the deafening boom of the handcannon heralding a cloud of dark smoke that blocked out the world. More shots rang out from both groups, a man screamed, then a motorcycle buzzed past the buckboard with Pig swinging an ax coated with slimy human entrails. Behind him a slaver doubled over to clutch at his missing stomach and collapse sideways.

Dropping the black-powder blaster, Dragon started to reload the predark revolver with his last few rounds. In wild confusion, the bikers and the horsemen circled about each other, firing their blasters nonstop, knives and axes flying about as the two groups battled to the death in the desert valley.

WITH THEIR BLASTERS held at the ready, the three companions crawled along the sandy ground, edging closer to the ancient blast crater. Stopping a few yards away, J.B. checked the rad counter on his lapel and relaxed when there was only background rad showing. Good. They needed those bikes, but he had no wish to charge into a hot pit to get the Red Cough. Nothing was worth that kind of misery.

The sounds of battle were still going strong when they reached the clump of tumbleweeds. This close, the companions could see that the desert plants had been lashed together with rope to keep them from rolling away on the breeze. A wise precaution, but having somebody hidden as a guard would have been a smarter move.

Easing to the weeds opposite the combat, J.B. gently parted them just enough to peek through. Three cannies sat on the big bikes, resting their arms on the handlebars, grisly human trophies dangling from strands of rawhide. Every bit of chrome was covered with dull tape and the glass windshield had been replaced with a wooden board bolted to the frame. They all had throwing axes dangling from their belts, along with revolvers riding in low holsters.

"How's it going?" one of the bikers asked, rotating the cylinder of the wheel gun in his hands. The Colt .22 had little stopping power, but the cannie had found an entire box of cartridges in a crashed mil wag. What his grandie called an Apee, or, sometimes, an APC. It was the find of a lifetime, so he was nursing the fifty live brass along for as long as he could.

"The slavers are coming this way," a tall cannie replied, shifting his position on the Harley. "We could attack them from behind—"

"No," the other snapped. "Dragon told us to wait right here, so here we stay until he signals for us to join the fight."

"But they might all be aced by then!"

"So? That only means we eat sooner." His stomach rumbled loudly just then in perfect harmony with the rumbling from the tainted clouds overhead. Fearfully,

the cannie glanced skyward, then relaxed. Those were
the wrong type of clouds for acid rain. Besides, it wasn't
anywhere near spring. Let the sky moan like an angry
slut. The noise would help cover the sound of their engines starting just before they charged the last of the
slavers. Then the feasting would begin!

Staying low to the ground, the companions separated
to move around the blast crater in different directions.
Leaving Doc near a scraggly yucca tree, J.B. headed for
a pile of boulders when there came the soft sound of
crunching sand and a cannie walked around a boulder
zipping up his pants.

The two men stared at each for a full second, then
the cannie clawed for his ax as J.B. stepped aside and
Doc lunged into view to plunge his sword directly into
the man's throat. Red fluid gushed from the hideous
wound and the cannie grabbed his neck, cutting off two
of his fingers as they slid along the sharp blade. He
looked into the Doc's face with dull comprehension,
then eased to the ground and went forever still.

Sliding out the blade, Doc waited until he heard a
whip-poor-will from the other side of the pit, then he
and J.B. grabbed the aced cannie and threw him over
the wall of weeds. The warm corpse crashed between
the parked two-wheelers, splattering them with blood.
The cannies spun at the grisly arrival and gasped in
shock.

That was when Krysty stepped into view firing her
AK-47 blaster. A moment later, J.B. and Doc appeared
from opposite sides of crater, triggering their own rapid-
fires. The 7.62 mm Kalashnikovs and 9 mm Uzi tore the
startled cannies apart, their lifeblood spraying into the
air. Riddled with slugs, one of them staggered around

still horribly alive, then yanked a predark gren from inside the bloody tatters of his shirt. Shooting from the hip, Krysty fired a single round and a black hole appeared in the middle of his forehead. Sighing deeply, the cannie dropped, his lifeless finger curled around the pin.

Kneeling, Krysty recovered the gren, while Doc and J.B. dragged the other bodies off the bikes. Briefly, they checked the corpses for any more grens, but there was only their axes and handcannons. Since the companions had much better weapons, those were left behind. Carrying too many weapons would chill you in the Deathlands even faster than having none. However, Doc did appropriate a cardboard box half full of .22-caliber copper-jacketed rounds. Those would make excellent trade goods at a ville.

Across the valley, the battle raged on. The smoke was getting thick around the buckboard, making it hard for both sides to see clearly. The bikers stayed in constant motion, firing their blasters and swinging axes. The slavers fought back with whips and handcannons, the flame from the muzzles of their weapons stabbing through the billowing smoke like angry lighting. One cannie stopped to pull out a Molotov and light the fuse, but a slaver discharged a scattergun, peppering the front of the big bike, blowing the tire and splintering the wooden shield. His hand raised to throw, the cannie shrieked as he drew back a bloody stump, blood pumping from the ragged tatters of flesh dangling from his wrist. Then the Molotov hit the ground at his boots and whoofed into flames. Covered with fire, the man insanely beat at the fire, his cries becoming louder and more frantic, until the gas tank of the bike hissed loudly, the fuel starting to boil from the rising heat.

"Run!" Pig screamed, stopping his bike. Kicking at the ground with both legs, he turned the bike and started to race away.

The rest of the cannie bikers followed his example, and they got a few yards away when the damaged Harley exploded, spraying out machine parts and human organs.

Taking advantage of the noisy distraction, the companions climbed onto big Harleys, kicked the engines into life and twisted the handlebar throttles until the bikes were roaring with power.

A slash of Doc's cane cut away the restraining rope, and as the tumbleweeds rolled away, the companions raced out of the pit. Charging along the dusty ground, they curved around the loudly fighting groups and went straight for the eighteen-wheeler Mack with the big painted eye.

Standing in the rear of the war wag, a cannie smiled at the appearance of the bikes, then frowned. Those weren't his people!

"Outlanders!" the cannie shouted, pulling a Molotov from a wooden box. He used a thumbnail to flick a wooden match alive and started to apply it to the oily rag fuse when he jerked backward to slam into the splintery planks edging the predark flatbed.

Dumbfounded, the cannie stared at the gaping hole in his chest, unable to comprehend why there was no pain from such a ghastly wound. Sliding into death, he dimly heard the report of the Steyr from the distant sand dune before eternal silence filled his darkening universe.

Sputtering in rage, the driver yanked out a rusty .45 autoloader and worked the slide just as the side window shattered, his head bursting apart from the arrival of the 7.62 mm round Ryan fired from the sand dune.

Rapidly braking to a halt near the cab of the truck, Krysty jumped off the stolen bike and yanked open the door to clamber up the step, then the seat, to reach the roof. Staying clear of the protective nails jutting from the thick planks, the woman sprayed the cannies in the rear with her Kalashnikov. Coming to a halt near the driver's door, J.B. hosed the interior with his Uzi, the two cannies crying out in surprise as the bullets forced them into a short death jig, their lifeblood splattering the windshield.

Without bothering to slow, J.B. hopped off his bike, climbed into the cab and pushed aside the corpses to start the engine. There was a struggling whine, then the big Detroit diesels came to life, blowing blue-gray smoke from the double exhaust pipes.

Stopping behind the war wag, Doc leveled his AK-47 and looked around frantically, his heart pounding. In the pandemonium near the buckboard, a man turned in his direction. Doc swung up the rapid-fire, but before he could shoot the man doubled over clutching his stomach. Once more there came the sound of the deadly Steyr.

Suddenly a hatch swung open in the planks and there was Krysty holding her Kalashnikov and a gory knife. On the bloody floor, a muscular cannie groaned softly and went still.

"Change of plans," she snapped, wiping the knife on her sleeve before sheathing the blade. "There's no room for the bikes!"

"Then hasten thy chariot, Hermes!" Doc replied, hastily getting inside and closing the hatch.

Krysty didn't know the quote, but understood the tone. Going to the front of the wag, she thumped a fist twice on the metal roof. Promptly, the war wag lurched forward, rattling and clanging across the rocky ground.

Starting to turn toward Ryan and the others on the hill, J.B. cursed as a group of cannies looked up at the noise of the approaching vehicle.

Realizing that they were being jacked while they were in the middle of a fight, the cannies raced toward the companions.

A bald woman whose arms were covered with tattoos almost reached the big wag when the bike toppled over, juice gurgling from a new hole in the fuel tank. Stunned at the sight, the woman stood still for a moment, then the war wag plowed directly into her.

The limp body went flying to land ahead of the wag, and J.B. drove over the cannie, the heavy tires smashing her flat.

Heading around the battle, the Armorer saw that more of the cannies were running toward the war wag as it rumbled past, their faces darkly grim. One cannie pulled back his arm to throw an ax, then spun, his throat pumping out blood like a broken fountain. As the sound of the Steyr arrived, the cannies and slavers both dived for cover.

Sticking an arm out the broken window, J.B. fired a couple of bursts from the Uzi at the group, then ducked behind the door. A heartbeat later, incoming rounds hammered the side of the Mack, shattering the sideview mirror, punching clean through the wood shutter covering the door and scoring a bloody path across his left calf. Nuking hell! Snarling at the pain, J.B. switched legs and started working the gas pedal with his other foot.

In the rear of the wag, Doc and Krysty looked around frantically for a blasterport, but apparently that particular invention was unknown to the cannies. But there were boxes nailed to the floorboards to make steps so that you could get higher than the protective planks and fire at folks outside.

"Have to do this the hard way," Krysty said, dropping a nearly spent clip to insert a full one.

Going to a firing step, Doc did the same. "On your mark, dear lady."

She nodded. "One, two…" But the wag jerked hard to the side, throwing them to the filthy floor, and there came the dull explosion of a gren.

Scrambling to their feet, the man and woman raced to the rear wall and climbed on the boxes to peek over the top. Several cannies had reclaimed their bikes and were racing in hot pursuit. Then a flight of arrows sailed overhead from the side of the war wag, closely followed by scattergun boom, lead shot peppering the wooden armor with a rattling sound.

"It seems that the last of the slavers has expired and now the cannies have turned their full attention on us!" Doc muttered, crouching to flick the selector switch on the AK-47 to full-auto.

"Too bad for them," Krysty retorted, doing the same. "One, two, three!"

Standing up together, they fanned the rapid-fires at the scurrying people until the clips ran empty, then they ducked again. Incoming lead pounded the wooden planks, throwing splinters with stinging force. Then something hit the side of the war wag with a clunk. A moment later there was a huge explosion behind the wag, a hail of something very hard hammering the planks.

Pulling the pin on a gren, Krysty tossed it over the wall. As the charge detonated, she rose and began shooting at the nearest biker. The stuttering rounds chewed a path across a wooden shield, then sent up puffs of dust from the ground. A tall cannie lost his hat and another fired back with a crossbow. The barbed quarrel hit the top plank only an inch below Doc's face. The scholar recoiled, then fired back in grim resolve.

As the rapid-fire cycled empty, Krysty dropped the blaster and drew her S&W wheel gun. It didn't have the range of the longblaster, but it was much more accurate. Squeezing off careful rounds, Krysty saw the lead smack into the wooden shields on the lead bike, but fail to get through. Fair enough. Taking a stance, she fired again, slower, more deliberately. A tire blew on a bike, sending the rider flying, then another rider dropped his crossbow as blood gushed from a minor shoulder wound. The bike wobbled, almost toppling over, but the cannie managed to right the two-wheeler and come on even faster.

Deciding to follow the success of the redhead, Doc slung the rapid-fire over a shoulder, set the selector pin on the LeMat to the 16-gauge shotgun, stood and fired. The front tire of a second Harley disintegrated into rubbery shards, the nose dropping to stab into the sand. As the bike flipped over, the howling cannie went flying as if launched by a catapult, and impacted onto the rear of the war wag with a grisly sound. After a moment Doc checked, and the corpse was dangling from the wooden armor, held in place by the rows of sharp nails.

Holstering her blaster, Krysty checked her pants' pockets, then her shirt. "Lighter!" she demanded, holding out a hand.

Searching his frock coat, Doc tossed over a butane lighter, one of several the companions had found in a New Mex redoubt. She made the catch, just as the war wag jogged to the right, then the left. There was another loud explosion, this time so close that loose sand rained down into the rattling eighteen-wheeler. Going to a box of Molotovs, she lit the oily rag fuses on several, tucked away the lighter, grabbed the box and heaved the entire thing over the back wall of the flatbed. Tumbling away freely, the box crashed on the ground behind the Mack war wag and the twelve firebombs exploded, combining into a towering inferno.

Arching wide around the fiery obstacle, one of the bikers jerked his head back as a 7.62 mm round from Ryan's Steyr took him squarely in the face. Almost casually, the cannie slid off the bike, the two-wheeler continuing onward for several yards before the front wheel twisted and it flipped, tumbling along the ground, throwing off broken machine parts.

Finding himself alone, the last cannie biker shouted something unintelligible over the sputtering diesel engine of the Mack war wag, then veered sharply away, zigzagging across the rough terrain. Twice the sandy ground kicked up along the escaping bike, then the cannie swung behind a stand of cacti and was gone from sight.

Angling out of the valley, J.B. drove the wag onto the desert and around a couple of sand dunes to finally find Mildred. He braked to a halt near her, the backpacks and extra supplies piled around her boots.

"Anybody hurt?" Mildred asked, looking closely at the dirty people. Their clothing was matted with fresh blood, but none of it seemed to be from them.

"Nothing serious," Krysty replied coolly, reloading her S&W blaster and tucking it back into the holster. Then she did the same for the AK-47 and slung it over a shoulder.

"I caught one in the leg," J.B. said, hanging an arm out of the window. "But it's just a scratch."

"You sure?" Mildred demanded.

"Yeah." He grunted. "No biggie."

But seeing the man's obvious discomfort, Mildred yanked open the door to inspect the wound. Thankfully he had been right; it was only a flesh wound. Yanking a clean cloth from her med kit, the physician tied it around the bloody pant leg as a temporary bandage. Later on she would clean the scratch and give it a couple of stitches if necessary. But for now, that would do.

A sharp whistle announced Ryan's arrival, the big man sliding down the slope on the seat of his pants, the Steyr held tightly in a raised hand.

"Five of them are still sucking air," he stated, working the bolt on the Steyr to remove the spent ammo clip from inside the longblaster. "Couldn't get a clear shot once they figured out where I was hiding."

"Damn!" J.B. snarled, closing the door again. He flexed his injured leg and it did feel a little better. Millie could handle a bandage the way he did plas.

"However, I did spot more tire tracks," Ryan added.

"Delphi?" Krysty asked from over the planks.

He nodded. "Could be."

"Great!" J.B. said. "Then get your ass in the Cyclops and let's roll!"

Ryan smiled. Cyclops was a pretty good name for a war wag.

Just then, a hail of blasterfire sounded, dust kicking up from the top of the dune.

"Good shots," Jak admitted grudgingly. "They got bikes?"

"Nothing that looked in working condition," Ryan answered, dropping in a fresh rotary clip; the clear plastic was slightly cloudy with scratches, having been used a hundred times before over the years. But the five live rounds inside were still visible. The Kalashnikovs and the Steyr took the same size ammo, but it had been a trip-long time since the man had found any replacement clips. When these were gone, the longblaster would have to be individually loaded before every shot.

"Horses?" Jak asked pointedly.

"Chilled, or on fire and running for their lives."

"On fire?"

"Yep."

"Damn." The teenager snorted, throwing his bedroll up and over the wall of planks.

But Doc caught it and dropped the roll inside. "No need for that. There's a hatch in the back," he said, jerking his chin in toward the rear.

Heading that way, the albino nodded, and the companions quickly relayed their supplies and spare blasters inside the Cyclops, along with the precious toolbox, and a couple of the nuke batteries. When he had the chance, J.B. planned to wire them to the wag headlights to make a nukelamp. It was a hundred times brighter than a flare, and would last until the halogen bulb died. The downside was they weighed more than a wheelbarrow and exploded if dropped into water. But the nukelamps were still much better than tallow candles.

Dragging out the corpses, Ryan took the gunner seat, with J.B. staying at the wheel. Going to the rear, Jak and

Mildred climbed through the hatch and into the fortified eighteen-wheeler. The physician could see that the wag had started out as a flatbed, designed for hauling concrete abutments, steel girders and other heavy cargo. The truck probably had an industrial transmission and reinforced frame, which made it damn near perfect for a war wag.

"Head for the dry riverbed," Ryan directed, hefting the rapid-fire to a more comfortable position. "That's the direction the tire tracks go."

"Sure they're not from this wag?" J.B. asked, starting the engine.

Brushing back his hair, Ryan frowned. "No way. This heap has worn tires. The ones from the redoubt were brand-new."

"Fair enough," J.B. said, shifting into gear. "Let's haul ass!" With a shudder, the Cyclops lurched forward a couple of feet, then settled into a steady chugging as it began to build speed rolling across the hard sand.

Chapter Ten

Charging into view, Dragon and the rest of his crew reached the top of the sand dune, their longblasters sweeping for the hidden sniper. But nobody was there anymore, only some empty brass glinting in the sunlight along with a lot of footprints.

"Son of a bitch got away!" Dragon snarled.

"And there they go," Pig growled, pointing to the north.

Holding a hand to his forehead to shade his eyes, Dragon stared hatefully at the moving dust cloud kicked up by the heavy war wag. The bastards seemed to be heading for the dried riverbed, which was both good news and bad, he thought. If the outlanders went south, the banks were much too steep for the wag to get out again until reaching the Great Salt, and if they went north…

"Gone," Big Suzy muttered, lowering her handcannon and ax. The nicked blade was smeared with blood, with tufts of hair sticking out. "The fragging Cyclops is gone! Black dust, we spent years putting the thing together, jacking tires, learning how to make shine, fixing the radiator…"

With a sputtering roar, the fat blonde raised both fists and shook them at the sky. "Shitfire!" Savagely, she turned on Dragon. "You! You said this was gonna be a peach! Easy pickings! Now we're stuck on foot in the middle of mutie country!"

"Shut up," Dragon muttered in a dangerous voice. "Shut up right now, bitch."

Defiantly, Big Suzy snarled at the cannie and took a step forward, her hand raising the ax slightly, then she met his cold gaze and went pale. "Hey, ya know," she muttered, lowering the blade, "I was just talking...."

The man turned away from her and looked again at the vanishing dust cloud. Yep, he thought, they were heading north. Shit.

"Hey, what're those?" Hammer asked suspiciously, his big hands twisting on a longblaster.

Walking over the crest of the dune, the cannies looked down the other side. Parked at the bottom of the dune were half a dozen strange wags. The stripped-down speedsters had a metal cage around them for some reason, and seemed to be completely undamaged.

"Why the frag would they leave those behind?" Ratter asked, sucking thoughtfully between his prominent front teeth.

"Let's find out," Dragon said cautiously, starting down the sandy slope. "And watch for boobies! These mutie lovers are tricky!"

Reaching the ground, the cannies spread out so that any mines or pit wouldn't catch all of them. Circling around the speedsters, they found nothing that seemed dangerous, and finally Dragon walked up to one and gave it a kick. Nothing happened.

Through the gridwork cage, he closely inspected the workings of the speedster, from the raised engine to the collection of nuke batteries. There were splotches of dried blood on the floor and dashboard, along with tufts of charred hair and some leafy vines. These had recently been in a fight with something large and hairy.

"Nuke me, they came from the north," Dragon muttered in surprise.

"Green Hell?" Hammer squeaked. "But that's full of those four-arm muties!"

"Which explains the cage," Pig added, rubbing the back of his neck. "They drove through the jungle in these things?"

"Seems like," Dragon said, easing open a hatch. The cannie froze at the sight of the wiring going to the nuke batteries, then relaxed with the realization that if the bars were live, he'd be a pile of smoking ash by now.

Sliding behind the wheel, the cannie looked over the controls, and soon found a newly installed button on the dashboard. That had to trigger the batteries. Smart. A sizzle cage. Trip smart.

Experimentally, Dragon checked the gears, then turned the ignition switch. The engine started immediately, then died with a sputter. He tried a few more times, but there was no response.

"These things are simply out of juice!" Dragon cried in delight. "Shitfire and honeycakes, boys, we're back in biz!"

Stepping from the speedster, the man grinned at his crew. "Pig, Suzy, check over the stiffs and scav every weapon you can, especially any grens or firebombs!"

"What about the meat?" Ratter asked, running blunt fingers through his greasy, unkempt hair.

"That's your job," Dragon ordered. "Take only arms and legs, and stack 'em in the rear. Lots of room back there with the batteries."

The man shrugged. "Sure, no prob."

"What about me?" Hammer asked timidly, shifting his boots in the loose sand.

Placing a hand on the shoulder of the tall man, Dragon beamed a smile. "You get to dig up those extra cans of juice we buried in the blast crater. Haul 'em over and fill the tanks."

"Sure, I can do that," Hammer said eagerly. He really didn't mind doing most of the heavy lifting, because he was the biggest and the strongest. That was only fair.

"As for me…" Dragon looked upward. "I'll stay on top of the dune and watch for muties."

Nervously, the other cannies glanced toward the sky. Already vultures were circling high above the valley, attracted by the smell of blood. Soon the screamwings would arrive, and then the stickies.

"After we get these rolling, what should we do next?" Suzy asked, scratching under a fat breast. "Head back to the caves to start smoking the meat, or haul ass to Waterton and sell the flints?"

Head back to the cave… What was she, an idjit? Dragon thought. "Frag that noise!" he snarled, casting a hard look to the north again. "We're going after the coldhearts that jacked our damn war wag and get it back!"

Just then, the faint sound of hooting was carried to them on the desert wind. As it faded away, the cannies rushed to their assigned tasks, Dragon clicking back the hammer on his stolen musket as he started up the dune once more. He knew a trick or two with nuke batteries that would make the thieves wish they had never been nuking born. He could almost hear their pleadings for death already.

THE DESERT GOT ROUGHER as Cyclops approached the bank of the riverbed, the land rising and falling in low curves like waves at sea. Nukescaping, Ryan realized, and checked the rad counter on his lapel, but the device registered only the usual background level.

"Okay, hold on to your ass!" J.B. shouted out the broken window.

As the war wag reached the irregular bank, the Armorer twisted the steering wheel sharply, trying to angle in for an easier descent. But the sun-baked mud crumbled under their weight and the lumbering eighteen-wheeler tilted dangerously, almost tipping over.

Shifting gears, J.B. alternated between the gas and the brakes, trying to get the Cyclops under control. The wheels spun freely in the air, the engine roaring with power. Then the other tires got purchase and the war wag lurched forward to go over the bank and fall a couple of feet on the dried mud with the force of a meteor. Everything loose went flying, the windshield cracked, the shutters hanging over the tires flipping up to smack against the splintery planks with a deafening crash. Then the war wag went lolling from side to side, rapidly building speed as it raced along the smooth riverbed.

"So that's what skydark felt like," Ryan said out of the corner of his mouth. "No wonder so few of us survived."

"We've gone through worse," J.B. muttered, ignoring the pain in his leg to shift gears. The dried mud was smooth and even, perfect for high-speed driving.

In the rear section of the fortified Mack, the rest of the companions dragged themselves off the floor and started putting everything back into place. Backpacks and bedrolls were scattered around, one of them missing entirely, and the nuke batteries had slid straight to the rear of the wag, hitting the wood so hard they made impressions into the planks. A headlight was also smashed and a couple of small kegs had broken open, covering the floor with loose black powder and lead balls that rolled dangerously underfoot. Plus, several crates had flipped over, disgorging mounds of broken flints, musket parts, spare motorcycle parts and a staggering collection of dried human remains, mostly fingers and sexual organs.

"Cannies," Mildred muttered in disgust.

"Aced now," Jak replied, taking a box of body parts and emptying it over the side of the war wag. Then he changed his mind and also tossed away the box.

"Most of them, anyway." The physician sighed, rolling up a sleeve. "Come on, let's clean this rolling abattoir before we catch the plague."

Finding some old clothing in a plastic box, the companions used the rags as brooms and swept the floor clean of powder and shot, shoving it out the rear hatch. Once they could safely walk again, the companions did a thorough search of every box, barrel and crate, finding a fair assortment of empty brass, a dozen Molotovs, a hammer and spikes for repairing the wooden armor and more trophies. In short order the companions cleared away all of the grisly items, including a rope of what seemed to be horsehair, but nobody could tell for sure, so over the side it went.

"Ashes to ashes, dust to dust," Doc stated, throwing away the last box of horrible dried things.

"Amen," Mildred added solemnly.

Opening the Molotovs, the companions checked to

make sure the bottles were full of shine, not fuel, then used it to liberally clean their hands and to wash the badly stained floor. Some of the cannies had been aced hard, and left behind more than their fair share of bodily fluids, not all of it blood.

Settling down to let the thick fumes evaporate, the companions dutifully checked over their blasters, then started carving small blasterports into the thick planks. By the time that was accomplished, the air was refreshingly clean and the companions literally breathed a deep sigh of relief.

"At least we have a lot of spare arrows," Mildred said with a touch of satisfaction. "That's something, after losing all of that black powder."

"Those are not arrows, madam, but quarrels," Doc corrected, raising a finger as if about to point to the blackboard. "A crossbow uses quarrels, not arrows."

"What dif?" Jak asked, arching a snowy eyebrow.

"An arrow has a smooth shaft, but a quarrel is notched to fit the guide of a crossbow and stay in place."

Mildred snorted a laugh. "Well, thank you, Fred T. Janes."

"Who, madam?" Doc asked, puzzled.

That brought the physician up short, and she tried to think of some way to explain about the creator of various military guides, but finally decided that the concept was just too complex. "Never mind," Mildred said, hiding a little smile. "Not important."

Slowly, the long hours passed, and the sun was dipping toward the horizon when Jak proposed making dinner, the suggestion greeted with a resounding lack of interest. The memory of the trophies was still sharp in their minds, and that ruthlessly killed the others' appetites. With a shrug, the unflappable albino teen went to a corner of the flatbed, opened an MRE envelope and dug into the hundred-year-old spaghetti with gusto.

Twilight was beginning to claim the world when the end of the riverbed came into view. Gingerly using his throbbing leg, J.B. slowed the wag as they came to a marshy field filled with what appeared to be wheat or some other kind of cultivated grain. Easing the Cyclops into the flooded cropland, J.B. was relieved to find the water only a couple of inches deep. However, the plants grew so close together, his view was reduced to less than a few feet ahead. If they were still following the riverbed, it was impossible to say.

"Fireblast, we're driving blind," Ryan muttered, glaring at the waving wild abundance around them. "There could be stickies, or a bastard cliff, only a couple of yards away and we'd never know about it until too late."

"At this rate we'll be in here until we run out of juice," J.B. replied with a scowl, his hands tight on the wheel. "How big was the size of the average predark farm? Couple of miles?"

"More like ten or twenty. Sometimes a lot more."

Scowling, the Armorer's muttered reply consisted entirely of vulgarity.

Standing in the rear of the war wag, the rest of the companions were resting their arms on top of the spiked wood and using their vantage point to scan the rustling vista of waving plants. None of them could see any order to the plants, let alone predark ruins, abandoned grain silos, bridges, homes, barns or any other sign of the prior owners. Just endless acres of the gently waving plants. There were some mountains on the western horizon, but where the cropland ended and the rocks began, nobody could say for sure.

"Reach to foothills?" Jak asked uneasily, clearly hoping that somebody would disagree.

"Mayhap it does, my young friend," Doc rumbled in consternation, the LeMat gripped tightly in one hand as if he was drawing comfort from the Civil War blaster. "We should be thankful this is not Australia. I have read where some of their larger farms extend for hundreds of miles without a break."

"What is anyway, wheat?" Jak asked curiously, reaching out to grab a plant, but staying his hand at the last moment.

"Millet," Krysty replied, resting her arms on top of the wooden planks. "Makes good bread once it's been cracked." Then she frowned. "Funny, I didn't think it could grow in wetlands like a marsh."

"Must be a mutie strain," Mildred guessed. "So I wouldn't try eating any until I have run some tests. There are grains that get an ersatz kind of mold that contains a natural form of LSD, a powerful hallucinogenic, ten times worse than wolfweed."

"Worse?" Jak repeated. "Nasty."

"Any chance it might affect us by breathing?" Krysty asked, covering her mouth and nose with a hand. The millet had a rich earthy aroma that was very pleasant, but the woman had encountered perfumed flowers before that tried their best to eat her alive. In the Deathlands, the only place you were safe was the grave.

"No, impossible. You have to eat it," Mildred replied after a minute. "The mold was much too heavy to be airborne."

"Hey, back there!" Ryan called out the window, craning his neck. "Any sign of this field ending?"

"Not until we reach the mountains!" Krysty answered promptly.

"Well, let us know if anything comes into sight!"

"Will do!"

Soon the plants were so thick around the Cyclops the muddy earth below was impossible to see anymore.

"Dark night, there's no way we're ever going to find any tire tracks in this," J.B. declared, downshifting to a crawl. "Mebbe we out to stop and—" But the man was interrupted by strident whistling, closely followed by an explosion of steam from under the hood. The dashboard engine gauge swung fast into the red.

"Thick we blew a hose?" Ryan snarled, throwing open the door.

"Only one way to find out." J.B. sighed, turning off the engine. He waited a few moments, but the gauge stayed in the red. Yes, it had to be a hose. Then he thought, Or the water pump, or the thermostat, or a dozen other things. Who knew if the cannies knew the difference between a socket wrench and a sock?

"I'll check for the box," Ryan said, climbing out of the cab. Staying on the corrugated metal step a good foot above the murky water, he pushed the seat forward. Most predark trucks had spare storage there for small items, flares, shovels, tow ropes and the like. But the man found only some predark candy-bar wrappers, a crumbling yellow sex mag, a road flare reduced to waxy residue and a few rusty tools eaten through with corrosion. Clearly, the cannies had not even been aware that the seat moved, or else they would have taken the mag.

"Nothing useful in there!" Ryan called, pushing the

hinged seat back into position. "I'll get the tools and gray tape." The Trader called it duck tape, but Mildred always said "duct." Weird.

"And a bucket!" J.B. snorted, sloshing around to the front of the war wag. Steam was rushing out from around the hood. If it was just a hose, they'd be moving again in less than an hour.

As Ryan pushed some plants aside to slosh away, J.B. tugged on his fingerless gloves and checked for traps. Sure enough, there was a boobie, a spring-loaded blade set to chop off questing fingers. Using a lock pick, the Armorer easily disarmed it and cast the pieces aside. Bastard amateurs.

Tromping around the hulking flatbed, Ryan noticed some furtive movements among the muddy roots of the millet. Had that been a rat? Most likely, considering the combination of shallow water and abundant food. But that would be in their favor. Rats attacked people when they were starving, but with all of this millet around these rats looked fatter than the ass of a baron's favorite gaudy slut.

Bunching up a handkerchief for protection, the man raised the hood and a wave of steam wafted out. It was definitely a split hose, J.B. noted, waving a hand in front of his face. His glasses were misty from the moist heat, but he could see the rent through the billowing cloud. The war wag had to have picked up some lead back in the valley. Stepping away, he used the handkerchief to wipe his glasses. There was nothing he could do but wait until the engine cooled enough to wrap some tape and twine around the split, then refill the radiator.

Going back into the cab, J.B. turned on the heater.

The power gauge flickered as the batteries engaged, then waves of hot air blasted from the vents under the dashboard. This was a trick the Trader had taught him long ago. If you were short on time and a radiator was boiling over, then just turn on the damn heater. They used the hot water cycling through the engine block to warm the interior of the wag. It sounded craz, but turning on the heater helped cool down an engine. That could buy you extra minutes of driving, which sometimes was all the difference between sucking air or feeding the worms.

Reaching the back of the Cyclops, Ryan thumped a fist on the hatch, and it was opened by Krysty, holding the tool kit and a bucket.

"Figured you'd need this." The woman smiled as she stepped down into the marsh. The dark water crested high on her blue cowboy boots, obscuring the embroidered spread-winged falcon design.

"Don't forget these," Mildred added, offering a fistful of relatively clean rags. "They'll do for filtering the marsh water."

"Thanks," Ryan said, taking the rags.

Just then, a plump creature scurried between the man and woman, then darted under the war wag.

"Damn, that was a big rat," Krysty said, touching the strap of the AK-47 slung over her shoulder.

"Mother of God... That's a rat," Mildred whispered, going pale. "Don't move! Everybody stay perfectly still!"

Starting to turn away from the hatch, Ryan and Krysty froze motionless at the physician's whipcrack tone. Warily, they glanced around at the thick rows of millet, their hands creeping toward their blasters. There was nothing in sight but the millet and the rats.

"Easy now," Mildred said, slowly moving the scattergun forward and gently working the pump-action. "Back in the wag, and close the hatch. Easy! No sudden moves!"

As if encased in solid ice, Ryan and Krysty turned and stepped back into the Cyclops. The instant the jamb was clear, Mildred slammed the wooden portal shut and worked the bolt.

"John, get the fuck out of the water!" the physician bellowed at the top of her lungs, spinning and running to the front. Climbing onto a wooden box bolted to the planks as a firing step, she rose above the wall and pointed the S&W M-4000 at the hairy lumps waddling among the muddy stems of the millet.

"John!" she screamed, a touch of panic tightening her throat. "John Barrymore Dix, where the hell are you!"

"Right here, Millie," J.B. said calmly, climbing into view on the roof of the cab. "Damn near lost my hat when I heard you shout like that."

"Thank goodness." Mildred looked over the man intently. The cuffs of his pants were damp, but it only looked like dirty water. "Did any of them bite you? Or scratch? Even a small bite could be fatal!"

Fatal? Now, the other companions scrambled onto the firing steps and prepared their blasters, gazing at the sea of rustling millet with newfound caution. What had the physician seen that none of them had noticed? Snakes? Millipedes? They had fought the big insects before, and that one time had proved to be more than enough.

"No, Millie, I'm fine," J.B. replied, sitting cross-legged on the roof. Scowling at the waving cropland, the man swung up his Uzi and worked the arming bolt. "Okay, what's the prob? Are there stickies here? Swampies?"

"Gator?" Jak asked, scowling at the swampy ground. The plants grew too close together for a gator to move around easily, but the teenager could not think of anything else that could have frightened the woman.

"By the Three Kennedys, I wish it was a gator," Doc rumbled, his face registering alarm. "Good call, madam. I might never have recognized the rodents fast enough before they had swarmed through the hatch and into the war wag. I have only seen an illustration of them in the newspaper." Keeping the rapid-fire in hand, the man also drew the LeMat. "Now, we at least have a fighting chance at life!"

"What mean? Just rats." Jak sniffed in disdain, easing his grip on a Kalashnikov.

"Worse than that," Mildred said grimly, the gentle wind riffling through her beaded locks. "These aren't rats, but solenodons!" At their puzzled expressions, the physician explained.

Indigenous to Cuba, the tiny rodent was acknowledged by many as one of the most deadly animals on the planet. In Mildred's day, solenodons had been hunted to the brink of extinction.

"The bite of a solenodon is toxic," the physician added tersely, studying the small animals scurrying through the greenery. So peaceful and tranquil before, now the field of millet seemed a buzzing deathtrap. How many of the deadly little creatures were moving around the trapped companions? Hundreds, maybe thousands. She swallowed hard. They wouldn't have enough bullets to stop them all if the rodents attacked.

"Is there an antidote to their bite?" Ryan asked, furrowing his brow. "Cut the bite, suck out the poison? Burn it with black powder?"

"No."

The one-word answer sent a chill through the companions. A single bite from a predark solenodon meant unstoppable death, and these muties were ten times larger.

"Solenodons," Doc repeated. "Even the pharaohs of Egypt never faced such a plague as this!"

"It was their size that almost threw me," Mildred confessed to the man. "They're just so damn big! But once I saw that head…" She shivered.

"How soon till we can move again?" Ryan asked

"Half hour, mebbe more," J.B. answered, shifting his position on the roof. "And I still have to patch the hose and refill the radiator!"

"Do we also have to fill the tanks or do we have enough juice to leave?" Krysty asked in real concern.

"No prob. We're good for at least a couple of miles," J.B. said without much enthusiasm. "It's getting the water that concerns me. How much is in the canteens?"

Walking over to the bedrolls, Mildred lifted the containers and shook. "Six canteens, each about half-full. Say, three quarts."

"Barely enough," the Armorer replied. "Nothing from the prior owners?"

"Sorry, no. They must have kept their canteen of water on their bikes."

"Shit!" the man cursed.

"No, you mean, piss," Ryan countered. Taking two

canteens, he unscrewed the tops and poured the contents of one into the other. "Okay, people, fill 'er up. Every drop will help."

"Shine, too," Jak added. "Small amount won't hurt much."

"Any chance it'll ace the smell of boiling urine?" Mildred asked hopefully, tying not to grimace.

"Nope. Make worse."

"Swell."

"Mayhap providence shines upon us and this new breed of solenodon has no venom," Doc said hesitantly.

"Could be, but I'd hate to be the one to find out," the physician returned. "Look, we're probably safe inside the Cyclops, as long we don't annoy them. Stay quiet, and make no noise. Let the engine cool, do the repairs and drive out of here nice and slow. Everything will be fine once we're far enough away from here."

Jerking her head toward the south, Krysty frowned. "Don't think we have that option anymore," she said, listening intently. "Engines are coming this way. A lot of them."

Rushing to the other side of the war wag, Ryan pulled out his Navy telescope. Sweeping along the riverbed, he easily found a large dust cloud coming their way. Adjusting the focus, he saw the six caged speedsters they had left by the sand dune.

"Fireblast, it's the cannies," Ryan stated, compacting the scope. "Bastards must have had a cache of juice somewhere for those bikes, and they've come to get their war wag back." The one-eyed man spoke calmly, but he was furious inside for not having considered the possibility and smashing the speedsters before leaving.

Now the companions were trapped in a chilled wag, surrounded by a field full of poisonous muties.

His mistake might chill them all.

Chapter Eleven

As the huge black doors to the redoubt in southern Arizona opened wide, Edgar Franklin paused to frown at the dark tunnel. There should be a guardian here, and Everbrites along the ceiling. Clearly something was wrong.

For a brief second the TITAN agent panicked, thinking he had walked into a trap set by Delphi, then he saw the destruction along the tunnel. Scorch marks pitted the curved walls, the mold on the bricks, marking where the tunnel had been three feet deep in water but wasn't anymore. There had been some kind of a major fight here, and his suspicions automatically went to Delphi. Only who had he been trying to kill?

Suddenly a huge shape moved in the darkness, lumbering toward the man.

Calmly, he studied the creature. It was a translucent blob, vaguely resembling a worm, but inside the living jelly was an armature of steel and twinkling lights, the metal flexing and bending. Franklin did nothing as the colossal thing approached. Towering over the human, it seemed ready to strike, then the thing stopped dead.

Reaching out a hand, Franklin paused, and the jelly parted to expose the armature. As he stroked the cool metal with a fingertip, the internal circuits read his fingerprints and a hatch cycled open the display a small control panel. Tapping in a code on the keypad, a tiny rainbow-colored disc about the size of a quarter jutted from a slot.

Taking a small box from his belt, Franklin inserted the mini CD and watched as the blast doors opened again, this time revealing Ryan and the other companions. Hitting fast-forward, the man skimmed through the numerous battles with the companions until the guardian was destroyed in a massive explosion.

"Well done," Franklin said, turning off the video disc. The agent was impressed in spite of himself. There were very few people in the world who could tackle a guardian and live. Yet these postwar vagabonds had done so with little more than raw bravery and a stolen APC. Most impressive. Turning off the monitor, Franklin waved a hand at the guardian and the deadly jelly flowed to cover the armature once more.

"Stay," he commanded, pointing at the floor.

The guardian bowed slightly and did not follow as the man casually strolled along the tunnel. The Type 4 guardian was not quite as smart as a Cerberus cloud, but then it was harder to kill, and lasted much longer. Two very valuable attributes. Plus, it was also harder to find. A Cerberus always reeked of ozone and you could smell one approaching from a hundred feet away. Try as they might, there was nothing Overproject Whisper could do to correct that flaw, and so the other types of guardians had been created to see which functioned the best as a possible replacement. So far, the question was far from being settled.

After a hundred or so feet, Franklin reached a huge crater in the floor, the rim broken and sagging. Now this was a recent addition. More handiwork of the vagabonds? Going to the crumbling edge of the crater, Franklin looked down and saw only darkness. Using a thumbnail to flick the side of a ring, his entire hand began to glow and he aimed the palm into the pit. The brilliant halogen beam stabbed deep into the murky recesses showing the crumbled foundation and broken stalactites, of all things. How utterly bizarre.

Listening closely for any movements, Franklin could only hear the running water and the occasional squeal of a rat. Obviously some sort of a river had been formed below the access tunnel, probably runoff from the nearby mountains, the rushing flow undercutting the floor until it was so weak that the weight of the stolen APC had caused it to crash through. And they survived a fall of over a hundred feet? Odd.

"Attend me," Franklin said in a normal tone. A few minutes later the guardian undulated into view and paused for more instructions.

"Fix that," the man commanded, gesturing at the hole. "And reinforce the foundation so there will be no further collapses."

Obediently, the guardian oozed away, gathering loose bricks and other debris inside its translucent form. Franklin nodded at that. Good enough.

Proceeding to the end of the tunnel, the TITAN agent studied the black rock wall for any signs of a breach, and decided that the vagabonds had not left or returned this way. Going to a seemingly discolored section of the brick wall, he pressed a palm there and a panel opened in the rock face, exposing a small keypad. Tapping in the standard exit code, he stepped back as the wall disengaged and rumbled apart, admitting a blinding display of bright golden sunshine.

As his eyes darkened to the hard exposure, Franklin walked out of the tunnel, his shoes crunching softly on the loose sand. A featureless desert extended to the horizon, and there was only the low moan of the wind to disturb the harsh landscape.

Franklin made a curt gesture with his right hand and a small compact needler dropped into his palm. Checking over the tiny weapon, he tucked it up the sleeve once more, then started walking due north. Roughly a hundred miles away was the last known location of Delphi, a new city that the locals called Two-Son ville. It was there he would begin the hunt for the rogue cyborg, and Dr. Theophilus Tanner. The council had chosen him, and he would not fail.

A MOIST WIND BLEW OVER the green field of millet, the fronds rustling around the stalled wag like a sea of autumn leaves.

"Okay, we gotta move. Give me those bastard canteens!" J.B. ordered, extending a gloved hand.

Rushing forward, Mildred stood on a firing step and reached out to press the straps into his grip. Their hands lingered together for a trifle longer than necessary, then the private moment passed and they were all business again.

"We'll keep them off your back," Krysty promised, sliding the Kalashnikov off her arm and working the bolt.

"Damn well better," J.B. growled, scooting along the roof and onto the front windshield.

"Here!" Jak called, tossing over a brown bottle.

Turning just in time, J.B. made the catch, saw it was shine, nodded thanks and tucked the container into one

of the large pockets of his leather jacket. Then, grabbing the raised hood, he artfully swung around the
dented metal, out of sight.

"All right, we gotta keep them as far away from the
wag and J.B. as possible!" Ryan said, placing aside
the Kalashnikov and swinging up the Steyr SSG-70
longblaster. "It'll be even worse if the cannies toss a
firebomb in here and set off one of these mucking barrels of juice." Clusters of steel drums were lashed
into place at each of the four corners, the old rusty
fuel drums looming dangerously among the companions like imprisoned foes just waiting to turn on their
captors.

"If one of those ignites, the cannies wouldn't need
to cook their dinner tonight, that's for damn sure,"
Krysty added, cracking open her S&W revolver. Inspecting the load, the woman noted the five rounds:
two predark, three reloads, all of them dumdums. She
closed the weapon with a soft click.

"We could dump the fuel," Mildred began, then
stopped herself. That would only leave the war wag
even more vulnerable, sitting motionless in a spreading
pool of diesel fuel. Grimly, the physician made a hard
decision and laid aside her precious med kit. She might
need to move fast, and the weight would only slow her
down. Slinging the AK-47 over a shoulder, she worked
the pump on the S&W M-4000 and moved to the front
of the wag. If any of the cannies wanted J.B., they'd
have to go through her first! For a moment she wondered what her Baptist minister father would have
thought about that, then she dismissed the thought. The
Reverend Mr. Wyeth never had to defend his congrega-
tion from a horde of slavering cannibals. But she felt in

her heart that if the occasion had arisen, her peaceful father would have sent them all straight to hell.

Bending to reach into a box, Jak pulled out several throwing axes and walked around the interior wall of the flatbed, stabbing them into the planks here and there.

Loosening the LeMat in his holster, Doc understood. Those were in case the cannies got inside the wag and the fight went hand-to-hand. The dire thought steeled the time traveler, and he went to the left wall of the flatbed to start emptying his frock-coat pockets of grens and ammo clips.

Ever so softly, the sound of racing engines increased as the disturbances in the millet fanned out, the location of the speeding wags only detectable from the trembling wakes left behind.

Good thing the millet was so high, or else we'd be visible for miles, Krysty realized, setting a muddy boot on the box that served as a firing step. Whispering under her breath, the woman said a fast prayer to Gaia.

"Think they might be stupid enough turn on the cages?" Mildred asked hopefully, studying the waving millet.

"Sure hope so," Ryan answered roughly, the Steyr moving to track the distant movements in the plants. "In this watery marsh, that would fry their asses faster than swimming in a pond in Washington Hole."

In spite of the situation, Mildred almost smiled at the image of the cannies getting thoroughly poached in a boiling, radioactive lake. The overconfident politicians in Washington, D.C., had to have been utterly shocked when they'd got hit by that long microsecond burst of hard reality. There was nothing in the world quite as sobering as atomic missiles shooting toward you.

A metallic clang erupted from the other side of the raised hood, J.B. muttered a curse, and something splashed into the soupy marsh. Instantly there was a low trilling from the muddy water, the musical tones rising in volume and steadily spreading outward until they seemed to fill the entire field.

"That solies?" Jak demanded, looking over the wall.

Down among the swampy roots, the plump creatures were running around, clearly excited about something. The dropped wrench? Then the teenager saw a faint trace of red in the dark water and he recognized it as blood. The stain seemed to be coming from the front of the war wag. J.B.'s wounded leg had to be bleeding again!

As Jak turned to tell Mildred, there was a commotion in the nearby plants and a speedster shot past the Cyclops only fifty feet away.

"They here!" Jak bellowed, sending off a long burst from the Kalashnikov. The hail of hot lead glanced off the protective cage around the speeding wag…and then it was gone, swallowed whole by the sylvan field.

"Okay, no need to be quiet anymore," Krysty snarled, burping the AK-47.

Aiming toward the crest of the wakes going through the millet, Ryan and the others sent converging streams of hardball ammo into the field. If they hit anything, there was no way of knowing. But as they reloaded, there came back an answering fusillade from the black-powder muskets, puffs of dark smoke rising to pinpoint each cannie. Lead miniballs hammered the thick wood planks edging the flatbed as well as life brass from rapid-fires, and the companions stood on the firing steps to train their weapons on the greenery near the telltale muzzle smoke. But again there was no cry from a chilled cannie.

Grabbing a gren, Doc yanked off the tape around the arming lever, pulled out the ring and whipped the explosive charge forward as hard as he could. The mil sphere disappeared into the waving millet a dozen yards away, and there was a loud detonation, dirty water, uprooted plants and aced solies soaring high into the sky.

Lightning flashed across the darkening sky as the engines of the speedsters changed direction toward the blast. Trilling loudly, the carpet of solenodons also raced away to investigate the noise.

"Chew 'em up!" Jak shouted, jerking the arming bolt to clear a jam from the Russkie rapid-fire. The little solies seemed to like fire and explosions just as much as stickies.

"How are you coming along there, lover?" Mildred asked, not looking in that direction. There was a flutter in the plants and she fired a burst with no results. Damnation, the very plants that were protecting them from the cannies were also making it near impossible to chill the enemy. The irony was almost poetic.

"Tell you in a tick!" J.B. shouted in reply.

With his leather jacket draped over the engine, the man was lying on his belly with outstretched hands knotting a length of primacord fuse around a canteen. Lowering the container to the ground, he let it fill, then hoisted it up and poured the murky fluid over the outside of the radiator. Reeking steam hissed off the hot metal. Fanning away the reeking fumes with his hat, the Armorer did it again and this time got a little less steam, the muddy water clinging to the metal for a fraction longer.

Lurking in the plants nearby, the solies watched the incomprehensible behavior, unsure of exactly what was happening or how to respond.

A speedster burst out of the millet, the cannie inside holding a homemade scattergun. Jerking into action, Ryan and Krysty fired their Kalashnikovs in unison, just as Ratter discharged his blaster. The boom sounded louder than doomsday in the field as a barrage of broken glass and bent nails peppered the planks, splintering the wood near Doc. Turning sharply back into the millet, the cannie wheeled away and startled voices were raised out among the wild plants.

Continuing to burp rounds from the AK-47, Ryan caught a minor disturbance in the plants to his right. Firing a figure-eight burst in that direction, the one-eyed man heard an answering cry of pain and a speedster charged out of the millet to violently crash into the eighteen-wheeler. The entire war wag shook from the impact, and Big Suzy was thrown from her seat to smack into the protective cage.

Bleeding from the nose, the stunned cannie clawed at the steering wheel when Mildred delivered a thundering dose of double-aught buckshot. Suzy was blown open, falling backward onto the nuke batteries. As her blood gushed onto the terminals, there was a loud crackle. Quickly, Mildred looked away just before the entire cage was covered with a dazzling display of electric sparks. Galvanized, the corpse jerked wildly, the muddy water sloshing over the rubber floor mats, bubbling. A hundred solenodons in the nearby roots went stiff. Then the terminals were burned clean and the short-circuit vanished. The charred body fell to the floor mats, the distorted features burned into a silent scream.

The plump little forms started bobbing in the swirling muck and a trill was raised from the other solies, but this time sounding different.

"One down," Mildred said, working the pump to chamber another 12-gauge cartridge. Then rapid-fires spoke from within the waving forest of plants and something hummed past her head. Ducking, the physician rose again a foot to the left and fired the S&W randomly into the plants before ducking back down again to reload.

Ignoring the sound of blasterfire coming from the fortified flatbed and the millet, J.B. decided that the radiator was cool enough to make the repair. Placing the dirty canteen on top of the manifold, he wrapped his hand in a thick wad of cloth and pressed down hard to twist the radiator cap. If it was too hot, the man knew that he would be hit in the face with a geyser of boiling coolant and probably go blind, but he was running out of time. As the cap came free, there was an exhalation of trapped gases and some mixed gurgling, but nothing else.

Grinning in victory, J.B. quickly got one of the clean canteens, unscrewed the cap and poured a little of the redoubt tap water directly into the copper-lined mouth of the radiator. As it sank into the interior there was some burbling and a little steam. Careful as if mixing a batch of plas, the Armorer added more water in small amounts. Almost there…

SPRAYING A LONG BURST from the AK-47 in a flat arc across the plants, Ryan moved the muzzle back and forth. Clipped-off leaves formed a whirlwind in the air, and a cannie cried out shrilly. A musket boomed and a miniball slammed into the planks near the one-eyed man, sending out a spray of splinters. He burped the blaster twice toward the musket's discharge, then turned to send a long burst in the opposite direction. This time he clearly heard the rounds hit the steel cage and somebody bitterly curse.

"Fuckers smart," Jak drawled, inserting a fresh slip. "Shoot on move, hard track."

Not bothering to reply, Ryan cut loose toward what he hoped was another of the speedsters, and the weapon stopped cycling with a misfire jammed in the ejector port. As the man worked to clear the port, a clay jug sailed into view with a short sizzling fuse.

"Incoming!" Doc roared, swinging the Kalashnikov toward the bomb. The ceramic container broke apart in the air, raining black powder and what looked like human teeth onto the green plants.

Another jug flew toward the Cyclops and Krysty got it with a single round. Then a speedster zoomed past the rear hatch and the portal shuddered from a hammering miniball.

"Fireblast, this was their wag and they know every bastard inch!" Ryan cursed, putting a burst into the disappearing speedster. A nuke battery in the rear split apart and there was a gushing roar of chem and electricity, but the driver still seemed alive and the caged wag was still moving as it wheeled out of sight.

Two more jugs were airborne, and the companions fired every weapon to just take them out in time. There came more double booms from the massive flintlocks, then a long pause, closely followed by loud banging from the primitive handcannons. The leafy green stalks were brutalized by the heavy miniballs, and the wooden planks bucked from the impacts. The homemade armor stopped most of the lead, but one miniball punched through and grazed past Krysty, missing her by a couple of inches.

Going pale, the woman dropped the Kalashnikov, her face contorting into a rictus of unimaginable agony as a fistful of her animated hair floated down to the dirty floorboards. Reeling blindly, Krysty collapsed to her knees, shaking and moaning.

Chapter Twelve

Caught by surprise, Ryan stopped shooting for a moment at the sight, then put his back to the woman and kept firing. Getting that much of her hair clipped had to have felt like having all of her fingers hacked off. Eventually, Krysty would be okay, but she was out of the fight until further notice. Come on, J.B., he railed. Get this fat wooden bitch moving again!

Bullets and miniballs zigzagged through the smoky air constantly, and the tattered stalks were starting to fall over to create an open space around the war wag, which was the last thing the companions wanted. Switching tactics, the companions started tossing the grens, trying to make the field impassable for the speedsters. But the companions had done their work too well and the stubborn little speedsters merely jounced over the rough ground plowing down more of the bedraggled millet.

Night was starting to descend and J.B. thanked his lucky stars that the headlights were turned on. This half-ass repair was tough enough without trying to do it in the dark! Flinching as he accidentally put some weight on his wounded leg, J.B. suddenly noticed the tiny rivulet of blood running down his leather jacket to drip into the marsh water below. A dozen or more solies were down there lapping at the life fluid and snapping at one another to get more.

Grabbing the roll of gray tape, he wrapped it around the stained bandage on his leg, ignoring the pain that caused. When there was no more seepage, J.B. put the roll aside and, with a shaking hand, started pouring some more water into the radiator. It steamed less this time, the water bubbling up and over the rim to flow down the sides and drip into the muck below. That sent the solies scurrying away, but they came back again sniffing for the source of the delicious red fluid....

Running low on grens, Ryan got a box of Molotovs and pulled out one, lifting the oily rag tied around the neck of the bottle as a fuse. Lobbing it gently onto the soupy ground, it landed with a smack, and then he fired a single shot. The bottle shattered and the chems inside ignited to form a pool of fire that brightly illuminated the area. Hissing in rage, the solies scurried away from the blaze.

Coming out of the millet, a speedster veered away from the flames, and Jak took out a headlight with his Kalashnikov. Mildred got the other, and the snarling cannie driver turned away to speed into the thickening darkness.

The rest of the companions followed Ryan's example and soon there were a dozen fires dotting the green plants. The noise of the speedsters lessened as they withdrew, but the companions knew they'd be back as soon as the flames died. And there were only a couple more Molotovs, nowhere near enough to erect another ring of fire. Right now they had the advantage, but when the Molotovs were gone, the cannies would highlight the eighteen-wheeler with their headlights, blinding the people inside, and that would be the end of the matter.

The muskets and rapid-fires sounded once more and

the wooden armor of the front cab was hit several times. Then a miniball glanced off the hood and it shook wildly. Moving fast, J.B. jumped off the engine into the marsh and missed getting decapitated by the thickness of a prayer. The hood was still vibrating when he jumped out of the water and grabbed the splintery wooden planks just as solie snapped at his boot. Kicking the mutie in the head, he heard bones crunch. As the body toppled over lifeless, the other solies converged on the twitching corpse to rip off gobbets of flesh. Scrambling frantically back onto the battered hood, J.B. swung around his Uzi and put a spray into the marsh, chilling a score of the little monsters.

Suddenly the field was alive with answering cries, squeals, grunts and trills coming from every direction at once, and a wave of solies attacked their dying brethren. Catching his breath, J.B. desperately looked around, trying to figure out how he was going to get back under the hood that he was currently standing on top of without becoming chum for the insanely carnivorous solenodons.

Deciding that this was his chance, Ryan kicked aside the locking bar of the hatch and jumped into the mud.

"Are you mad, sir?" Doc bellowed, rushing forward to haul the man back inside.

But Ryan took off at a run, zigzagging past the fires and piles of fallen plants. It was time for the cannies to get a taste of their own medicine.

As he sloshed through the muck, solies rose from the cloudy water trilling and hissing. Immediately Mildred's ZKR target pistol barked repeatedly, and several of the fat muties burst apart, spilling their guts into the mud. The other solies turned away from the man to consume their fallen brethren, and Ryan pulled the SIG-Sauer and kept heading for the bobbing headlights.

Zooming around, the speedsters had plowed crude roads through the millet, and he stayed along the side of one, ready to dive for cover if one of the wags appeared. The shadows were becoming black, and the man was starting to question the judgment of his plan when he came upon a speedster sitting in a small clearing, the cannie inside the cage laboring to load a musket.

Ryan fired once and the cannie toppled over, his brains splattered across the dashboard.

Backing away from the engine, Ryan put two more slugs into the fuel tank. As the juice poured into the mud, he fired again, the muzzle-flash igniting the fuel fumes with a whoosh. Quickly, he ran into the millet as the flames raced back into the ruptured fuel tank inside the cage.

Still moving, Ryan heard the speedster explode into a fireball, the blast illuminating the night.

A curse came from the plants to his right, and Ryan bent low to sprint that way through the sticky mud to find himself looking directly into the face of the big cannie. Jerking back in surprise, Hammer paused in confusion before going for his handblaster. But the delay was fatal, and Ryan sent a whispering man-stopper directly into the cannie's left eye. The man barely reacted, sitting there as if trying to decide what to do next, then sighed and went motionless, one hand still on the steering wheel. Repeating the performance with the gas tank, Ryan was yards away before the second speedster detonated.

Back in the cab of the Mack, J.B. yanked out the clip

from a Kalashnikov, then worked the bolt to make sure there weren't any live brass in the chamber. Slinging the empty rapid-fire across his back, the Armorer pulled a gren from his munitions bag, primed the charge and tossed the bomb just ahead of the war wag. The blast shook the millet for yards, and a dozen solies screamed in death, the fiery blast sending a score of the muties sailing away, the bodies burned, broken and bleeding.

Instantly jumping from the cab, J.B. raced to the front of the vehicle, raised the hood again and crawled back on top of his leather jacket over the engine. Only moments later, a swarm of solies arrived to savage the chilled carcasses of the dead. Whew! That had been close, he thought.

Shoving his Kalashnikov between the battery housing and the hood, J.B. checked to make sure it was firmly in place, then got another gren ready and lobbed it into the field as far as he could. The blast flashed bright and the solies around the wag paused at the noise, then scampered away in droves.

Free for a few minutes, the man lay down again and went hurriedly back to work. Drying the damaged hose with a handkerchief, J.B. carefully closed the rent as if it were a wound in living flesh, placed the piece of rubber floor mat, then began to wrap gray tape around the opening. There was a terrible clang as another miniball hit the hood, punching cleanly through the rattling metal. Ducking low, J.B. hoped for the best as he continued to work.

When J.B. had enough layers in place, he added a few more purely as a precaution, then used his teeth to rip the roll. Trying to ignore the sounds of battle from all around, the Armorer started lashing the twine around the tape in neat rows. He didn't know if this sort of jack-leg fix would be able to take the pressure of a big Detroit power plant, but it was the best he could do under the circumstances.

KEEPING A SHARP WATCH for Ryan in the darkness, Krysty was shoving one of the last clips into her AK-47 when the tattered plants parted and a speedster rolled into view, the big tires crushing solenodons into the soapy mud. The animals squealed as they were chilled, sending out a wave of trilling from the other muties.

Dropping the AK-47, Jak whipped out his Colt Python handblaster and started banging away at the cannie as the man lit the oily rag fuse on a Molotov. Then a wave of solies came boiling out of the marsh, climbing all over the fat man, their claws and teeth slashing at his rawhide clothing.

Cursing in shock, Pig dropped the firebomb and tried to yank one of the snarling muties off his chest, but they were already burrowing into his flesh, red blood streaming down his body and onto the Molotov. Squeezing one of the muties in both hands, Pig crushed the creature until its spine audibly snapped, but that only made the others scamper over his face, snipping at his mouth and eyes. Shrieking in pain, Pig blindly swatted the creatures when the Molotov shattered and flames filled the speedster. Flailing madly, the burning cannie could only scream as the solenodons kept digging into his chest, the torrent of blood tinged green with the venom from their sharp fangs.

Aiming for the cannie, Jak changed his mind and went back to loading the Kalashnikov. This was not the time or place for mercy. They weren't out of this nuking field yet, and might need every round they had to escape alive.

"Chill you all!" Dragon snarled, firing a hogleg pistol. The weapon boomed loudly, flame lancing out through the billow of smoke. A tire on the flatbed blew and the machine titled slightly.

As the companions tried for the driver, the muzzleflashes of the Kalashnikovs bloomed in the blackness. Dragon killed the headlights and took off, the tires spinning freely as he zigzagged through the slick mid. Shouting impossible threats, the cannie leader began circling the war wag, firing his musket, then switching to his predark wheel gun.

As another tire blew, Mildred realized what the cannie was doing and cursed his intelligence. If he took out enough of the tires, the big wag wouldn't be able to move, trapping the companions among the solies forever.

As Dragon swung past the cab, the Uzi chattered, the 9 mm rounds ricocheting off the cage throwing out bright sparks. Then the cannie smashed a Molotov on a dented bumper and the burning liquid engulfed the left front tire.

Stepping into view from the plants and smoke, Ryan kicked a solie out of the way and swung up the Steyr to fire once at the speedster perfectly silhouetted by the flames licking at the front of the war wag.

Dragon was slammed backward into his seat from the 7.62 mm rounds, blood gushing from his shoulder, the wheel gun firing skyward to hit nothing.

Ryan dived to the side as the speedster raced past, veering out of control. Then Dragon slammed on the brakes, shifted gears and executed a sharp turn to come straight back again. Crouching in the filthy water, Ryan squeezed off a shot. It clanged off the steel cage, and Dragon thrust out an arm to raise a throwing ax, the dancing firelight flickering off the polished steel as if it was already coated with blood.

Firing twice more, Ryan ducked below the ax and put a round directly into a spinning tire. The rubber exploded off the rim just as Dragon turned to make another sharp turn and the speedster flipped over, tumbling along the swampy ground to finally stop upside down.

Tangled inside the cage, Dragon tried to reach the hatch when the first wave of solies arrived, the blood dripping from his shoulder a clarion call to the little muties. Trilling in delight, they poured through the openings of the cage and covered the man, biting and clawing.

Snarling curses, Dragon crushed the animals in his hands and threw aside the pulped bodies. But more and more of them came out of the millet, tearing open terrible wounds and then tugging out the intestines of the still-living man. The cursing changed to insane shrieking as the cannie fell to his knees into the bloody mud, the solies burrowing inside his chest cavity with only their lashing tails visible.

Yanking out the Kalashnikov that held up the hood, J.B. swung around the hood and onto the roof, then kicked it hard with a boot. The hood crashed down with a noise like metallic thunder and for a split second, every solie in the field stopped making noise.

Scrambling back into the cab, J.B. tried to remain calm as he twisted the ignition switch. The diesel sputtered and died. Pumping the gas pedal, he tried again.

Sheet lightning crashed overhead to silhouette a figure at the passenger-side window. Swinging up his Uzi, J.B. nearly fired until he saw it was Ryan trying to get inside the cab.

"Move this piece of shit!" the one-eyed man roared, firing his SIG-Sauer downward. A solie squealed.

More rodents appeared to converge on the partially consumed bodies, white bones gleaming from the bloody tatters of the clothing. Muskets lay useless in the gory mud, and one speedster lay on its side, the engine still running, the rear wheels spinning freely an inch above the mud. A solenodon climbed on top the warm machine and began to slash the leather seat.

Twisting the ignition switch once more time, J.B. was rewarded by a roar of power and the wag lurched forward. It jerked into the field of millet, the flames dying on the left front wheel in the watery mud before the tire loudly blew and the cab titled hard to the left. Struggling to control the massive war wag, J.B. alternated between the brakes and the gas, constantly shifting gear. Speed was their only hope now, but the faster they went, the less control he had.

Dark night, J.B. thought. This fragging thing has eighteen wheels and the cannie had to ace one of the two tires that mattered.

Shouts and blasterfire came from the fortified section of the flatbed as a few solies scrambled up the splintery wooden sides to attack the companions in the rear. Mildred blew the head off a solenodon as it came over the top, and Doc blew apart two with one blast from the shotgun round in his LeMat. But the explosions and blood only drew the attention of more of the plump animals and the bloody mud darkened with their furry bodies.

"Krysty, wake up!" Mildred shouted, thumbing fresh cartridges into the S&W scattergun. She only got two into the blaster when several of the solies scurried over the top of the planks. She shot from the hip, the bodies blown into hamburger from the stainless-steel fléchettes. The other solenodons inside the wooden walls momentarily turned their attention away from the companions to attack their fallen brethren, and everybody frantically reloaded.

Hissing in rage, a solie scrambled over the wall near Jak and leaped for the teenager from behind. In midair, the mutie exploded into fur and guts.

Spinning, Jak saw a trembling Krysty brace herself by grabbing on to a barrel of juice, the smoking S&W Model 640 tight in her fist. The woman was deathly pale, her animated filaments hanging limply as if ordinary hair, but her face was grimly determined, and the pocket blaster swept the interior of the flatbed for new targets.

Fuming with frustration, J.B. tried to get the wag to move faster, but the flat tire was flopping loosely on the rim, making the front suspension shimmy so hard the steering wheel was almost jerked out of his hands. The noise of the tire was louder than the engine and attracted the solies more than grens. Dozens of the muties attacked the loose rubber, only to be crushed under the shuddered rim. Then furry heads popped into view above the battered front armor. Leaning out the window, Ryan shot the solies off the hood, angling the rounds carefully to make sure that he didn't ruin the repair job on the radiator. But he was fast running out of ammo, and there didn't seem to be any end to the swarm of solenodons.

Trying their best to not fall over from the constant jerks and bouncing of the war wag, the companions in the rear shuffled together and put their backs together to form a circle. The floorboards were littered with spent brass and aced solies, but the little muties kept coming over the walls in ever-increasing numbers. The companions were firing their blasters nonstop, chewing the top of the plank walls into splintery ruin as they chilled the muties before they could get over the top.

Slapping in his last clip, Jak saw a solie make it over the wall and drop successfully inside to land on top of a barrel of diesel juice. He couldn't shoot it there! If he missed, the whole wag would go up in flames! As the solie braced for a leap, the teen hurriedly jerked his hand forward and a knife blade pinned the squirming creature to the wooden wall.

Holstering his empty LeMat, Doc broke formation to grab a Kalashnikov lying on the bedrolls, and a solenodon landed on the sleeve of his coat. Trying to shake it off, the man cursed as it slashed at the fabric, the greenish venom spreading across the worsted material. With no other choice, Doc grabbed the animal by the tail and flung it over the rear wall…then looked in horror at the tattered sleeve. His bare forearm was visible through the tear, a pair of scratches traced along the skin, but there was no blood and no sign of venom. Shaken by the near miss, Doc snatched up the AK-47 and worked the arming bolt to rejoin the fight, more determined than ever to keep the deadly muties out of the vehicle. But the rapid-fire was empty and there were no spare clips in sight.

Casting away the useless blaster, Doc pulled out his sword and hacked a solenodon in two, then speared another completely through, the blade entering the mouth and coming out the rump. Flipping the twitching body free, Doc began slashing at the muties, lopping off their heads the instant they came into view over the planks.

Dropping a spent clip from the SIG-Sauer, Ryan reloaded and kept firing, blowing a solie off the hood, then firing across the interior of the cab and blowing one apart as it tried to attack J.B. behind the wheel.

With a wrenching noise, the shredded tire came off the rim and the wag noticeably increased in speed. Now able to release the steering wheel for a second and shift to a higher gear, J.B. accelerated the wag, plowing through the millet until the tall plants began brushing the solenodons off the outside of the vehicle. Soon there were a lot less of the hairy muties making it over the planks, and then none at all.

Heading west, J.B. breathed a sigh of relief. Ryan started to hastily shove loose brass into a spent clip for the SIG-Sauer when he saw in the rearview mirror that the solenodons were still coming after the war wag, the narrow path of crushed millet plants flattened behind the big vehicle thickly carpeted with the plump muties. There didn't seem to be any end of the things, and on the dashboard, the engine temperature gauge slowly began creeping back toward the danger zone.

Chapter Thirteen

Standing on the edge of a cliff, Delphi was admiring the scenic view on the other side of the chasm. Nevada was such a beautiful state with all of the white-water rivers, soaring hills and jagged mountains. Even the nuclear war had done little to damage the majestic landscape.

Oh, a few of the hills were missing, and a couple of the mountains were a lot smaller, the cyborg admitted to himself. But such minor alterations were trivial compared to what had been done to the rest of the world. Washington, D.C.; Paris; Berlin; Tokyo…dear heavens, there were sections of Europe so devastated that they would never recover. But the colossal defenses of Cheyenne Mountain, the supreme headquarters for NORAD, had spared most of the West from the atomic ravishing of the war, even if Cheyenne Mountain itself was a glowing hellzone of tortured strontium nuclei and cesium-rich lava fields. But this was why he had chosen the Lehman Caves of Nevada as his base of operations. There was little nuke damage and numerous predark ruins to scav for supplies if necessary. And it had proved necessary.

Glancing over a shoulder, Delphi checked to see how the work was progressing. A short distance away, the four war wags of his convoy were parked near the main entrance to caves. A squad of his troopers was attaching tow chains to the boulders blocking the entrance, while Cotton and the others stood guard with the Kalashnikovs.

Delphi smiled at that. This was the only way in, or out, of the labyrinthine maze of the Lehman Caves. Locks could be smashed, guards dogs slain, sec men bribed and land mines tripped. Ah, but simple boulders could only be removed by heavy machinery. High explosives would only make the front entrance to the caves collapse. True, the use of granite boulders was cumbersome and crude, but aside from moving to a redoubt, this was the only way to be sure that his home was completely undisturbed. And more important, undiscovered by any agents from TITAN or Coldfire.

Long ago, the cyborg had established numerous such disguised locales throughout the Deathlands as rewards for the coldhearts he hired to do special tasks. Now the caches were his lifeline, a few precious depots of ammo, fuel and tech.

If only I had thought of adding some spare parts for myself, Delphi thought. That would have saved me from traveling the so-called Deathlands to dig up a chip here and a circuit board there, on top of using the jungle redoubt to raid the laboratories of Coldfire and TITAN.

But at least he now had enough supplies to finish his original mission: find Doc Tanner. That would get him reinstated with Coldfire, and then his real work could continue from this deplorable interruption of… How long had it been? He really didn't like to think about it too much. The facts only depressed him.

Glaring hostilely into the windy cavern below, Delphi felt the call of nature and loosened his clothing and began to relieve himself into the wind. The cyborg was mostly mechanical parts these days, even more so after tangling with Doc Tanner, but a few pieces of him were still quite organic, especially the one part held in his hand. There were cybernetic replacements for both males and females, but none of them functioned quite as well as the original equipment.

Softly, there came the sound of a footstep from behind.

Unable to decide if he should zip up first or turn around, Delphi paused for a moment, and froze motionless as he felt the cold sting of sharp steel pressed to his bare throat.

"Don't move, outlander," the huge man muttered, his breath reeking of ketones, diseases and shine. "I been watching this cliff for weeks, waiting for you to come back. And now you have, wags and bags and all, sweet as a gaudy slut to her bed." The gigantic man cackled insanely. "Now give me your blaster or I'll cut you like a mutie dog!"

"My troopers…" Delphi began.

"Are a hundred yards away! And if those big blasters turn in our direction…" With unnatural strength, the man pushed Delphi closer to the edge of the cliff until the deep chasm yawned only inches from his shoes. The cyborg was impressed. To possess such colossal strength, the coldheart clearly had more than a touch of mutie in his blood.

"One nudge, and you're flying, feeb!" the giant whispered hoarsely. "Now, give me those blasters!"

"No, I don't think so." Delphi snarled, mentally activating his new force field. As if moved by a wall of invisible steel, the man was shoved away from the cyborg to go straight over the edge of the cliff and tumble away screaming.

Finished emptying his bladder, the cyborg rearranged his clothing and walked away from the cliff toward the waiting convoy. His sensors said there were no more hidden coldhearts in the rocks. It was silly of him not to check more regularly, but it didn't seem to be necessary anymore. Even after Tanner had nearly slain him, and half of his systems were damaged, such primitive attacks had not been a real danger. Now, he was stronger than ever.

Walking around a boulder, Delphi found himself confronted by a dozen of his troopers from the convoy, with Cotton Davenport in lead. They looked concerned, and the Kalashnikovs in their hands were poised for combat. The rapid-fires seemed rather bulky and ungainly from the addition of a 30 mm gren launcher under the main barrel, but the man held the big-bore blasters with confident ease.

"We heard a scream, Chief," Cotton said as a question, glancing around. "Is there trouble?"

"No," the cyborg replied coolly. "No trouble. I aced a screamwing. Is everything loaded?"

"Yeah, sure," Davenport answered hesitantly, slowly easing her stance to rest the AK-47 on a broad shoulder. "The boulders are ready to move on your word. A screamwing, you say?"

"Well, it certainly looked like one." Delphi chuckled, strolling away. "Let's get inside and load up for another trip, a very long one this time. Weeks, possibly months."

The group of troopers registered surprise at the pronouncement.

"Months?" Cotton asked. "Shitfire, Chief, we could cross the world in that. Where we going?"

"A place called Front Royal in Virginia," Delphi said with a frown, starting for the caves. "We're going to find a certain…cannie by the name of Doc Tanner." That last part had been off the cuff, but the lie sounded good. "He aced a lot of my friends, and now it's payback time."

"Fuckin' hate cannies," a trooper growled. Several of the other troopers grimly nodded in agreement. All of them had lost kin to the cooking pots of the stinking cannies, and more than a few of them carried deep scars from viciously fighting the flesh-eating devils.

"Cannies gotta get chilled, that's the nuking truth," Cotton agreed wholeheartedly. "You sure this Tanner is at, ah, Fort Royal?"

"Front Royal," Delphi corrected. "And no, I'm not sure. It's simply the best place to start." Then the cyborg made a snap decision. "However, if we don't find him in Virginia, then we'll hunt for him elsewhere. Underground."

"Underground," Cotton repeated slowly, then glanced at the boulders blocking the entrance to the cave. "You mean, in some sort of cavern like we have?"

"Oh, much better than this." Delphi snorted, and started to tell them about the redoubts, but stopped just in time. That knowledge would come later. First, he had to get Tanner, and when he was accepted back into Coldfire, then, and only then, could the cyborg unleash his army of primitives into the mat-trans system and openly declare war on his masters!

They abandoned me, Delphi raged internally. Left me to perish among the primitives as if I was a failed experiment, a mutie with too many legs, or a bioweapon that refused to kill. Well, never again would the cyborg allow others to hold such power over his life!

But first the cyborg would have to creature Tanner. He was the key to everything! Victory, revenge…and salvation.

SUDDENLY THE PLANTS WERE gone in front of the lumbering wag and J.B. hit the brakes, squinting into the night to see if there was more ground ahead or only empty air. Sharp cliffs rose around them in jagged profusion, and for past few miles the low rumble of a waterfall grew steadily louder.

Illuminated by the flickering yellow beam of the sole remaining headlight was a hard, flat scrubland with only a few tufts and clumps of the millet growing sporadically amid the uneven barrens. In the distance, mist ruled the night, and the waterfall could be heard from somewhere nearby.

"Dirt never looked so good." Ryan exhaled, sitting up straighter in the seat. "This might be a good place to fix the bastard tire."

"I hear that," J.B. growled, flexing his cramped fingers. His arms ached from trying to maintain control of the shuddering wag, and his shoulders felt like a solid knot of congealed muscle. "Okay, let us— Son of a bitch!"

Glancing in the sideview mirror, Ryan grimaced at the sight of a dozen solies coming out of the tall millet and into the wan moonlight. Fireblast, he'd never seen anything like it before in his life.

"Wait here," Ryan commanded, throwing open the door and hopping down to the ground.

Approaching the handful of solies, Ryan armed the

AK-47 and skillfully put a single round into each fat mutie. Standing in the chill night air, he warily studied the field of millet for any more of the little bastards. Then a whistle sounded from the rear of the wag.

"That looks like the last of them," Mildred said, her ZKR blaster held in a two-handed grip. "Persistent little things, aren't they?"

"Indeed, madam," Doc agreed, a hurricane lantern held in one hand and the LeMat in the other. "King Sisyphus was a slugabed in comparison to these arduously diligent solenodons."

Cocking an eyebrow, Mildred stared at the man in unabashed amusement. "Refresh my memory," she said. "Exactly what the hell did you teach in school again?"

"English literature, but I was a most voracious reader of, well, everything."

"I guess so." She chuckled, shaking her head.

There came the sound of wood scraping against wood, and Ryan looked up to see Jak peering over the plank wall, also holding a lantern and Kalashnikov.

"Solies might be circling," Jak suggested uneasily. "Catch from side."

"No, impossible. They're too stupid for such complex thinking," Mildred stated firmly, holstering her blaster. "I don't care how many folds their cerebral cortex may have, the heads are simply too small for them to be intelligent."

"Runts smart," the teen insisted, referring to a race of humanoid muties they had encountered once. The underground dwellers had been scarcely three feet tall, but with full human intelligence. The companions survived tangling with the little warriors only because of superior firepower.

"And they were human muties with heads twice the size of these rodents," Mildred replied. "Or whatever a solenodon technically is. I don't know what genus, or class, they belong to."

"Genus, pain. Class, in the arse," Doc muttered in dark humor, resting the longblaster on a muddy shoulder. The weary companions looked like zombies fresh from the grave, their muddy clothing ripped and splattered with solie blood. All of their boots bore deep scratches from the fat muties, only the anti-landmine steel plates in the U.S. Army footwear saving them from being poisoned by the green venom of the resilient rodents.

"Hey, J.B., ace the engine!" Ryan shouted over a shoulder.

"No prob!" the man answered from the cab. The rumbling diesel died away.

Several minutes passed as Ryan listened closely to the sounds of the night, but the big man could only hear the ticking of the hot engine and the pervasive rustle of the wind-stirred millet.

"All right, that was the last of them," Ryan declared, easing off the bolt on the Kalashnikov and draping the rapid-fire over a shoulder. "Might as well fix the fragging tire before we go any farther. Jak, stay on guard. Mildred and Doc, rustle everybody up some chow. J.B. and I will…" He frowned, feeling his gut tighten. "Where's Krysty?"

"Asleep," Mildred answered quickly. "She's sleeping in one of the bedrolls. That bullet she took through her hair drained her. She needs to rest."

"Yeah, let her sleep," he said with surprising gentleness. "J.B. and I can fix the wag by ourselves."

"Although we'll probably wake her anyway with the repairs," the Armorer said gruffly, walking into the glow of the lantern and wiping his hands on a rag. "There's a spare tire, but no spare rim, and the one we have is more warped than a boiled boomerang."

"Any chance you can fix it?" Mildred asked hopefully. "Hammer the rim back into shape?" She had tremendous confidence in John's ability to repair damn near anything made of metal.

"Good enough for it to hold a seal? No way. If we were back at the redoubt, I could probably do something, but not out here." J.B. scratched under his hat. "Now I might be able to shift a couple of tires from the back and put them on the front, but that all depends on how many we have left."

"Why two?" Jak demanded, brushing back his snowy hair. "Only one flat."

"Because the front tires are totally different from the rear," J.B. explained patiently. "They're for steering the cab, while the ones in the flatbed are for supporting the cargo. They don't turn like the ones up front, and we need a match pair to make the cab steer smoothly. Dark night, the front suspension is banged up enough from our ride through that damn marsh! On top of which, the rear tires are bigger than the others, so we'll have to trim the damn planks, too."

"Fair enough," Jak said in acceptance. "Radiator fixed."

"Yeah." J.B. shrugged. "That's something at least."

Just then, there came a high-pitched whistling from under the hood and white steam blasted onto the ground under the engine, quickly slowing to a bubbling dribble of hot water.

Casting an angry look at the teen, J.B. tugged his fedora on tighter and tramped toward the cab, muttering nuke-hot curses.

It was dawn before the companions got the Cyclops back under way again. Transferring the tires had been hard work, but the flatbed had built-in jacks for disengaging the locking mechanism of the cab, and the toolboxes had contained a wide assortment of wrenches, hammers and crowbars. This time, J.B. used a leather belt and some pieces of wood to reinforce the damage hose, with Mildred helping by treating the busted hose like a broken leg. Doing a recce, Doc had located the waterfalls and used the canteens to fill the radiator, plus make a pot of black coffee. The mil brew was strong and bitter, but it banished their exhaustion, at least for a little while. When the work was finally done, everybody had a meal and caught a couple of hours of sleep. Their clothing was filthy, stiff with dried blood, but the companions were awake and rested.

Starting the engine, Ryan listened to the machinery for several minutes before revving the diesel, trying to blow the repair. But the pressure stayed steady, the engine temp keeping well within the operational limits. Satisfied, he shifted into gear and the Mack moved smoothly forward, the replacement tires seeming to work just fine.

With an exhausted J.B. catching some additional sleep in the back, Krysty was riding in the cab. Resting an elbow out the window, the redhead was chewing a stick of hundred-year-old gum from an MRE pack, seemingly her old self again. A Kalashnikov rested across her lap, and a cannie throwing ax lay on the seat between her and Ryan, along with a canteen of lukewarm coffee.

After some discussion, the companions had decided to try for Two-Son ville in the Zone. There had been no trace of Delphi after the watery marsh, but since the friendly ville was roughly in this direction, it seemed the logical place to go. With the accursed cyborg on the move again, they'd need someplace to use as a base of operations, and they were sure of a friendly reception from Baron O'Connor, as well as Sec Chief Stirling. On the downside, there was no way they had enough juice to reach the ville, but the reserve barrels of diesel in the flatbed would take them most of the way. That was good enough. With luck they could find a ville and trade the war wag for some horses, or buy more juice. Aside from the dried human trophies, the cannies had kept a lot of the personal possessions of their victims. There were boxes of boots, pocket combs, harmonicas and such in the back. Along with several kegs of black powder, a bag of sharpened flints, a box of assorted knives, several axes and a dozen flintlock blasters. As long as nobody recognized the war wag of the cannies, they were in good shape. Jak had tried to use some shine to remove the painting on the front planks, but it was made of some predark stuff that stubbornly resisted being erased, so the teen had settled on hacking up the giant eye with an ax.

"Mayhap we should call the wag Justice," Doc said, chuckling. "Because now we are blind."

"Or the Stygian Witch," Mildred shot back amiably.

"Singular? Most inappropriate."

"How about Norad?" Jak suggested, trying to join the conversation. "They blind."

Mildred dutifully considered that. She had been puzzled hearing that curse for the first time, but it made sense, too, seeing how the North American Air Defense had really dropped the ball in protecting the nation. Blind Norad was one of the most vulgar phrases that existed in the Deathlands. Yeah, it fit, all right, but just seemed too disrespectful to the military personnel who had died standing their posts in Cheyenne Mountain. Their regrettable sin of omission had been paid for a thousand times over in a thundering moment of nuclear fury.

"Okay, what about—" she began when there was a crackle of lightning, a low rumble of thunder, and it stared to rain.

Horrified, the companions darted for cover under tarpaulins and plastic sheets. But after a few minutes, there was no reek of sulfur, and they were delighted to discover it was merely water coming down instead of deadly acid rain. Taking advantage of the storm, they used the tiny bars of complimentary soap that came with the MRE food packs to scrub their clothes while still wearing them, and washed as much of the bloody mud out of their hair as possible. Feeling greatly refreshed, the companions continued the lumbering overland journey in the no-name wag, expertly catching the fresh rain to refill the canteens once more.

"I still like Justice." Doc gamely tried once more, screwing the cap on a sloshing canteen.

Her sodden array of beaded locks hanging down like a drowned tarantula, Mildred irritably snorted. "Oh, shut up, ya old coot."

Slowly the long miles rolled by and eventually the scrubland changed into a pine barrens, the stunted trees becoming larger and growing closer together until forming a thick forest that was impossible for the rig to traverse.

Braking to a halt, the companions waited for the rain to cease, then J.B. used his minisextant to pinpoint their location and check a map. They were very close to the Utah border, pretty much in the middle of nowhere, but he located a predark highway to the south only a couple of miles away. If it still existed, it should take them past the forest and more than halfway to Two-Son ville.

Heading to the south, Ryan soon found the remains of the highway. The gray asphalt was badly cracked, weeds growing out of every crevice, and there were a lot of potholes. But it was still passable and went in the correct direction.

Crossing a granite bridge, Ryan saw the sprawling ruin of a predark city at the bottom of the gorge. A partially melted skyscraper rose above the flattened stores and burned homes, and a lay on its side amid the neat rows of parked civilian cars at a shopping mall. Ryan gave the ruins only a glance. He had seen similar things. When the nuke war came, the titanic explosions annihilated anything near them, but everything else just a little farther away was sent tumbling. Once he'd found an intact iron bridge smack in the middle of a grassy field, the closest water a hundred miles away.

The rad counter on his lapel began to move into the red, and Ryan shifted to a higher gear to leave the vicinity fast, not slowing down until the bridge was far behind them.

Fragrant pine trees grew thick along the ancient highway, a brown carpet of dead nettles so thick on the ground that it sometimes hid the asphalt. There was a lot of wildlife in the area, and Ryan saw several wolves racing through the trees, but then they were gone.

Willow and birch trees began appearing among the

stately pines, along with something that resembled oak, and then a new variety of tree came into view.

Climbing on a firing step, Doc grinned, showing his eerily perfect teeth. "Maple trees!" he cried, beaming in pleasure. "Those are maple trees! The same as we had back in Vermont."

Viewing the trees made the man think of home, and Doc briefly considered asking Ryan to stop so that he could harvest some of the wonderful sap. They had axes and buckets, what else was really needed? But then he remembered it took hours to gather the sap, after which it had to be thoroughly boiled and then reduced. A full bucket of raw sap yielded only a cup of syrup.

Without a proper thermometer, he'd need some white vinegar to cut the froth in case of overboiling. Egad, I might as well wish for the moon on a string. And besides, it was the wrong time of year.

"Maple syrup." Mildred sighed, smacking her lips. "It's been a long time since I have even thought about pancakes." Once in a redoubt, she had found an MRE pack claiming to contain pancakes and syrup, but the hard crunchy stuff inside had seemed more fitting to repair busted tank armor than as breakfast fare. Pancakes were no longer part of her life, any more than traffic jams and cable TV. Gone, and better forgotten.

"Pancakes?" Doc said as if he had never heard the word before. "Waffles, madam! Those are the only proper milieu for maple syrup!"

"Fair enough." She chuckled. "Shall we stop off at a waffle house for the breakfast special?"

"If you find one that's open, I'll pay."

"Deal!" She laughed.

Lying curled in a corner, J.B. grunted. "Will you two

please shut up?" he demanded from under his fedora. "I'm trying to fragging sleep!"

"Of course, John, sorry," Mildred apologized.

Reclaiming his seat, Doc sighed. "Waffles," he whispered longingly.

"Pancakes," Mildred replied softly with a grin.

"Gumbo," Jak added, lost in his own thoughts of home.

In the cab, Krysty sharply jerked her head to the right as something flashed by in the distance. "Pass me your longeyes, will you, lover?" she asked, leaning out the window.

Keeping a firm grip on the steering wheel, Ryan did so and she extended the telescope to its full length, studying a woody hill on the right side of the highway. Looking in that direction, Ryan could only see the misty forest.

"Something wrong?" he demanded tersely, slowing slightly as the highway began to curve.

"There's a ville up there," she said, compacting the antique. "I wonder if…"

Snarling a curse, Ryan savagely slammed on the brakes and desperately downshifted. Bucking hard in response, the Mack tilted sharply and nearly flipped over as the wheels locked, then the tires began sliding freely across the thick layer of pine needles.

For a split second, Krysty saw a thick tree trunk lying across the highway, then they hit and there was only noise and chaos.

Chapter Fourteen

A cool night wind blew over the desert carrying the faint smell of the nearby Great Salt, which had been greatly altered since the nukecaust. The setting sun only a reddish blur behind the thick cloud cover in the sky, the muted light made the landscape appear as if it was bathed in blood. Suddenly sheet lightning crackled amid the billowing clouds of chems; a moment later strident thunder rumbled downward like the voice of God.

Rudely awakened, a screamwing stirred in its nest atop a tilting skyscraper, then launched itself out the window to glide into the thickening shadows, eyes hungrily sweeping the ground below for anything edible. Alive would be preferable, but there were young to feed, so anything organic would do.

Landing briefly on top of a sagging billboard, the winged mutie squawked in disappointment at the discovery that the hard, shiny, smooth frame was not organic. Anointing it with feces as a reminder to not check the dead thing again, the screamwing took off, wheeling through the air as it investigated rooftops, alleyways and schoolyards. But not even the lizards and rats seemed to be out this night. The screamwing was starting to think that she would have to slay one of her young and feed the body to the others to keep them alive, when she caught a movement near the edge of the tall stone things. Darting in that direction, the mutie caught the smell of living flesh on the wind and folded back her wings to streak down from the mottled sky, her deadly beak poised and ready to strike as she headed straight for the two-legs ambling across the hot sand.

STOPPING TO REMOVE the cap from his canteen, Edgar Franklin heard a soft beep from the proximity sensor under his loose clothing. Damn, a screamwing! Those were dangerous. Closing the canteen, the man drew his needler and looked up, his eyes filtering out the background light until spotting the deadly little mutie coming at him at over a hundred miles per hour. Most impressive! Locking on to the target, Franklin fired once from the hip and holstered the weapon. A few seconds later a handful of burned feathers and bones rained down upon the hard-packed sand covering the dusty street.

Stepping over the smoking corpse, Franklin took out the canteen again and sipped the water inside while continuing his journey through the predark ruins. He was dressed in loose rags and mismatched boots, his backpack made of more patches than original material. A long, jagged scar had been carefully pasted on his face, calluses on his hands, and his teeth stained a mottled brown to simulate rampant decay. The man could barely recognize himself, which was good. That might buy him a few seconds of indecision before Delphi attacked if they should meet. If? Make that when. And in a contest between cyborgs, a split second could make the difference between life and death.

The old corroded Colt .45 revolver at his hip was fully functional, but it was purely window dressing, to make him appear the part of an itinerant wanderer. His backpack held only a few meager possessions, plus the mandatory trade items, a glassine envelope containing a single AquaPur tab, spent brass suitable for reloading and a carefully ripped and then taped wall poster of a naked predark woman. She was most pleasing to view, and would buy him out of a lot of trouble in most villes.

Under his dirty clothing, Franklin carried a small arsenal of weaponry, several of which were surgically embedded into his body, including a self-destruct charge. If Franklin should die, anything near him—especially Delphi—was going to be obliterated by an HE charge of staggering power.

Shuffling along the barren streets, Franklin marveled at the excellent condition of the buildings: post office, bookstore, hair salon… A lot of them had intact roofs, many of the signs were still legible and there was even glass in some of the windows! Just incredible! Although every pane had been sandblasted to a milky white by the never-ending desert breeze. The same with the cars. Every inch of paint had been removed from the chassis; only the models made of fiberglass retained their original colors, the touches of metallic green and iridescent blue strangely incongruous amid the rest of the beige and gray landscape.

It was plain that World War Three had been very kind to the city of Tucson, not a single nuclear bomb detonating anywhere near the sprawling metropolis. All of this damage was clearly man-made, probably from the rioting mobs searching for food and killing scientists….

Damn it! Franklin raged. I must remember to speak in contemporary terms! The nuke war was called skydark, and nobody killed anymore, they aced, or chilled, and scientists were always referred to as whitecoats. If he had said those thoughts out loud to the wrong people some ville sec man would have fragged him on the spot and put his ass on the last train west.

Turning a corner, Franklin saw a gap in the row of buildings, cracked bricks and broken masonry strewn across the street, the foundation reduced to merely a blackened crater. The cyborg raised his hand to check the map on his PDA. Yes, this was the place where the local baron and his sec men had destroyed a nest of the modified stickies created by Delphi. What a gargantuan waste of time and effort that had been. Intelligent muties. The phrase was an oxymoron. The gene-blasted things were incapable of advanced learning. So what was the point of Delphi trying to make them smarter? Had he actually been trying to force them to evolve, or merely to hail him as their god? It was pitiful.

Walking through the penumbra of a movie theater, Franklin saw the dying light of the sunset glint off something shiny in the distance and stopped in his tracks. Ah, there it was at last! Two-Son ville had to be very close for him to see a reflection from the greenhouses surrounding the Citadel.

Easing closer, the man paused at the sight of a vast field of broken foundations and cracked asphalt. A dozen buildings had to have been brought down in the middle of the city to create this large empty field. But the pieces of the structures had not been wasted. In the middle of the clear zone was a walled city—a city within a city—the outer wall rising ten yards high, the top sparkling with broken glass and barbed wire. In these dark days, it was a most formidable barrier. The front gate was colossal, composed of overlapping pieces of metal and wood: railroad ties, car doors, sheet iron, everything and anything the locals could find.

A ring of concrete K-rails formed an irregular pattern in the ragged field. Franklin knew those were positioned to break the rush of the muties or any human invaders in war wags. There was a term for it, a shatter zone, he dimly recalled. Obviously these humans had not fallen quite so far as those in Florida or Oregon. Rising high behind the massive wall was a truncated skyscraper, the roof cut at a sharp angle, clearly damage done from the nuclear wind of skydark. That was the so-called Citadel, home of the baron and his family.

Backing away slowly so he wouldn't attract attention in case there was anybody watching the ruins, Franklin eased around the corner once more until the ville was out of sight. Looking around, he spotted an empty hardware store and went inside. The shelves were vacant, of course, but more important, there were the remains of an old campfire. Perfect. That would lend a lot of credence to his story.

Sliding off his backpack, the agent of TITAN started making camp. When night fell, the light of his campfire would attract any stickies in the crumbling city. One would do in a pinch, but twenty would be much better. A nice hooting mob of muties charging through the ruins and intent upon his blood murder.

Pulling out the Colt, the cyborg cracked open the cylinder to check the position of the four dead rounds. Yes, a dozen or so stickies would be perfect. Then he could start his real work.

IN A RESOUNDING CRASH, the planks across the front of
the war wag smashed into kindling as the Mack rammed
into the tree trunk like a runaway express train. Chunks
of bark and a million nettles filled the air as the headlight shattered, the windshield cracked, both fenders
buckled and the hood flipped up to expose the roaring
diesel engine. The two companions inside the cab were
thrown onto the dashboard, and the people in the rear
were tossed around like rag dolls, pelted and hammered
from every direction by flying boxes, barrels and crates.

With the tires smoking in protest, the flatbed swung
sideways to also crash against the barrier blocking the
highway, the colossal pine tree rolling back a few yards
along the cracked asphalt.

Locked into position, the brakes squealed in protest
as the big rig shuddered to a rough halt, the transmission banging and bucking loudly, clouds of white steam
flooding from the ruptured radiator hose.

Minutes passed and nothing moved inside the crip-
pled war wag. There was only the sound of the gentle
breeze blowing through the pines trees edging the highway and the slow drip of hydraulic fluid onto the pine
needles from a cracked pump. Then with a low groan,
the hood came back down with a ringing crash.

Scrambling up the hill, a gang of grinning people
quickly headed for the busted vehicle. They were
dressed in forest camou, with leafy branches lashed to
their squirrel-fur jackets. Their boots were merely thick
layers of cloth held in place with strips of green rawhide. The garments were crude, the hide badly cured.
But bare steel knives were thrust into knotted rope belts,
and everybody sported a club and a homemade blaster.
The primitive blaster was composed of only a thin tube

attached with strong twine to a block of wood. A precious .22 round was stuffed into the tube and nailed to the back was a spring-driven mousetrap with a nail attached to the killing bar as a firing pin. The weapons looked haphazard, almost comical, as if they were about to come apart at any second, but each deadly blaster was adorned with a neat row of notches, indicating the owner's number of successful chills.

"Shitfire, we got a big one this time!" Dexter cackled in delight, the leader of the coldhearts waving the homemade weapon and checking for any movement from the passengers or driver. The wag was enormous, the biggest he'd ever seen.

"Dulle, Inga, watch for any sign of Levine and his sec men!" Dexter barked, almost dancing with excitement. "Martin, Betty, Spencer, check the cab!"

As the others spread out, Martin went to the passenger door and yanked it open. "We got a slut!" he called, then spun as his teeth went flying across the highway.

Yanking back the wooden stock of the Kalashnikov, Krysty flipped it over and pulled the trigger, but the rapid-fire did nothing. Gaia, the slam it got against the dashboard must have broken something inside.

Casting it aside, the redhead pulled her S&W .38 and shot the coldheart in the chest. The dumdum round made a small hole in the squirrel-skin jacket, but came out his back the size of a fist, pieces of flesh and bones spraying onto the pine needles.

"What the… Holy nukes, she aced Marty!" Dexter gasped in disbelief, bringing up his blaster. "Chill the slut!"

Taking aim, the coldheart thumbed the pressure plate of the mousetrap, the killing bar snapped forward and the nail struck the predark .22 brass. The blaster gave a bang, and a soft lead slug smacked into her wheel gun, sending it spinning away.

Flexing her stinging fingers, the woman cursed at the lucky shot and turned to race after her wheel gun. She could see it plainly lying on a patch of asphalt, the burnished steel reflecting the dappled sunlight. But before she could reach it, Betty threw her club in a sideways motion. Spinning through the chill air, it slammed into the woman just as she was going for the weapon. Stunned, she fell to the ground fighting for breath.

"No need to chill the slut," Betty boasted proudly, walking over to the supine companion. "Alive, you feebs can ride her for weeks before we sell her to the slavers for muskets and flints!"

The stocky blonde grabbed Krysty by the collar and hauled her up, and the snarling redhead buried her knife into the belt of the coldheart, twisting the blade to widen the chilling wound before yanking it out. Groaning into death, Betty stumbled aside and Krysty dived for the wheel gun, coming up with it held in a two-handed grip. But the coldhearts had already taken refuge behind the fallen tree spanning the highway. The woman knew a round into the tree would force the rest of them into sight, but there were four shots left in the gun, and four coldhearts. She had several speedloaders on her, but positioned out in the open, those might as well be empty for all the good they'd do her right here and now.

Just then, the cracked windshield of the Mack was blown into pieces, the tiny cubes of green safety glass showering across the hood as Ryan fired his Kalashnikov on full-auto. The 7.62 mm rounds hammered along the top of the fallen tree, throwing off bark and splinters.

Clutching his bleeding face, Dulle stood and turned to run, but Krysty shot him in the back. The coldheart flopped down out of sight.

Instantly, Krysty broke for the flatbed, snapping off a couple of shots just to keep the coldhearts from getting a good bead. As the woman darted behind the trailer, there was a bang and a chunk of the wood armor cracked loose to strike her on the shoulder. Slamming against the rear hatch, Krysty panted for breath and frantically reloaded. Damn, those sons of bitchs were good shots!

More bangs came from the coldhearts and Ryan replied with several short bursts from the AK-47. Then something launched into the air from inside the fortified flatbed. The glass bottle arched across the highway and crashed behind the tree trunk to erupt into a whoosh of flames.

Screaming madly, a coldheart stood, beating at the fire with her hands and blaster. The weapon was triggered and a gout of red blood blew out of her thigh, but the burning woman never seemed to notice as her piteous wails became louder, her long hair igniting to completely engulf her face.

From out of nowhere, a horn sounded a single loud note and the remaining coldhearts broke from cover to race down the slope toward the pine trees. Taking careful aim, Ryan waited until they were all in plain sight, then executed each of the runners with a neat round in the back of the head.

Incredibly, the leader of the coldhearts still kept moving, although no longer for the treeline. Weaving drunkenly, he turned, his face slack and mouth drooling slightly.

Getting a bead on the coldheart, Ryan could see that while the body was still breathing, there was nobody inside the riddled head anymore. But before he could shoot, Krysty fired her .38 and the mindless man jerked to fall over like a puppet with its strings cut.

"Everybody okay?" Mildred asked from the rear of the flatbed, her face smeared with red from a bloody nose.

"Been better," Ryan replied gruffly, rubbing his aching stomach. When the Mack hit the tree, he had slammed into the steering wheel, completely knocking the air out of his lungs. He felt like he'd been kicked by a mule.

"Better than them, anyway," Krysty retorted, dropping the spent brass into an open palm and tucking it away into a pocket for later reloading. Then she used a speedloader and dropped five live brass into the cylinder of her wheel gun.

That was when a group of armed men and women charged out of the pine trees from the other side of the highway. Running in formation, every person was carrying a longblaster of some kind, everything from a BAR to a flintlock, the only identical feature of their mixed clothing being a rawhide fringe hanging from their gunbelts. Stopping near the splintery end of the tree, the armed newcomers glanced at the dead bodies on the asphalt.

"Nuking hell, the outlanders aced Dexter's gang!" a sec man cried out. "Hip, hip, hurrah!" The rest of the party raggedly joined the cheer.

That caught the companions by surprise, and they exchanged puzzled looks when a big man on a horse galloped out of the woods. Reining in the stallion, the rider was broad and tall, with black hair and a full beard with sideburns hanging down in oily ringlets. The man wore a uniform of some kind with the insignia removed, and there was a blaster on each hip. His dark clothing was clean and his leather boots shone with polish. Nobody had to tell the companions that this was the local baron.

"So what the hell happened here?" the baron demanded. "Looks like Dexter and his mutie-loving feebs tried another jacking, and this time got jacked themselves."

Krysty walked over to stand by her lover. "That's about right," Ryan drawled, resting the stock of the Kalashnikov on a hip. "You the baron here?"

"Mind your tongue, outlander!" a sec man snarled, advancing a step. "He's the lord baron to the likes of you!"

"At ease, Sergeant O'Malley," the baron commanded, not even looking at the fellow. "Yeah, I'm in charge of Pine ville. The name is Levine, Avarm Levine."

"Ryan Cawdor."

"And I'm guessing you're the leader of this group?"

"Close enough," Ryan said with a shrug, then introduced Krysty and the other companions standing behind the wooden planks of the flatbed. Their blasters were in plain sight, but not pointed directly at the newcomers.

"So, Lord Baron, I gather that we did you folks a favor by taking out these bastards," J.B. said, resting an arm along the top plank of the wall, his Uzi held in a casual grip. Just because folks smiled nicely, didn't mean shit to him. Mildred and Doc liked to quote some old poem about outlanders who smiled but were still coldhearts. Although they called them smiling villains. Yeah, the Armorer had met more than a fair share of those over the years, that's for sure.

"Did us a favor? Hellfire, we're gonna throw a party tonight over this chilling!" Levine barked in laughter, looking in frank pleasure at the sprawled bodies. Already the corpses were covered with insects industrially hauling away the fresh food. "These mountain men have been jacking most of the wags that come this way for years. Not every one, but enough. Raping, taking slaves, stealing everything they could. We've been hunting them for a dozen winters and this is the closest we ever got. Only folks that ever chase 'em away was John Rogan."

The sec men nodded in agreement at that, but the companions went stiff.

"Come again?" Ryan asked softly, the wind blowing across the highway and stirring the bed of pine needles. "What was that name?"

"Trader Rogan," the baron repeated. "John Rogan. He runs a convoy through the Great Salt and around Bad Water Lake. Sells blasters, ammo, panes of glass, crop seed, some tools. Just about anything useful. Even books, sometimes."

"Does he indeed, sir?" Doc muttered, frowning deeply. Some time ago, Delphi had hired a group of four brothers to try to track down the companions to murder Ryan and capture Doc. The cyborg had equipped them with electric motorcycles, working radios, M-16 assault rifles, grens and a host of military gear. They had been John, Edward, Alan and Robert, the Rogan brothers.

The companions had chilled the coldhearts, but now Delphi was using one of their names. In an attempt to disguise his real identity? Who was the cyborg hiding from? Doc wondered. There was a moment of dizziness. What had he just been thinking about? Oh yes, Delphi was pretending to be the aced coldheart John Rogan. Most curious.

"Sure, we've heard of the guy," Ryan hedged. "Dresses all in white?"

"Yeah, that's him." Levine nodded, leaning forward to rest an arm on the pommel of his saddle. "Hell of a trader. His convoys help keep this ville alive. Sold us meds once that stopped a dose of the Black Cough that nearly wiped us out."

"Did he?" Mildred asked, puzzled.

"Bet your ass," O'Malley retorted belligerently. "Saved my wife and babe, and never asked for jack."

"Some folks say he's the Trader," another sec man added proudly, putting a lot of emphasis on the last word. "You know, the one that fought in the Mutie Wars? But Rogan says that was somebody else." He shrugged as if unable to figure out the truth of the matter.

"Does he? Interesting," the physician muttered, pinching her cheek thoughtfully. What in the world was going on here? Could Delphi have changed that much after fighting Doc? Had some of the damage altered his brain patterns, maybe even changed his thinking? Or was this some complex trap to ace the lot of them again? That seemed a lot more likely. Well, whatever the damn cyborg was doing, Mildred felt absolutely sure that it would only be beneficial to Delphi and nobody else. Certainly not these people.

"Be a great honor to meet him," Ryan said with a straight face. "When is he due here again?"

"Couple of weeks."

The one-eyed man tried not to grimace. Damn. They had to be at the end of his route, which logically meant if they hurried, the companions could hit him from the rear. A nuking good idea with one big flaw. Annoyed, he glanced at the battered war wag. It had stopped dripping fluids from underneath, but looked as if a hard fart would make it fall apart.

"Well, we aced them, but they got us first," Ryan stated, slinging the Kalashnikov across his back. That was an old trick of the Trader, the real one. Holster your blaster in the middle of cutting a deal and the other fellow would be more interested in doing business. "Any chance you got a mech or a blacksmith in your ville?"

The baron's horse snorted loudly and shifted its hooves on the cracked pavement. "Got both," Levine said, stroking the muscular neck of the animal. "Be glad to have you stay here for a while. Till first snowfall, if you like. I offered a month of food and shine for anybody who got one of the coldhearts, so I owe you that much at least."

"Besides, everybody would like to meet the people who sent Dexter on the last train west," a tall sec man added. "Shitfire, there, One-eye, I'll buy the first round of shine myself!"

"Shut up, fool," O'Malley growled, watching the outlanders as if they were about to start spitting poison.

"Think we need to drag it up the hill with some horses, or will it roll?" the baron asked, frowning at the war wag. "I'd say no, but I've been wrong before."

"Let you know in a tick." Getting into the cab, Ryan tried the ignition switch and there was only a fast series of clicks. Changing the setting on the choke, he pumped the gas pedal hard and tried again. There were more hard clicks, then the engine caught with a throaty sputter, banging and clanging until settling into a fitful chugging.

Quickly, Krysty got back into the passenger seat. "Lead the way!" she shouted out the broken window, holding the door closed by draping an arm outside.

"Sergeant O'Malley, stay here with two others to clear the damn highway!" Levine shouted, wheeling his horse around. "Everybody else with me. Double-time, boys, unless you want to drag it home!"

Walking sullenly, the sergeant stepped out of the group with two other sec men, and the rest of the armed norms broke into a fast trot, heading back toward the dense woods.

Grinding through the gears, Ryan followed close behind. Once off the highway, he saw a crude dirt road snaking through the sloping pine trees, going to a large ville standing prominently on the crest. Not surprisingly, the outer wall appeared to be made entirely of logs. Although there was something odd about them that the man couldn't quite see from this distance.

"What do you think, lover?" Krysty asked out of the corner of her mouth. "Should we wait here for Delphi, or go after him once we're back on the road?" The war wag jerked hard, almost throwing open the side door. "That is, if we can fix this rolling pile of shit."

"First I want to know more about why Delphi is treating these folks like they were blood kin," Ryan muttered, fighting to keep the sputtering engine turning over. "Then we'll decide on where, and how, we chill his ass."

"Fair enough," Krysty muttered, hugging the rapid-fire. "Think they might actually be kin?"

"There's no way to tell for sure. Could be. But more important, we need to know how many sec men he has, what kind of blasters, how many wags and such. I'd prefer a stand-up chilling, but I'll settle for drilling the bastard the way I did Silas if that's what it takes."

"A hell of a shot." The woman smiled.

Ryan shrugged in dismissal. "The wind was with me."

She laughed at the false modesty. "I just hope the bastard cyborg hasn't made any more smart stickies."

"I hear you." Ryan snorted in agreement. Already, the engine temp was creeping upward so he turned on the heater. Brutal heat gushed from the air vents, banishing the slight chill in the air until the two people felt as if they were sitting inside a glowing rad pit.

The long trek up the hill was noisy and arduous, the diesel constantly stalling and flooding. But eventually Ryan got the shuddering machine onto level ground and the struggling engine smoothed out a little. Not much, but enough so that the temp gauge lowered a hair.

"This is a joyous day, boys!" Baron Levine shouted from his horse. "Let me hear you tell the ville!"

Obediently, a corporal pulled out a battered old harmonica and started blowing a snappy tune. Keeping in time, the marching sec men and women began to sing loose harmony.

"Sec men stand upon the wall,
when coldhearts come, we'll ace 'em all!
Blaster boom at first alarm,
outlanders fall to buy the farm!"

"A battle hymn?" Doc asked in amazement. "My word, I have not heard one of those since the War Between the States!"

"Never heard." Jak snorted. "Good song. Like."

"Many Jewish families sang after the Sabbath dinner on Friday." Mildred smiled. "After a couple of thousand years, they got pretty damn good."

"Guess so."

"I was always puzzled why it was called benching."

"'Cause sing on bench?" Jak asked, brushing back his snowy hair.

"Honestly, I have no idea."

"Dinner over. Sing on bench. Occam," the teen said with the certainty of youth. Occam was something Doc used to talk about, some predark whitecoat who said the simplest answer was usually the correct one. A person could load that into a blaster.

Surreptitiously, Doc and Mildred exchanged amused looks over the albino teen's casual reference to the philosophical axiom of Occam's Razor.

"Guess we're rubbing off on him," the physician whispered.

The song went on for several stanzas, boasting of bravery and nightcreeps, cannies and muties.

"Very nice." Doc beamed, restraining from applauding.

"Yes, it was. And I fully expected it to become vulgar at some point," Mildred said, sounding oddly pleased. "Hard to imagine anything not, these days."

"The wit and wisdom of Henry David Thoreau would not be found very entertaining in these dark days, my dear Doctor." Doc sighed, leaning against a barrel. "You know, I never even considered trying to buy my way out of the pit by singing. I know quite a few battle hymns, both British and American, plus a few Prussian and French songs. Change a word or two, here and there, and *voilà!*"

"Wa-la?" Jak asked, furrowing his brow.

"It is a predark word meaning there you have it, or there you go."

"Gotcha, I suss."

"Another good word, my young friend."

Turning her head away, the physician tried to hide her amusement. Languages were living things that changed constantly. In only a hundred years, twentieth-century English was nearly as incomprehensible as Babylonian, and it had been the same back in her time period. Nobody said to-morrow as separate words any-more, it was always "tomorrow." Farewell was origi-nally "fare thee well," and goodbye was a contraction of "God's blessing be upon you." Briefly, the physician wondered what the future would bring. Then Mildred frowned. Nuking hell, this was the future.

The thick forest ended a hundred feet away from the ville, the rocky ground dotted with low tree stumps, the air redolent in the thick smell of pine. Anybody, or thing, trying to reach the ville would cross that open ground and be an easy target for the ville defenders.

This close, Ryan could now see what had caught his attention at the bottom of the hill, and gave a low whistle. The log wall of the ville rose about twenty feet and was completely covered with intricate carvings of griz bears, bull moose, mountain lions, soaring eagles and fiery mushroom clouds. Naked sec women beheaded stickies with swords, volcanoes spewed lava and giant worms battled predark army tanks. Some of the designs seemed new, while others were darkly weathered.

Only the front gate was different, the smooth surface covered with sharp sticks draped with concertina wire. Sec men walked along the top of the decorated wall, and guard towers rose from behind, along with numerous thick plumes of smoke. This was obviously a heavily populated ville. A gallows hung over the wall at one point, a rotting corpse dangling from the noose, squawking birds pecking off bits of the decomposing flesh. The arms ended at the wrist, the hands missing, clearly indicating that the crime of the deceased had been theft.

"Gaia, I've never seen anything like these carvings before," Krysty said, not sure if she found the decorations offensive. The only purpose of a wall was to keep out coldhearts and muties. Nothing a damn thing more. To make them pretty seemed inappropriate somehow. Almost…obscene.

"Must be a bitch doing fresh ones every time the wall gets damaged from a fight," Ryan observed, downshifting the gears. The engine rebelled and he fought to keep control. The man guessed there was really nothing wrong with making a ville wall pretty. He'd just never seen it done before.

These elaborate carvings told him much about the locals. Unless they had a lot of highly skilled slaves, which was highly unlikely, the people in the ville didn't mind hard work, and that meant they were good fighters. Not because of physical strength, although that always helped, but because of the discipline involved. Willing workers made good fighters. One just seemed to go naturally with the other. Ryan frowned at the thought. Could this be the source of Delphi's convoy hands? It was a disturbing possibility.

Chapter Fifteen

As the baron galloped toward the ville, the front gate swung open exposing an inner bulwark of crushed rock topped with a muzzle-loading cannon. The sec men and women behind the cannon crisply saluted the baron as he rode by with the running sec men close behind.

Rattling and clanking every inch of the way, Ryan directed the war wag through the gate and angled around the bulwark to enter the ville. The amassed sec men behind the bulwark didn't salute this time, and watched the clattering wag in close scrutiny, scarred hands resting on the holstered blasters by their sides.

As the Cyclops shuddered past the formidable gate, Mildred could only stare at something nailed to the wooden jamb. A small roll of paper, or maybe parchment, tilted slightly off center.

"Madam, am I mistaken," Doc said softly, "or was that a Jewish prayer scroll on the gate?"

"Sure looked like a mezuzah to me," Mildred said with a wide grin. "Maybe this mountaintop ville was a winter ski resort before the war. Or at least a winter retreat. Perhaps a lot of Jewish people left the big cities around Christmas to get a break from the nonstop barrage of carols for a holiday they don't celebrate. Possible."

"Then skydark hit in January, trapping them here,"

Doc mused. "So they turned the ski resort into a fort to survive." Made sense, he supposed. The companions had encountered villes ruled by Aztec priests, the Amish, a Russian czar…so why not a religious group such as the Jews? After civilization crashed, the world had been up for grabs and a lot of folks reached out to seize a handful for themselves. It was nice to know that a couple of villes were being run by thinkers and scholars, instead of the usual amoral sociopaths.

As the war wag started down a wide street paced with bricks and loose gravel, every civilian in sight stopped whatever they were doing to gape at the machine with ill-disguised contempt. Ryan could hardly blame them. The Mack was literally held together by duct tape now, and could come apart at the seam at any moment. Privately, the man was impressed that the war wag had made it this far without bursting into flames. Whatever else was true about the desert cannies, they had definitely been good mechs.

"Where did you get all of those fancy rapid-fires?" a sec man shouted up to the cab over the banging engine. "Got any more brass for them? What would you take in trade?"

But Ryan said nothing, pretending he couldn't hear over the laboring diesel.

As the war wag rambled along, Krysty noted a shallow gutter running down the middle of the street. That could be for gathering drinking water or to pool the rain to extract the sulfur to make black powder. Possibly both.

Not surprisingly, wood seemed to be the primary construction material in the forest ville; nearly every building was made of hand-hewn beams, the lintels adorned with intricate carvings, ranging from obscene to comical. Only the roofs were different: a wild conglomeration of plastic sheeting, sheet metal and crude clay tiles, anything capable of withstanding the deadly acid rain.

Closely watching the passing crowds, Ryan saw that there were a lot of people carrying crossbows, but only the sec force had blasters. Good. If the companions had to leave in a hurry, that would aid their departure a lot, Ryan decided.

The sounds of the ville filled the air: drunken singing from a tavern, the shrill laughter of gaudy sluts, a couple of bare-chested men fighting in an alleyway surrounded by other men placing bets. A group of children ran dangerously in front of the war wag chasing a dog with a piece of plastic in its mouth. A blind man sat cross-legged on the street, darning a sock.

Somewhere a man was singing, a woman sobbing and somebody playing a badly tuned guitar. The air smelled of boiling soup, freshly sawed wood, spent black powder, curing leather hides, fresh bread, horse dung and, of course, the all-pervasive aroma of pine.

"Look, over there!" J.B. said excitedly.

In the alleyway between two stores were a lot of junk cars and trucks, piled three, sometimes four, layers deep. Among them were a couple of large vans, a tractor, a snowplow and a Mack truck cab. The tire and rims were gone, the gas tanks rusted through and full of buzzing bees. But the wreck was exactly what they needed. That was, if any of the hoses were in good condition. There was even a windshield only mildly scratched.

"Bingo. Is glass hard to install?" Mildred asked in a worried tone.

"Nope, easy as pie," the Armorer replied amiably. "Just have to make damn sure it doesn't drop!"

"Straw on floor," Jak commented as if that settled the matter.

"Not a bad idea at that," J.B. admitted, pulling a bit of cigar from his shirt pocket to inspect the stubby roll, then tuck it away. "Hopefully our flintlocks and black powder will fetch a good price from the baron. We're bastard sure not trading any of our modern pieces."

Slowing his mount to an easy trot, the baron rode around a corner. As the war wag followed, Ryan saw a large corral full of horses and a couple of large barns. One of them had the outline of a horse painted above the doors, while the other had a castellated gear. Nobody needed to know how to read to figure out which was for horses, and which for wags. At the approach of the noisy wag, the horses started uneasily nickering, more than a few rearing up to slash the air with their hooves and loudly whinnying in disapproval.

Coming to a halt, Baron Levine slid to the ground and pointed at the barn doors. A couple of the sec men rushed forward to throw them open wide, showing a large interior covered with sawdust, the walls lined with neat rows of parked vehicles, brown delivery vans, Beamers, a police car and a lot of snowmobiles.

"Park it in the back!" the baron shouted over the laboring engine. "Near the grease pit!"

Applying the brakes, Ryan got the huge vehicle through the doors without hitting the jamb, then braked to a complete stop in the middle of the barn. Shifting out of gear, he twisted off the engine and listened to it sputter on for almost a full minute before finally going still.

Throwing open the doors and hatch, the companions

clambered out of the war wag, only Jak staying in the rear to guard the supplies and spare blasters.

"Ya know, outlander, I had a dog make similar noises once," a sec man said, hooking thumbs into his palomino-colored gunbelt. "Shot the poor thing myself out of sheer kindness."

"Then boiled it for soup, I suppose?" Krysty asked, crossing her arms.

The man grinned. "Of course. Why waste a perfectly good dog?"

"Sounds like a mitzvah of mercy," Mildred quipped, hefting the med kit over her shoulder.

With that, every sec men in the barn turned their attention to the physician, and the baron slowly raised an eyebrow. "And how do you know that holy word?" he demanded politely, his grip tightening on the leather reins.

Privately, Mildred cursed herself for the slip. What was common knowledge back in her time was probably forbidden arcania nowadays. "An old friend used it a lot. Said it meant a good deed or act of kindness."

"It does," Baron Levine replied, easing his stance. "And I'm pleased to know there are others of our faith still alive in the world. I assumed we were the last of the Israelites."

"No, there are others. Not a lot, but some," Mildred stated.

"Are there?" the baron said, nodding. "Good news indeed." Patiently, he waited for a couple of minutes hoping she would say more, but when it was clear that she was finished talking, he dismissed the topic with a shrug. They would talk further on this matter later, when they were alone. He'd make sure of it.

By now a crowd of villagers had gathered outside the

barn, most of them with small children. They all craned their necks for a better view of the war wag and outlanders, but nobody dared walk into the barn. Wags and blasters were only for the sec force, even if they didn't work. That was the law. Villagers were not allowed to even touch such things.

"Lord Baron, there were some wrecked wags back in the ville," J.B. said, taking off his hat and slapping it against a leg to shake off the dirt. "Do we talk to you about doing a scav for spare parts, or somebody else?"

"Unfortunately for you, those belong to Sergeant O'Malley," the baron said, sounding apologetic. "But I'll see that he accepts any fair offer you make."

"What about the homemade blasters of those coldhearts?" Ryan asked pointedly. "Those should come to us for doing the chilling. That enough?"

Now some of the sec men began to grin and nudge one another.

"Yes, those blasters would be enough for anything you want," the baron said, rubbing his chin. "That is, if he can also have their clothing, boots and knives. Do we have an accord?"

Trained by the Trader, Ryan knew a good deal when he heard it. "We have an accord," he said, making sure to repeat the odd word.

"Done and done," Levine stated, tilting his head slightly. "Let's go to my home so that you can wash and meet my wives. I'm sure they will be eager to meet the people who have removed the thorn of Dexter from the side of our ville."

Ryan shook his head. "We'll be happy to come for dinner, but we're sleeping here with the wag."

"Yes, I see," the baron said, narrowing his eyes. "Fair

enough, I suppose. I could offer to put guards on the barn to protect your belongings, but they would be my guards, so what's the point? You've earned our trust, not the other way around."

He paused, then shouted, "Sergeant Cuthbert!"

"Yes, my lord?" a broad sec man asked.

"Send in some braziers and charcoal to keep our guests warm through the night. I'll see to the banquet tonight."

"At once, sir!"

"In the morning we can…" The baron stopped talking.

At the doors, the crowd parted to allow a hunchbacked woman to shuffle into the barn. At her appearance, the villagers and sec men ceased all conversations and became so still that the cawing of the crows feasting on the hanged thief could dimly be heard.

Her long hair was the deepest black, nearly ebony, with only faint wings of silver at her temples. Her dress was worn but clean, her moccasins layered with different colored patches. The hump on her back was pronounced, nearly bending her double, and she walked stiffly and with obvious difficulty.

Stepping a few yards away from the companions, the wrinklie raised her head to show that her eyes were pure white.

"What is it, Haviva?" the baron asked in a surprisingly gentle voice.

"I have a message for the newcomers," the blind woman said softly, almost in a whisper. "Those who walk the invisible road that spans the world below the ground."

The sec men and villagers looked perplexed by that

cryptic declaration, but the companions became tensely alert. They didn't know who the woman was, but that had sounded like a pretty good description of the gateways hidden in the subterranean redoubts.

"Everybody out!" the baron commanded, gesturing broadly and pulling his horse along. "The doomie needs to speak privately with the outlanders!"

All of the others quickly left the barn; only the baron remained. Nothing happened in the ville without his knowledge and consent, and that included future events.

The companions stayed in place, closely watching the wizened hunchback. They had encountered muties before with the gift of seeing into the future. Doomies were usually sickly, as if their frail bodies could not support the terrible weight of the knowledge in their minds.

When the double doors were closed and bolted, Doc brought over a burlap sack of sawdust and placed it behind the hunchback. Fumbling with a clawed hand, Haviva found the lumpy bag and sat with a grateful sigh, as if completely exhausted from the torturous ordeal of standing.

"Which of you is the leader?" she asked.

"That's me," Ryan answered, brushing back a stray lock of his dark hair. "What do you want to tell us, old one?"

Raising her head, Haviva directly faced the man. "In the sand," she whispered. "There is a key hidden in the sand that opens the door that cannot be approached. You must find that key in order to slay the ancient giants!" Sweat broke out on her brow and trickled down her lined face. "The giants want only good, to help all of humankind. Their hearts are pure! But their plans will fail, and we shall pay a terrible price in new fire!"

New fire. Did she mean there was going to be a second skydark? Ryan wondered. And what were these giants she spoke about? Some predark tank or warship? Those were often called giants. And what was this door that could not be approached? That couldn't be a redoubt. They went through those all the time. Just then, some dim memory flickered, then vanished just as fast.

"Where are the giants?" Ryan asked, casting a glance sideways at the baron. Levine was listening to the conversation in total confusion. Good. The less the man knew, the better.

"But you know where they are!" Haviva went on. "You have seen their home. That is the door!"

"The door that can't be approached." Ryan snorted in disbelief. Okay, enough of this shit. She had him going for a moment, but this was going nowhere fast. The idjit doomie was making no sense at all.

"No, I speak the truth!" Haviva insisted, as if hearing his unspoken thoughts. "The giants have sent a holy warrior to find the machine that walks like a man! But they must not succeed, or else that death will forge a chain that ends us all!"

The machine that walks like a man… Delphi? Now she had Ryan's total interest. "How do we find the holy warrior?" he demanded. "Is he also part machine?"

"He does not matter, only his servants," Haviva muttered, looking upward into the infinite. "Friends will kill you by trying to save you! Enemies will save you by trying to kill you!" She grabbed his arm, her fingers digging in hard. "Find the key, open the door and kill the ancient giants! Stop the new fire!"

"Do giants have name?" Jak demanded gruffly.

Nodding, the doomie reached out a hand to move a bony finger through the dirty sawdust on the floor, making a small circle, then a large oval that cut through the middle, and on the left side she made a crude star.

Astonished, Mildred scowled at the pattern. That looked like the astronomy symbol for the planet Saturn. But if that was correct, then what did the star represent? One of its many moons?

"TITAN!" Doc roared. With a badly shaking hand, he aimed the blaster at the design. "That is the symbol of TITAN!"

Moving fast, J.B. used his boot to wipe the symbol from the floor. Breathing heavily, Doc continued to stare at the floor, then slowly turned to walk away, whistling as if he didn't have a care in the world.

Stunned, Krysty was speechless. The man couldn't even look at the symbol.

"Tell me, Haviva," Mildred said urgently, licking her lips. "Do these ancient giants… Are they… Do they speak softly?"

"Yes!" the doomie cried. "You understand! The giants whisper!"

Jerking back, Mildred recoiled from the words as if physically struck. Doc had told them that the time-trading project had been a division of Overproject Whisper. Did they send people to the future? Were there giants hunting for Delphi, and if they found him it would somehow trigger a second skydark? Did that mean the companions had to save Delphi to prevent another nuclear holocaust?

"Enough of this shit!" Ryan demanded, taking the hunchback by the shoulder. "Where is the bastard door? Where's the key?"

"But you have seen them both," Haviva whispered faintly, her misshapen body starting to sag. "You see them all the time...."

"Where? When have I seen them!" Ryan demanded, putting as much force into the words as he could muster.

"In...your dreams..." she exhaled, strangely slumping over.

Releasing his grasp, Ryan watched as the woman eased to the floor and went still.

"Sleep? I wake," Jak declared, reached out to shake the hunchback.

"Don't bother," Baron Levine said, staying the teen. "When she stops, that's all you'll ever hear on the subject again. The strain of seeing the future is becoming too much for her. Every year our doomie says less and sleeps more. Soon..." He shrugged. All things died. Not even a baron could do anything about that.

Kneeling, Mildred suspiciously placed two fingers on the carotid artery in the throat of the hunchback, checking for a pulse. "Haviva is not asleep," the physician said, slowly standing. "She's gone."

"What? Impossible!" the baron roared, going to the woman and shaking her hard. "Haviva! *Haviva!*" But there was no response from the hunchback.

"I'm truly sorry," Mildred said, feeling helpless. "I wish there was something I could do." The canvas med kit seemed to be a slab of cold granite hanging at her side.

"She died giving you this warning," Levine muttered. "It's like Haviva was waiting for you to arrive before she could allow herself to finally...let go."

"Pity it didn't make any sense," Ryan said evasively, and instantly regretted it. From the dour expression on the baron's face, he was deeply insulted by the lie. Damn.

Scowling darkly, the baron pulled a knife and put a small cut into his left sleeve, then sheathed the blade. "Goodbye, little one," he whispered, giving a tug to slightly rip the material.

Recognizing the gesture for what it was, J.B. respectfully removed his hat and Krysty said a short prayer to Gaia. The others bowed their heads. Then, going to the wag, Mildred retrieved a blanket and draped it over the dead woman. The hunchback hadn't been under her care, yet the physician still felt like she had just lost a patient.

"Enough! Life goes on. I'll send in some sec men to remove the body," the baron growled, turning to head for the door. "As for you folks, get to work on your damn wag! I gave you a month, and my word is stone. But after that you're no longer welcome in my ville!"

"But, Baron…" Mildred began, then stopped, knowing it was futile to argue to anybody at a time like this.

Unbolting the door, Levine threw it open and walked outside, then turned to look at the covered form on the floor. "Thirty days," he growled, and strode away shouting orders.

"Taking hard," Jak said, easing his grip on the Colt Python. "Think they kin?"

"Doesn't matter," Ryan said, wearily rubbing his face. It had been a long day and it wasn't over yet. Fireblast, he was tired. "We were planning to leave long before a month passed, so this hasn't really changed anything. Recce the ville, fix the wag and then go after Delphi."

"But if chilling the cyborg will start another skydark…" Krysty began hesitantly.

Impatiently, Ryan cut her off with a gesture. "The doomie said the person sent by what Doc called TITAN couldn't chill Delphi. She didn't mention us at all."

"True," the redhead agreed hesitantly. The predications of a doomie did not always come true. Time flowed like a river, not a concrete road. It was forever changing, flowing, taking on new patterns. The mere fact that they had gotten a hint about what was to come might change the outcome all by itself.

Nothing was absolute or carved into stone. Time was sort of like plas, soft, malleable and always deadly. Mildred and Doc said that it had to do with free will. Ryan and J.B. believed it was because knowledge was the ultimate weapon. Jak didn't give a nuke. And as for her, well, Krysty considered the future a gift from Gaia. It could be changed if you were worthy and tried hard enough.

"Swell. Now it's a race to see who aces the cyborg first." J.B. returned his hat to the accustomed position. "Us, or these assholes from TITAN."

"If the doomie was telling the truth."

"A big if."

"True."

Pulling out a scrap of paper and a pencil, Mildred licked the stubby point and made a copy of the design. A circle, an oval and a star, the symbol for TITAN. For some reason, the design seemed familiar. She'd seen it someplace before, but where?

"So, what is this town you've been dreaming about?" Krysty asked curiously. "Don't think you ever mentioned it before."

After making sure they were alone, with nobody hidden or listening, Ryan told them all about his reoccurring dream from the Mutie Wars.

"Dark night, I always did wonder what happened when you fell off that hill," J.B. said, removing his hat. "Hell of a tale." He smoothed the brim of his fedora with strong fingers. "Sounds like you saw something that you shouldn't have and got chased away, like a dog pissing on a ville wall. Whoever these folks are, they could have aced you easily enough."

"Just dropping me back in the nuking lake would have done it," Ryan agreed honestly, crossing his arms.

"But the only thing you ever saw was the ville," Mildred added. "Which logically means it must be someplace special. Perhaps a predark fortress, or even the master redoubt."

"Where all soldiers go?" Jak demanded in surprise.

"Maybe."

Taking a seat, Ryan frowned. Now there was an unsettling possibility! Tangling with the cyborg was going to be a tough enough fight, but if this was another Anthill, or even a redoubt full of predark soldiers, they'd be walking into a rad pit of trouble. Uneasily, he looked at what remained of the design in the dirt. Just for a second there was a flicker of memory about the white building in his dream, then it was gone.

Studiously glancing at the flatbed and Mack sitting quiescent only a few yards away, Mildred frowned. "It might even be the laboratory that Doc escaped from."

The words hung thick between the companions, filling the air like invisible chains to focus their attention upon the tall, elderly-looking man standing alongside the war wag, his head bowed in somber contemplation.

"That would explain a lot of things," Krysty agreed, biting a lip thoughtfully. "Well, the little doomie hung on just long enough to pass us this warning. Sounds like we'd be triple-stupe fools to ignore it. Doesn't matter if it's the home base for this TITAN person, or just a hardsite for Delphi. We have to do a recce."

"Fair enough," Jak said resolutely. "If help Doc, kick nuke in ass. Know where is?"

"Not really, that whole damn journey is blurred in my head," Ryan answered, sounding angry. "But you were there, J.B. Any chance you recall me falling off a cliff during the Mutie Wars?"

"Yeah, I do," J.B. said. "Happened just that one time, about a hundred miles from here, at a place called Lake Powell."

Tensely alert, Ryan waited for some internal reaction to the name, but nothing happened. Good. Mebbe the warning from Haviva had somehow freed him from the mind block he seemed to have about the damn place. He had no idea why people from this TITAN group were after Delphi, but the one-eyed man felt certain that the mystery would be answered once they got inside that white adobe building with the symbol for TITAN above the door.

Chapter Sixteen

The crackling firelight cast dancing shadows across the sandy street, the reddish glow inside the predark store making it resemble the bloody mouth of some hungry beast.

Sitting near the campfire, Edgar Franklin tossed another piece of wooden door onto the flames, causing an explosion of hot embers that swirled and danced upward to the smoke-stained ceiling. Twilight had come and gone. Now black night ruled the predark ruins, softening the angular contours until it seemed like a vast stone canyon full of arroyos, buttes and rills. A cold wind blew among the old buildings, softly stirring the loose sand to the sound of distant rain. From somewhere within the concrete maze, an owl hooted, and then a tumbleweed rolled along the boulevard, moving past the gaping storefront as if it were late for an appointment. Franklin added another piece of wood to the fire. Even in death, the great city maintained the precious illusion of life.

About an hour ago, a couple of mangy wolves had padded up to the store to peer inside, the reflected firelight making their eyes shine eerily bright. Unfortunately, the animals were much too scrawny to be considered a decent threat, so he killed them with the needler and let the screamwings savage the bodies until there wasn't a trace of them remaining aside from a few dark stains on the dusty sand.

Picking up a galvanized aluminum pot, the cyborg poured some coffee into a cracked ceramic mug and took a sip. The pungent black brew was strong and bitter. There was a packet of powdered hot chocolate secreted inside the folds of his clothing, but that was being saved for a trade item. In somber retrospect, it seemed to the man that the entire world had become one huge prison where the strong preyed on the weak and food was the only real currency. Well, food and weapons.

Finishing the mug, Franklin tossed the dregs onto the fire and impatiently rubbed the container in the sand to clean it enough to go back in his pocket. It was nearly midnight and he was becoming quite impatient. The ruins were supposed to be filled with stickies, but he had heard rumors of something called the Metro being used to eradicate most of the muties. Perhaps it was true. Pity. But if nothing of sufficient size arrived soon, he would have to take matters into his own hands, wounding himself with a knife, and staggering to the ville claiming he was attacked by coldhearts. It would be much more believable if he was seen being chased by some stickies, but need drives where the devil must, as the old saying went.

Just then, something large stirred in the darkness outside the store, and the cyborg strained to hear shuffling steps and then the telltale swish of a tentacle lashing through in the air. A stickie? Tensely, the cyborg waited, but there were no more sounds of movement. Damn, even one stickie would have been better than—

Throating an inhuman cry, a shambling mockery lurched from the darkness and into the red firelight, a dozen ropy tentacles thrashing around, a billowing white mist obscuring the body of the oncoming creature. For only a brief moment, Franklin vaguely saw the face of the thing, the skull obscenely split in two as if two or more heads had merged together, or perhaps were in the process of separating.

With a guttural cry, Franklin stood and quickly backed away. Nuking hell, a howler! The bedamned monstrosities were one of the horrors of the Deathlands, and nobody knew what they were aside from death incarnate. The whitish mist surrounding them was a powerful neurotoxin, and even a drop on bare skin paralyzed a person. True omnivores, howlers ate anything they could reach, and only a single one of them had ever been successfully chilled without resorting to a nuclear device.

As the howler moved through the empty doorway, Franklin drew his needler and fired a long burst at the misshapen thing. The discharged pins hit the howler in the chest, if it had a chest, and punched clean through doing no visible damage. Shit!

As the beam winked out, the cloudy mutie howled in unbridled fury and charged, the deadly tentacles lashing out in every direction. Stepping to the side, Franklin fired again, sweeping the weapon's lambent beam sideways to try to cut the howler in two, but with no results. The fléchettes passed through the mist-shrouded body as if it were a hologram.

Keeping to the middle of the store, its tentacles spreading wide to prevent any possibility of the prey slipping past, the howler moved directly into the campfire, seemingly unaffected by the crackling flames.

That broke his resolve, and Franklin turned to pelt

toward the rear of the store. He had to get outside. He needed room to maneuver! But reaching the fire exit, the cyborg found the metal door would not open, no matter how hard he tried. Then he saw the jamb was bent, warped from the collapse of the upper stories. Firing his weapon at the howler for a moment, Franklin then turned the beam on the door to start cutting out a crude circle. As the beam chewed through the predark steel, the needler in his grip became uncomfortably hot, the weapon designed for single shots, not continuous operation. The noise of the tentacles grew steadily louder, and he felt a painful stinging start on the back of his neck. *Curse Coldfire for never sharing the secret of their force fields!*

Glancing nervously over a shoulder, Franklin saw the thing was dangerously close, the white mist billowing outward, discoloring the rubber floor tiles. Pulling the Colt, he fired the two live rounds at the mutie, the muzzle-flash temporarily parting the swirling mist and giving him a glimpse of the creature underneath. No...impossible!

Gagging on vomit, Franklin threw himself at the portal with all of his strength. There came the sound of tortured metal, and for one terrible second Franklin thought the door would hold, then with a loud crack it swung free, throwing him haphazardly to the ground.

Scrambling to his feet, the TITAN agent sprinted into the cold darkness, the sand crunching under his shoes as the cyborg propelled himself frantically toward the ville. All considerations of trying to trick his way inside were gone, replaced by the heartfelt desire to get his ass safely behind that big wall.

Bursting out of the alley, Franklin took the corner at

full-tilt and started to charge across the shatter zone. Dodging past the concrete K-rails, the cyborg tucked away the needler and fumbled to empty the dummy shells from the Colt and thumb in live rounds. From behind, the undulating cry of the howler kept coming his way, sending a chill down his spine.

Taking refuge behind a three-foot-high K-rail, the cyborg rested the blaster on top of the concrete divider and put three booming rounds directly into the cloudy horror. The muzzle-flash lit up the night, and the howler responded by heading toward him faster.

"Help! Help me! Open the fragging gate!" Franklin screamed, triggering the last three rounds one at a time, before dropping the brass and struggling to reload. Moving backward, he bumped into a divider and dropped some of the brass. Panic seized him and Franklin closed the partially loaded cylinder to click on three empty chambers before firing two thundering rounds at the howler, then turned and ran for the ville.

Straight ahead, he could see dim shapes moving along the top of the wall, and then there came some flashes of light from the pinnacle of the Citadel. Mirror flashes? Damn, these primitives were more advanced than he'd believed possible!

Suddenly the sec men on the wall disappeared and Franklin felt a wave of dismay, when there was a flurry of movement in the dark sky above. Hitting the wall, he turned and started reloading the Colt again just as several objects fell to the rocky ground just in front of the grabber, the glass bottles shattering and bursting into pools of flame.

His hands shaking from the effort to smoothly load the wheel gun, Franklin cursed their abject stupidity.

Fire had no effect on howlers! Then more objects came pelting down to land in a rough circle around the shambling creature, each metallic tube tipped with a short length of sizzling string. Pipebombs? The Molotov cocktails had been thrown only to highlight the target!

A split second later, powerful explosions filled the night, knocking over a K-rail and sending the howler flying for several yards. As it landed, more pipebombs dropped around it in a precise pattern, and the series of deafening blasts seemed to shake the world.

Closing the cylinder of the Colt, the cyborg was impressed. Those blasts had been way too powerful for black powder, or even gunpowder. Could they have found a stash of predark dynamite? No, these were better than that, but not quite as strong of TNT or C-4 plastique, which left… He smiled. Guncotton! Fulminating guncotton! It seemed that some unsung genius in the ville had rediscovered the ancient Civil War explosive. And why not? It was only a mixture of cotton filaments and nitric acid. If you knew how, it could be made from bedsheets and silver jewelry. Once again his estimation of the ville went up. Smart. Clearly, these were extraordinary people. Perhaps this ville could be used for some of his own plans. Afterward, of course…

A fusillade of blasterfire came from the sec men on top of the wall, closely followed by another bombardment of pipe bombs. Lashing insanely, the howler seemed to be trying to attack the explosive charges, its tentacles cracking K-rails and kicking up a storm of loose sand and rocks.

Then there came the sound of heavy machinery slowly building in tempo, then the night was slashed apart by a sliver of light that slowly expanded. The gate was opening!

Dashing forward, Franklin snapped off two more rounds at the mutie in passing, then dived through the narrow crack to land on hard ground.

All around him sec men were shouting orders, blasters discharging, and the thumping motors altered pitch, the massive gate slowing down to now rumble closed. Scuttling away from the ever narrowing crack, Franklin saw the howler reach the opening and thrust out a tentacle just as the gate resoundingly closed.

The tip nipped off, the piece of ropy length fell to the ground and wiggled around mindlessly until a sec man skewered it with an arrow from a crossbow. Lifting it warily, he swiftly climbed a broad flight of wooden stairs to the top of the wall and tossed it back into the night. An angry cry came from the other side of the gate, then the titanic portal shuddered as something rammed it from the outside.

"Still here?" a sec woman demanded scornfully from on top of the wall. "Then try this, fucker!" Lighting a fuse, she threw down a pipebomb and stepped back. A few seconds later there came a loud explosion from the other side, and then ringing silence.

"Well?" a big man asked, holding a sawed-off shotgun in both hands.

The sec woman looked down and grinned. "He got the message, Chief!" She chuckled triumphantly. "The howler is moving back to the ruins."

"Fair enough. All right, ease off the cannon," the sec chief commanded, letting down the two hammers on his blaster before sliding it into a holster at his side. There was also a BAR strapped across his back, and a large knife tucked into his left boot. His face was heavily scarred, the overlapping patterns almost obscuring some sort of a blue tattoo on his throat.

Only a few yards away from the gate, Franklin saw a sandbag nest filled with sec men holding blasters and Molotov cocktails. Aiming at the gate was a large muzzle-loading cannon, a stiff fuse jutting from the end like questing antennae.

"You heard the chief," a plump blond woman said, lowering her torch. "At ease, ya bastards. The howler got one look at Betsy here and pissed itself!"

There came a scattering of laughter from the armed guards and they slung the BAR longblasters over their shoulders, the burning rags tied around the neck of the Molotovs yanked loose and dropped into a plastic bucket full of water to hiss into extinction. Barely visible behind the sandbags was a pyramid of wrought-iron cannonballs, along with several lumpy cloth bags.

Franklin identified canister rounds. During the Civil War, such items were made of thin sheets of tin and filled with hundreds of musket balls. But these homemade versions probably contained only small bits of junk, broken glass, bent nails, busted pieces of pottery, anything the ville couldn't readily use. But fired from the maw of a black-powder cannon and the barrage of debris became a shotgun blast of devastating potential over a short distance.

Most likely about six feet past the open gate, the cyborg guesstimated. He didn't know if the hammering could have slain a howler, but it would have shredded anything else, and at the very least, the sheer force of the multiple impacts would have thrown the mutie back outside again so the gate could be closed. Clever. Then the cyborg did a double-take at the sight of two of the men carrying canvas bags slung over their shoulders, the sides decorated with a large red cross. What the hell was going on in the ville?

"Now, as for you," the chief sec man said, crossing his arms and glowering downward. "Can't say you've earned a lot of friends here, rist, bringing a fragging grabber down our throats."

Rist…tourist? Sprawling on the ground, Franklin pretended to pant from exhaustion. Yes, of course, the genesis of the word was obvious: tourist. Tucson had once been a vacation city, but after skydark, outsiders would have been extremely unwelcome, and the word became slang for a nonresident. However, this was when the cyborg noticed just how many sec men were standing near the gate, their hands full of blasters, Molotov cocktails, pipe bombs and torches. That was disturbing. TITAN did not have the secret of force fields like Coldfire, and there was enough weaponry here to dispatch him without much effort on their part.

"I…had no choice," Franklin started, trying to shift uneasily under the stern gaze. "I was…" *Don't say compelled, idiot! Small words, always use small words!* "My dreams forced me here."

"Your dreams," the sec chief said slowly, as if testing the words for a hidden trap. The fellow didn't look crazy, but the sec boss had been fooled before.

"I'm here to find a man called Silver," Franklin explained, slowly rising to his feet. "I had a dre— A friend of his is in terrible danger and needs help."

"Yeah? Well, I'm Chief Stirling," the big man declared. "Steve Stirling. Been told that's a kind of silver." The sec boss kept a hand near his double-barrel blaster. "What's the name of this friend of mine?"

Dusting off his clothing, Franklin shook his head. "I don't know his name for sure," the TITAN operative lied. "But it's got something to do with the rain."

"Rain?" Stirling laughed.

"Yes. He is tall, very tall, with black hair and only one eye. Carries a curved knife like nothing I have ever seen before."

A hush fell over the crowd of sec men and suddenly not one of the blasters was pointed at Franklin anymore.

"Nuking hell, that sounds like Ryan," Stirling whispered. "Not *rain,* you feeb, Ryan!"

"And he's in trouble?" a barrel-chested sec man demanded, advancing a step. "Where is he? Talk fast, rist!"

"I do not know where," Franklin said, dramatically gazing into the sky. "When I sleep, there are dreams and I see distant faces, events, wars, births…they mostly come true…"

A sec woman gave a low whistle.

"So you're a doomie?" Stirling demanded.

"No!" Franklin denied hastily. "I'm no mutie! I'm a norm! Ain't nothing like that thing outside!"

Moving his hand off the blaster, Stirling snorted. "Blind Norad, there ain't nothing like a howler this side of hell, and we got lots of folks in here with a little mutie blood in 'em. So don't worry about that. The baron has never hung a rist for being different. What's your handle?"

"Adams, Eric Adams. And I ain't no doomie!"

"Sure, sure," Stirling said soothingly. "You just have dreams sometimes and they come true. Hey, no biggie, right? Everybody dreams." The chief sec man had an idea what was going on here, but if this Adams really was a doomie, then he needed to be handled as gently as a newborn colt. Doomies were incredibly rare, and even more valuable. Advance warning of a drought, or acid rain or mutie attack could save the whole fragging ville. Of course, there were folks who sometimes only pretended to be doomies to try to get food and shine from the baron. But the cure for that was easy: slit the tendons so the liar couldn't run, then toss him naked to the next stickie that happened by the ville.

"Sounds like nuke shit to me, sir," Lieutenant Edward Rogan muttered in a deep growl. In his grip was a shiny blue Webley .44 revolver, and a machete hung under his left arm in a leather shoulder holster. The brass was loaded with black powder now, but worked as good as ever.

Advancing a step, the colossal lieutenant nearly made Stirling look small. The barrel-chested giant had countless small scars on his face until it seemed barely human. A gold ring dangled from his left ear, and he walked with a pronounced limp.

Turning, Franklin looked directly at the much larger man. "The river was deep enough to spare your life, but not your leg," he said softly, trying to sound like he was in a trance and not merely repeating data he had memorized. "And you lay unconscious for a night and a day before this man—" he pointed at the chief "—came along to drag you out of the mud, and build a fire…"

"Bah, everybody knows that story." Stirling grunted. "We tell it over shine at the gaudy house. Now a real fragging doomie…"

"You worked for the machine that walked like a man," Franklin continued, as if not hearing the interruption. "He gave you and three others predark things, machines with wheels, and rapid-fires! He stood behind glass that could not be broken and called himself Delfy."

"Delphi," Rogan groaned, his face contorting into an unreadable expression. A hand gripped his blaster, and he let go slowly. Nuking hell, so this feeb was a real live doomie! There was no way anybody else could know those things, especially about the invisible wall that protected Delphi from blasters and knives. He'd never even told Chief Stirling that detail, and he owed the sec boss his life.

"Guess you really are a doomie," the sec chief said, seeing the conflicting emotions on the face of his friend. "So, what's this about Ryan being in trouble?"

"Frag that drek." Rogan's eyes glinted in open hatred. "Do you know anything about Delphi?" The giant man couldn't care less about Ryan and the others. They had tried to ace him, and he'd survived only because of that nameless river and Chief Stirling. It'd been a fair fight, and he held the outlanders no grudge. But Delphi was different. That was a personal matter, and the last Rogan brother had sworn a blood oath to find and chill Delphi no matter the cost. Even his own life.

Stirling stepped between the two and grabbed Franklin by the arm. "Tell me about Ryan first," he demanded. "Where is he? What's the trouble? Talk fast, and I'll fill your pockets with live brass! Dozens of rounds! Tell me!"

"D-dozens?"

"Guaranteed! Now talk!"

"My dream was about both," Franklin whimpered, finding it easy to sound frightened by the sec man. His grip was like iron. Perhaps there was just a touch of mutie blood in him, eh? "To the far north, past the Great Salt is a ville by a lake. The rocks are bloodred, the water dark green, and there they shall meet, Rain and Delfy, but only one will walk out of the predark ruins alive... Sometimes it is the one-eyed giant, and sometimes the man dressed all in white...."

"Sounds like it ain't been decided yet," Stirling mused thoughtfully. "And I can make the difference?"

"Yes! But only if you hurry!" Franklin said excitedly. "And it may already be too late, unless you get there before..." Slumping his shoulders, the TITAN operative began panting for breath as he had seen real doomies do after a vision.

"Before what?" Rogan demanded gruffly. "Talk, rist!"

Making a vague gesture with his hands, Franklin shrugged and reeled a little bit, stumbling to stay on his feet.

Damn all doomies! They were weaker than breadcrumb coffee! Chief Stirling snapped his fingers, and a couple of sec men rushed over to take hold of Franklin and help him to the sandbag nest. Sitting, the TITAN operative began to breathe shallowly, and he wiped his face with a trembling hand. Apparently the locals believed his act, as they moved away to hold a hushed conference. Only the plump blond sec woman seemed to be keeping a close watch on him, as if expecting trouble.

"Shitfire, Chief, we owe Ryan and his people a triple lot for their help with those muties," a sec man declared resolutely. "If they're in for a shit-storm, then count me in to help!"

"And me!" another sec man added, followed by a chorus of eager voices.

"Cut the chatter," Rogna barked, rubbing the scars on his neck. "The doomie said the dream was for only the chief and me." The old wound still hurt sometimes when the acid rain came, and he always took it as a sign of danger. But was the doomie a danger, or was it Delphi? There was only one way to be sure.

"Besides, the rains will be coming soon," Stirling added. "Which means we'll be hit by coldhearts seeking shelter, new muties, cannies looking to get fresh supplies of meat.... The rest of you have got to stay here to guard the ville."

"Mebbe we should check with the baron," a sec woman offered, glancing toward the Citadel rising from the center of the ville. "He owes Ryan a blood debt for saving Daniel and—"

"Tell him in the morning," Stirling retorted, cutting her off abruptly. "However, I'm leaving right now."

"Sir?"

"You heard me." Putting two fingers into his mouth, the sec chief sharply whistled across the courtyard. "Hey, Hannigan!"

Masked by shadows, the door to a predark auditorium swung open exposing a fat man holding a lantern. Behind him were wooden stalls holding the ville horses and mounds of green hay.

"Yes, sir?" Hannigan asked sleepily, fighting back a yawn.

We were tossing pipes, and he was sleeping? Lazy fragging bastard, Stirling thought. "Get my horse saddled! And pack a week's worth of food! Plus a dozen pipe bombs!"

"No, get a couple of horses ready!" Rogan countermanded. "Along with one of the new med kits, plenty of water, and fill the fragging saddle bags with every pipe bomb they can hold!"

"Ah…Chief?" Hannigan asked uncertainly, glancing at Stirling.

Stirling and Rogan looked hard and long at each other, then the chief nodded grimly. "You heard the lieutenant!" he bellowed. "Now move your ass!"

"Yes, sir!"

A few minutes later, the stablehand returned with the mounts, the iron horseshoes clanking against the cobblestone streets. Dutifully, Stirling and Rogan checked over the packs, then climbed into the saddles.

"Okay, Sergeant Hassan, you're in charge until we get back," Stirling commanded, tightening the reins. "Give us a moon. After that, consider us aced. But don't send any rescue parties! This is a private matter, and not ville biz."

"I'm sure Baron O'Connor would say different," the sergeant muttered, stroking his beard. "But since I can't talk to him till the morning, that's too nuking bad for me, I guess."

"Yeah, you'll be a grunt by dawn," Stirling agreed.

The sec man dismissed that cavalierly. "Been there before, and still made sergeant faster than you."

"Fair enough," Stirling said, extending a hand. "Protect the baron, and watch your back, old friend."

They shook. "You, too, sir."

Walking his dark stallion toward the gate, Lt. Rogan paused near the sandbag nest. "You better be right about this, Adams," he growled in his unnatural voice. "Because getting chilled by a howler ain't nothing compared to what I will do to you if this is some sort of trick."

Incredibly, Franklin believed the threat. The big man radiated an aura of danger that was almost palpable. "Avoid the hollow lands," he suggested in reply. "And watch for a painting of a winged horse."

"A what?"

"A red horse with wings. You shall find what is needed there."

Starting to ride away, Rogan shot the man a suspicious look as if questioning his sanity, then faced the gate. "Open 'er up!"

With the sound of working machinery, the massive gate began to lumber aside.

"You sure about this, Chief?" a sec woman asked, scratching her cheek.

Checking the load in his sawed-off scattergun, Stirling said nothing. Delphi had walked right up to the man as he lay bleeding in the grass, then walked away chuckling. *The nuke-sucker laughed as he left me to board the last train west.* The memory burned in his mind. Was he sure about going after Delphi? Hell yes.

"Any sign of the howler?" Rogan shouted up to the guards on the wall through a cupped hand.

"Clear as shine!" a sec man replied loudly. "But there's something moving in the ruins to the west!"

"Stickies?"

"Can't tell!"

Fair enough.

Bunching the reins in one hand, Rogan drew the Webley and thumbed back the hammer. He wasn't afraid of getting chilled, only of failing. Delphi had gotten his entire family aced, and now was his chance for payback.

As the gate cleared the wall, the two sec men kicked

their horses into a gallop, riding through the narrow opening and into the featureless night.

As the sec men at the controls shifted the gears, the gate slowed its rumbling passage, stopped, soon closed with a muffled boom.

Hassan hitched his gunbelt. "Pierpont, Smith, check the juice lines on the diesels! If we need the gate hot again tonight, I want it primed and ready! Everybody else, check your blasters!"

As the sec men hurried to their assorted tasks, Hassan strode over to Franklin. "On your feet, rist," he decided. "I gotta keep you off the streets until dawn. Then we both go report to the baron."

"Yes, of course," Franklin said, reclaiming his feet. "Any idea where—"

"Sir?" a voice said from the shadows.

Drawing their blasters, the sec men turned fast, then relaxed and holstered their weapons. A young woman stood at the murky edge of the light coming from the alcohol lanterns. She was pale and slim, with long ebony hair tied into a loose ponytail. Her clothes were clean but heavily patched, and a coiled bullwhip hung at her hip. Oddly, the grown woman was cradling a pre-dark doll in her left arm as if it were a living child. Some time ago a child she'd grown to love contracted the Black Cough and died. Devastated by the toddler's untimely death, the final straw in a life filled with hardship, the woman had lost her grip.

"What do you want, feeb?" a blond sec man snarled rudely.

"I came to bring my brother his dinner," the woman replied, proffering a wicker basket. There were some raw vegetables inside, along with a small loaf of bread and some smoked meat. "I heard something about Ryan… Is there any word about my husband?"

"Husband?" Franklin asked in shock. There had not been anything in the file about Ryan or any of his companions getting married. This could change everything.

"Yes, sir," the woman said with a dreamy smile. "I'm Emily Tanner. My husband is Doc Tanner, Theophilus Tanner." Then she lovingly looked down at the bundle of plastic and rags she held. "And this is our little daughter, Lily."

The TITAN operative was speechless. What was this? Had Operation Chronos trawled Emily Tanner successfully from the past? Then he noticed the scorn in the faces of the sec men, and the wild glint in the woman's fevered eyes as she adjusted the rags around the doll. Ah. The poor woman was insane, and had fixated on Doc Tanner for some reason. Wait a moment, the dinner was for her brother…. Could this be Lily Rogan? In his last report to Coldfire, Delphi had expressed a belief that Tanner might have had a brief sexual liaison with the former gaudy slut. Now she was insane and believed they were a couple with a child? How very interesting.

"I'm truly sorry," Franklin said, trying to sound believable. "But Doc Tanner…Tanner was chilled, aced by Delphi."

The wicker basket hit the ground and the young woman went deathly pale as she tightly hugged the doll to her chest. "No," she whispered almost too softly to hear.

"Yes, ma'am," Franklin lied. "I'm afraid it's true."

Going oddly still, Lily Rogan turned and walked stiffly into the darkness and out of sight.

Damn, he had hoped for a better reaction than that! Oh, well.

"They're all aced," Franklin said softly, gazing upward at the cold and distant stars. "Or will be." Just for a moment, there seemed to be a subtle movement in the heavens, and then it was gone, lost in the infinite black.

Chapter Seventeen

Night had conquered the rocky vista of the Nevada plains, and the four wags of the convoy were parked in a rough square around a pair of crackling campfires.

A dozen men were sitting around the double fires, stitching holes in their clothing, smoking predark cheroots, sipping real coffee and sharpening knives. Staying along the shadowy edge of the firelight, a pair of troopers patrolled the campsite, their arms cradling shiny new BAR longblasters. A harmonica played softly, and somewhere in the rocky plateaus, a hellhound snarled defiantly at the moon, the response of the mutie triggered by its distant canine ancestors.

The double fires had been Delphi's idea, to prevent a coldheart, or mutie, from extinguishing one fire and leaving his man to fight in darkness. Oh sure, the wags had headlights, but first someone had to find the wags and get his ass inside.

"Well, time to stretch my legs before sleep," Delphi said, pretending to yawn and stretch. "Be back in a tick."

The music stopped and several of the troopers looked up from whatever they were doing.

"Want some company, Chief?" a bony norm man asked, lowering a harmonica. "Never wise to wander about alone in these parts."

"Hell, sir, nobody should ever go anywhere alone," Cotton Davenport added grimly, working the freshly oiled bolt on her BAR.

In dark harmony, a hellhound sounded its battle cry at the cold and forbidding sky once more.

"Nothing out there I can't handle," the cyborg stated confidently.

Reluctantly, Cotton grunted at that, knowing it to be true. The chief was lightning-fast with his handcannons. "Ten minutes, and then I come get you," she replied gruffly. "Don't care if you're in the middle of a dump, or choking the chicken. Don't want you out of my sight for too long, sir."

Bemused, the cyborg smiled tolerantly at the woman. Her devotion to his welfare was as touching as it was misguided. When it became necessary to terminate this group, he would make her death as painless as possible. "Give me an hour," he said, hitching his gunbelt.

"Nope," Cotton said, shaking her head. "Fifteen minutes."

"Twenty."

She paused, then shrugged. "Done."

"Done," Delphi replied with a half smile, and rose to walk away into the night.

"Him and his crazy walks...." A trooper chuckled, spooning more beans from a tin can.

"Aw, shut your piehole and go check on Jeffery on the lead wag," Cotton growled, returning to her military ablutions. The receiver of the longblaster was sticking slightly for no reason that she could discover, and it was making her ornery.

Sensing this was not the time or place to challenge the woman, the trooper stood and headed for the nearest war wag, still regularly eating the predark baked beans.

As soon as the cyborg was out of the light, Delphi activated his force field and breathed a sigh of relief as the soft glow of the immaterial barrier permeated the darkness. He never really relaxed until he was safe behind the impenetrable force barrier or inside a redoubt. There were just too many things in the world these days whose sole purpose in life seemed to be hilling and eating people.

I helped create a few, but not this many! Delphi denoted sourly. It was almost as if Nature was responding to the Nuke War in a concentrated effort to remove the annoying species that had so damaged the world.

When he was far enough away from the enclave of war wags, Delphi illuminated his eyes and swept the darkness for signs of stickies. He had heard a soft hooting earlier that evening, and knew they had to be somewhere in the area. Not close enough to be a threat to his wags and troopers, but possibly near enough to reach in a short walk.

A cold wind blew over the barren landscape carrying the smell of ancient concrete dust, which meant a ruin of some kind was relatively close, so he headed in that direction. Soon enough, he found the tattered remains of a truck stop, the restaurant and pumps reduced to only jagged teeth rising from the hard crystalline ground, the soil obviously fused solid from a nuke hit.

Wolfweed grew thick in the area, along with some more of the trip-cursed millet. Staying alert for any solies in the area, Delphi inspected the thicket of weeds and was delighted to find a score of stickies sleeping in a pile at the bottom of a rad crater. His built-in Geiger counter registered lethal radiation, but that meant nothing to his shield, and the cyborg walked confidently through the weeds to pause at the edge of the depression.

The force field kept his smell from the muties, but the soft sound of his shoes on the fused ground caused them to stir, and one big stickie raised her misshapen head to sleepily glance around and then stare directly at the unexpected sight of a juicy two-legs standing right alongside their crib. Food!

Standing upright with surprising speed, the hulking female raised both of her sucker-covered hands and inhaled deeply to sound a warning hoot, when Delphi raised a hand and played a colorful beam of light over the amassed muties. In an instant, all of them were awake. Several of the young scurried away in terror, then all of the adults formed a defensive wall between the children and this strange two-legs. One male hooted softly, more in puzzlement than anything else, his mind swirling with bizarre images and ideas.

Taking heart at that, Delphi doubled the power to the Educator, then tripled it. *Come on, my broken children, learn, think…learn to think! Put up a rock, pick up that broken truck axle…raise it as a club. See your enemies fall under the blows! Think, my children! Learn to think!*

One of the stickies started to reach for the axle shaft, then shuddered and dropped to the ground, a thick fluid running freely from his ears and mouth. Then the big female soiled herself, and all of the children began to bleed profusely from their horribly human-looking eyes.

Infuriated at the reactions, the cyborg viciously increased the power of the Educator to the maximum level. Wildly going into convulsions, the family of stickies toppled to the radioactive ground, frothing and twitching.

When the bodies stopped bleeding, Delphi turned off the Educator and fanned the pile of corpses with his laser, quickly reducing them into charred ashes and blackened bones. Failure. Another failure! But then, stickies were hardly even self-aware enough to be called sapient, much less sentient.

Turning away from the slain muties, Delphi strode purposefully back to the campsite. Clearly, these creatures had simply been too crude to accept the advance training. Perhaps I pushed them too hard? he wondered. Or too fast? But it really made little difference. He had been able to fix everything that had been damaged by that grenade blast from Tanner, but apparently not the Educator. That sophisticated piece of equipment was beyond any of his makeshift repairs. Such a pity. It seemed to kill the stickies now, instead of awakening their minds.

A subtle motion in the gloomy shadows made Delphi drop into a combat stance, his needler and crystal rod sweeping for targets. But then Cotton stepped into view from behind a boulder, bracketed by two other troopers holding longblasters and oil lanterns.

"You're early," Delphi said, holstering his weapons.

"Heard a hoot and thought there might be stickies around," Cotton replied, studying the darkness as if searching for any hidden dangers. "Guess I was wrong."

"No, there were stickies," Delphi grunted, mentally engaging the internal lock on the Educator inside his palm. "Just not anymore."

"Fair enough," Cotton said in acknowledgment.

However, as the group moved around the boulder and into the twin nimbi of the crackling firelight, it occurred to Delphi that the Educator now made a splendid torture device. Adjusted to a very low setting, a person might last for hours, maybe even days, writhing in hideous torment under the probing beam of the malfunctioning Educator.

It would take me years to extract a fitting revenge from Tanner, the cyborg thought hatefully. So I will make sure his friends die first, crawling and begging for mercy, until I finally turn the beam upon him!

Delphi felt himself actually smile. Days of screaming, yes, that would be sufficient. Now all he had to do was find his nemesis....

IT SOON BECOME APPARENT to Ryan and the others that it was a wise decision to leave the mountaintop ville as soon as possible. The work on the war wag should have taken them only a few hours, but it was nearly a week before it was ready to roll, and for good reasons.

Although Baron Levine had kept his word and food was delivered to them every day, whenever he wasn't around it smelled odd, and Mildred was soon convinced that the cooking had been liberally seasoned with feces. As for everything else—machine grease, replacement planks, rawhide strips, shine—the local civies started asking for more and more jack until the prices were astronomical. More than once blasters were drawn, and the sec men had to intervene—reluctantly. No chillings had occurred, but it was only a matter of time. The companions had done nothing to cause the passing of the little doomie Haviva, but apparently she had been beloved by everybody from the baron down to the gaudy sluts, and now the whole ville blamed them for her boarding the last train west. The onus for the passing was lashed around them like an infernal millstone.

When their food supplies began to run low, Jak went out hunting and brought back wild rabbits, along with every pocket jammed full of shiny green leaves. Mildred and Doc recognized the plants as kudzu, a common weed in their time that grew faster than ivy and was harder to kill than horseradish. Yet the albino hunter insisted the leaves were not only edible, but also tasty. After an experimental nibble or two, the rest of the companions had to agree with that assessment. The kudzu leaves were as sweet as cactus fruit, and left a pleasant aftertaste in the mouth. After that, somebody always went along with Jak to help carry back extra foliage. Soon the rear of the war wag was well stocked with smoked meat, kudzu, wild carrots, tree crabs, acorns, pine nuts and barrels of spring water that had been carefully boiled under Mildred's harsh scrutiny, just in case the locals had gotten to the bubbling spring outside the ville walls before the companions had discovered its location.

Ryan's rad counter proclaimed the water clean of radiation, but that was the least of the companions' worries. Every night, something large would patrol around the ville, never coming close, but always there. The sec men on the wall were unable to find the thing in the torchlight, and even alcohol lanterns augmented with pieces of broken mirrors were insufficient to the task. Norm, mutie or machine, there was no way to tell, but the presence of the midnight visitor aced any notions of slipping away in the darkness. When the companions left the ville, it would have to be during broad daylight.

That meant the war wag had to be in shape for combat, which meant more time on repairs, and hunting, and so on.

But finally everything was ready, and the companions drove the heavily patched wag out of the barn and through the beautifully carved gates of the ville. The scowling sec men watched them depart with clear pleasure, and several of the guards raised their blasters slightly, but they withheld firing, more frightened by the devastating power of the predark Kalashnikovs than the anger of their baron. The hatred of the locals was almost palpable.

"So long, Shangri-La," Mildred said with a sigh, watching the gates close. A moment later, they loudly locked, and then locked again. Exodus in stereo. "Aside from the people, that was a nice ville. The baron was nice, the water clean, plenty of game in the woods and no slave pens."

"Seen better," Jak drawled, tucking a leaf of kudzu into his cheek as if it was a chaw of tobacco.

Trundling down the sloping hill with Ryan at the wheel, J.B. in the passenger seat, the big rig jounced along the forest trail and back onto the predark highway. Every indication of the attempted jacking and fight was gone; even the thick carpeting of pine needles had been removed, exposing the jigsaw of cracked asphalt to the cruel light of day.

"I was most sure that the sec men were going to try to chill us once we were out of sight of the ville," Doc rumbled, easing down the hammer of his LeMat and holstering the blaster. "I am extremely pleased to be proved wrong."

"Why waste powder on outlanders already leaving?"

Krysty stated, her long crimson hair flexing in the morning breeze.

"Too true, madam. Waste not, want not. We are as aced to them now as we could ever be."

Heading west once more, Ryan slowed the Mack and kept a sharp watch on the bushes growing along the roadway. A loaded AK-47 rested on the patched bench between the men, along with a box full of grens. The Molotovs were gone, every precious drop poured into the fuel tanks of the lumbering Cyclops. The big diesel was running smoothly again, but it consumed juice the way a rapid-fire did brass.

"Anything?" Ryan asked tersely, steering with one hand, the other tight on the gearshift. The transmission fluid was a mix of different types of oil and a few pre-dark chems that J.B. added to prevent frothing. It worked, but shifting gears required a lot of muscle.

"No, we're clear," J.B. answered, shifting his glasses to a more comfortable position on his nose. "Guess they really are going to let us leave alive."

"Wise move," Ryan stated, going to a higher gear to accelerate the wag. The repaired engine roared with power and black smoke steadily chugged from the overhead exhaust pipes.

The forest was cool and thick with shadows that morning, the cloud coverings in the sky a brilliant orange that almost resembled early daylight. Soon, the dried brown pine needles covered the road once more, and Ryan eased up on the engine a little, deciding that traction was more important than speed. Doc often recited some old poem about such things, but the man could never remember it correctly. Something about being soft?

"Monkeys," J.B. muttered, gazing out the open window. "Something to do with a monkey."

"Softly, softly, catchee monkey." Ryan chuckled. "Thanks, that was preying on my mind."

"No prob." J.B. chuckled. "I..." He stopped to frown, then sniffed hard. "Do you smell smoke?"

Quickly, Ryan looked over the dashboard, but the few remaining gauges that were still working seemed to be fine. "No trouble with the engine. Mebbe we're just cooking some grease and oil off the engine block." Then he caught a whiff, dark and pungent, almost sweet. Wood smoke!

Suddenly a huge crowd of animals surged across the highway—deer, wolves and a cougar—all moving fast. The sight was unnerving. Mortal adversaries like that would only travel together to escape from a greater danger—earthquakes, floods or their worst enemy, fire.

Just then, something thumped twice on the roof of the cab. "Get this shitbox rolling!" Krysty yelled from the rear of the war wag. "The forest is on fire!"

"Where?" J.B. shouted backward. "Behind or ahead?"

"To the sides. Both sides!"

Fireblast! Forcing himself not to look, Ryan concentrated on driving and shoved the stick to the highest gear while tromping on the floor pedal. The big engine responded and the war wag surged forward with renewed speed.

"Think the locals did this?" J.B. demanded, tightening his grip on the Kalashnikov. Billowing plumes of dark smoke were starting to come through the trees, slowly turning day into twilight.

"Nobody who lives in a wooden ville would set the

bastard forest on fire," Ryan admonished. "This must be just a coincidence. A lightning strike or something."

The Armorer said nothing, but the expression on his face clearly stated his opinion of the matter.

"Yeah, I know," Ryan muttered, hunching his shoulders. The war wag was still accelerating, but the engine gauges were starting to creep upward again, too.

More animals charged across the highway in front of the Mack, and a flock of birds and screamwings flew overhead cawing, tweeting and hooting their terror. Taking a gentle curve down the side of the mountain, Ryan ran straight into a river of smoke, the dense band of gray as impenetrable as any fog. Cursing bitterly, the one-eyed man turned on the headlights and twin halogen beams stabbed outward to pierce the swirling fumes and dimly illuminate the road surface. Mentally, the man praised J.B. for installing those nukelamps under the hood. The beams were a hundred times brighter than regular wag headlights, and didn't drain the batteries. Without them, he'd be stone blind right now, lost in the murky gloom.

The smell of burning pine was getting stronger, and the companions started coughing. Pulling out handkerchiefs, they quickly wet the cloth with their canteens and tied the crude masks over their faces. That eased the coughing, but their eyes still stung from the pungent wood smoke.

Shrieking in agony, something dashed out of the burning bushes covered with writhing flames. The companions tracked the griz bear with their weapons, but, blind from the searing agony, the bear charged right back into the forest and disappeared in the roiling smoke.

Slowly, the companions were becoming aware of a faint noise, a low crackling that steadily grew in volume. Waves of heat were coming from behind them and to the right, and there were brief flashes of reddish light dancing between the densely packed trees. The fire was almost upon them.

Another mob of wild animals raced across the pre-dark highway, squirrels, conies and a host of other small animals. Then something large came out of the smoke to slam hard into the wag, cracking a headlight. Ryan savagely twisted the wheel to avoid the blurred shape, and the startled face of a bull moose flashed past J.B.'s window.

The Armorer burst into laughter at the sight, then blinked and fired off a burst from the AK-47.

"What'd ya see?" Ryan demanded, trying to look to the right and watch the road at the same time. Just then the wag gave a thump as it rolled over something small and not quite fast enough to escape both the fire and the speeding war wag.

"Could have sworn…" J.B. started, squinting hard into the cloying smoke. Then he jerked back and triggered the Kalashnikov again. "Son of a bitch!"

Before Ryan could ask, he saw it, moving through the smoke and flames like some impossible colossus. It was huge and irregularly shaped, the shell glistening as if wet and rippling with a rainbow of colors. Then the smoke parted for a moment, and Ryan looked directly at the huge thing. It was the droid from the redoubt, but the machine was radically altered. It had only four telescoping legs now, the body was the chassis of the egg-shaped war wag and there was a projector of some sort perched on top. In a moment, it was gone, left behind the racing Mack. Then something stepped onto the highway and started following after the war wag with remarkable speed.

"Fireblast, the bastard thing must have fixed itself!" Ryan snarled, veering wildly away from the machine. "How is that possible? I smashed the comp!"

"I don't think it is the droid," J.B. retorted, yanking a gren from the box. "But the war wag! Doc said the damn thing was almost sentient. Delphi talked to it like a person!"

"Then the bastard thing was functional the whole time we were there!" Ryan snapped, dodging another throng of terrified creatures. "Fragging machine must have been playing possum, pretending it was aced to hide from the nuking droid!"

"So after we aced the droid and left, it took all those spare parts and rebuilt itself!"

"Either that, or this is another droid!"

"No fucking way!" This was the same LAV, he recognized some of the burn marks from the redoubt. So the bastard machine had been tracking them all these miles, gathering parts and metal to make jackleg repairs. Ryan wouldn't be surprised if there were a few pieces of the speedsters and the two-wheelers mixed in there by now.

Striding purposefully behind the war wag, the LAV started lancing out shimmering beams of light. Wherever the scintillating rays hit, a tree burst into flames, the raging fire constantly building in intensity.

With a guttural cry, Doc dropped down fast, and a beam hit the rear of the war wag, the new green planks smoldering, the pine sap popping and snapping. In a tick it was through and bored out the other side, just missing the cab.

"Ryan, stay away from the maple trees!" Krysty bellowed, snapping off wild shots at the dimly seen machine. "If they're juicy with sap and get too hot, too fast—" The woman was cut off as a maple tree violently exploded, the noise louder than a gren. A dozen other trees began to topple over from the unexpected blast, a hurricane of sparks swirling outward.

"Fucker," Jak cursed, instinctively reaching for his Colt Python, then releasing the checkered grip. There was nothing the handcannon could do against this sort of threat.

Swinging up her ZKR target pistol, Mildred took a stance and snapped off three fast shots. Two of them ricocheted off the egg-shaped chassis, but the third directly hit the crystal lens of the laser. Instantly, the LAV answered back, the energy ray slicing through the thick smoke to punch a hole in the wooden planks, passing within a scant inch of the physician.

"Son of a bitch must have reinforced the focusing lens!" Mildred spat, lowering her blaster. "If the smoke wasn't lowering the coefficiency of that beam we'd all be aced for sure!"

Uncaring about the tech talk, Jak and Krysty both put several bursts from their Kalashnikovs into the machine. But if the 7.62 mm hardball mil rounds did any damage it was impossible to say. The air was thick with smoky embers and the LAV kept constantly on the move, staying behind trees and only stepping into the clear to attack with the laser again. More than once it missed the bucking war wag completely, but every hit added more holes in the planks. In short order, the machine wouldn't have to guess where the people were behind the wood; it'd be able to see them quite clearly.

Off in the distance, another maple tree loudly exploded, the LAV pausing at the sound before continuing after the war wag.

Digging into a pocket, Jak unearthed a spare clip for the AK-47 and whipped it at the approaching machine. The curved magazine landed amid some burning shrubbery. As the LAV walked past, the live rounds started loudly cooking off. Pivoting, the machine began peppering the shrubbery with the laser until there was no more banging.

"Stupe," the albino teen said, searching for another clip.

Taking advantage of the brief distraction, Doc went to the front of the flatbed, thumped twice on the roof of the speeding cab and stuck out his hand near the passenger window. J.B. didn't waste any breath asking what the scholar wanted. He simply passed up a gren.

Returning to the rear, Doc guessed the distance, then passed the sphere to Krysty.

Slinging the Kalashnikov over a shoulder, the woman took the gren and pulled the pin, but kept her hand tight on the arming lever until the war wag stopped bucking for a single instant. In a blur, she whipped her hand forward and the gren sailed high to disappear in the smoky air. A split second and it reappeared to bounce off the top of the LAV and explode thunderously.

The machine rocked from the detonation, one of its spidery legs bucking. But then the LAV righted itself and surged forward, the laser flashing nonstop. A dozen more holes were scored through the planks, and a rear tire blew, throwing everybody to the corrugated floor, which gave Mildred an idea.

Scrambling back to her feet, the physician grabbed a flat tire from a pile of rubbish they had been planning to fix, and heaved it over the side. The tire landed near a fallen tree and began to smolder, thick smoke coming off the burning rubber to spread out in a black cloud. Covered with the fumes, the LAV paused in confusion, and Jak threw another gren. Once more, the machine attacked the fiery bushes, all the time falling farther and farther behind the war wag. The laser stabbed out blindly and only succeeded in setting more trees ablaze.

The heat was becoming oppressive, and breathing was a chore. But all the companions could do was dampen their cloths and keep firing.

The horn sounded from the cab, and the companions looked in that direction to see Ryan waving an arm. Krysty rushed over, and he passed her a pipe bomb.

"Curve up ahead!" Ryan shouted, pointing that way.

"On it!" Krysty yelled in return, and went to the corner of the flatbed to find a likely candidate. She found one almost immediately. There was a huge pine tree covered with flames and leaning dangerously close to the road.

As the war wag raced past, she gently tossed the gren right at the base. They were only a few yards away when the charge exploded, ripping apart the base of the giant pine. In a splintery crash, the tree fell across the roadway only moments before the LAV reappeared from the stifling chaos of the conflagration. The companions held their breath but the machine didn't even pause as it headed past the fiery tree and took off in a new direction.

"Fuckin' stupe," Jak said with a lopsided grin. "Whowee, that close!"

"Amen to that, brother." Mildred sighed, brushing back her beaded locks.

Suddenly the flatbed jounced hard and the companions heard a gurgling splash. Clear water dripped through several of the laser holes, and looking over the riddled planks they saw that the Mack was forging through a shallow creek. The air was just a touch cooler here, and they all breathed easier while checking over their blasters.

The sky above them was a solid blanket of gray from the rampaging forest fire, the noise of the burning woods deafeningly loud. In every direction, maple trees were detonating every few seconds now, throwing up geysers of flaming branches and shattered bark.

Fighting to keep control of the big rig, Ryan twisted the steering wheel sharply to avoid a burning tree as it came crashing down into the creek. The water temporarily extinguished the flames and the charred branches scraped along the side of the vehicle as it passed by. The damp wood burst into flames once more, fed by the boiling sap inside the battered tree trunk.

Hitting a mud hole, the cab listed and the front tires spun freely, then found purchase. The wag lurched forward to glance off a broken slab of ancient concrete. Cursing steadily, Ryan brought the it back under control just in time. More slabs of concrete were lying on the shore, which offered an interesting possibility. Angling out of the creek, Ryan jounced the vehicle up the bank and the wag was soon shuddering along the cracked remains of a predark road. It was just one lane, not a broad highway like before, but the farther they got from the creek, the better the condition of the concrete slabs. Within minutes, the fire was left in their wake, the road surface humming below their tires.

"No sign of the LAV," J.B. said, craning his neck out the window to look behind. "But that doesn't mean anything. It tracked us for a hundred miles, and waited a week for us to come out of that ville. For my taste, that's just too bastard smart for any comp or machine!"

Glancing into the dirty sideview mirror, Ryan said nothing. The fire was still coming their way, and the engine was close to overheating again.

The road turned abruptly to the right, and the one-eyed man yanked the wheel hard to keep from going over the edge of a cliff. The tires squealed in protest, the flatbed fishtailing out to smash into the low wall of loose boulders that served as a safety fence. The rear of the wag rebounded as the impact sent a massive stone rolling for several feet, and then they dropped out of sight.

Gaining the roadway once more, Ryan frowned to see that they were running parallel to a deep chasm. He listened for the boulders to hit bottom, but there wasn't a sound. Only a soft whispering wind.

"Dark night, that must be bastard deep," J.B. observed sourly, craning his neck for a better look. "Better move off this quick and get us some combat room, just in case that LAV finds us a second time."

"No need," Ryan declared, shifting to a lower gear. The transmission stuck, and he had to pump the clutch and shake the shift to get the grinding gears to finally engage.

Squinting through his glasses, J.B. frowned then broke into a ragged grin. Less than a mile up ahead was a thin black line extending across the chasm.

"Hot damn, a bridge!" J.B. cried in delight. "Now we're cooking with microwaves!"

Shifting gears once more, Ryan almost smiled at the twentieth-century expression. J.B. and Mildred were starting to sound like each other more and more these days.

As the wag drew closer, Ryan could see the bridge was actually a box trestle made of riveted iron. Perfect. Even weakened with age, a trestle should still be strong enough to support the war wag. But soon the one-eyed man could see that the bridge was not designed for civilian traffic. It was for a railroad! There was no pavement, only rusty steel rails and wooden ties with open spaces between them that showed only air.

Sounding the horn, Ryan warned the others just before ramming onto the railroad tracks. The wag shook wildly as if hit by a barrage of cannonfire, but he got it moving in the right direction, the tires scraping along the steel rails, bouncing from one wooden tie to the next. The needles of the gauges on the dashboard began to jump around madly, making it impossible to see if the rattling was doing any damage to the beleaguered diesel engine. The hood was shaking so hard, the man half expected it to come loose and crash into the windshield.

But Ryan forgot about such minor considerations as the entire bridge gave a low moan, and a brown snowstorm of rust flakes sprinkled down from the quivering girders over the aged tracks.

Chapter Eighteen

As the rain of corrosion covered the windshield, Ryan activated the wipers. But only the passenger side worked.

"So far, so good!" J.B. said unnecessarily loud, studying the tracks ahead for any obstructions. Bridges were a good spot for coldhearts to try to jack travelers. He'd seen it done many times before. "None of the wooden ties have fallen away yet, so I think we're fine. Just keep moving!"

Bracing himself, Ryan shoved the gas pedal to the floorboards and threw the transmission into high gear. The war wag promptly accelerated, and bizarrely the shaking eased somewhat. Must be going too fast to fall between the ties anymore.

Halfway across the trestle, Ryan risked a glance outside and saw a white-water river at the bottom of the chasm, jagged rocks thrusting up from the turbulent cascade like the broken fangs of prehistoric beast. A few moments later they were through the trestle and Ryan banked the steering wheel sharply. The war wag lurched violently, and then was rolling smoothly along a flat grassy field.

"Park anywhere. I want to check for damage," J.B. said, releasing his death hold on the dashboard.

"No prob." Ryan braked to a stop.

Throwing open the cab door, J.B. hopped to the
ground and rubbed his sore leg. It still hurt a little from
the graze he got back in the dunes, but only a little. Then
a piercing whistle came from the rear of the wag.

"Incoming!" Krysty shouted, and several of the Kalashnikovs started chattering.

Slamming open the door, Ryan swung out of the cab
with the SIG-Sauer in his fist. Just across the bridge,
smoke was starting to pour out of the trees, announcing the arrival of the fire. And deep within the murky
interior something large was smashing a path through
the foliage. The LAV had found them again!

Emerging into view, the spidery machine paused
near the railroad tracks, sending out a white ray of some
kind to play along the ancient steel.

Switching blasters, Ryan worked the arming bolt on
the AK-47, dismayed at how light it felt. Half a clip
wasn't going to stop that droid. Nothing they had would,
except...

As the machine advanced to the trestle, a flickering
glow started coming from the woods, dark smoke rising to taint the sky. A scattering of animals burst from
the forest to race past the LAV, but it completely ignored
them, staying with the railroad tracks until they reached
the bridge. Looking upward, the machine swiveled in
their direction and the laser began to strobe, the rainbow beam lancing out to hit the gridwork of old beams
and punching white-hot holes in the riveted steel. Moving fast, the companions took cover, but the crisscrossing girders of the box trestle offered no clear view of
them from the other side.

"We could run," Mildred said loudly, "but there's no
place to hide. I see only open countryside for miles."

"Stand here," Jak declared grimly, hefting a pipe bomb. "Finish now!"

"Everybody out of the wag!" Doc bellowed. "Keep on the move! Do not offer a group target!"

Advancing to the mouth of the box trestle, the LAV paused, temporarily stymied by the fact it was too large to enter the trestle, then it reached out with two legs and crawled on top of the bridge to scuttle forward, the laser needling out to stab holes in the ground all around the war wag.

The fragging thing was trying to herd them back into the wag for a group chill, Ryan realized in cold certainty. Just how smart was this thing?

"Nuke running," he declared firmly. "J.B., we got no choice. Use it!"

"Yeah, I know," the Armorer said unhappily, digging in a pocket as he walked closer to the bridge.

Pulling out a metal canister, he yanked the ring, flipped off the arming lever and heaved with all of his might. Tumbling through the air, the gren landed on top of the trestle, and promptly rolled through the gridwork of girders to land on the open array of rails and ties.

"Gaia," Krysty whispered, her hair flexing wildly. "Don't let it fall through!"

As if her battlefield prayer was answered, there came a brilliant white flash, followed by a hurricane of wind dragging the companions toward the bridge. They dropped flat and dug in their fingers to stay in place. Next there was a crumpling noise unlike anything they had ever heard…and then silence.

Rising from the ground, Ryan adjusted his eye patch. The LAV was gone, and so was the entire bridge, along with large chunks of the cliff on both sides.

"So that's an implo gren," Mildred said in low astonishment. "Never actually watched one explode…I mean, implode before. Impressive. I have absolutely no idea how the thing works."

"Nobody does anymore." Going to the edge of the cliff, Krysty looked carefully over the edge and saw only the rushing white-water below. Nothing could be seen in the river. The droid and bridge were simply gone, compacted to the size of pebbles in less than the tick of a chron.

"Well, there's no going back now, even if we wanted to," J.B. commented dryly, tugging his fingerless gloves on tighter. "But without that implo gren, we don't have a chilling edge on Delphi."

"Yeah, we do," Ryan growled. "He doesn't know we're coming, and that'll be enough."

"Unless he also has encountered a doomie," Doc rumbled in dark consternation.

There was no possible reply to that, so the companions said nothing as they clambered back into the wag. Starting the engine, Ryan headed west again. According to the map J.B. had checked, Bad Water Lake was about sixty miles away. With luck, they could be there by early dawn.

Mebbe I'll even get a chance to recce that white building, the one-eyed man contemplated. Although he had a gut feeling it'd be a triple-smart move just to blow the place to nuking hell.

WITH BRAKES SQUEALING, the lead war wag of Dephi's convoy came to a halt on the pebbled beach of the huge lake. A few moments later, the other three wags crested a low rise and stopped alongside the motionless wag, forming a ragged line. Some loose stones tumbled away from studded mil tires to splash into the scummy green water. They dropped through the thick covering as if it was mist and vanished from sight, the scum rippling outward for a few yards, almost appearing to be alive from the subtle disturbance.

Jagged red rocks rose from the hidden depths of the lake like the teeth of a dragon, ancient and weathered. Sharp cliffs edged the huge lake most of the way around, leaving only a scant few breaks in the sandstone palisades where the sloping pebble shore could be easily reached. Several miles wide, the lake stretched across the horizon, a foamy vista of dark green, the thick layer of slime broken only by the occasional red dagger of rock or the bleaching bones of an aced traveler. There was no sound of birds in the air or of waves on the shore, the scum making the water too thick to lap against the hard stones.

With a low hydraulic sigh, the side of the lead wag cycled open and Delphi stepped onto the beach, Cotton and a few other troopers close behind. A soft breeze ruffled their clothing and hair, the dank air ripe with the pungent smell of filth and decay.

"What a rad pit!" Cotton exhorted, hitching her gunbelt. "No wonder we never came this way before."

"Guess that's why the locals call it Bad Water Lake," a trooper drawled, scratching his unshaved neck. The man felt itchy just looking at the colossal quagmire.

Another trooper grunted in agreement. "Shitfire, I'd rather walk across a rad pit naked than dip a toe in this stinking drek hole!"

"I heartily agree," Delphi muttered in annoyance, running a hand across his smooth blond hair. The cyborg did not recall the lake being in such a poor condition. Had it gotten worse, or were his memory circuits faulty? Briefly, he tried to access any still-functioning satellites overhead, but there was only the steady crackle of static from the thick layer of radioactive isotopes blanketing the world just behind the storm clouds.

Suddenly a low swell lifted the scum and moved across the lake only to disappear down into the secret depths once more.

"What was that, the tide or something?" a trooper asked nervously, tightening the grip on his BAR longblaster.

"Something," Delphi answered in droll amusement. "There are muties in the deep parts of the lake. They rarely come to the surface, but when they do, it is best not to be around."

"I zero that, Chief," a sec woman replied with a grim expression.

"Ever seen one of 'em, Chief?" a trooper asked curiously. "I heard tell of sea muties before. Krakens, they were called. Nothing but tentacles and teeth."

But Delphi said nothing in reply, his eyes narrowed in somber contemplation. Teeth in the water. No, surely the warning had been for the rodents in the millet field.

"Mannheim, Caruthers, Beltran! Keep a finger on the triggers of the autoblasters!" Cotton shouted over a shoulder, unwilling to take her sight off the Stygian pool. "If anything comes into view from that pest bog, blast it!"

In response, there came a chorus of metallic clicks from the Vulcan 20 mm rapid-fires on top of each wag as the safeties were released.

Crossing his arms, Delphi scowled. The four war

wags were all modified forms of a LAV 25, Piranha-class transport, and were waterproof, capable of float-ing for days. But there was no way in nuking hell he was going to risk crossing this stagnant pool of toxic chems just to save a few days. No, they'd have to take the long way around. Unfortunately, both directions were equally unappealing. To the north were mountains with deep ravines that might be impossible to cross, not to mention snow avalanches, and to the south was the Great Salt, and more stinking muties than he could think. Impossible terrain or nonstop combat. Damned if we do and damned if we don't, he thought.

"Okay, Chief, which direction do we try?" Cotton asked, squinting sideways.

Weighing the options, Delphi started to reply when an internal alarm sounded inside his head. What in the... Son of a bitch, the LAV had just been destroyed! And less than a hundred miles to the east! He looked in that direction. But how was that possible? The nearest ville would be...Pine ville. But the cyborg had estab-lished that was a secure zone, a fallback position in case he ever needed to hide from TITAN. The LAV was pro-grammed to never approach the ville under any circum-stances.

Which left only four distinct possibilities. The ma-chine might have suffered some sort of malfunction and actually was in fine shape but was simply unable to broadcast anymore. That made the most sense. Sec-ond, that some natural disaster had destroyed the LAV, a volcano or an earthquake. Not an unreasonable pos-sibility. But with the on-board protocols in effect, that seemed rather far-fetched. Third, an operative of TITAN could have found the machine and destroyed it. Delphi didn't like that idea very much. It would mean that TITAN was now on the move against him, aggressive instead of reactive. He'd have to start watching for traps. The fourth possibility was the least likely, almost ridiculous, but the more Delphi considered it, the more it seemed to make some sort of horrible sense.

Ryan, the cyborg raged silently. The LAV had to have been destroyed by Ryan, Tanner and the others! Logically that meant they had been hunting for him from the Colorado redoubt where the LAV had been in storage. Which also meant they were now heavily armed with AK-47 assault rifles and grenades. More than an equal for his troopers. The cyborg flexed his hand, feeling the weight of the damaged Educator buried inside his plastic skin. But not for his war wags, and certainly not for him.

"Everybody back in the wags!" Delphi bellowed. "Get razor, people, we're heading south!"

"Across the Great Salt?" Cotton gasped, taken aback. "North would be a lot easier."

"And slower," Delphi retorted. "We have more than enough firepower for anything, or any thing, that gets in our fragging way."

"If you say so, sir," the woman relented hesitantly. "But why the rush? Why not take the time and go around the long way?"

"Let's just say that I heard a hoot," Delphi replied, giving a carefully calculated half smile.

The rest of the troopers grinned back, taking heart at his bravado.

Blind Norad, they were dumber than stickies.

"Besides, have I ever steered you wrong before?" the cyborg added.

"No, sir, you haven't," Cotton replied, straightening her shoulders. "Okay, Chief, give the word and we'll follow you right into nuking hell!"

Good, Delphi mentally noted, starting back to the waiting machines. Because that was exactly where they were heading.

Straight to hell.

REACHING THE CREST of a low desert hillock, Chief Stirling paused to look around the desolate countryside. There was a blast crater to the south, the rill of lava thrusting upward like a picket fence of spears. But there was no glow in the air above the crater, so it was probably safe for the two men to stay in the area. Just not for too long, the sec chief amended privately.

The weathered ruins of a predark city rose on the horizon to the west: concrete bridges broken off in midspan, the crumpled remains of buildings littering the grounds. In every direction around the ruins were scattered pieces of broken tech, debris thrown wide of the nukestorm and embedded by the pervasive desert sand: a white enamel sink with the faucet still attached, the rim of a car tire, a topless female mannequin, the bent hatch to a tank, a gravestone, a stuffed bear.

Removing the stopper from a canteen, Edward Rogan took a small sip of the lukewarm water and held it in his mouth for a minute to allow the tissues to absorb the fluid before finally allowing himself to swallow. As with everything else, there was an art to staying alive in the desert.

"What a drek hole," Rogan commented, scowling at the landscape. There was nothing in sight but desolation. Not even any trees to offer shade, or a trickling creek. It was the type of place a man would ride through on the way to somewhere else.

"Seen worse, but not by much," Stirling replied, pulling down his neckerchief. Pouring a few drops of water into a calloused palm, the man vigorously rubbed the water over his face. Damn, it was a hot day! And there was still a long way to ride before reaching Bad Water Lake. What they would do then, he wasn't sure. But if Ryan and the others were in some sort of trouble, he'd just head for the sounds of chilling and watch out for flying lead.

Snorting in reply, Rogan started to take another sip, but paused at the sound of thin metal fluttering in the wind. Only there was no wind to be felt this day. Not even a breeze.

Easing a hand to his Webley, the huge sec man looked warily over a shoulder to see what made the noise, then he paused to blink in surprise.

"Well, nuke me." Rogan chuckled. "Looky there!"

Turning fast, Stirling leveled his sawed-off alley-sweeper, then lowered the weapon when he saw an old, predark sign sticking out of the side of a small sand dune. Surrounded by tumbleweeds, the worn metal was heavily corroded with rust, but there was still just enough paint on the surface for him to see the vague outline of a red horse with wings. A red-winged horse.

"Son of a bitch," the sec chief whispered, resting the double-barrels on his shoulder. "Just like that doomie told us about. Think we should have a recce?"

But Rogan was already off his mount and throwing the reins over a clump of cacti festooned with colorful flowers.

"Yeah, guess so," Stirling relented, and did the

same to his own stallion to join the norm standing near the sign.

"Okay, now what?" he asked bluntly.

"How the frag do I know?" Rogan muttered, then squinted against the harsh sunlight. There was a dark shadow behind the tumbleweeds.

Approaching the plants as if they were a pit full of stickies, Rogan saw they were plastic and lashed into position with thick nylon rope.

"Markers," Stirling whispered, swinging up his sawed-off again and clicking back the two hammers. "This is a cache for somebody. Mebbe coldhearts or slavers."

Or Delphi, Rogan mused, but he did not say that thought out loud. The chief did not know that he had once worked for the Delphi, only that he hated the bastard and wanted to ace him personally. That alone was enough of a bond to make the two men friends. The sluts could yak about love, but hatred kept a man strong, like powder in a blaster.

Going to the largest tumbleweed, Rogan looked around carefully and grunted upon spotting a spring-loaded mantrap in the sawgrass. Moving back a few feet, he found a stick and tossed it onto the pressure plate of the trap. The rusty steel jaws closed with a resounding bang that made it leap off the ground and rattle the chain that anchored it to a wooden hatch set flush to the hard sand.

"Watch for another," Stirling warned knowingly, running a hand over his blue tattoo. "Nobody but a stupe leaves only one trap."

Nodding, Rogan used his machete to probe the edge of the hatch until finding the locking mechanism. Twisting the blade, he felt the lock give and jerked back fast as a scattergun boomed from the tunnel below. Dropping flat, the two men heard objects humming past them overhead for a few seconds. Then there was only silence and a spreading dust cloud that expanded until it was thinned down to nothing. The noise echoed across the sandy desert for a long time.

Easing their heads over the jamb, the two men looked down into the tunnel to see a worn iron ladder attached to a cinder-block wall, electric lights glowing dimly from the concrete ceiling. The sec men exchanged excited looks. This was no trader's cache, but a baron's bolthole!

Tossing down another stick, Rogan saw there was no reaction from the walls or floor of the predark tunnel. But Stirling held the man back and threw down a heavy stone. It hit the floor and cracked apart setting off another blaster hidden inside the wall.

"Bastard really protected his stuff well," Rogan said in grudging admiration.

"Almost too well," Stirling agreed, titling back his hat. "If we find any more traps, mebbe we should move on."

"No prob there. I like my guts where they are right now, safe inside me."

"You can load that into a blaster and fire it, my friend."

Testing the ladder with more sticks and stones, the two men made it down to the floor where they found a trip wire. Stepping over the wire, they crept around a corner and gasped.

The next room was a storehouse of blasters and munitions. Plastic pallets lined the floor, and metal shelv-

ing covered the walls, every inch of the depot packed
with mil supplies: combat boots, vacuum-packed fatigues in clear plastic bags, web holsters, ammo, grens,
a pile of canvas satchels marked C-4 and a row of plastic tubes of unknown function. In the corner, a dusty
canvas sheet was draped over something large and irregularly shaped.

"Rapid-fires!" Rogan snorted in delight, taking an
M-16 assault rifle down from a wall rack. "She's packed
with gel, but looks in perfect shape!"

Already at the pallets of grens, Stirling was checking over the explosive charges for any signs of rust or
corrosion. But they seemed to be in the same perfect
condition as everything else. As if the cache had only
been filled a few days ago. That stirred a dark suspicion
at the back of his mind, but how anybody giving them
a fortune in blasters could be a bad thing he had no idea.
But instincts honed in a hundred battles told him this
whole cache was some sort of clever trap. Stirling just
wasn't sure who it was set to ace.

"LAWS!" Rogan laughed, lifting one of the plastic
tubes. "These are fire rockets that fly farther than arrows
and are hot like a dozen bombs!"

Easing down the hammers on his double-barrel, Stirling gave a low whistle. "A man could take over a ville
with this lot," he said in a carefully measured tone.

As if sensing trouble, Rogan turned. "You saved my
ass," he said bluntly, "and I gave Baron O'Connor my
word. Never meant much before, but it does to *you*." He
said the last word strongly, thrusting out a finger. "I
want this stuff so I can chill Delphi, then we give the
rest to the baron. Got no interest in becoming one myself. Savvy?"

"Natch," Stirling said after a moment. Then he grinned. "So let's loot the place, amigo! With these sorts of blasters, Delphi is gonna be eating dirt by noon!"

"Fragging hope so," Rogan muttered darkly, going to the corner and yanking away the canvas sheet. "Mebbe this is a flame-thrower or a— Nuke me!"

With the soft sound of powerful hydraulics, the sec hunter droid slowly rose to its full height and took a single step toward the startled men, the thick steel arms extending to proffer the spinning metal blades.

Chapter Nineteen

The smoke slowly faded into the distance behind the companions as their battered war wag lumbered along the rolling hillside. Evening was darkening the world before they reached flat ground once more and stopped to refuel. The big barrels of diesel were tapped, the juice flowing into plastic buckets with a cloth stretched over them to filter out any dirt or debris that might have gotten mixed into the precious liquid.

"Watch for any flashes of light," Ryan warned, standing guard while Jak and Doc emptied the buckets into the rusty steel fuel tanks of the big rig. "Anything bright could be a war wag coming this way."

"Or a laser targeting us for a missile strike," Krysty added ominously, working the arming bolt on a Kalashnikov. Standing in the rear of the flatbed gave the woman much greater visibility, and she was keeping a close watch on the setting sun. That was the direction Delphi would attack from if possible, hiding his advance in the dying glare.

"If see, what do?" Jak asked, lowering the empty can to the ground and wiping a sheen of sweat from his brow.

"Do?" Mildred repeated. "If a contrail starts arcing into the sky, we jump ship and run like the blazes!"

"Thank you, Sister Mary Sunshine," Doc said sarcastically, an AK-47 resting in his hands.

"Even paranoids have enemies, Theophilus," Mildred said, then chuckled, keeping a tight grip on the Kalashnikov. It had a massively greater range than her ZKR target pistol, and while the scope was low power, it was better than nothing. Mikhail Kalashnikov had invented a damn fine weapon.

It was funny, the physician realized, back in her time this was the chosen weapon for the enemies of America: the Soviet Union, Vietcong, Arab terrorists, Colombian drug lords and the like, and here it was the protector of civilization. The irony would have been amusing if it wasn't so damn heartbreaking.

"Full," Ryan announced, tossing the empty fuel can over the splintery wooden armor of the flatbed. It landed with a hollow clatter on the corrugated floor. "Let's roll while we still have some daylight left."

"Miles to go before we sleep, eh, Doc?" J.B. said with a smile, trudging into the rear of the big rig.

"Indubitably, sir," Doc answered, stoically still on guard. "And as the poet so wisely added, we also have many promises to keep err we dare to sleep."

"Like acing Delphi," Jak noted grimly, flipping his jacket over a shoulder and climbing into the cab. It was his turn to drive, and he was looking forward to operating the big rig. Ever since he saw his first wag, a steam jenny powering a water pump, the albino teen had liked machines. He considered them to be just like blasters. Not good or bad. Just tools. It all depended on who was holding the controls.

After removing his jacket and setting it aside, Jak started the engine and ran a check over the controls while Doc got in the passenger seat to ride shotgun. The albino teen hunter knew everything had to be okay with the rig, or else Ryan or J.B. would have told him.

Doc saw the condition of the teenager, and wisely slipped off his own frock coat and folded it neatly on the front seat. Even though night was coming, the air was steadily getting warmer. The companions were approaching the Great Salt, a vast crystalline plain of sizzling desert and sun-baked rock where nothing grew but the body count.

Rumbling black smoke from the overhead exhaust pipes, Jak worked the gearshift and brake, and the Mack lurched into motion, starting across the barren flatlands and steadily building speed as they headed directly into the setting sun.

"Miles go before sleep," Jak said, shifting gears. "Know any other poems?"

"Certainly!" Doc said with a smile, the barrel of the Kalashnikov protruding out the open window. "I have every sonnet written by Shakespeare memorized! Along with most of Milton's 'Paradise Lost,' Dante's 'The Inferno,' the collected works of Walt Whitman, Emily Bronte, Alfred Lord Tennyson—"

"Anything *good?*" the teen interrupted, putting a lot of emphasis on the last word.

"But they're all excellent…" Doc started, sounding puzzled, then thoughtfully pursed his lips. "Ah, you mean ribald! Well, there is a most disrespectful limerick about a rather special fellow from Nantucket…"

"Heard it. Others?"

"Not really, no."

"Damn."

Settling into the monotony of long-distance travel, the two men turned their talk to battle plans for con-

fronting Delphi. Slowly the storm clouds followed the
sun over the horizon and the black velvet of night filled
the sky, the stars twinkling brightly around a low, bloodred moon. Around midnight, the companions stopped
for food and a bathroom break, and to pour the last of
the juice into the fuel tanks. The barrels were dead-
weight now, bone-dry empty. In less than a day, they
would be back on foot. In preparation for that, Mildred
and Krysty started making backpacks of food, while
J.B. and Ryan sorted through the collection of blasters,
taking only those in the best condition. There was a
minor excitement when a solie was found hidden under
a wooden box they had been using as a seat, but the
deadly little mutie was long dead from starvation. However, the knowledge that it had been living among them,
waiting for release to strike was rather disturbing. Stabbing it with his panga, Ryan flipped the corpse over the
side and cleaned the blade.

Just then, a soft hooting came from the darkness and
the companions scrambled to get back inside the war
wag. Hastily starting the engine, Jak drove away fast,
the headlights sweeping across a group of stickies for
only a second before they were left behind. The hoots
came louder for a minute as the muties gave chase, but
the sounds faded as the wag picked up speed. Soon
there was only the noise of the diesel and the hum of
the predark tires on the hard-packed sand.

"At least they weren't holding any weps," Ryan
stated, easing the safety back on his SIG-Sauer and holstering the blaster.

"Thank Gaia for that." Krysty sighed, her hair flexing as if anxious. "That's something I never want to see
again."

"Another good reason to chill that damn cyborg," Mildred muttered in unaccustomed anger. "The world is quite screwed up enough as it is without his insanity to help things along!"

"I zero that," J.B. stated, releasing the pistol-grip safety on his 9 mm Uzi blaster. "The Trader always said that if something wasn't broke, then don't try to fix it!"

"Amen to that, brother!"

Soon there was the faint smell of salt in the air, waxing and waning with every tuft of the breeze. But the smell got steadily stronger as the ground changed from stubby grassland to sandy barrens and finally into a desert. The companions pulled neckerchiefs around their mouths to keep out the loose windblown salt. The granules stung their eyes, but there was nothing they could do about that, so it was ignored like so many of life's small pains.

"This is it, the start of the Great Salt," J.B. said, resting his folded arms on the top plank of the splintery wall. "Dark night, we haven't been here since…" He paused to frown.

"Not since we last tangled with Delphi," Ryan finished. "Yeah, I know. What the frag is it about this particular slice of hell that keeps drawing us back again and again?"

"Just coincidence. There isn't anything special about it," Mildred declared firmly. "After all, this is just desert, miles upon miles of hot, dry, sandy nothing."

"Mebbe," the one-eyed man muttered uneasily. "But it does make me wonder sometimes."

"Anything look familiar, lover?" Krysty asked, scanning the plains and dunes around them. The heavy tires of the wag were kicking up a huge dust cloud. In the daylight, they'd be visible for miles. Hopefully, the same would be true for Delphi.

"Familiar? No, rocks are rocks," Ryan replied. "There's nothing special about anything in the Great Salt, and it's been a long time."

"I seem to recall that we had just left some partially melted ruins and were trying to reach the mountains when the stickies attacked," J.B. said, stroking his chin. "We were near a gorge…an arroyo? No, it was a cliff overlooking a huge green lake…."

Studying the ground, Ryan felt foolish looking for the tire tracks of War Wag One. But that had been many years ago. The one-eyed man frowned in concentration. *But I've been here long before our encounter with Delphi,* he realized, feeling the years slip away. *I rode this sand with a Colt on my hip, and my missing eye still giving me headaches just before a rain storm.*

With a squeal of brakes, the war wag came to an abrupt halt that almost threw the companions to the floor. After a moment, they recovered and looked over the plank wall to see that the Mack was stopped near the edge of a cliff. Dully illuminated by the bloated moon was a vast shimmering expanse of gray that stretched outward from the cliff for miles.

"We're here," Ryan said, feeling an odd surge of excitement in his stomach. "Bad Water Lake."

"Can't see a thing. Jak, ace the lights!" Doc commanded.

Obediently the headlights went out and darkness covered the land. It took several minutes for their sight to adjust to the gloom, then Ryan went to the rear of the flatbed to unbolt the hatch and hop to the ground.

Walking carefully to the edge of the cliff, the companions kept their blasters at hand as they stood facing the huge lake. Long minutes passed, and there was only the sound of the wind and the ticking of the cooling engine block. Nobody spoke as they studied the seemingly endless expanse of gray. There was no reflection of the moonlight on the waves, so there was obviously something covering the water, chems mebbe, or scum.

We've seen similar things before in the Oarks, and Pacific, Mildred noted, crossing her arms. Once, very long ago, Bad Water Lake had been called Lake Powell. She caught a special about it once on the Travel Channel. Built to power some hydroelectric dam whose name she couldn't recall, Lake Powell was one of the biggest reservoirs in predark America, and one of the largest in the world. The rough and craggy shoreline was longer than the entire west coat of North America from Alaska to Mexico. There had been several attempts to stock the artificial lake with fish, and they'd all failed until somebody got wise and seeded the lake with plant life first for the fish to eat. Then the lake had become a sportsman's paradise. But that was before skydark.

Now, a cliff extended along the lake like the wall of a ville, impossible to traverse. Here and there were broken canyons, deep recesses where the cliff crumbled down to the shore of the lake, offering limited access. The rock formations were beautiful, rising and flowing along the shores as if formed by the hands of a loving sculpter. Gigantic boulders were perched miraculously on top of small peaks, and a soft wind whistled through arroyos as if they had been carved to become musical instruments. Dotting the distant shoreline were the hulking wrecks of houseboats, huge vessels, two, three stories high, the gold trim and silver brightwork still shiny in the Utah sun. And covering everything was a thick layer of green scum that looked as hospitable as an open grave.

"So have the mighty fallen. This had been a playground for millionaires in my time," Mildred said, resting both arms on the railing. "They all tried to build fancier boats than their neighbors, the vessels soon becoming ridiculously expensive. Several of them were worth millions of dollars...a baron's ransom," she deftly translated for the others. "They had jets instead of propellers, plasma-screen televisions, fireplaces, wine cellars, heliports, everything you could possibly think of, and then some."

"Then the war hit," Ryan said in a tolerant voice. "These millionaires probably turned against each other for the last supplies of fuel and food."

The physician shrugged. "Some would have had some weapons on board in case of thieves or pirates. It was rare, very rare, but it did happen sometimes."

"And so their Bacchanalian paradise ended like this," Doc intoned dourly. "To become a sargasso of death and destruction. The damn fools probably had enough to start a proper ville, and live in safety, but no, they each wanted it all, a thousand little barons fighting over the last few scraps of civilization until they destroyed themselves."

"Pride goes before a fall."

"As does stupidity, madam," Doc growled, the cool wind ruffling his silvery hair. "And as the good book suggests, I do not suffer fools gladly."

"Corinthians 11:19," Mildred replied, settling the matter.

"Hey, what there?" Jak asked, pointing.

Everybody turned in that direction. Far off in the distance was a large block shape sitting motionless in the gently rippling sea of gray.

Pulling out the longeyes, Ryan extended the Navy telescope to its full three feet and studied the scummy lake until finding a sandy island located in a small cove. Son of a bitch, there it was, exactly as he remembered. A couple dozen adobe buildings clustered around an open plaza. Ryan thought the ville had been on shore, but there it was, smack on the island. He had to have gotten lost tumbling off the cliff. This was the ville from his dreams.

No, this place was real. I have been there and walked those streets! Ryan frowned. Then a split tick later, I awoke miles away.

"Any islands here from your time, Millie?" J.B. asked, adjusting the position of the wire-rimmed glasses on his nose.

"No, this is something new," the physician stated, taking hold of the canvas strap of her med kit. Clearly, from the rock formations, the water level of Lake Powel had lowered over the intervening century. But enough to form an island? The land mass would have had to be only a dozen or so feet below the surface.

In spite of the weak moonlight, the one-eyed man could still make out a lot of the features of the little ville. It was surrounded by sand dunes set so perfectly around the adobe buildings they were obviously fakes. The streets were empty, devoid of wags, carts of any kind. The only movement came from some torn curtains fluttering in the evening breeze. A large Yucca tree grew inside a broken house, the branches going out the windows, the roof seriously off-kilter. Not a damn soul was in sight. No sec men or civilians. Not even a horse, dog or chicken was visible. Just a couple of fat Gila lizards lounging near some cactus plants. Forked red tongues lolled from the open jaws, and the rainbow-speckled hides of the lizards glinted brightly in the moonlight as if they were made of polished metal.

"Easy swim to island. Any sharks?" J.B. asked, scowling at the featureless gray expanse.

"No, just game fish," Mildred replied. "Nothing dangerous that would frighten the tourists like pike, or barracuda. Much less a great white!"

Just then, something broke the surface of the lake, causing a low swell to rise and move across the water for a long distance, then disappeared into its depths once more.

"Then again, I could be wrong," Mildred relented sagely, rubbing the back of her neck.

"Don't…don't I know this place?" Doc asked so softly the words were almost lost in the breeze.

That made Ryan pause and lower the Navy telescope. Those were almost the exact same words the old man had said when they'd met for the first time. Suddenly the one-eyed man had the feeling that huge pieces of the puzzle about skydark and the redoubts were moving closer together, almost near enough for him to get a glimpse of what was actually happening….

Squinting hard, Krysty suddenly pointed. "What's that?"

Bright lights suddenly appeared across the bay.

Moving fast, the companions dropped flat to the ground, drawing their blasters and clicking off safeties.

Adjusting the focus on the scope of his Steyr, Ryan swung back and forth in gentle arcs until locating the array of lights.

"Wags," he whispered unnecessarily, knowing the distance was far too great for the sound of a voice to carry. It would probably take a blaster shot a second to get there, if it could reach that far.

"How many?" J.B. demanded, wiggling his glasses for a better view. But it was hopeless. To him, the lights were merely bright smeary blobs.

"Four sets of headlights," Ryan reported, sucking a hollow tooth. Then he got them in focus. Shitfire, those were LAV 25 armored personnel carriers. Two of them had 20 mm Vulcan miniguns mounted on top, while the others had something else, but he wasn't sure what they were. The hulls were camou-colored, the splotches of green, red and brown dotted with gray smears from soft lead bullets ricocheting off the resilient predark armor. All of the machines were equipped with tires and treads, making them able to drive on land or across water. Suddenly that island didn't seem so distant or unreachable.

"Whoever these folks are, they riding in LAVs," Ryan stated bluntly. "Two with a Vulcan, and two with what looks like…" There was a bright flash of red and orange. "Yeah, they're flame-throwers. A screamwing attacked and they fried it in flight."

"Damn good shooting," Mildred praised in a growl. "This has gotta be Delphi."

"Makes sense."

"Gaia, we have no chance against four of those predark war wags," Krysty stated bluntly. "Remember those electric motorcycles Delphi gave the Rogan brothers to try and ace us? If these are mil versions of anything like those, I say we scrub this recce and leave."

"I agree," J.B. said, the words tasting like ash in his mouth. "We are outclassed and outgunned. I'd go up against one, or even two of them, but four…" The man didn't finish the statement. He really didn't have to.

Infuriated, Ryan was forced to agree and started to say so when door opened in the rear of the armored wags and people climbed out and into the light. There was a score of men in matching camou jumpsuits, along with a busty blond woman carrying several blasters. She seemed to be in charge; everybody jumped when she pointed at something. Then a thin man stepped out of the crowd and walked to the very edge of the cliff to stare down at the island.

Cold adrenaline flooded Ryan at the sight. The fellow was tall and thin, with blond hair plastered against his head. His clothing was different from the others', a smooth tan in color clear. A holstered blaster at his hip, and there was some sort of glass, or crystal rod, tucked into a shoulder holster. Walking along the precipice, the man moved with a slight limp, then he turned away from the others and raised a hand and studied the glowing palm in private.

"Delphi," Ryan whispered, putting a wealth of raw emotion into the single word. Working the arming bolt of the Steyr, the Deathlands warrior set the crosshairs directly on the chest of the hated cyborg. The wind was puffing from the left, which wasn't good, but he could compensate. The range was extreme, but he'd once aced an enemy even farther away. One pull of the trigger and it was all over. Doc would be free, and the danger ended. The coldhearts would fight among themselves over control of the LAVs, probably destroying the machines and one another. It couldn't be better. Then I'd be free to recce the blasted island, Ryan thought.

Pulling in a long breath, he held it for a moment, then

stroked the trigger. The muzzle-flash was still visible when he tracked the longblaster to the left, where the wounded man would fall, and he fired again, then shifted to the right and fired twice more.

The shots were executed swiftly, and Ryan rode out the recoil of the last shot as the first 7.62 mm hollow-point round arrived like silent thunder. Doubling over in pain, the cyborg grabbed his stomach as blood gushed from the hideous wound. Stumbling to the left, Delphi recoiled as the next rounds arrived, but there was no blood, and he didn't seem affected in any way.

That was when Ryan saw two black blobs hovering in the air just in front of the cyborg, and instinctively understood those were his bullets. Fireblast, the bastard had turned on his force field! the one-eyed man thought.

Slowly straightening, Delphi removed his hands from the bloody cloth, apparently undamaged, and brushed away the bullets hovering in front of him like flies stuck in amber.

The big blonde and the other uniformed sec man were running around in confusion, firing their BAR longblasters at nothing in particular. Swinging his head back and forth like a droid scanning for targets, Delphi suddenly paused and looked directly at Ryan far across the midnight bay, and smiled.

The sight was unnerving, but Ryan fired two more rounds directly into cyborg's face, the 7.62 mm slugs slamming to a dead stop inches away from his grinning visage.

Delphi shouted something over a shoulder, and the two war wags with cannons on top began to spit flames.

Bursting into action, the companions rose to race away from the edge of the cliff, but the rain of 20 mm shells arrived a heartbeat later and the ground erupted in powerful explosions. Salty dust filled the air as a section of the cliff broke away with Ryan yards away from safety.

"Gaia, no!" Krysty screamed, advancing a step. But there was no reply from within the swirling dust cloud.

Chapter Twenty

From within the moonlit cloud, a hand raised into view and grabbed hold of the sawgrass. As they clenched into a fist, blood seeped from between calloused fingers as Ryan pulled himself over the precipice and got an elbow onto solid ground.

Finished reloading, the 20 mm miniguns began to hammer away once more as the rest of the companions rushed forward to grab the one-eyed man and haul him away from the crumbling edge. Scrambling to his feet, Ryan charged for the war wag a second before the shells arrived, the barrage of detonations throwing up gouts of flame and creating a dense swirling cloud of dirt and salt.

Taking refuge behind the war wag, the companions heard a low rumble and another section of the weakened cliff broke away to plummet to the shore in a stentorian cascade. After a few minutes, the incoming fusillade of shells stopped and an eerie silence covered the land. There was only the panting of the companions and the soft pattering of loose rocks tumbling off the cliff to the shore below.

"Dark night, that was close." J.B. exhaled, wiping his face with the back of a gloved hand. "Too damn close for my taste!"

"Well, I wasn't going over a second time." Ryan

coughed, then hocked and spit brown onto the rocks. "That was for nuking sure!"

"Now what?" Jak asked in real concern, hefting his Kalashnikov rapid-fire. "Blasters chew Mack apart when get close!"

"And there's no damn cover to hide behind!" Krysty cursed. Each of the companions was coated in grainy white, looking like something that escaped from a shallow grave.

"Doesn't matter if we run or stay to fight," Doc rumbled darkly. "In just a few moments, we shall be in plain sight."

"Which leaves us only one choice," Ryan declared grimly, pulling a butane lighter from his coat pocket.

THE SOUND OF ENGINES filled the air, constantly punctuated by random blasterfire as the four predark war wags rolled along the edge of the cliff. Oddly, the dust cloud located where the outlanders had been was thicker than ever, the grayish white of the salty sand rapidly becoming an impenetrable brown.

"I don't like this," Delphi muttered, squinting at the thickening clouds. "Full stop!"

"And hit the headlights," Cotton added grimly, looking suspiciously through the windshield. Between the airborne salt and smoke it was impossible to see a thing in the night. Visibility was less than twenty paces.

"Sure thing, Chief," Jeffery said, braking the lead war wag to a full stop and pulling out a switch on the dashboard.

Instantly, four sets of brilliant beams stabbed out into the thickening fumes. There were only vague shapes shifting in the dark cloud, then flames rose high, adding a bright halo of illumination that silhouetted what remained of the big Mack rig and wooden flatbed.

"Holy nuking hell, their wag is on fire!" Jeffery shouted in delight. "No chance of the bastards getting away now!"

"Mutie shit, it's a trick!" Cotton growled, grabbing the mike from the ceiling. "All wags, triple red! This is an ambush! Repeat, this is a—"

But that was as far as the woman got before the LAV 25 to their left violently detonated, a staggering fireball expanding from within in a titanic roar. Broken pieces of the armored chassis and bloody chunks of flesh slammed into the other three wags, denting one and smashing the front windshield of another.

As the wag was buffeted by the concussion, Delphi suddenly realized what had happened. Ryan and the others couldn't run, or hide, so they'd set their own wag on fire to create a protective smoke screen in order to ambush the convoy. The plan was audacious, almost insane, but it had worked, and in a single instant the cyborg had lost a quarter of his fighting forces.

Enjoy your victory, Ryan. It's your last, Delphi railed silently.

"Open fire!" he bellowed into his hand, the words bizarrely echoing throughout the three remaining predark wags.

It took only a heartbeat for the gunners to unlimber their blasters, and soon crisscrossing streams of 20 mm shells were randomly hammering the murky ground, throwing more dirt and salt into the air, making it even more difficult to see. Jeffery cut loose with the flamethrower, the hissing column of fire licking across the landscape in hellish fury.

Suddenly the burning wooden wag lurched into motion and charged forward to ram into a LAV 25. The front grille of the Mack crumbled from the impact, the lightweight metal and chrome doing no damage to the heavy steel-alloy armor of the predark war machine. But the big diesel engine surged with power, the burning tires dug into the loose soil and the Mack began forcing the LAV sideways, heading directly for the cliff.

"Ace the driver!" Delphi screamed, pulling out his crystal wand and pointing it at the flame-enshrouded cab. But there was nobody in sight behind the wheel. Bastards had to have rigged it somehow, the cyborg guessed, tightening the grip on his weapons. Jammed a stick on the gas pedal and lashed down the steering wheel. Not a bad trick, but surely the LAV could easily escape such a crude trap!

Black smoke gushing from the louvered exhaust ports, the LAV lurched into action, trying to angle away from the ragged cliff. But the smashed chassis of the Mack was tangled on the armor frame of the LAV, and the battling machines began to curve into the dense cloud and out of sight.

"Harrison, shoot the outlander wag with your cannon!" Delphi yelled into his glowing hand. "Blast yourself free!"

"No need, chief!" the trooper shouted over the sound of grinding gear. "I can get us free!"

"That was an order!" Cotton bellowed, hunched over as if charging into a fight. "Use the fragging cannon!"

"Not going to waste brass for a lousy… Nuking hell!"

As Delphi switched his eyes to the ultraviolet spectrum, the cloud dramatically thinned and he clearly saw the struggling LAV and Mack truck go over the edge.

"Harrison, talk to me!" Cotton demanded, fearing the worst. "Harry!" But there was only silence.

"It's too late," Delphi said simply, his words almost a whisper.

Piercing screams came from the ceiling speaker of the control room, closely followed by a deafening series of metallic crunches, shattering glass, indescribable banging, clanging, then a watery splash and silence.

Stunned beyond words, Delphi could only stare at the empty section of cliff. It was incredible! Ryan and his people had taken out two of his armored personnel carriers in only a few minutes! How was that possible? Just for a second, the cyborg tasted fear, then he shrugged off the useless emotion.

If I want to live, think fast, and move faster, Delphi rationalized. This was it, chilling time. No more finesse or clever plans. Just bare-knuckle bloodletting. Get clear of the smoke, establish a new firebase, lay down suppression fire, bracket the targets, then kill them all.

"Wags, retreat at full speed!" Delphi commanded into his hand. "Don't turn around, just move!"

"Get the fuck out of this cloud, people," Cotton roared into the mike, "or we're shit in a can!"

Working the controls, Jeffery didn't even bother to reply as he threw the transmission into Reverse and tromped on the gas pedal. With a low rumble, the LAV's engine engaged and the mil wag started moving swiftly away from the murky cliff. But it traveled only a few yards before something bounced off the windshield, then exploded, hard shrapnel peppering the armored hull. A thin crack appeared in the predark plastic and bitter smoke began to seep into the control room.

Grabbing Cotton, Delphi hauled the sec woman to

the floor as two more grens hit the windshield and violently detonated. The resilient mil plastic shattered into a million jagged pieces as it blew into the vehicle, cutting Jeffery into shreds, his death cry lost in the sound of the razor-sharp debris ricocheting off the interior walls, gunracks and seats.

The shards were still falling as Dephi and Cotton crawled along the short passage out of the control room and to the rear cargo area. There were four other troopers standing near the exit hatch with longblasters in their hands, unsure of what to do.

Still in gear, the LAV continued to roll along backward, without direction. Every bounce shook the damaged transport, and loose items rolled around the corrugated floor to get dangerously underfoot. Strapped into position, the side gunners hung limply in their chairs, red blood dribbling from their tattered clothing, pointed pieces of windshield sparkling from the countless small cuts covering their gory bodies.

"Grab whatever you can, boys," Cotton ordered, taking a mixed bag of ammo and grens from a peg on the wall. "These nuke-suckers really screwed the mutie when they tangled with us!" There was a trickle of warmth on her cheek, but the sec woman stoically ignored the minor wound as she loaded a clip of tracer brass into a BAR.

Wordlessly, the men nodded and started to fill their pockets with brass and grens.

"Stay low, and only shoot when you clearly see the outlanders," Delphi commanded. "I don't want any of my people aced by friendly fire." Actually, he didn't give a damn if they died. He just did not want them getting in the way when he went after Ryan and Tanner. When this was over, he'd chill everybody.

As Cotton and the other troopers got ready, Delphi yanked a panel off the wall, exposing a series of glowing buttons. "Ready?" he asked.

Taking a deep breath, Cotton worked an arming bolt. "Rock and roll, chief."

Pressing the buttons in order, there was a series of dull thuds from the corrugated floor, and a section slid aside to reveal sandy ground streaming past the opening. Without a pause, the cyborg dropped through to hit the dirt and go flat. A moment later, Cotton dropped from the LAV, followed by the others in tight formation. Salty dust filled the air, and it was hard to see clearly, but a moment later, the shadow of the LAV 25 was gone and they were clearly bathed in the bright halogen headlights.

Frantically, Delphi and Cotton dived to the side, but the others moved too slow and blasterfire tore three of them apart before they could get out of the lethal illumination.

Triggering their Browning Automatic Rifles in tribursts, the troopers hammered the swirling cloud with heavy rounds. But there was no answering cry of pain to announce a hit.

Listening hard for any sound of the hated outlanders, Delphi watched the LAV 25 veer off randomly to slam into a dune. The rear hoisted upward and the wheels left the ground. Stuck in place, the machine continued to run, the front wheels starting to dig down into the crystalline soil, throwing more salt and sand into the air.

Moving away from the shuddering vehicle, Delphi saw the cliff had collapsed completely to form a sort of rough steps leading down to the polluted lake. At least

I have an avenue of escape if necessary, the cyborg noted bitterly, flexing his hand. The situation was quickly getting out of his control, and a wise man knew when it was time to go. Not yet. He still had a lot of chilling to do first. But soon.

Struggling to shove a fresh clip of brass into the open breech of his longblaster, Caruthers flinched and dropped the weapon to grab his throat. Blood was spurting out in pulsating arcs, a leaf-shaped throwing blade buried to the hilt in the side of his neck. As the dying man toppled to the ground, Delphi calculated the angle of trajectory to throw the blade and sent a sizzling ray from the crystal rod in that direction, followed by a burst of fléchettes from the needler. If he hit anybody, there was no way to tell. How had this battle turned so fast against him? The convoy had four armored vehicles to Ryan's old piece of homemade junk, and yet the outlanders were winning! It was impossible! Intolerable! The cyborg scowled. He should have been traveling with a hundred hunters, instead of leaving them to guard the redoubt. Those would have done the job, easily slaying Tanner and the others.

Then a fiery flower blossomed in the cloud. Delphi recognized it as the muzzle-flash of a Kalashnikov and instantly raised his force field. The hail of hardball rounds loudly zinged off the immaterial barrier, more coming from another direction in the night, and then still more. He replied with the needler and laser, only realizing at the last second that the bright energy beam was how they were finding him. Reluctantly, he sheathed the rod and flexed his hand to activate the malfunctioning Educator. It hummed to life inside his flesh, and he moved it in a slow arc, blindly trying for

a chill. A gren came falling from above to detonate over
the cyborg, the hot shrapnel churning the ground around
his shield but completely failing to penetrate.

"Here I am, Tanner!" Delphi shouted. "Come and get
me!" But the only reply was another thrown knife, two
grens and more blasterfire.

Murky figures moved toward the trapped wag and
the last LAV 25 unleashed a shuttering stream of 20 mm
shells to pepper the ground and sloping dune. An an-
guished cry told of a hit, but Cotton grimaced when she
recognized the voice as Mannheim's. Shitfire, another
man lost! The trooper tried to kept mental count of the
aced, but it was hard to think. The noise of the furious
battle was becoming deafening. Hot lead was flying in
every direction. Grens detonated louder than thunder,
and the 20 mm blaster constantly burped short bursts
into the fray. But then Cotton detected a new sound
among the chaos, low and dull, almost mechanical. And
it was coming straight toward her.

Chapter Twenty-One

As Cotton swung up the BAR, she pulled out the sawed-off 12-gauge and started forward grimly. The smoky cloud was starting to thin, and the woman scowled at the unexpected sight of two men on horseback riding toward the fight. For a single moment, Cotton thought they might be coldhearts, but then she saw that their clothing matched and that they were packing rapid-fires. They had to be sec men! But where had they come from? There wasn't a ville around for a hundred miles! But it didn't really matter. If they weren't her men, they had to be chilled. That was a lock.

Staying low, Cotton tried to get a bead on the new-comers when something metallic came into view trailing after the two big men. Nuking hell, she thought, it was a predark machine of some sort! The large cylindrical body was made of shiny steel, and there were armored treads underneath, rocketing the thing forward almost as fast as a horse could run. Which meant it was a lot quicker than any person on foot. There was a smooth dome on top bristling with antennae, and the thing sported two crazy red eyes that spun around in every direction. Flexing metal arms extended from the sides, each of them tipped with spinning buzz saws.

"Mother of night, a sec hunter droid!" Delphi gasped, firing the HK needler and the laser at the war machine.

The sizzling red beam struck the droid and seemed to be absorbed, but the stainless-steel fléchettes bounced off wildly, some of them coming back to impact the cyborg's shield. In the gloom, a distant figure cried out, his intestines slithering out of a tattered belly like a tangle of oily snakes. Focusing on the fellow, Delphi cursed when he saw it wasn't Tanner or Ryan.

Just then, two horseback riders galloped past the cyborg, firing M-16 assault rifles at point-blank range. But the 5.56 mm hardball rounds rebounded harmlessly from his force field, and he shot one of them in the arm with his laser, the other with the needler, before they vanished into the billowing cloud. How bizarre, the cyborg thought. One of them resembled Edward Rogan. But that was impossible. The Rogan brothers had all been chilled and buried long ago. He paused. Or had they? Quickly, the cyborg set the laser to full-power, minimum aperture, and swept the battlefield, trying for a quick chill.

Incoming lead and steel pounded the shield from several directions, and another rain of grens was augmented by a large homemade pipe bomb. The combined detonation rocked the cyborg, almost making him fall, then inspiration hit, and Delphi reached out with his EM implants to seize control of the droid and turn it against the outlanders. But try as he might, there was no answering signal from the droid. It spun around and charged directly for him, as if locked on to his broadcast.

Standing his ground, Delphi stabbed out with the laser and needler, the duel weapons savaging the droid, removing an arm and melting an eye. But the machine kept coming, as unstoppable as the rising moon.

"The metal thing is after the chief!" a trooper bellowed, swinging up his BAR and firing a tri-burst at the machine. "Chill the fucker!" The hail of hot lead hit the chrome dome, doing scant damage. Then the machine saw the man, the twin saw swinging in opposite directions. They heard the horrible sound of steel cutting flesh. The trooper shrieked for a brief moment, then blood sprayed high as he fell to the ground in ragged pieces.

"Nuke-sucker aced Jimmy!" Cotton yelled. "Light it up!"

The servo motors of the LAV 25 whined into life as the 20 mm Vulcan swiveled on top of the war wag and then the blaster started vomiting flame. The shells hit the ground near the machine, throwing out gouts of sand. Nimbly, the droid dodged to the side, then grabbed the predark APC in a deadly hug. Sparks flew like fireworks as the spinning blades dug into the steel armor, slowing chewing a path inside the machine. Rounds poured from the blasterports, the muzzle-flames stabbing outward, but the angle was wrong and the BAR longblasters couldn't get a bead on the attacking droid.

Withdrawing the blades, the droid wrapped its arms around the barrel of the Vulcan minigun and yanked the rapid-fire free to the sound of screeching metal. The sec man operating the weapon screamed as his hand came away minus fingers, life pumping from the ragged nubbins of flesh. Tossing away the minigun, the droid plunged the buzz saws through the unfortunate man.

Lurching into action at the ghastly sight, Cotton sprinted back to the LAV trapped against the dune. Clambering inside, she activated the flame-thrower and aimed the blazing column of jellied fuel at the sec hunter droid and fired. Covered in flames, the droid reached out to grab the fluted nozzle of the weapon and crush it tight. From inside the wag there came a rattling hiss, then the seals blew and the interior of the wag was flooded with burning chems. Cotton screamed briefly, then the fuel tanks ignited and the wag detonated along with the ample stores of munitions, the double explosion ripping the droid apart, the sparkling debris flying through the cloudy air along with the tattered norm counterparts.

The rain of destruction fell across the churned ground as a horse ran past Delphi without a rider, and the cyborg knew the two newcomers were now on foot. Fools. Trying to lure them close, the cyborg trained the Educator on a galloping horse. Galvanized as if hit by lightning, the animal went stiff, the muscular body shaking all over. Foam began to drip from its mouth, and its legs buckled as the stallion toppled over to commence jerking irregularly, some long plastic tubes sticking out of the saddle bags breaking apart and spilling out pieces of predark rockets. Turning off the device, Delphi saw the animal go limp as drops of red blood started to bead its hide.

"Hear that, Tanner?" The cyborg laughed. "You're next, old man! And then I'll go back in time to pleasure your wife!"

But the outrageous lie yielded no results. Either Doc Tanner had not heard the threat, or he didn't believe it, which was much more likely. A blind fury boiled within the cyborg. Cotton was chilled, the LAVs were destroyed, time to end this now!

Expanding his force field to the maximum range,

Delphi moved relentlessly through the swirling fumes, triggering his weapons at anything that moved, no longer caring if he aced some of his own troops.

KEEPING THE SLAB OF BROKEN plank in front as a shield, Ryan stayed low and fired the Kalashnikov at the small area of clean air that moved within the swirling, acrid fumes of the burning wag and tires. The damn cyborg never realized that the force field that protected him also made him easy to spot. The plan had been to try to lure Delphi to the cliff and throw him into the lake. Doc had said that his force field stopped working when it got wet. But the cyborg was crafty and was keeping as far away from the crumbling edge as possible.

A wounded trooper lunged for Ryan and he fired the AK-47, blowing away his throat. As the corpse sagged to the ground, the twitching hand triggered the BAR, a trio of rounds hitting the plank and slamming it out of Ryan's grip. The wood went airborne and disappeared in a new volume of smoke from the three burning LAVs. Fireblast!

Working the bolt on the Kalashnikov to clear a brass jammed in the ejector port, Ryan found the clip empty and tossed the rapid-fire away. That had been the last reload. Now he was down to the Steyr, SIG-Sauer, a few grens and the panga.

A heated barrage of rounds told him that somebody had more ammo for their BAR, and Ryan stayed low as he moved across the sandy ground. His eye was stinging badly from the airborne salt, but there was nothing he could do about that right then except ignore the pain. Pieces of smoldering metal and steaming chunks of bodies lay everywhere, spent brass lying golden among the silvery grains of salt and sand.

The telltale boom of the LeMat proclaimed that Doc had also run out of brass for the predark AK-47. Then the Uzi chattered, a brief stutter of flame pinpointing the location of J.B. in the smoke. A red beam lanced across the battleground toward the Armorer, and he ducked, barely in time. Breaking into a full run, Ryan pulled out the panga. Come on, feeb, use that las just once more time, Ryan urged silently.

A dark shape rose from behind a chilled horse and steel flashed mirror bright as a trooper stabbed at Ryan with a BAR, the bayonet gleaming like polished death. The bayonet knocked the Steyr aside, and the one-eyed man swung the panga to slice his attacker across the chest. Lurching away, the trooper tried to aim the long-blaster, but seemed unable to find Ryan even though the Deathlands warrior was only a yard away. Attempting to pull the trigger with shaking hands, the pale trooper staggered, drool flowing from his slack mouth.

Knocking aside the BAR, Ryan mercifully leveled the Steyr and shot the man in the forehead. Blood, brains and bone went flying.

The faceless corpse hugged the rifle like a child did a favorite toy for protection from the monsters in the night. Then a lambent energy beam stabbed out of the roiling smoke and hit the corpse. The clothing burst into flames, and Ryan jerked aside to throw a gren. It vanished into the gloom, and a few seconds later it detonated, the sound of the explosion mixed with a startled cry. Encouraged by that, Ryan prepared another gren and started forward, the Steyr leading the way.

THROWN BACKWARD by the explosion, Delphi hit the ground hard and struggled onto his feet just in time for a roaring giant to charge out of the smoke. The startled cyborg recognized Edward Rogan and immediately shot the huge man in the chest with both the needler and the laser. But as the body collapsed to the ground, Delphi saw the sizzling fuse dangling from the canvas satchel strapped to his back, along with the clearly printed words *U.S. Army, C-4 plastic explosive, demolition charge.*

Spinning around fast, Delphi tried to run when the world became solid white as the trip-hammer explosion engulfed him completely. Suddenly airborne, he seemed to float for a very long time through the moonlight before crashing onto the pebbled beach. The force field flared from the impact, but held, as strong as ever. Climbing to his feet, the jubilant cyborg laughed in triumph at the knowledge that he missed landing in the scummy water by less than a foot.

Glancing upward, Delphi saw Ryan and the companions standing on the cliff above, then a hail of dark objects flashed past the cyborg to splash into the polluted lake.

"Missed!" Delphi said with a sneer, raising the crystal rod to chill his adversaries when the barrage of grens and pipe bombs loudly detonated, throwing a foamy wave of dirty water over Delphi. Erupting into sparks, the force field visibly wavered and then vanished.

Horrified, the cyborg looked down at his dripping wet hands, then quickly aimed the laser just as the companions fired their assortment of blasters.

Pain tore through Delphi and his internal systems went into emergency function, closing off arteries and rerouting blood as microfilaments raced to close the gaping wounds in his chest and limbs. More grens hit the beach to roll into the lake, the explosions soaking him again and again, as he stumbled away, bleeding, unsure of where to go or what to do next. A LAW rocket streaked through the gloom, then a pipe bomb landed nearby. He kicked it away to bounce off a boulder and disappear into the thick green scum. The blast sent a column of steam and slime skyward, and he clumsily dodged the falling hail of hot filth, his strength returning with every beat of his artificial heart. The blood had stopped gushing from the bullet wounds, and his vision was clear once more. Breaking into a frantic run, the cyborg pelted along the pebble beach, thinking only of escape.

Bullets kicked up the stones along the shoreline, ricochets throwing out sparks as more grens detonated in the lake behind him. Only a faint spray reached Delphi, moistening his tattered clothing, washing away the red blood tinged with hints of yellow. His force field fluttered in response, struggling to come back online. Just a few more seconds and he would be safe. It flickered again, bright sparks dancing all around the cyborg. Yes, almost there!

Then something large fell from the sky, and Delphi instinctively ran away, trying to gain as much precious distance between him and it as possible. The thing hit the beach with a resounding thump, and he saw it was another satchel charge. The fools missed the lake entirely!

Then the awful truth hit Delphi one second before the twenty-four blocks of predark C-4 plas ex violently detonated. The satchel charge had been exactly on target.

Chaos ruled Delphi's mind as he was blown sideways to splash into the lake. Floundering in the mucky water, the cyborg sank to the bottom as his struggling force field dropped completely. But the depth was only a few yards. He still had a fighting chance!

Struggling to hold his breath, Delphi clawed for purchase on the smooth pebbles lining the shallow water, grabbing hold of something round and full of holes. Panicking at the thought of another gren, the cyborg illuminated his eyes and stared in mindless terror at the charred skull. There was just enough tattered flesh left for him to identify Edward Rogan, the teeth grinning evilly in the dappled water. Then it hit him. *Teeth in the water!*

Casting the horrid thing away, Delphi surged forward and broke the surface to desperately pull in a lungful of air. Brushing away the sodden hair from his face, the cyborg could not see anybody nearby, and he sloshed for the beach. Choppy waves were spreading out fast, and hazy gray smoke lingered over the turbulent water.

Lying on the shore were more pieces of Rogan, a boot with a foot inside, a bent machete and a gunbelt with an undamaged Webley still firmly in the holster. Excellent! Racing toward the beach, Delphi almost made it out of the water when he heard the sound of galloping hooves. Jerking toward the collapsed section of the cliff, Delphi saw two men riding a horse across the loose soil. Ryan and Tanner!

The cyborg grinned in delight. Excellent! Now he could chill the fools and take their horse for his escape. Raising his hand, Delphi aimed the Educator, and his hand flinched as a hole was blown clear through the palm. A rolling boom echoed from the cliff overhead, telling of a sniper, and pain racked Delphi as fat blue sparks started crawling over his flesh from a short-circuit. Mentally, the cyborg screamed for the autorepair systems to fix the device, but there was no response.

Staggering away from the shore, Delphi tried to raise his force field to no avail when something tightened around his leg. Looking down, the cyborg saw it was a slimy tentacle extending out of sight under the scummy waves. Other tentacles were wiggling along the bottom to haul away the scattered bits of Rogan. The fresh blood had to have attracted the attention of some underwater scavenger! Glancing at the Webley only yards away, Delphi attempted to break free of the undulating limb, but the grip was like iron. Thrusting his damaged hand into the water, he hoped the short-circuit might drive the mutie away, but the tentacle only tightened more, nearly crushing his leg, and began to inexorably pull him away from the shore and deeper into the toxic chem lake.

Reining in the wounded horse, Ryan and Doc jumped to the ground and advanced upon the cyborg, steadily firing their blasters. Lead plowed into the scummy water, blowing away small pieces of the cyborg. Hydraulic fluid and blood seeped from the punctures, staining the lake mottled colors.

"Wait!" Delphi yelled as the waves lapped at his chest. "Save me, and I'll tell you the secrets of the redoubts! I know it all! I know everything!"

Ignoring that plea, the two grim men continued to trigger their weapons as the tentacle bodily hauled Delphi back under the water and out of sight.

Turning on his eyes, the cyborg saw that the creature seemed to be composed of nothing but tentacles and a large sloppy mouth that opened and closed constantly. Fumbling for the decorative knife on his belt, Delphi unexpectedly felt the hard slaps of hot lead hit him again. Suddenly he understood that the outlanders were not trying to ace him, but to cripple him. Served to the lake mutie like tossing a dog a bone!

Madness overwhelmed the cyborg as his laboring lungs began to throb with the need for air. Then his internal systems came online, and flapping gills opened in his neck, brining new strength with a rush of oxygen. Redoubling his efforts to escape, Delphi slashed at the tentacle. Incredibly, the ropy limb withdrew, only to be replaced by a dozen more tentacles that wrapped tightly around his arms and legs, pinning the cyborg helpless. As if it were some ancient Kraken from predark myths, the aquatic mutie dragged the squirming Delphi into the shadowy depths of the lake and stuffed him whole into its gaping mouth.

Screaming curses, Delphi thrashed madly as a thousand tiny fangs pierced his flesh and hardened gums began to slowly grind, ripping away layer after layer of clothing, skin and muscle. Pain filled his world. Still alive and horribly conscious, Delphi began traveling down the putrid gullet as searing stomach acids washed over his helpless form as the cyborg entered a new type of hell.

Chapter Twenty-Two

"And so ends Delphi," Doc said, holstering the smoking LeMat. "I would have preferred to take his life personally, but nothing is perfect."

"Near enough." Ryan grunted, holstering the SIG-Sauer and sliding the Steyr off a shoulder to work the arming bolt. Patiently, he waited for the cyborg to rise again from the scummy waves. But after a few minutes, the man eased his stance and clicked on the safety.

"Satisfied, my dear Ryan?" Doc asked, arching an eyebrow.

"Near enough," the one-eyed man replied, almost smiling.

A clatter of loose stones from behind made the two men turn and grab for their blasters, but the noise only proved to be the rest of the companions clambering down the sloping embankment of loose salt and sandstone. Everybody seemed undamaged, except for Chief Stirling, who had a bloody arm stuffed into his shirt for support. A LAW rocket was strapped across his back, the launching tube cracked but still serviceable.

"That pays a lot of debts," the sec man boss stated, giving them a hard smile. "Never thought I'd see the day. When Rogan and I found that fragging droid in a cache of predark blasters, I thought I was on the last train west for sure." The man grinned. "Then the nuking thing gave a bow like we were barons and asked for orders."

"So you told it to come along, and help ace Delphi," Mildred guessed, hefting the med kit slung over her shoulder.

"Yep. Worked, too, although damned if I know why."

"How find?" Jak asked, his long hair billowing in the breeze.

"Doomie told us back in Two-Son."

"Thank Gaia for that," Krysty said, finishing reloading her S&W revolver and closing the cylinder.

"Yeah, good thing doomies are on our side," J.B. drawled, resting the Uzi on a shoulder. "Be a triple-bitch to fight an enemy who knew what you were going to do, even before you did!'

"Got that right," Stirling agreed, rubbing his arm.

"I can fix that," Mildred said, reaching into her med kit. "Only take a few minutes."

"Sounds good," the sec man replied, easing the limb from within his uniform. "It's going to be a long walk back to Two-Son without horses or wags."

"First, we have to recce that island," Ryan said, walking to the edge of the beach. Now that Delphi was gone, he couldn't take his sight off the place. So near. He was almost there. Adjusting his eye patch, Ryan noted that down here he could even see the white adobe building with the strange design above the doorway, and now he knew what the symbol stood for.

"Get ready, TITAN," the man whispered softly. "Here I come—"

There was a flash of bright light and a moment of disorientation.

As his vision cleared, Ryan blinked at the sight of

snow covering the landscape, reaching all the way to the craggy black mountains on the horizon, the snowcapped peaks and tors, challenging the heavens above. The sun was high overhead, and a shaggy goat stood on a nearby tor, chewing on some flowery weeds growing out of a small crevice. Fireblast, it happened again!

Hastily looking around, the Deathlands warrior was relieved to find the rest of the companions standing waist-deep in snow only a few yards away from the towering black doors of a redoubt.

"Dark night! What the fuck just happened?" J.B. blinked, startled. He removed his fedora to brush back his hair and jam the hat back on good and tight. "Must have been TITAN's defense mechanism. Mighty nice of them to send us here, rather than the moon."

"Where is here?" Jak asked with a scowl, trembling from the bitter cold. "Alaska?"

"Tell you in a sec," J.B. replied, tugging the minisextant out from under his sandy shirt.

"More important, where is Chief Stirling?" Doc asked, his words foggy in the cold air. Hastily, the old man began to button his damp coat.

"Probably back at Two-Son ville," Mildred guessed, stuffing her hands into pockets. "And I strongly suggest that we get our damp asses out of the cold before we all catch pneumonia and die."

"Well, I see no place else to go," Krysty observed dourly. Walking to the keypad, she tapped in the entry code. After the usual pause, the massive blast doors rumbled aside and a great exhalation of warm air rushed out to greet the companions.

"Okay, this is…Siberia," J.B. said slowly, then double-checked the figures. "Yep. We're smack in the middle of nuking Siberia, about a thousand miles from Moscow."

"You sure about that?" Mildred queried. "Why would there be a redoubt here?"

"Who knows?" the Armorer replied, tucking away the minisextant. "We've been in redoubts outside Deathlands before. Who knows why any of them were built."

"Siberia. The other side of the world," Mildred said in a soft voice that was almost a whisper. "You know, to anybody with brains, this would be seen as a warning to never trouble the folks on that island again."

"Guess so. Last time they sent me back to the Trader," Ryan added, studying the landscape. "This time, halfway around the globe. Brass will get you powder that the next time, we'll be aced. Chilled to the bone."

"So the next time, we get them first," J.B. said confidently, walking into the access tunnel. "Smash the island to drek, before getting close. We'll figure out something."

The companions hurried into the redoubt's access tunnel.

Stomping the snow off his shoes, Doc looked at the distant Russian mountains lost in somber contemplation. Cort Strasser was aced, as was Silas, and now Delphi. When would enough blood be spilled to pay his debt to the universe? When would sufficient lives be lost to redress the balance?

"When will I be allowed to go home!" Doc bellowed, shaking a fist at the morning sky. The shouted words echoed across the snowy field and down into the river valley, seeming to repeat forever. But if the universe heard, or cared, there was no reply.

With a sigh, Doc turned away from the barren wasteland and started into the foreign redoubt to rejoin his friends, the only real family he had anymore. A few moments later, Krysty keyed in another code and the titanic blast door closed with a hollow boom.

THE MOON WAS STILL HIGH in the nighttime sky when the green layer of scum covering Bad Water Lake started to ripple around the small island. Then, incredibly, the land mass began to slowly move away from the pebbled beach until it was in the middle of the lake, very far away from the dark shore.

Moments later, a dozen Krakens moved below the scum, creating low swells and they assumed positions around the island like sec men standing guard. As if compelled by a will of its own, the green scum expanded to fill in the ragged patches, and a strong wind blew in from the hills, throwing loose sand over everything on the cliffs.

Soon, every trace of the battle was erased as if the fight had never happened, and a thick silence settled over the huge artificial lake, undisturbed except for the sound of the low wind and the slap of the dirty waves against the rocks.

BACK IN TWO-SON VILLE, Edgar Franklin leaned against a low cinder-block wall and sipped warm beer while he watched the workmen toil in the ville's greenhouses. Safe behind the wall of glass, the thriving green plants seemed almost unnatural set amid the endless desolation that surrounded the walled city. In spite of himself, the cyborg was mildly amused. Not even the legendary Dante ever imagined a lush garden in the center of Hell.

Finishing off the ceramic mug of homemade brew, Franklin set it aside and started toward his room in the basement of the gaudy house. Thankfully, everything had gone according to plan, and the grand scheme of things was finally back on schedule. He had completed his assigned task, and Delphi was dead. In the morning, he was supposed to meet the baron, but instead, he would slip out of the ville at dawn and return to the redoubt, then jump back to his base and resume his regular duties. The traitor had been destroyed, but TITAN's bid for control of the Deathlands had only just begun.

Epilogue

Mildred's Journal

The light from the campfire was low and reddish, almost as if the world had been painted with blood. A warm breeze was blowing across the Great Salt, and Dr. Mildred Weyth was sipping a hot cup of coffee, the companions taking a much-needed rest. Under her anxious fingers was a small leather journal. She had found it in the redoubt and decided it would be perfect for a codex, a sort of catalog of all the useful information that she learned during their travels. She could also record a few observations.

Not anything I would ever need, Mildred noted, but something to help some future generation to stay alive and thrive. Even in these blighted days knowledge was power, often more useful than a loaded blaster.

Opening the journal, Mildred took out a scavenged predark pen, gathered her thoughts and carefully began to write.

For those who come after me… In this journal I will list all of the useful knowledge that I have gained over my long and bloody travels through this strange new world. For example, boiling excrement and mixing it with clean sand makes a perfectly good soil for growing plants.

She then drew a crude picture to show how window glass from predark houses and office buildings could be used to build greenhouses to keep off the acid rain. That started a new train of thought, and Mildred described how to make black powder, and how to convert that into the much more powerful gunpowder, and then how to make fulminating guncotton. It was tricky, but John had taught her how and now she could pass on that knowledge.

Lifting the pen from paper, she frowned. There was so much data, so much vital knowledge that she wanted to impart to future generations, but there was no way for her to list it in any kind of order. Things would simply be listed as they occurred to her. Random knowledge for a random world. Somehow, that seemed only proper.

Pine ville is located in western Colorado, north of the Great Salt. It is a peaceful ville with a fair baron. Do not be afraid to go there in times of trouble. But the sec men are tremendous fighters, so don't piss them off!

She paused again, feeling the warm breeze move her hair.

This is the third ville I have encountered with a rule by law, rather than the drunken whim of madmen. They are Front Royal in Virginia, Two-Son ville in New Mexico, New Mex, I suppose, just

below the Great Salt, and Pine ville. Slowly but
surely, a few people are carving out slices of
civilization from this savage wilderness. Seek
them out, there is strength in numbers, and use
this codex to aid the struggle for peace.

She paused again.
"Millie?"
With a jerk, the physician looked up and saw J.B.
running stiff fingers through his rumpled hair. "Some-
thing wrong?" she asked in concern.
"Nope, it's just your turn to get some sleep," he said
with a smile, taking his glasses out of a shirt pocket and
putting them on. "What are you writing?"
"Just a poem," Mildred lied, closing the journal and
cinching it tight with a leather strap.
"Dirty?" John asked hopefully.
"Now, why ever do you ask?" She laughed, rising to
kiss the man good-night.
The task took longer than expected, but nowhere
near as long as they both would have liked. Eventually,
Mildred left the man to his work. She didn't know why
she had lied to her lover about the journal, but in retrospect, it now seemed a wise precaution. She suspected
that her companions wouldn't approve of her writing
about the redoubts as the knowledge might be used
against them someday.
And that was correct, she admitted privately. This
codex could end up biting them all in the ass. But it was
a chance she would have to take. Her father would have
called it a moral imperative.
If I hide knowledge away like a baron did his guns
and food, hoarding it for my own personal use, then I'm

as guilty as the fools who destroyed the world, damning the innocent to lives of brutal hardships, needless toil and abject misery.

Was the book dangerous? Hell, yes. Was it necessary? Also, a resounding yes.

Mildred admitted to herself that most likely nobody would ever see the codex, much less find it useful. But Ryan had taught her to prepare for what an enemy could do, not what they might do. Hope for the best, plan for the worst. I'll add more as often as I can, until the book is full, she vowed.

The predark physician stood gazing at the starry sky, then looked into her soul. Somehow, there had to be a way to end the bloodshed and warfare, to return peace to the world, and she vowed to do whatever she could to try to make the dream come true.

Because in spite of everything—nukes, muties, droids and coldhearts—hope still survived, even there, deep in the heart of the Deathlands.

Don Pendleton's Mack Bolan®

Patriot Play

A violent group known as The Brethren
have allied themselves with foreign
terrorist organizations and are planning
direct collision with the U.S. Administration.
With federal agencies at a standstill, a
determined President needs a direct, no-
mercy solution and Mack Bolan is ready.
Partnered with Able Team's leader
Carl Lyons, Bolan returns fire on a
relentless search-and-destroy mission
against an organization driven by
warped ideology to claim absolute power.

**Available March
wherever you buy books.**

TAKE 'EM FREE
2 action-packed novels plus a mystery bonus
NO RISK
NO OBLIGATION TO BUY

GE0

Look for

THE SOUL STEALER
by AleX Archer

Annja Creed jumps at the chance to find a relic buried
in the long undisturbed soil of Russia's frozen terrain.
But the residents of the town claim they are being
hunted by the ghost of a fallen goddess said to ingest
souls. When Annja seeks
to destroy the apparition,
she discovers a horrifying
truth—possibly leading
her to a dead end....

**Available May 2008
wherever you
buy books.**

ROOM 59

A research facility in China has built the ultimate biological weapon. Alex's job: infiltrate and destroy. His wife works at the biotech company's stateside lab, and Alex fears danger is poised to hit home. But when Alex is captured, his personal and professional worlds collide in a last, desperate gamble to stop ruthless masterminds from unleashing virulent, unstoppable death.

Look for

out of time
by
cliff RYDER